MEANT FOR LOVE

GANSETT ISLAND SERIES, BOOK 10

MARIE FORCE

Donna,

Enjoy Alex & Jenny!

Marie Force

Meant for Love
Gansett Island Series, Book 10

By: Marie Force
Published by HTJB, Inc.
Copyright 2013. HTJB, Inc.
Cover Design by Diane Luger
Print Layout by Isabel Sullivan
E-book Formatting Fairies
ISBN: 978-0985034184

marieforce.com

View the McCarthy Family Tree here. marieforce.com/gansett/familytree/

View the list of Who's Who on Gansett Island here. marieforce.com/whoswhogansett/

View a map of Gansett Island. marieforce.com/mapofgansett/

The Gansett Island Series

Book 1: Maid for Love (*Mac & Maddie*)
Book 2: Fool for Love (*Joe & Janey*)
Book 3: Ready for Love (*Luke & Sydney*)
Book 4: Falling for Love (*Grant & Stephanie*)
Book 5: Hoping for Love (*Evan & Grace*)
Book 6: Season for Love (*Owen & Laura*)
Book 7: Longing for Love (*Blaine & Tiffany*)
Book 8: Waiting for Love (*Adam & Abby*)
Book 9: Time for Love (*David & Daisy*)
Book 10: Meant for Love (*Jenny & Alex*)
Book 10.5: Chance for Love, *A Gansett Island Novella* (*Jared & Lizzie*)
Book 11: Gansett After Dark (*Owen & Laura*)
Book 12: Kisses After Dark (*Shane & Katie*)
Book 13: Love After Dark (*Paul & Hope*)
Book 14: Celebration After Dark (*Big Mac & Linda*)
Book 15: Desire After Dark (*Slim & Erin*)
Book 16: Light After Dark (*Mallory & Quinn*)
Book 17: Victoria & Shannon (Episode 1)
Book 18: Kevin & Chelsea (Episode 2)
A Gansett Island Christmas Novella
Book 19: Mine After Dark (*Riley & Nikki*)
Book 20: Yours After Dark (*Finn McCarthy*)
Book 21: Trouble After Dark (*Deacon & Julia*)
Book 22: Rescue After Dark (*Mason & Jordan*)

More new books are alway in the works. For the most up-to-date list of what's available from the Gansett Island Series as well as series extras, go to marieforce.com/gansett.

AUTHOR'S NOTE

Welcome back to Gansett Island for Book 10 in the Gansett Island Series! A reader recently asked me if I'd ever imagined the series going to ten books when I first wrote *Maid for Love*. Absolutely not, I replied. I don't plan that far ahead on anything, so it's as much of a surprise to me as it is to anyone that the McCarthys are still going strong at ten books. It's all thanks to you, the lovely readers, who write to me every day to tell me how much you love the island and its people. And because of you, I hope to continue writing the series for a long time to come.

I have a confession to make. This one might be my favorite one yet. We've waited a long time for Jenny to get her story, and I'm completely in love with Alex Martinez, who turned out to be Jenny's perfect match—even if it doesn't seem that way in the beginning! He's a little rough, a little coarse, a little gruff and a whole lot of sexy, and I adored writing both of them. I hope you enjoy Jenny's long-awaited second chance at love.

You'll also see more of Grace and Evan in this story as well as series favorites Seamus and Carolina and Dan and Kara. Of course, Mac and Maddie are back, too, because it wouldn't be a Gansett book without them! If you're having trouble keeping up with the Gansett Island cast, view the Who's Who on Gansett Island.

Next up is a special edition we're calling *Gansett After Dark*, which will feature Laura and Owen's wedding along with some catch-up stories for each of our past couples as well as a few new ones. You'll meet some other members of the extended McCarthy family as well as the Lawry siblings. I'm looking forward to writing that one!

Special thanks to team HTJB: Julie Cupp, Lisa Cafferty, Holly Sullivan, Isabel Sullivan and Nikki Colquhoun, as well as my faithful beta readers Ronlyn Howe, Kara Conrad and Anne Woodall. Thank you also to my editor, Linda Ingmanson, proofreader Joyce Lamb and cover designer extraordinaire Kristina Brinton. I so appreciate everything all of you do to help me produce my books! Thanks to Sarah Spate Morrison, who is always willing to answer a medical question. Dan, Emily and Jake put up with me when I'm writing, and Brandy and Louie keep me company and provide snuggles on demand.

My eternal gratitude goes to my amazing readers, who are so incredibly generous in their support of my books. You make my world go round, and I'm thankful for you every day.

xoxo

Marie

CHAPTER 1

The dream was always the same, the last perfect moment before life as Jenny Wilks knew it ended forever. She and her fiancé, Toby, in their cozy New York City apartment, enjoying breakfast, the morning paper, the news on TV, talking about everything and nothing. He'd asked about their dinner plans, and she'd reminded him her parents were coming the next day, so they needed to clean their apartment.

He'd groaned in protest, and she'd laughed at him, as she always did. She was a neat freak, and he was a certified slob. She loved him anyway, even when she had to pick up after him. Every time she had the dream, she tried to recall those final minutes, wanting desperately to know what they'd said to each other.

It was the one thing she couldn't remember, and the one thing she *needed* to know.

Toby got up to leave for work in Lower Manhattan, leaning in to kiss her the way he did every morning. He looked gorgeous and successful in the suit that had been cut just for him, as he rubbed his freshly shaven cheek against hers. "I'll—"

A roar of noise startled her out of a sound sleep, setting off a panic deep inside where the lingering trauma still resided. An engine, close by… In a cold sweat despite the oppressive heat, she launched out of bed and ran for the window to find a shirtless man standing on the back of the biggest lawn mower she'd ever seen. At—she glanced at the clock on her bedside table—*5:45 a.m.*! Was he serious?

Next to the clock was a framed picture of Toby that brought back the dream in startling, vibrant detail that made her eyes swim with tears and sparked fury that had her running for the lighthouse's spiral staircase. Down she went to the first floor and then one more level below to the mudroom and out into the pearly predawn, where the air was thick with heat and humidity.

She burst into the yard, screaming as she went, *"Hey! Hello! Do you know what time it is?"*

The dark-haired man wore a bulky headset over his ears and couldn't possibly hear her over the roar of that…*thing*…he was driving. It was massive—and very, very loud. His skin glistened with sweat as day three of the heat wave from hell began on Gansett Island.

Jenny looked around for something, anything she could use to get his attention and zeroed in on the bumper crop of tomatoes that had begun to ripen on the vines she'd planted earlier in the summer. Without giving a single thought to what she was about to do, she grabbed a handful of pulpy tomatoes and began flinging them at the man's bare back.

The first two went wide, missing the target, but the third one hit him square between the shoulder blades, splattering on contact. Excellent.

Recoiling from the direct hit, he cut the engine on the beast, threw off the headset and jumped from the platform, spinning to face her. "What was that?" Looking around, he noticed the remnants of the first two tomatoes on the ground next to him. *"Are you throwing tomatoes at me?* What the hell?"

"I could ask you the same thing! Do you have *any idea* what time it is?"

"Ah…five something?"

Despite her rage, she couldn't help but notice a muscular chest and belly, dark chest hair, tanned skin and khaki shorts that hung from narrow hips. He wore work boots with dark socks that peeked out the top of them. "Five forty-five. *In the morning!*"

"Thanks for clarifying. Do you mind leaving me alone? I've got a long day ahead of me, and you're the one who complained to the town that we hadn't been out to cut the grass. Well, we're here to cut the grass."

"Not at five forty-five in the morning you're not."

"Ah, yeah, I am."

She took a step closer to him. "No, you're not."

He took a step in her direction. "Yes, I am."

The fourth tomato in her hand went sailing toward his head.

He ducked at the last second, avoiding a direct hit. "Are you completely insane?"

As he looked her up and down under the cover of sunglasses, Jenny realized she was wearing next to nothing as she faced off with the angry lawn guy. The lighthouse didn't have air-conditioning, and the heat had been unbearable, thus the short nightgown she'd worn over tiny panties. She crossed her arms over her unrestrained breasts.

"Look, lady, I'm sorry if I woke you up, but I need to get back to work if I'm going to keep this already screwed-up day on schedule."

"You're not turning that…*thing* back on at six o'clock in the morning! I thought I was being attacked or something."

"Right. Attacked. On Gansett Island, where it's so unsafe."

Jenny knew what it was like to be attacked in a place where she'd always felt safe, a thought that brought back the images from the dream, reminding her of what she'd missed out on thanks to the roar of his lawn mower.

Who knew when or if she'd have the dream again? It had been more than a year since the last time Toby had "visited" her slumber. "You never know when a safe place can become unsafe." As she uttered the words, her chin quivered and her eyes swam with tears.

"Oh my God. You're *not* going to cry!" He tipped his head for a closer look at her. "Are you?"

"No, I'm not going to cry." She really had no intention of crying, but having that particular dream threw her out of sorts for days every time it happened. Being blasted out of a sound sleep on top of it was a recipe for emotional overload.

"Good." He ran his fingers through straight, silky, dark hair, a gesture that made his muscles tighten and bulge, not that she was looking or anything, and then he lifted his sunglasses to swipe at the sweat on his face, revealing dark brown eyes. She couldn't help but notice how exhausted he looked. "Listen, I'm sorry I woke you up," he said in a more conciliatory tone. "I wasn't thinking about someone actually living here. I need to get this done while I can. Since you're already awake, would you mind if I got back to it?"

The exhaustion that radiated from him had her softening, too. Slightly. "And you won't show up here again at this hour?"

"I won't show up here again at this hour."

"Fine."

"Fine." He treated himself to another good look at her barely covered body before he stalked back to his Sherman tank of a lawn mower and fired up the beast.

Damn, that thing was loud! Jenny covered her ears and headed into the lighthouse, kicking the door shut behind her because that made her feel like she'd gotten the last word on the matter. She went up the spiral stairs to the kitchen and poured a glass of ice water that she ran over her face, hoping to cool her fevered skin. This heat was unbelievable and heading into another day with no end in sight.

Trying to ignore the impossible-to-ignore sound of the mower, she took the ice water with her when she went up another level to her bedroom and stretched out on the bed. She turned on her side so she could see the photo of Toby and stared at his boyish grin, wishing she could go back to sleep and return to the dream, back to the last minute in time when everything was still right in her world.

What had he said to her before he walked out of their Greenwich Village apartment into a crystal-clear September day and disappeared off the face of the earth? If only she could remember. At times over the last dozen years, she'd considered hypnosis to jog her memory, but she'd never taken it that far. The dream did this to her every time.

It made her start to wonder again, which tended to set her back a few steps in the never-ending cycle of grief.

It was less raw and gritty now than it had once been, but it was always with her, as much a part of who she was as the dark blonde hair that refused to grow past her shoulders or the tiny mole next to her upper lip or the brown eyes that were too close together, in her opinion. Toby used to laugh at her inventory of "flaws." He said she was the most beautiful creature on the planet, and he was the luckiest guy in the universe because she loved him. How exactly did one "move on" after experiencing the all-consuming love of a man like that?

She'd been trying to move on lately, accepting dates with guys her well-meaning friends had fixed her up with. So far she'd been out to dinner with the very nice—and very tall—Gansett Island fire chief, Mason Johns. They'd had a good time together, but there'd been no real spark. She almost hoped he didn't call her for another date so she wouldn't have to turn him down.

Linc Mercier, the Coast Guard officer who ran the local station, had called to ask her to dinner tomorrow night, and she'd accepted his kind invitation. She'd met Linc a few times through her friends Mac and Maddie McCarthy and newlyweds Tiffany and Blaine Taylor. Linc seemed like a nice enough guy, and he was certainly handsome, but again, she didn't look at him and think, *wow*, the way she had the first time she met Toby at Wharton when they'd been MBA students together.

Maybe she'd never feel that particular emotion again. Maybe she should accept that she'd been lucky to feel it once, which was far more than some people ever got. She stared at the photo of Toby and thought of the phone call he'd made after the plane hit the South Tower. He'd said he was so sorry to do this to her and that he wanted her to be happy, that her happiness was the most important thing to him.

She blew out a deep breath, mad at herself for wallowing in the past as she had far too often in the last twelve years. Toby was gone. He wasn't coming back. She'd accepted that a long time ago. Now it was time to get busy seeing to what he'd most wanted for the rest of her life—true happiness. It was out there somewhere, and she was determined to find it, if for no other reason than she owed it to him.

IF ALEX MARTINEZ was looking for further proof of how totally his life had gone to shit, Exhibit A could be the sticky remnants of flying tomatoes drying on his back in the sizzling heat. He'd have full-blown spaghetti sauce ready to eat by the time he finished cutting the grass.

As he rode the biggest mower they owned over the acres of land that surrounded the Southeast Light, the sun beat down on him relentlessly. He guzzled the last of the water he'd brought with him. The scorching heat wasn't doing much for his already surly disposition. He'd gone from cultivating new breeds of orchids and other exotic plants at the U.S. Botanic Garden in Washington, DC, to cutting grass on Gansett Island, regressing to his former life as a sixteen-year-old.

He'd left the respect of his colleagues, along with his ascending career in horticultural sciences, to come home to help his brother, Paul, run their family business on Gansett and manage their mother's rapid plunge into dementia. A year ago, she'd been running the business their father started on the island more than four decades earlier. Now he and his brother were doing their best to keep the business afloat while dealing with their mother's illness, too.

At times Alex felt like his head was going to explode from thinking too much about the staggering array of demands on his time, as well as the overwhelming challenge of trying to care for their mother within the confines of the small island they called home. If they'd lived on the mainland, he and Paul would've investigated long-term residential facilities by now, especially after their mom strolled out the front door of their home recently and walked miles into town on bare feet.

That incident had scared the hell out of both brothers and brought home the very real need for more qualified medical care than they could provide, even with the amazing support of Dr. David Lawrence, the island's doctor.

If one good thing had come from the tomato-chucking incident, he'd discovered that he was, in fact, still a man who could be moved by a sexy woman, even when she was spitting nails and hurling tomatoes at him. That was one hot lighthouse keeper, he thought, remembering the way she'd looked in the baby-doll nightie that barely covered all her most important assets. Too bad she was so unfriendly. He might've been interested in getting to know her better—as if he had time for such frivolous pursuits. Who was he kidding?

God, he was overheating, and he was only halfway done with this massive lawn. Thinking about the way she'd looked in that barely-there nightgown wasn't doing much for his temperature. Filled with frustration and unable to remember the last time he'd had sex because it had been so long ago, Alex shut off the mower and crossed the wide expanse of lawn he'd already cut to the lighthouse, where a hose lay coiled on the grass.

He turned on the water, let it run until it went cold and then stood under the spray until he began to cool off. While he knew he should get back to work, he stood there for a few extra minutes, relishing the refreshing shower. So little about his life was enjoyable these days that he had to take pleasure where he could find it, and this cold shower was feeling pretty damned good.

Alex pushed wet hair back from his face and startled when he saw the lighthouse keeper watching him take a shower under her hose. She'd put on a skimpy tank top and short-shorts that did awesome things for her legs. She was staring at him as if she'd never before seen a half-naked guy take a shower under a hose.

He expected her to chew him out for helping himself to her water, but then she licked her lips and something in him snapped. He dropped the hose, and his stride ate up the space between them until he was standing right in front of her.

Big brown eyes widened with surprise, but she held her ground as she gazed up at him.

"What are you looking at?" he asked.

"Not a damned thing. What're you looking at?"

He zeroed in on her lips, which were moist and very appealing. The entire package was very appealing. Well, except for the tomato incident. But he wasn't thinking about tomatoes just then. Strawberries came to mind as he stared at her ripe lips and wondered if they'd taste as sweet as they looked. "Nothing." Alex took another step that put him right in front of her.

Her lips parted with surprise as she looked up at him, probably trying to gauge his intentions. And what were his intentions, exactly? Damned if he knew.

"Who are you?" she asked.

"Alex." Since he had absolutely nothing to offer any woman, he gave her only his first name. "Who are you?"

"Jenny."

He'd begun to rethink his plan to steal a taste of those lips when she moistened them again and made his decision that much easier. "If you don't want this, say no."

"I, um…"

His hands curled around her hips, drawing a gasp from her as he tugged her against him. "That's not no. Last chance…"

She didn't say no. She didn't say anything as she continued to look up at him with big, startled eyes that had him thinking about melted chocolate. And then her hands landed on his bare chest, and he realized she was bringing him closer, not pushing him away.

He lowered his head and moved slowly, giving her time to say no at any point. She didn't. His lips landed on hers, and the impact was nothing short of incendiary. He told himself it was because it had been so long since he'd done this, but he suspected that wasn't entirely the case.

It was her and the sweet taste of her lips and the moan that came from her throat as she wrapped her arms around his neck. Holy shit. *Holy fucking shit.* He pulled her even closer, not caring in the least that she'd feel his instant arousal or that he was getting her wet. Her breasts flattened against his chest as her mouth opened to his tongue.

Oh my God. This was the hottest kiss he'd ever experienced, and he'd had his share of hot kisses. Just as he was sinking into her sweet-ness, though, she began to withdraw. He wanted to cry out in protest, but then she grabbed his hand and pulled him toward the door to the lighthouse.

"Not out here," she said, her voice hoarse and sexy.

As he followed her through the door, his gaze firmly planted on her ass, Alex gave thanks to the god of hot kisses that she wasn't done with him yet. And while he was at it, he said thank you, Jesus, too. In the mudroom, she spun around to face him, and that was when he saw that his wet chest had soaked her thin top, making her nipples visible. He took a good long look at that gorgeous sight.

Lust pounded through him as he reached for her at the same instant she reached for him. The second kiss made the memory of the first one pale in comparison. He reached down to cup her ass and lifted her in tight against his erection. When she wrapped her arms and legs around him and gave as good as she got, Alex decided he'd truly died and gone straight to heaven.

Hello, Jesus.

CHAPTER 2

*I*n all her life, Jenny had never done anything even remotely close to what she was currently doing in the mudroom with Alex, the lawn-mower guy. She'd never kissed a guy she wasn't involved with, let alone one she'd been throwing tomatoes at in a fit of rage only an hour ago. She didn't even know his last name and didn't really want to know. Somehow, rage had turned to lust, right around the time she saw him taking a shower under her hose.

He was smoking hot, and he knew how to kiss, too. *Christ have mercy*, the man could kiss. She kept thinking she should put a stop to this. Her emotions were all over the place after the dream and her thoughts of Toby, so this probably wasn't the best idea she'd ever had. But damn if she could bring herself to call a halt to it, especially right when it was getting interesting.

Shifting ever so slightly, he pressed her back against the wall, which freed up his hands to move from her waist to her ribs, stopping just below her breasts.

Jenny wanted to beg him to keep going, but since he was currently sucking hard on her tongue, she couldn't exactly use her words. So she used her body, arching her hips into tighter contact with the hard column of his erection and placing her hand over his, urging him to keep going.

In addition to being one hell of a good kisser, the man could also take a hint. His big hand covered her breast, and Jenny nearly passed out from the surge of pleasure that coursed through her when he roughly pinched her nipple. Her audible gasp ended the kiss, but he didn't stop what he was doing to her nipple.

Right when she feared that he was going to end the encounter, he tipped his head and went to work on her neck, licking and nibbling and sucking lightly on the skin just below her ear. Jenny had forgotten how much she liked to be kissed there. He rolled her earlobe between his teeth, biting down harder right as he squeezed her nipple again. The combination made her cry out. She wasn't sure if she was asking for mercy or begging for more.

He leaned his forehead against her shoulder, seeming to summon control or sanity or something that would help him deal with this situation.

Jenny was oddly moved by the sexy stranger and curled her hand around the back of his neck, hoping to offer comfort and keep him from getting away. Not yet anyway.

"How did we get here?" he asked.

She breathed in the scents of freshly cut grass and tomatoes that clung to him. "I'm not quite sure."

"One minute I was borrowing your hose, and the next..."

Jenny smiled at his summary of events. "I don't do things like this."

"Like what? Like this?" He tweaked her nipple again, making her gasp and squirm against his tight hold.

"Yes, like that. And this." She dragged him into another torrid kiss, this one skipping right over the preliminaries and going straight to open mouths and tangled tongues.

His hands were under her shirt now and moving up, pushing her bra out of the way to cup bare skin. The work-roughened calluses on his hands sent her halfway out of her mind when they made contact with her nipples. He played with her breasts until she was on the verge of explosive release, which had never happened to her before. It usually took much more than that to get her to that point, but it had been such a long time since she'd experienced this kind of desire. A very long time indeed. Sudden thoughts of the last time she'd been kissed with such unrelenting passion brought visions of Toby to mind and had her pulling back from Alex as sanity returned.

"What?" he asked, his voice rough against her ear. "What's wrong?"

"Nothing." *Everything.*

"Do you want to stop?"

"We probably should."

"Yeah, I guess." Even though he agreed, he didn't sound like he wanted to. He removed his hands from under her top, and Jenny wanted to cry from the loss as she slid down the aroused front of him. When her legs wobbled under her, he held her steady until she regained her footing.

"I, um—"

With his hands on her face, he kissed her softly. "Don't."

"I was only going to apologize for the tomatoes."

"Don't do that either. I've never had a woman throw tomatoes at me or made out in a lighthouse. And here I thought this day was going to totally suck."

She smiled up at him, dazzled by his gorgeous brown eyes, the darkly tanned skin, the scent of freshly cut grass and the ripple of muscles under her hands.

"Thanks for letting me borrow your hose."

"Is that like a metaphor or something?"

"Or something." He kissed her nose and then her lips, lingering for a full minute of pure lip-on-lip contact. "I gotta go."

She let her hands drop from his shoulders. "I know."

"I'll see you around, Jenny the lighthouse keeper."

"See you around, Alex the lawn mower."

He kissed her again and was gone, leaving her to sag against the wall as she tried to comprehend what had just happened here. Jenny reached under her tank to adjust her bra, which rubbed against abraded nipples. Through the window, she watched his long stride eat up the yard as he made his way back to the beast. When he bent to retrieve the discarded headset, she zeroed in on the flex of his ass as a bead of sweat rolled down her back.

She might've never done anything like that before, but she sure did hope she'd get to do it again. Soon. After all, the grass needed to be mowed regularly, right?

Jenny blew out a deep breath and tried to find her scattered senses as she went upstairs to check on the brownies she'd put in the oven for the lunch she and some of her friends were taking to Sydney Donovan, who'd recently had surgery. Thankfully, the brownies hadn't burned while she was heating things up with Alex in the mudroom.

Alex… She liked his name. She'd always liked that name. Naturally, she was filled with curiosity about him. Who was he? What was his story? At their age, everyone had one. Some, she knew, were better than others. Of course, she could ask her friends, who would probably know every detail about him and his life. But as she took the brownies out to cool, she decided she'd keep this morning's interlude to herself. Who knew if it would happen again, and her friends had gone to so much trouble to arrange the dates with Mason and Linc and were working on others. Why would she sacrifice the chance to meet some nice guys because of what would probably turn out to be a one-time lapse in judgment with the lawn guy?

She wouldn't. It would be stupid to share what'd happened with Alex with her friends. First of all, she'd hate for them to think she was loose or easy, which she wasn't. At all. Or at least she never had been. Until today. Anyway, she didn't want them to think she was that kind of girl, and she didn't really want to *be* that kind of girl.

Girl. Woman. Whatever. She'd never been loose with guys and had no intention of starting now. If anyone had told her yesterday that this day would unfold the way it had, she would've called them crazy.

Jenny stood in the kitchen for a long time, attempting to collect herself. She needed to go out to the main road and open the gates to let in the tourists who swarmed the lighthouse property every day. It was one of the more popular spots on the island, and it was time to open for the day.

She usually walked the half mile to the gate and back because she enjoyed the exercise. Except she'd have to walk by *him* as he worked on the lawn. So she made an exception to her usual routine and grabbed her car keys. She could easily blame the heat for her cowardice, she thought as she got into her car and blasted the air-conditioning.

In her former life in New York, she couldn't have conceived of a life without air-conditioning. And for the most part, she was fine without it at the lighthouse. She could always count on a cool ocean breeze, but the unusual heat wave had made for some sweaty days and nights. And it had led a sexy lawn guy to take a shower under her hose.

She giggled when she remembered the punch to the gut she'd experienced watching the water sluice over his muscular frame. God, the guy was H-O-T, and the combination of the heat and the view had positively fried her brain cells. That was the only possible explanation for her wanton behavior.

If you don't want this, say no.

The memory of his gruffly spoken words was like a flashpoint of heat that even the air-conditioning blasting in her face couldn't overcome. She hadn't said no. Rather, she'd said *yes, yes, yes*—not with words, but with actions so brazen he probably thought she was a total slut. But he hadn't seemed put off by her behavior. If anything, he'd encouraged it.

Jenny blew out an uneven deep breath as she felt him watching her drive down the long dirt lane that led to the road. She continued to feel his eyes on her as she unlocked the gate and swung it open. How in the world had he gotten his truck and that beast of a lawn mower onto the property? He must have a key, she decided. *Great…*

On the way back, she drove by the green Martinez Lawn & Garden pickup truck with the trailer attached for the beast and could tell he was still watching her. Martinez Lawn & Garden… She wondered if he was an owner or an employee and hated herself for wanting to know more about him. Owners of a company like that didn't usually do things like cut the grass, did they?

"Oh for God's sake, Jenny. Knock it off, and let it go. It was a couple of kisses. Stop making it into a federal case."

She was still muttering to herself when she stepped into the mudroom and stopped short as images from the carnal encounter flooded her mind, making her mouth water for another taste of him. This was utter madness, and it was enough already.

After stomping up the stairs to the bedroom, she sat at her computer to record the weather conditions and seas on the Coast Guard website she reported to every day, which was another of the regular duties required of her position. The job wasn't exactly the best use of the MBA she'd earned at the University of Pennsylvania's Wharton School of Business, but she liked her life at the lighthouse and on the island, where she'd made friends she greatly enjoyed.

They kept her busy and engaged in island life, which was exactly what she needed after years of floundering following Toby's death. She finally felt rooted again and ready for the next phase of her life, whatever that might be. The morning passed quickly as she replied to several emails from her parents and sisters, who worried about her far more than they should—not that she hadn't given them ample reason to worry over the years.

Her parents were talking about coming to visit this summer, and she hoped they would. She'd love to show them "her" island and introduce them to her new friends. Speaking of her friends, it was time to get ready to go to Syd's. She'd offered to arrive early so Syd's husband, Luke, could go to work for a few hours.

Suddenly, she realized she could no longer hear the beast and went over to the window to look out at the lawn, which was devoid now of the mower and the hot man who ran it. He was gone. That was fine. She had to go, too. But as she drove away from the lighthouse on her way to Syd's, she wondered if or when he'd be back.

JENNY ARRIVED at Sydney and Luke's oceanfront home a short time later. She was accustomed now to the breathtaking views the island afforded, but theirs was one of her favorites. Carrying the brownies she'd baked, Jenny tapped on the glass door and heard Syd's dog, Buddy, bark inside.

Luke came to the door and smiled when he saw Jenny there. "Oh, good, you're here. Syd can't wait to be rid of me."

"That's not true," Syd called from her perch on the sofa. She had decorated the room in shades of navy and cream and made the most of the exquisite view. Jenny absolutely loved this room. "He can't wait to go to work."

"Also not true," Luke said with a wink.

"Glad to see you two lovebirds getting along so swimmingly," Jenny teased.

"We've been spending a *lot* of time together," Sydney said. "And not the fun kind of time." Her long red hair was piled into a messy bun on the top of her head, and other than the dark circles under her eyes, she looked great.

Luke bent over the sofa to kiss his wife. "We'll be back to fun in a couple of weeks. In the meantime," he said to Jenny, "she's under orders to take it easy. No heavy lifting or strenuous activity."

"Got it," Jenny said. "I'll take good care of her. Don't worry."

"Call me if you need anything," Luke said to Sydney. "I can be home in a couple of minutes."

"Go already, would ya? Honestly, I can't get rid of him." This was said with a warm smile for her handsome husband.

"Never let it be said I can't take a hint. Back in a couple of hours."

"We'll be here," Syd said.

"Thanks again, Jenny," he said on his way out. "I appreciate the break from the ball and chain." He quickly shut the door so he could get in the last word, which left Sydney shaking with silent laughter.

"Hurts to laugh," she said.

"You two are funny."

"We've been together around the clock for more than a week. I knew he was dying to get back to the marina but would never say so. Thanks for coming over to babysit me. I told him I was fine by myself, but he wouldn't leave me alone."

"He's very sweet."

"Yes, he is. He's been an absolute rock through the whole thing. All this hassle and who knows if it'll even work?"

"It went well, though, right?"

"The doctor said it all went perfectly. Couldn't have asked for better. He was able to successfully reconnect both of my fallopian tubes."

"So why don't you seem more excited? You want a baby, don't you?"

"I do, but…"

"But what?"

"It's scary to think about having a baby and then worrying all the time about something happening to it. I don't know if I could survive that again. But I'm trying to follow Luke's lead and think positively. He says I've used up my lifetime supply of bad luck."

"I have to agree with him."

"I do, too. But it's still scary."

"Could I ask you something that might seem weird and out of the blue?"

"Of course you can. You know that."

The two women had bonded initially over their mutual experience with tragedy and had become close friends. Syd had been the first to reach out to Jenny after she arrived on the island and had connected her with a vast circle of friends she'd come to adore. Jenny hadn't felt so at home anywhere since she lost Toby and was forever thankful to Syd for making the overture.

"Do you ever dream about Seth and the kids? As if they're still alive?"

"Not as much as I used to right after the accident, but occasionally. Why? Do you dream about Toby?"

"Same as you. It used to be more frequent when it first happened, but now it's only once in a while, and it always messes me up for a couple of days afterward."

"It messes me up, too. I felt so bad because I had the dream when

Luke and I were on our honeymoon. Of all the times for a blast from the past."

"Oh jeez. What did you do? What did *he* do?"

"He was great about it, like he is about everything. He just rolls with whatever comes his way and keeps me calm, too. I tell him that's his special gift—instilling calm."

"It's a good gift." Jenny thought of Alex and how he'd instilled passion rather than calm.

"Yes, it is. Anyway, the honeymoon dream threw me for a loop for a couple of days. It's always a shock to wake up from the dream and remember what happened."

Jenny nodded in agreement—and in understanding. "I had the Toby dream this morning. Same thing."

"What do you dream about?"

"It's always the same thing. The last morning we spent together. I want so badly to know what he said to me before he left, and what I said to him, but I wake up before I get there. Every time."

"Do you think it would make a big difference to know what you said?"

"Intellectually, I know it won't make any difference. He'll still be dead, you know? But I'd like to know."

"It would give you closure."

"If there is any such thing."

"I don't like that word very much for the same reason."

"That's one thing I've come to understand in the last twelve years. I'll never get true closure, but peace is possible, and so is happiness and joy and other things I thought I'd never experience again."

"Love is possible, too, Jenny."

"Maybe so." Jenny couldn't help but think of the fiery encounter with Alex. That had been a long, long way from love, but it had reminded her that she was still very much alive and still very much a normal woman.

"So no sparks with Mason, huh?"

"Afraid not. He's a very nice guy, though."

"Yes, he is. Doesn't mean he's the one for you. Who's next?"

"I'm having dinner with Linc tomorrow night."

"Ohh, he's so cute. I bet you'll feel sparks with him."

"I guess we'll see." Sparks… Was that what she'd felt with Alex? No, that had been a full-fledged flame. She wanted so badly to tell Sydney about what'd happened with him but decided not to. It felt intensely private, and not only because her behavior had been so far out of character. The minute she told someone else about it, it wouldn't belong just to them anymore. And for now, she wanted to keep it between them.

That led to another, far more startling thought: What if he told people? He wouldn't do that, would he? How could she be certain he wouldn't? She didn't know him at all. With those worries churning in her belly, she made a cup of tea for Sydney and chatted with her about a wide variety of island gossip.

"So Daisy actually turned down the house she was offered?" Jenny asked.

"That's what I heard. David wants her to move in with him, and they're talking about that."

"Good for her—and for him. I've always thought he was a nice guy, despite what happened with Janey."

"I've thought so, too. He was certainly good to us when we were weighing our options before I had the surgery. He referred me to the surgeon in Boston, someone he knew from his residency."

"No one is all good or all bad, right?"

"That's been my experience. Daisy surely seems happy with him."

"What's up with her ex-boyfriend?"

"He's back in jail for violating the restraining order. Even though Daisy wasn't home, the neighbors saw him kick in her door, so that counts as a violation. His bail was revoked."

"Thank goodness he's back in jail where he belongs."

"No kidding. Poor Daisy. Imagine a man of his size beating up a woman her size—or any woman, for that matter."

"I can't imagine it. I refuse to."

A knock on the door preceded Maddie coming into the house. She carried Hailey in her car seat and set her down on the floor by Jenny. "Be right back with the food I brought."

"Let's get you out of there," Jenny said to Hailey, who beamed up at her with a smile full of baby teeth. Relying on her years of aunt experience, Jenny unclipped the straps and lifted Hailey out of the seat. At ten months, Hailey was sturdy and chubby and showed no signs of the trauma she'd experienced at birth. Like her older brother, Thomas, she had light blonde hair and big blue eyes.

"You're a natural," Syd said.

"I've got three nieces and two nephews. Lots of practice." Jenny snuggled the baby in close, breathing in the scent of baby shampoo and lotion. She'd once expected to be a young mother but had long ago accepted that she probably wouldn't have children. That was another thing that had been taken from her on a cloudless September day.

Maddie returned, carrying a huge bowl, a baguette and a bag.

"What did you make?" Syd asked.

"A big salad and some spinach dip."

"That sounds so good," Syd said with a sigh. "I'm going to gain thirty pounds from this surgery if you guys keep bringing food over."

"That's what friends are for," Jenny said with a smile for Syd.

Syd stuck out her tongue at Jenny, and then Hailey stuck her tongue out and made raspberry noises that had both women laughing.

"What're you two teaching my daughter?" Maddie asked when she came in to sit with them.

"Things she needs to know," Jenny said, keeping her hands on Hailey as the baby pulled herself up to the coffee table.

"Uh-oh," Syd said, "she's cruising."

"Yeah," Maddie said. "That started this weekend."

This was said without Maddie's usual enthusiasm for all things involving her family. Jenny exchanged glances with Sydney.

"What's wrong, Maddie?" Syd asked.

"What? Nothing."

"Come on," Syd said. "It's us. We know you better than that."

"Nothing's wrong. Really. Do you want something to eat yet? The others should be here soon."

"Maddie…"

"It's ridiculous in light of what you're going through. It doesn't even count as a problem." Despite her words, Maddie's eyes filled, and she turned her full focus on Hailey.

"Tell us what's wrong," Jenny said. "You might feel better."

"It's stupid, and I feel foolish for even being upset about it."

"Tell us anyway," Syd said. She and Maddie had been friends since a summer job scooping ice cream during high school.

"I thought I was pregnant. In fact, I was sure I was pregnant. And I'm not. See what I mean? What do I have to be weepy about? I have two perfectly healthy kids, and neither Mac nor I wanted to be pregnant again yet, so it doesn't count as an actual problem."

"Sure, it does," Syd said. "You're sad that something you thought was happening isn't."

Maddie closed her eyes and shook her head. "It's crazy to be upset about not getting something you didn't even really want in the first place."

"I think I actually followed that," Jenny said.

"Mamamamamama," Hailey said, chewing on her fist as she teetered on new legs.

"Mama is here." Maddie reached for her daughter and hugged her close, despite Hailey's efforts to get free.

Laura McCarthy poked her head in the door. "Is this where the party is?"

"Come in," Syd said.

Laura stepped through the door, followed by her fiancé, Owen Lawry, who carried Laura's five-month-old son, Holden, in a car seat. "He's not staying," she said, using her thumb to point to Owen. "He wouldn't let me drive myself or carry Holden, so I had no choice but to let him bring me over."

"We're glad you're here," Jenny said, "no matter how you got here."

"She forgot to mention she's been sick all morning," Owen said.

"Okay, too bad you gotta go now, *honey*," Laura said, her hand on

Owen's chest as she steered him backward toward the door. She let him kiss her before she sent him out the door and shut it behind him. "He's driving me batshit crazy."

"He's worried about you," Syd said. "We all are."

"I'm pregnant," Laura said, "not dying. Although sometimes I feel like I might be dying."

"That's got to be so miserable," Jenny said, keeping an eye on Maddie, who was still wrestling with her emotions.

"I'm sorry," Laura said to Syd in particular. "I don't mean to be bitching about being pregnant in front of you."

"You're bitching about the sickness, not the pregnancy," Syd said.

One of the things Jenny loved best about Sydney was her endless empathy toward others, even after losing her husband and children so tragically.

"What's wrong, Maddie?" Laura asked.

Jenny watched Maddie wipe tears off her cheeks.

"Absolutely nothing. Nothing at all. I'm a hormonal mess today."

"And she's a little disappointed, I think," Syd said.

Maddie shrugged. "Maybe a little."

"Oh," Laura said, "so you're not pregnant?"

"Apparently not."

"I thought you didn't want to be," Laura said, her brows knitting with confusion.

"I didn't want to be." Maddie sniffled as Hailey patted her face. "Until I wasn't."

"You know that's seriously messed up, don't you?" Laura asked.

"Yes! I get it. Believe me. Mac was having a total meltdown at the thought of me being pregnant again before we were ready to even talk about another baby. He'll be thrilled to hear it was a false alarm." Maddie wiped the tears off her face. "Anyway, enough about me. Let's talk about Syd and how she's going to be the next one to get pregnant."

"Don't jinx me," Syd said with a teasing grin.

"I'm so sorry," Maddie said, breaking down again. She handed Hailey to Jenny and got up to leave the room.

Holding the baby, Jenny started to get up from the floor, but Syd held up a hand to stop her. "Allow me."

"Do you need a hand up?" Jenny asked.

"Nope. I've got it." Sydney moved slowly, but she rose to her feet and followed Maddie into the kitchen.

"I've never seen Maddie like that," Jenny said to Laura. "She's always so upbeat."

"I know. It's not like her."

Stephanie, Abby and Grace came in, carrying covered dishes and bringing laughter and noise and chaos, which required Jenny's full attention as she tried to steer them away from the kitchen to give Maddie some privacy.

"What's going on?" Abby asked.

"Maddie's having a rough day," Jenny replied. "Syd is with her."

"Hope everything is okay."

"I think it will be."

They arranged all the food on the dining room table next to the paper plates, napkins and plastic forks Sydney had provided. As they filled their plates, talk turned to their friend Janey Cantrell, who'd recently delivered her son two months premature in an emergency C-section.

"I talked to Joe this morning," Janey's cousin Laura said. "P.J. is doing well and off the ventilator, which is a huge step forward."

"And how is Janey?" Grace asked.

"Recovering slowly, but doing better every day," Laura said. "The doctors told her she needs to take it very easy for a month or so until she's fully recovered. She lost a lot of blood."

"She's so damned lucky to be alive," Stephanie said. "They both are."

"No kidding," Laura said. "I can't even think about what happened without feeling like I'm going to break out in hives or something."

Grace patted Laura's arm. "It's better if you don't think about it."

"Imagine your ex-fiancé saving your life—and your child's—the way David saved them," Stephanie said. "What a crazy scenario for all of them."

"Thank God David was right there when she had the emergency and knew what to do," Grace said.

"Seriously," Jenny said. "A stroke of luck for sure."

Maddie and Sydney came into the room and greeted the new arrivals. "Sorry to be such a basket case today," Maddie said. Her eyes were red and puffy from crying. "I feel like such a jackass for bawling all over you guys. Blame it on the hormones."

"No apologies needed," Laura said. "We all have those days. I feel like all I do lately is cry and puke. It'll be a miracle if Owen shows up for our wedding."

"Oh, shut up," Stephanie said, laughing. "He can't wait to marry you."

"I can't imagine why. I've done little more than breed and puke since he's known me."

"Apparently," Sydney said dryly, gesturing to Laura's rounding belly, "you've done a few other things, too."

Jenny cracked up laughing along with the others and helped Hailey as she made a huge doughy mess of the roll she'd chosen from the table.

"I'm so sorry to dump and run," Maddie said as she took a seat on the floor next to Jenny and Hailey. "Have you gotten to eat yet?"

"We're doing just fine, aren't we, Hailey?"

"Mamamama." Hailey dropped the doughy mess on the floor and reached for her mother, dragging handfuls of wet bread into Maddie's hair.

"Wow," Jenny said. "She moves fast."

"Why do you think I require two showers per day?" Maddie asked, cuddling her daughter close.

"Are you okay?"

"I'm fine. Today is about Syd. I feel terrible making it about me."

"You didn't. We all support one another. It's what I love best about living here."

"Yes, we do," Maddie said. "And we're so glad you're here with us."

"I am, too," Jenny said, humbled as always by the genuine friendship she felt among this group of women and the men they loved. "So have Tiffany and Blaine resurfaced yet after their big day?"

"I heard she was seen briefly at the store yesterday," Maddie said. "My mom and Ned asked to keep Ashleigh and Thomas for another night to give the newlyweds some more time to themselves. They can't go away this time of year, so I guess they'll take an official honeymoon in the fall."

"You know," Jenny said, "we never got to have a shower for her because the whole thing happened fast."

Maddie's eyes widened with interest. "You're right!"

"Who's to say we can't do it after the fact?"

"Absolutely no one, and how funny would it be if we bought her a bunch of stuff from her own store?"

"Hilarious! I'd be happy to have it at the lighthouse. We could do it out in the yard."

"Did the lawn finally get cut?"

Jenny felt like her face lit up like a neon sign at the mention of grass cutting. "Just today, in fact."

"Hey, you guys," Maddie said to the others. "Jenny just had the best idea. How about a bridal shower for Tiffany, complete with stuff from her own store?"

"Oh yeah," Stephanie said. "I'm digging that."

They spent the rest of the afternoon on Syd's back porch, planning the shower for the following weekend while enjoying the sunshine and company of good friends. Syd's dog, Buddy, was in the middle of everything, as was Hailey. While they all took turns holding Holden, the laughter and conversation never lagged.

"God, I needed this," Grace said as the party finally broke up around five. "I feel like all I do is work."

"Welcome to summer on Gansett," Stephanie said. "I'm off to the restaurant for another wild Saturday night."

"Oh, I forgot," Grace said. "I'm supposed to tell you that Evan and Owen are playing at the Tiki tomorrow night, and they want us all to come."

"We are so there," Abby said.

Everyone else agreed they were long overdue for a group night out at the Tiki Bar. They hadn't done that yet this summer.

Most of them had plans that night with their husbands, fiancés or boyfriends and were off to shower and change. Jenny remembered what it was like to have a regular Saturday-night date and missed being half of a couple. But she certainly didn't begrudge her friends their hard-won happiness. Each of them had been through the fire to get to where they were today, and they deserved all the good things life had to bring them.

However, as she drove away from Syd's house, Jenny couldn't help but be a tiny bit envious of what they had to go home to when she was on her way back to the empty lighthouse for another night alone.

CHAPTER 3

*T*welve hours after his day began, Alex drove onto the grounds of Martinez Lawn & Garden, where the retail store was closing for the night. Sharon, the young woman they'd hired to run the store for them this summer, waved to him as he went by. She'd been a total godsend to him and Paul as they managed the landscaping end of the business along with their mother's increasingly complicated medical situation.

He drove into the huge aluminum building where they kept their equipment and stowed the trailer, not bothering to remove the mower, since they'd be back out bright and early in the morning. Alex, who wasn't usually required to cut grass, was helping to work through the backlog and get back on schedule before they lost most of their landscaping customers.

He'd forgotten what an ass-kicker it was to ride the mower all day in the broiling sun, especially this week in the midst of the worst heat wave in recent history. Leaving the "barn," as they called the equipment shed, Alex eyed the house with wary trepidation. What would he find when he got there? Would his mother be awake or asleep for the night? Would his brother be agitated from dealing with her and generally out of sorts?

Alex hated not knowing what to expect, and he hated that he hated his life with an unhealthy passion. He'd had a great life in DC, including a job he'd loved, good friends as well as softball and basketball leagues he'd played in for years. But then came the call last fall from his brother, letting him know that their mother's forgetfulness had become something much bigger, and he couldn't handle it all on his own any longer.

In the course of two weeks, Alex had quit the job he'd loved, sold his townhouse and moved home to Gansett Island. And now he was back to cutting grass twelve hours a day and coming home every night to a host of challenges he'd never expected to face and was completely unequipped to manage.

The toot of a horn caught his attention. How long had he been standing in the doorway to the barn, staring at the house and dreading what he had to face there? Speaking of godsends… He waved to David Lawrence and his girlfriend, Daisy Babson, as they pulled up the driveway and parked outside the house.

Alex and Paul never would've survived the last year without David guiding them through the medical maze surrounding their mother's dementia. And Daisy had been a gift from above since his mother walked away from their home and landed in a rocker on Daisy's porch in town.

"Hey, guys," Alex said, going over to greet them.

"Hey, Alex," David said. "I've got good news. I heard back from two of the agencies on the mainland with potential candidates for the nurse position. One of them is very anxious to move to a new place, but the other said she'd need to see it first."

Alex released a deep breath that he felt like he'd been holding for weeks. Help was on the way. "When can we meet them?"

"I brought their emails and résumés with me so you and Paul can take a look. I figured if you like what you see, we can arrange something as soon as they can get here."

"That sounds great. I can't thank you enough for your help."

"I'm happy to do what I can. I think this'll be a great solution and

will allow you to keep your mom safely at home while giving you and
Paul some breathing room."

"That'd be nice. Air has been a bit hard to come by lately."

"I bet it has."

"How's your mom been today?" Daisy asked. "I brought her some
of the perfume she admired last night."

"I haven't seen her since this morning. I just got home. Come on
in. I know she looks forward to your visits." And in another of the
ultimate ironies of his life of late, his mother lit up with pleasure
every time she saw Daisy, whom she'd met just a few weeks ago, but
often seemed surprised to realize her own sons were now grown men.
"I don't know what we'd do without the ladies from the church who
stay with her while we're at work. And they cook for us, too.
Everyone has been so amazing."

Alex's throat closed around the lump of emotion that settled there
when he thought of the way the island community had rallied around
his family in their time of need. While he wouldn't have chosen to
move home, he was thankful for the warm embrace of their longtime
friends as he and Paul managed the daily crisis their lives had become.

"That's Gansett for you," Daisy said as they walked up the stairs to
the sprawling ranch house where Alex and Paul had grown up.
"Everyone is always willing to lend a hand."

"Daisy!" Marion cried when the three of them came in the door.
"I'm so glad to see you!" She hugged Daisy as if she hadn't seen the
young woman in weeks, when in fact it had only been twenty-four
hours since Daisy's last visit. She'd been incredibly faithful to his
mother since their inopportune meeting.

"I'm glad to see you, too. Your hair looks lovely. Did you have it
done today?"

"I don't know. Did I have it done today?"

"Yes, Mom." The strain around Paul's eyes and mouth were indica-
tive of a difficult day. "Chloe was here this afternoon."

"I did have it done today." Marion patted her gray curls lightly.
"Chloe came from town. My George always tells me to get my hair

done, because he knows how much I enjoy it. He's so good to me that way."

"Let's go outside on the porch." Daisy extended her arm to Marion. "I know how much you love the heat."

"I do so love it. I'm always cold."

Yearning for the coldest shower in the history of cold showers— for more reasons than one—Alex watched them go. His mother's constant insistence that his father was still alive was just another on a long list of painful things about her illness. Losing their father to cancer ten years ago had been among the worst things Alex and Paul had ever been through, and to hear her talk about him like he was still alive was a constant reopening of an old wound.

While they went out of their way not to talk about it, Alex knew it affected his brother just as profoundly.

David filled Paul in on the news about nursing applicants. Alex provided beers for all three of them while they pored over the résumés and emails from the two women. One of them disclosed in her email that she had a young son and was looking for a fresh start for both of them.

"Does your cottage have room for two people?" David asked, refer- ring to the guesthouse they were making available to whomever accepted the nursing position.

"There're two bedrooms," Paul said. "So that wouldn't be an issue. How soon can we get them over here?"

"That's up to you," David said. "I'll make myself available whenever you want me to meet with them."

"That's really good of you," Alex said. "I know we've said this a million times, but we never would've gotten this far without your help and support."

"Happy to do it. That's what friends are for, right?"

"Yeah," Alex said gruffly. "Thank God for good friends."

"And good beer," Paul said in a welcome moment of levity that made them all laugh. "I'll email both of them tonight and set up the interviews. I'll let you know when they're coming."

"You and Daisy probably have better things to do than come check on us every night," Alex said. "Not that we don't appreciate it."

"Daisy knows her special bond with your mom helps the situation, and she insists on visiting every night. But I'm happy to do it, too."

The kindness of those around them only added to the emotional battlefield inside Alex. On any given day, he experienced the full gamut from rage to despair to relief to gratitude to overwhelming love for the mother who'd given him everything to anger at the God who'd taken so much from her at such a young age. "I'd better hit the shower before I stink the place up," Alex said. "Thanks again for everything, David."

"No problem. Call me if you need me. Any time." David stood. "We're going to head out in a bit, so we'll see you tomorrow."

Alex nodded in appreciation and headed for the room that had been his as a child. Here he was at thirty-four, back in his old room, surrounded by high school trophies and other reminders of an idyllic childhood on Gansett Island. While this house and island were about the last place he wanted to be, he couldn't conceive of being anywhere else when his mom and brother needed him. It didn't do any good, he'd discovered over the last year, to wallow in thoughts of what could've been.

He was too busy on a daily basis dealing with what *was* to think too much about the life he'd left behind in Washington—or the woman he'd thought he loved until she made it clear she wouldn't be waiting around for him to deal with his family crisis. Apparently, he'd dodged a bullet there, but the loss of a relationship he'd enjoyed was just another thing to be bitter about.

He stepped under the icy-cold blast of the shower and let the water rain down upon him until he was completely numb and shivering, which was a welcome relief after sweating his balls off all day. He washed his hair, shaved the scruff off his face and finally allowed his thoughts to wander to the incredibly intense interlude he'd shared with the sexy lighthouse keeper.

Jenny...

He liked her name, and he'd really liked kissing her. He'd had a very long day with nothing much to do but drive the mower and think about what'd happened at the lighthouse that morning—and how much he'd like it to happen again. The somewhat anonymous aspect to their encounter had been another welcome relief. Everywhere he went these days, people asked about his mom, and while he appreciated the concern, it was nice to spend a few minutes with someone who had no idea what a catastrophe his life had become.

After at least thirty minutes under the cold water, he finally turned off the shower and wrapped a towel around his hips. As he found a clean T-shirt and board shorts, a plan began to form that he hoped he'd be able to execute. He went to the kitchen to find his mother watching *Jeopardy!* with the TV on full blast and Paul at the table, his laptop open in front of him and a new beer sitting in a puddle of condensation. It was so bloody hot, and his mother was cold all the time, so the AC was off.

"Were you rubbing one out in there, dude?" Paul asked with a snort of laughter.

"Oh my God. Shut the fuck up. I was trying to cool off after a day spent literally in hell. I've never been so fucking hot in my life."

"Alexander, watch your mouth."

His mother chose the damnedest times to be lucid and in complete control of her faculties. "Sorry, Mom."

Like he would have when they were teenagers, Paul covered his mouth to hide his pleasure in watching Alex get in trouble. Alex gave him the finger, which made Paul laugh out loud.

"I'm telling Mom," Paul said.

"Go right ahead."

While Paul drove him nuts sometimes, Alex had never been more thankful for his brother than since he moved home. He couldn't imagine facing this nightmare alone.

"Mrs. Garfield left a chicken thing in the oven," Paul said. "It's actually pretty good."

That was saying something, as the brothers had commented recently that they never wanted to see another casserole for the rest of their lives. Even so, as two guys who could barely heat soup without disaster striking, they were grateful to the women from the church who insisted on feeding them.

Alex ate the surprisingly good chicken and had two servings of salad before he assisted Paul with the nightly ordeal of getting their mom ready for bed. The two of them had done things—and seen things—no son should ever have to do or see, and they did it willingly, even if the routine took a vicious toll on both of them.

As close as he and Paul were, they never spoke of the indignities. They soldiered through because it was what had to be done, and it was what their father would've expected of them. And they did it because they loved their mother and were fully aware of all she'd done for them.

Though he was as exhausted as he'd ever been, Alex was also keyed up on adrenaline after dealing with his mother, and knew he'd never sleep this early. "Do you care if I take the bike out for a ride?" he asked Paul. After the recent walk-about, one of them had to be home with their mom, which was why they rarely made social plans for after work.

"I've got six weeks' worth of accounting to catch up on, which should take me every night this week and well into next, so go right ahead. I'll be here."

"Do you need help with the accounting?" It wasn't lost on Alex that his brother had shouldered a heavier portion of the burden for many months before he finally asked Alex to come home to help him.

"Nah, I've got it figured out, and it would take too long to show you the system. Easier to do it myself."

"You sure you don't care if I go?"

"I don't care, Al. I've got Sam Adams and the Red Sox to keep me company. Who could ask for anything more than that?"

The lighthearted statement contained far more truth than Paul had intended. Here they were, fairly good-looking guys in their mid-thirties with no sign of a wife or children for either of them, and no hope of such things when they couldn't make a single move without considering their mother's welfare first.

Yeah, Alex thought, as he went out to the barn where he kept the

Harley he'd brought home from DC with him, *the Martinez brothers made for very attractive marriage material.*

He'd expected to be married by now, maybe even have a couple of kids, too. But life hadn't worked out the way he'd planned, and who knew when he'd have time to think about a family of his own? He'd probably be too old and too bitter by the time he was able to go there.

Doctors had told them their mother could live for decades in her current condition. After losing his father so young, Alex was in no rush to live without his mom, but he couldn't visualize a future that didn't involve her daily care. What woman in her right mind would want to be a part of that?

"You're so fucking depressing to be around," he said to himself, taking advantage of the opportunity to swear to his heart's content. "Who'd want you anyway?"

Jenny had wanted him. The thought popped into his head so suddenly it nearly took his breath away and made his cock surge inside his shorts. He hadn't felt anything close to desire in so long he'd wondered if the old guy still worked. Today he'd discovered that everything worked perfectly, and God help him, but he wanted more of her.

He had no good reason to return to the lighthouse, and yet he could think of no good reason not to. Leaving the driveway, he pulled onto the main road, traveling in the opposite direction from the Southeast Light. The roar of the bike beneath him and the rush of the air through his hair made him glad he'd left the helmet at home. While he'd never ridden the bike without one in DC, he rarely bothered with the helmet here. Maybe that was stupid, but he felt safe here in a way he didn't anywhere else.

And it was too damned hot for the helmet. He rode out to the bluffs and back through town, making two complete circles of the island that took him past the Southeast Light twice. On the third circle, he turned the bike into the dirt road that led to the light and drove the bike around the locked gate. As he did that, he wondered if the roar of the bike would make her mad enough to throw something at him.

He chuckled, remembering her outrage and the splatter of a
tomato connecting with his back. That had definitely been a first.
He'd never made a woman mad enough to throw things at him, but
he'd also never behaved quite so spontaneously with a woman before
either. The last time he'd kissed a woman he barely knew had to have
been in college, but that didn't count, did it?

Still pondering that question, he roared to a stop outside the lighthouse, which was dark and sealed up for the night. The only light was
provided by the full moon that gave the entire place a yellow glow.

Great… Would he get the one-day award for waking the same
woman twice? He was about to turn the bike around and get the hell
out of there when the sound of activity above had him looking up.

She poked her head out the window to look down at him.

"Don't tell me I woke you up again."

"Okay, I won't. What're you doing here?"

What was he doing there? Alex had no idea. Well, he had *some*
idea… "I'm going swimming. You wanna come?"

"Now?"

"What's wrong with now?"

"It's dark."

"So?"

"Are you riding that thing without a helmet?"

"Yeah. So?"

"That's kind of stupid and so is swimming in the dark."

"Too hot for a helmet, and who says swimming in the dark is
stupid?"

"Everyone."

"You wanna fight with me or go swimming?"

"Can I do both?"

Alex smiled at her saucy reply. "Sure, knock yourself out and grab
a couple of towels while you're at it."

"Give me a minute."

"I've got all night." *Sure*, he thought. *I've got all night to* sleep, *which
is what I should be doing right now.* But sleep wasn't on his mind when
Jenny stepped out of the lighthouse a few minutes later, wearing a

short dress and flip-flops and carrying two beach towels. He could see her bathing suit tied around her neck and was suddenly very interested in whether it was a bikini.

If there is a God in heaven, please let it be a bikini. And PS, you owe me one.

She eyed the bike with trepidation. "Where is this swimming going to take place?"

"Here." He swung his left leg over the bike and stood, dwarfing her. How had he failed to notice earlier that he had a foot on her? Probably because he'd been too busy stuffing his tongue down her throat to pay attention to such trivial matters as height. "Come on." Gripping her hand, he led her around the lighthouse to the steps that led to the sand below.

"I don't think it's safe to swim down there at night," she said, pulling back. "There're rocks and stuff."

"Do you always do what's safe?"

"Yes. Don't you?"

"Not always. Safe is boring."

Apparently, she had nothing to say to that, which he took to mean she was considering whether or not she was safe in the dark with him. They navigated the stairs, aided by the light of the moon, and landed in the sand, where Alex kicked off his shoes and waited for her to do the same. At the water's edge, he dropped her hand to remove his shirt and then waited for her to pull the dress over her head, revealing what looked to be a pink bikini.

Thank you, God. We're almost paid up.

He spread the towels on the sand and held out a hand to her. "Ready?"

"I don't know if this is a good idea. What if we get caught in a rip current or something? No one even knows where we are."

"That's what makes it fun. It's you and me and the moon and the sea."

"All right, Dr. Seuss."

He turned his back to her and looked over his shoulder. "Hop on Pop. I'll keep you safe."

She laughed—hard—and then surprised him when she took him up on his offer, climbing onto his back and wrapping her arms around his neck. "Don't drop me."

"Wouldn't dream of it." Why in the world would he drop her when having her thighs pressed against his ribs felt so damned good? With his arms hooked under her legs, he walked into the water and eased them in slowly, staying close to the shore because he wasn't completely foolish about the risks of swimming at night.

"Ahhh, that feels good," she said as the cool water washed over them.

Was it his imagination or did she tighten her hold on him? No, definitely not his imagination. "Sure does. I thought I was going to burn up today."

"I couldn't deal with being outside all day in this heat."

"You do what ya gotta do." He held on tight as he lifted her up and over the gentle roll of the waves. The water was as calm as it ever was on the south side of the island, perfect conditions for a nighttime swim. "Could I let go for one second if I promise to come right back?"

"Sure." She released her tight hold on him and slid down his back.

Alex waited until she was standing before he let go of her and turned around to face her. "That's better." He drew her into his arms, arranging her legs around his hips. "Much, much better."

Her arms curled around his neck, infusing him with a strange sense of comfort, which was odd, considering he knew nothing about her other than her first name and where she lived. Maybe the comfort came from the anonymity and the relief of leaving his troubles behind for however long this latest interlude lasted.

"Did you think about what happened this morning after I left?"

"Not at all. Did you?"

"Nope. Just another day at the office. My female customers can't restrain themselves when I'm around."

Jenny snorted with laughter, which pleased him. That had been his goal. "They are only human, after all."

"Right? That's what I say, too. Although I've never had any of them throw stuff at me before."

"I refuse to apologize for that. You woke me up at an ungodly hour!"

Alex smiled at her indignation. Enough with the talking, he decided, tipping his head and going in slowly to kiss her. At first, he simply laid his lips over hers, waiting to see what she would do. Would it be like before, when the passion between them flared like fire finding dry brush, or would it simmer more slowly this time?

He quickly had his answer when her tongue dabbed at his bottom lip, setting off a chain reaction that made him groan and pull her in tighter against him. Her arms gripped his neck, and her breasts flattened against his chest.

This whole thing was insanity, and he hadn't done anything like it since he was in high school, when girls came on to him endlessly. Once in a while, he let one of them catch him—albeit briefly—but he'd always known everything there was to know about them. Even as he told himself this was insanity, he cupped her backside and squeezed.

Alex lost himself in the moment, allowing the sweet taste of her lips and the lush curves of her body to take him away from all his troubles and worries. Her hand on his face soothed and calmed him even if he felt anything but calm. He wanted more. He *needed* more.

Without breaking the kiss, he maintained his tight hold on her bottom and stood up to walk them to the shore.

CHAPTER 4

I've completely lost my mind, Jenny thought as she clung to Alex's muscular shoulders. Even as she questioned her sanity, she knew she wasn't about to send him away. The guy was like sex on a stick, and for the first time in her life, it didn't matter that she didn't know him. Nothing mattered but the way it felt to be held and kissed by someone who didn't know about her terrible tragedy, who didn't pity her from the word *hello*. He hadn't the first clue who she was, and she liked it that way.

As they emerged from the water, the heavy, sultry air only added to the erotically charged atmosphere. And when he laid them down on the towels, Jenny felt his muscles bulge and strain under her hands. He never missed a beat with the kiss, turning his head to deepen the angle, his tongue teasing and tempting her and making her forget the values she'd remained true to her entire life.

It felt too damned good to be held by a strong, sexy, confident man to think about values or future trips to the loony bin. She'd cross that bridge when she got to it. In the meantime, she was fully enjoying the protective way he held her, the sensual way he kissed her and the enticing strokes of his tongue, which were never too much but rather just right.

But suddenly it wasn't enough to be close to him. It wasn't enough to kiss him and touch him. She wanted more. Shifting onto her back, she tugged at him, encouraging him to move on top of her. She hadn't done anything like this in such a long time that she'd almost forgotten how to use her body to send the proper signals.

Jenny curled her leg around his hips, hoping he'd take the hint.

He did, and the pleasure flooded her. Almost of their own volition, her legs parted to welcome him into her embrace. The groan that rumbled from his chest only added to the heated desire that thrummed through her bloodstream. And then he shifted his hips and pushed the hard ridge of his erection against her, making her cry out from the punch of desire that slammed into her.

Alex broke the kiss, turning his attention to her neck, kissing from her ear to her throat and along her collarbone. He tugged at the bow behind her neck that anchored her bikini top. "Can I?" he asked gruffly.

The word *no* hovered on the tip of her tongue, but she couldn't bring herself to say it. She couldn't bring herself to say anything at all, so she only nodded and then held her breath as he eased the top away from her straining breasts. For the longest time he only looked at what he'd uncovered as the warm breeze had her nipples tightening unbearably.

Jenny squirmed under him, seeking relief of some kind or another.

"Easy," he whispered. "I'm not going anywhere."

It was the perfect thing for him to say. They had no time limit, no one waiting for either of them.

He bent his head over her chest.

"Wait."

His forehead landed on her sternum. "What's wrong?"

"You're not married or anything, are you?"

"Hell no. I wouldn't be here doing this with you if I had someone else. What about you?"

"Not married. Or anything."

"Now that we've got that cleared up, can we get back to what we were doing?"

Though she wanted nothing more than to get back to what they'd been doing—because it was about to get even more interesting—she felt the need to clarify one thing. "That's not exactly true."

"Which part?"

"The 'or anything' part. I've been dating. Some. Here and there. Nothing serious, though."

"Great. Glad we cleared that up. Green light to proceed?" As he spoke, his lips left a trail of fire over the tops of her breasts.

"One more thing."

His deep sigh relayed a world of frustration. "I'm listening."

She was almost afraid to say it because she didn't want him to leave. Not yet anyway. "I won't have sex with you."

"Who said I wanted to have sex with you?"

Jenny raised her hips a fraction of an inch, putting her sex in direct contact with his straining cock and drawing a tortured hiss from him. "You did."

His gruff chuckle made her smile. "I suppose I did, and I suppose I might've tried for a home run if you hadn't set me straight. But for now," he said, kissing his way to the valley between her breasts, "this is more than enough for me."

Jenny wondered if it would be enough for her and berated herself for taking the home run off the table. If only she wasn't so certain she'd hate herself in the morning…

When his lips closed around her nipple, she became quite certain she'd hate herself in the morning for saying no.

She grabbed handfuls of his long hair, holding on for dear life as he licked and sucked and bit. *Christ almighty*, the pain of his teeth clamping down on her sensitive flesh nearly finished her right off. He kept it up until she was nearly delirious from the pleasure, and then he shifted his attention to the other side.

The tight grip she kept on his hair had to be hurting him, but he didn't say anything, and she didn't dare let go. Jenny opened her eyes to look up at the star-laden sky as she arched her back, wanting to get closer to the heated torment of his mouth.

He stopped suddenly, his head dropping again to her chest.

"What's wrong?" Jenny tuned in to the heavy sounds of his breathing and the lap of the waves against the shore.

"Do you want me to stop?"

"Not particularly."

"So it would be okay if I kissed you here?" His lips landed on her belly, making her skin quiver.

"Mmm."

"How about here?" he asked, moving lower.

"That's good, too." *I'm not going to let him do* that, *am I? Apparently, I am. Oh my God, I have to put a stop to this madness. That's what it is. Utter madness.*

Alex untied the bows at her hips, and her bathing suit bottoms fell away, leaving her completely naked in the moonlight.

"Is this legal on Gansett Island?" Jenny muttered.

Alex laughed and continued to kiss her belly as he settled between her legs. "Do you honestly care?"

"I don't do this."

"Don't do what?"

"*This*. With men I barely know or men I just met or well, anyone."

"Well, that's a damned shame. Why not?"

"That's an awfully long story, and this isn't the time or the place."

"I wouldn't mind hearing your awfully long story sometime, but you're right about the time and place. I've got other things on my mind at the moment."

"I *can't*." But even as she moaned the words, she tightened her grip on his hair. She wasn't sure if she planned to pull him closer or push him away.

"Yes, you can." The rasp of his whiskers against her belly made a liar out of her as she arched into him, trying to get closer.

Fully aware of his destination as he kissed his way down her body, Jenny knew she had to stop him now, while she still could. She'd had sex a couple of times since Toby died, but she'd never allowed *this*. It seemed too intimate an act to do with a guy she didn't love. So why was she allowing Alex's broad shoulders to part her legs or his big, rough hands to cup her bottom to position her the way he wanted her?

For the longest time, he only hovered, as if giving her a final chance to truly say no. She didn't say no. She didn't say anything, because her brain refused to function properly. By the time he pressed his tongue into her folds, she was on the verge of begging him to hurry up.

Toby had been good at this. Alex was, too. He licked and sucked and *bit*... Jesus... And then he pushed two fingers into her, and she came hard, her legs shaking violently. He backed off, but only for a second before he was back for more, starting all over again as if he hadn't just delivered one of the most powerful orgasms of her life. In her right mind, she'd be wondering how he'd managed to keep the encounter entirely sand-free, but he'd done that as smoothly as he'd done everything else so far.

"I want another one," he said in that raspy voice.

"I can't."

"You said that before, and you did." He flexed his fingers deep inside her and bent his head to prove her wrong.

Usually she was too sensitive after the first one to go for two, but he powered through the sensitivity and had her coming again less than five minutes later. Utter insanity.

Apparently, satisfied with himself and his handiwork, Alex crawled up her body while keeping his fingers planted deep inside her. He sucked hard on her left nipple, making her moan, before continuing to her mouth, where he kissed her with deep thrusts of his tongue, which bore her flavor.

"You are so fucking hot." His coarse words, uttered against her lips, made her tingle all over. "Mmm," he whispered, stroking his fingers through the flood of moisture between her legs, "someone likes dirty talk. I'll have to remember that for next time."

Next time...

Those two words finally snapped her out of the sexual stupor he'd seduced her into. She pushed at his shoulders, wanting him off her immediately. Naturally, he resisted her efforts to dislodge him, flexing his fingers to remind her he was still inside her, as if she needed the reminder. "Please. Stop."

He immediately withdrew his fingers from between her legs and rolled off her onto his back. They stayed like that, side by side, breathing hard as the heavy night air washed over them.

Jenny's legs continued to tremble as her core pulsed with the after-effects of two scorching orgasms. Her eyes burned with tears that she refused to shed. She was thirty-seven years old and had never done anything even remotely close to this. She had no reason to feel ashamed and yet… Somehow that was exactly how she felt.

"Are you okay?"

He had to go and be sweet to her, which only made her feel worse. "I'm fine."

"What's wrong?" Alex raised himself up on one elbow so he could look down at her.

"Nothing."

"Are you having regrets?"

"Well, *yeah*. Duh."

"Why? We didn't do anything wrong."

"We barely know each other, and we're rolling around on the beach like a scene out of *From Here to Eternity*."

His soft chuckle was as sexy as every other damned thing he did. The man was truly a walking, talking example of sex on a stick.

Jenny sat up, covering her breasts with her arm as she felt around in the dark for her bikini top or bottoms, preferably both.

"Things are kind of screwed up for me right now," he said, "and I sort of like the fact that you don't know anything more about me than my first name and what I do for a living. But I'll tell you my last name, if you really want to know."

"No." The word was out of her mouth before Jenny could take a second to think it through. "If you tell me your last name, then I'll be tempted to call my friends tomorrow and find out everything about you. And that'll ruin everything. You're Alex Lawnmower to me."

Laughing, he said, "Okay, Jenny Lighthouse, but there's one other thing about me you already know."

"What's that?"

He cupped her bare breast as he kissed her. "I'm hot for you, and I want more."

She shook her head as she pushed him and his hand away. "No more. This was a one-time moment of madness, never to be repeated."

"You'll take away my will to live if you tell me we can never do this again."

"Don't make jokes about dying. Not to me, anyway."

"Why not?"

She bit her lip and shook her head. Telling him why not would change everything. "When you said things are screwed up, you don't mean because of a woman, do you?"

"Yes, but not in the sense you mean. It's family stuff, not romance stuff."

Strangely comforted to know he wasn't running from a bad relationship or worse—a bad marriage—Jenny located her top and tied it around her neck.

The brush of his fingers on her back tying the other part gave her goose bumps and made her nipples tighten with interest. *Down, girls. The party is over.*

His lips were soft against her shoulder, making her wish she was someone different, someone who could have a good time with a hot guy and not hate herself for it the next day. "It was more fun taking it off than it was putting it back on."

Jenny smiled in the darkness. He was sweet and funny and sexy and so much more than she was ready for. She'd only recently decided to give dating a whirl. Rolling around naked on the beach with a guy she'd only met that morning was way too far outside her comfort zone.

He helped her to locate the other half of her bathing suit, kept his back to her while she got dressed, shook out the towels and walked her back to the lighthouse without touching her again.

Jenny wasn't sure if she was relieved or disappointed that he'd kept his hands to himself. At the door, she turned to him, his arresting face illuminated by a floodlight. "I'll, um, I guess I'll see you when you cut the grass again."

His confident smile unnerved her. "If not before."

"Alex, really, I'm not in a good place for this sort of thing—"

He silenced her with a deep kiss that made a total and complete liar out of her. "See you around, Jenny Lighthouse." He let her go so suddenly that she had to reach for the door to steady herself as he handed the towels to her.

She held on to the door handle while he started the motorcycle and drove off in a cloud of dust. Her mother had always warned Jenny and her sisters to be wary of men who preferred motorcycles. Alex was exactly the kind of guy her mother had worried about—a bit reckless, a bit devil-may-care and a whole lot of trouble.

Jenny planned to take her mother's advice and stay far, far away from him.

By the end of the long, emotional day, Maddie was completely drained and feeling like a jerk for making such a big deal out of not being pregnant when she hadn't even wanted to *be* pregnant.

She cringed when she recalled her breakdown at Syd's. Like she had any right to be mourning an unwanted pregnancy in front of her friend, who was going to such enormous lengths to get pregnant after losing two children in an accident. "You're one hell of a good friend," she muttered to the darkness.

Her kids had refused to go to bed, and, sensing she was teetering on the edge of losing it completely, Mac had sent her outside with a glass of wine to decompress while he wrestled them into bed.

I have so much to be thankful for, she thought as she rocked on the deck that overlooked the ocean in the distance. Two amazingly bright and beautiful kids, her wonderful husband, who was so tuned in to her he could tell when she needed a break, a lovely home, her mom and sister close by and happily settled with men who adored them, her adorable niece Ashleigh, a future stepfather she'd come to love,

amazing in-laws and the kind of friends she used to dream of
having...

With so much happiness in her life, what right did she have to be
so decimated by such a silly thing as a false-alarm pregnancy?

"You have no right at all to feel this way. None."

"Talking to yourself, love?" Mac asked as he joined her on the deck,
dressed in only a pair of low-riding pajama pants that left his exquis-
itely muscular chest on full display.

Maddie took a long, hungry look at that most excellent man chest
and added it to her gratitude list. That chest and the man who
owned it were all hers, and he was the best thing in a life full of
amazing things. "I'm the only one who wants to hear my woes
today."

"I want to hear your woes every day. Are you going to tell me what
has you so wound up and weepy?"

"It's so stupid, and I feel like such a jerk because I bawled all over
Syd today when she's going through so much. I'm an idiot and a bad
friend."

"Madeline... You're going to piss me off saying something like that.
Who cooked dinner for Joe and Janey at least twice a week while she
was on bed rest? Who's stepped up for Laura to help with Holden
while she's been so sick? Who helped take care of Buddy while Luke
and Syd were on the mainland? Who has Ashleigh as much as her
mother does? Come on. You're an awesome friend and sister and aunt
and sister-in-law and cousin-in-law."

He pulled her up and slid into her chair, settling her on his lap
with his arms around her. Nuzzling her neck, he said, "You're the
most awesome wife and mother. You're the glue that holds our whole
unruly crew together, and everyone knows it."

Surrounded by him and his all-consuming love for her, Maddie
was finally able to confess her deepest sorrow. "I wanted that baby
we're apparently not having."

"I know you did. Shockingly, I did, too."

She raised her head from his shoulder. "You did? Really?"

"How could I not want another one just like the two we already

47

have? They're so freaking amazing, and what's one more in the midst of mayhem?"

"I thought you were mad about it."

"Why in the world would I be mad when it was my fault in the first place? You were drunk, I was sober, and I forgot the condom. What right did I have to be mad about anything?"

"Still... I didn't think it was what you wanted."

"You know how I feel about this island and crazy-ass pregnancies, especially after what just happened with Janey and P.J. That's the part I was freaked out about. Actually having another baby? Not so much." The chair rocked slowly under them, stirring the heavy air around them. "Goddamn, it's hot."

"So hot. There's not even the slightest breeze."

"Supposed to last another couple of days," Mac said.

"Thank God for central air."

"I was thinking we ought to shut it off in our room and have sweaty heat-wave sex."

For the first time in hours, Maddie laughed. "Leave it to you to want that."

"Come on. You know you want it, too. We can work around the monthly thing."

"The monthly thing was gone as fast as it came."

"Wait... so it only lasted a day?"

"Less than, actually."

"I don't want you to think I'm overly obsessed with what goes on down there, but doesn't it usually last a lot longer than that?"

"Yeah. It's probably the heat or something."

"Or something."

"What does that mean?"

"What if you really *are* pregnant, and the one-day period was a false alarm?"

The possibility hit Maddie like a lightning bolt to the heart. "That doesn't happen. Does it?"

"Might be time to pee on a stick, my love."

All of a sudden, tears were flowing down her cheeks in a flood that couldn't be contained.

"Hmmm, nonstop crying, emotional ups and downs…" Mac cupped her breast, making her startle from the almost shocking sensation that tore through her from the simple caress. "Sensitive breasts… I'm not a detective, but it seems like I might've witnessed these signs once before."

"Don't get my hopes up. I can't bear to not be pregnant twice in two days."

"Tomorrow we'll buy a test and get an answer." He kissed her neck and jaw, blazing a trail to her lips. "Since there's nothing we can do to resolve this dilemma tonight, how about I try to get your mind off it with some sweaty heat-wave sex?"

"That might help as long as you don't care if I cry the whole time."

"As long as you're crying from the pleasure, I'm fine with a few tears." He kissed her and patted her bottom to get her to stand. "Stay here. I'll be right back."

While he was gone, Maddie leaned against the rail, looking down on the yard as she thought of the possibility Mac had suggested. It was odd for her period to only last a day and not even a full day at that.

Mac returned carrying the handheld baby monitor, which he set on one of the teak tables that was part of their deck set. Then he set about removing the pads from two of the lounge chairs. He put them on the deck and held out his hand to her.

"Right here?"

"Right here."

She snuggled up to him on the makeshift bed, resting her head on his outstretched arm.

"I hate to see you sad about anything," he said.

"I'm sorry. I'm being crazy, and I know it—"

He kissed her soundly, silencing her words as much as her worries. "You're not crazy. You're adorable, and I love you."

"Don't be nice to me, or I'll start crying again."

"Fine then. You're a shrew and a hag, and I still love you."

She laughed even as tears filled her eyes. "How did I land such a fabulous husband?"

"You were very, very, *very* lucky."

"Yes, I was."

"We both were. And I'll tell you what, if it turns out you aren't pregnant, we'll try again next month." As he spoke, he removed her T-shirt and panties as well as his own pajama pants.

"I thought you never wanted to go through that again."

"I never again want to see you in any sort of pain or danger. That's the part I object to. Not the baby. So we'd do things differently this time. Make sure we're where we need to be way before you're due so there's no chance of any drama."

"Do you have any idea what it'd be like to have three kids under the age of five?"

"Worse than having two kids under the age of five?"

"I've heard it's way worse."

"You go from a man-to-man defense to a zone."

"Huh?"

"Sorry, basketball joke. Basically, it means they'll outnumber us."

"Yes, they will. And how about when they're all teenagers at the same time? What will that be like?"

"Will you be here with me?" Mac asked.

"Where else would I be?"

"Then it'll be as fantastic as the rest of our lives will be. It's all good, honey. As long as we have each other, they can't defeat us." As he spoke, he arranged them so he was behind her, his arm secure around her waist and his cock snug against her ass.

Maddie squirmed, trying to get closer to him, the position new and unfamiliar to her.

"It's getting sweaty around here," he said as he slid against her, the movement aided by the slight sheen on their skin.

"Mac… Hurry."

"I'm not in any hurry tonight."

The combination of the stifling heat, his nearness, the glide of his erection and the erotic thrill of making love outside had Maddie reaching for completion before he'd even touched her. He flattened his hand over her belly and worked his leg between hers. His hand slid from her belly to play with her breasts, tweaking her nipples and setting her on fire.

Her breasts were so sensitive that she almost begged him to stop touching her there, but he moved on, sliding his hand down to cup her mound as his cock nudged at her from behind. Maddie gripped the corner of the lounge pad, looking for something to hold on to as he inched into her in small increments that were nowhere near enough.

"Easy, honey. Relax against me."

"It's so hot," she said, moaning as the warm air heated her from the inside with every breath she took.

"Yes, you are."

She pushed her bottom backward, aching for more. "I meant the air is hot."

"That, too."

No matter how hard she pushed back, his hand on her hip ensured that he remained wedged just inside her. And then his fingers slid through the dampness above where they were joined, teasing and coaxing her toward release. He made her crazy with a combination of shallow thrusts and the small circular movements of his fingers.

She was on the verge of pleading when he rolled them to the left until she was facedown and he was on top of her, plunging into her now with deep thrusts and insistent fingers that swiftly took her straight to heaven.

He collapsed on top of her, both of them sweating profusely and breathing hard as he continued to throb inside her.

"Anything you want, sweet Madeline," he whispered in her ear, his breath making her shiver. "I'll give you anything you want."

Completely surrounded by him, she sighed with contentment. He always knew how to make her feel better. "I have everything I need as long as I have you and our family." As she said the words, she decided that no matter what the pregnancy test showed, she'd remember to count her many blessings.

CHAPTER 5

"That was freaking amazing," Josh Harrelson said through the microphone that linked the soundboard to the studio where Evan McCarthy had just recorded the first song for release under the Island Breeze label. "That's the one, man."

"You're sure?" Evan's insecurities were never far from the surface, especially when considering his own music.

"Ab-so-freaking-lutely. If that's not a huge hit, I don't know jack shit about this business."

"I thought you'd given up swearing," Evan said, relieved by the praise and amused as always by Josh's colorful dialogue.

"What did I say that was a swear?" He seemed genuinely baffled, which made Evan laugh.

"Not a damned thing." Evan checked his watch. Crap, it was getting close to two in the morning. "I gotta split before Grace sends out a search party."

"Wait till she hears that song you wrote for her. You're gonna get so lucky, dude."

Evan couldn't imagine getting any luckier than he already was, engaged to the most beautiful woman—both inside and out—he'd ever known, running his own business and getting ready to launch his own record label, right from his home on Gansett Island. Life was as good as it got, and Grace was the reason for most of his contentment these days.

High off the successful recording session, he wanted to see her and be with her and breathe in her intoxicating scent, even if she was sound asleep. He'd take her any way he could get her, he thought as he rode his brother Mac's ancient motorcycle home to her. Another bike went by in a blur on the other side of the road, passing him at high speed on the island's winding roads. Evan hoped the driver was someone local who knew the twists and turns, or he might end up wrapped around a tree if he didn't slow down.

Evan's cell phone vibrated in his pocket, but he left it there until he pulled into the parking lot at the pharmacy Grace owned in town and parked the bike at the foot of the stairs that led to their place behind the store. He pulled the phone from the front pocket of his jeans, and his eyes nearly bugged out of his head when he saw a text from his manager, Jack Beaumont. He hadn't heard from Jack in months, since his once-promising recording career blew up in a mess of bankruptcy filings, leaving his debut album locked in a court battle.

Are you up? Jack's message said. *If so, call me. Urgent.*

Evan glanced at the stairs, longing to be with Grace after sixteen hours at the studio, but he knew he'd never sleep until he found out what was so important that Jack had to text him in the middle of the night. He found Jack's number in his contacts and placed the call.

"Hey, Evan. Sorry to reach out in the middle of the night, but I just got the most incredible call, and I didn't want to wait to get in touch."

The unusually effusive tone in Jack's voice put Evan immediately on guard against whatever he might say.

"Are you there?"

"Yeah," Evan said. "I'm here. What's up?"

"I heard from reliable sources that the judge is going to issue some rulings tomorrow in the Starlight Records bankruptcy case. One of the rulings is about your album. He's going to allow it to be acquired by Long Road Records."

Long Road Records was owned by Buddy Longstreet, the reigning king of country music. A year ago, Evan would've sold his soul to the devil for this news, but everything was different now.

"Evan? Did you hear me?"

"I heard you. I'm just trying to process it." Visions of Grace, their incredible life on the island, surrounded by family and friends, the studio he'd poured his heart and soul into, the friend he'd persuaded to come to the island to be his sound engineer, the artists they'd booked through October to record there, the plans to turn their indie studio into a major hit machine… All of it ran through Evan's mind like film on fast-forward.

"I thought you'd be ecstatic."

"I am. Of course I am. It's just that I'm not sure what it all means."

"It means that Buddy Longstreet is going to get behind your album and your career and make you into a star like we always planned. That's what you want, right?"

Evan suddenly felt incredibly nauseated as memories of crippling stage fright came back to remind him of one of the reasons he'd been so relieved to watch his career go in an unexpected direction. "Um, I…ah… Listen, could we talk in the morning?"

"Sure." Jack sounded baffled and rightfully so.

"I'll talk to you then." Evan ended the call and sat on the bottom step, his mind racing with implications and scenarios and complications he hadn't anticipated. He'd considered the recording a lost cause and had tried to let it go during the months when he'd been too busy getting the studio off the ground to think about things he had no control over.

"Ev?" Grace's sexy, sleepy voice permeated the silence. "Are you down there?"

He stood and started up the stairs. "I'm here, baby."

Under the light of the moon, he saw her yawn as she tied a silk robe tighter around her waist. "I heard the bike, but then you never came up. I thought something was wrong."

At the landing, he hooked an arm around her and lifted her. "Nothing's wrong when I get to come home to you."

She squeaked with surprise and looped her arms around his neck, holding on tight.

Inside, they landed in a jumbled mess of arms and legs on the bed that was still warm from her body. The heat fired him up and cleared his mind of everything except for her.

"You're all charged up tonight." She ran her fingers through his hair in a gesture intended to calm him, but all it did was feed the fire. She knew his moods so well. Often after performing or recording, he was high on adrenaline. Tonight, he was high on her and everything she brought to his life.

"It's you. You do that to me."

"Right," she said, laughing. "It's all my fault."

In the faint glow of a nightlight, he gazed at her, drinking in every detail of her gorgeous face. "You know I love you more than anything, right?"

Her brows furrowed. "Of course I do. Are you worried I don't know that?"

He shook his head. "Just making sure."

With her hand curled around his neck, she drew him down to her. The instant his lips connected with hers, he forgot about everything but her. There was only her.

"You need to sleep," she said.

He tugged at the belt to her robe. "I need you more."

"Evan…"

"What, honey?"

"I love you more than anything, too. I love everything about our life."

"So do I." And he was loath to do anything that might endanger that life, even if it meant exchanging one dream for another. He didn't want to think about that now, though. Not when he had some precious time with his love.

A year ago, he'd thought his life was perfect. As he freed himself from his clothes and sank into her warm, welcoming body, he found true perfection. Every time he touched her, he knew perfection, and he couldn't imagine a day without her, let alone weeks or months on the road, promoting an album from a previous lifetime. All the years before her felt like they'd happened to someone else rather than him.

She caressed his shoulders, zeroing in on the tight knot of stress at the base of his neck. "You're so tense, Ev. Are you okay?"

"Mmm, I'm better now." Nothing in the world could compare to the sweet pleasure of making love with Grace. Everything about her appealed to him and had from the very beginning. They'd been together more than a year now, and every day was better than the one before.

Her hands slid over his back, clutching his ass to hold him deep inside while she climaxed. The tight squeeze of her muscles annihilated his control, and he cried out as he followed her. "Damn, that's so good." He captured her mouth in a deep, sensual kiss that revved him up again, like he hadn't just come as hard as he ever had. "It's always so damned good."

"I don't have anything to compare it to," she said lightly, "so I'll have to take your word for it."

Evan smiled as he kissed her again. "Trust me when I tell you, it's never like this." He kissed her again. "Ever."

Her arms encircled him, surrounding him with her love and her addictive scent. "When are you going to marry me and make a decent woman out of me?"

"I've been thinking a lot about that and asking around about the best place to go in the dead of winter when everyone will be ready to get off this island. I heard about a place in Turks and Caicos that I want to look into."

"We need a place that allows kids," she reminded him.

"That was on my list of criteria."

"I can't believe we're really talking about this."

"Let's do more than talk about it."

"What do you mean?"

"Stay there." He withdrew from her, got up and went to fetch her laptop from the desk and brought it back to bed with him.

"What're you doing?"

"Looking up the place I heard about." He typed into the search engine and clicked on the link to the resort. "Oh, look at that."

Grace sat up for a better look, oblivious to the fact that she was naked. A lot had changed in the last year, and now they were actually making wedding plans.

"I want to get married on the beach at sunset."

"That sounds perfect," she said with a sigh of contentment that pleased him.

He glanced at her. "Should we go for it?"

"Right now?"

"Why not?" He began to fill out a destination wedding question-naire. "How many people? You do the count: my parents, your parents, your brothers, my brothers, my sister, Joe, Abby, Stephanie, Maddie, Thomas, Hailey, P.J. Who am I forgetting?"

"Laura, Owen, Holden, the twins, your Uncle Frank, Shane."

"I have to invite my Uncle Kevin and his family, too."

"Aunt Joann?"

"Nah, she never leaves Gansett."

"Friends?"

"Tiffany, Blaine and Ashleigh. Oh my God, Ned! You have to invite him!"

"Jeez, he should've been at the top of the list—along with Francine. Getting to be a lot of people, though."

"We know a lot of people. Jenny, Syd, Luke."

Evan laughed as the numbers grew. "What's the count?"

"I lost count. Fifty adults, six kids.?"

Evan typed the numbers into the computer and hit enter. Then he clicked on the "Beach wedding at sunset" option from a pull-down screen, along with the month of January as his preferred month and hit Enter again. "Let's see what they've got."

They stared at the screen until the date of January eighteenth popped up as available.

"January eighteenth," Grace said.

"Are we going for it?"

She blew out a deep breath and looked at him. "You're sure about this?"

"I'm going to pretend you didn't just ask me that."

"Go for it."

Evan clicked on the link to Book This Date. "I need a credit card. Hand me my wallet, will you?"

Grace reached for it on the bedside table and gave it to him. "How much do we have to put down?"

"Twenty-five hundred to hold the date."

"That'll make it official."

"Certainly will. They're going to email us tomorrow to talk details."

"I can't believe we just did that," she said as he returned the laptop to the desk and got back in bed.

"What will your parents say?" he asked, accustomed now to how unsupportive they could be of their only daughter when she didn't fall in line with their idea of how her life should unfold.

"They won't approve, but who cares? It's not their wedding."

"Will they come?"

"I hope so."

"And if they don't?"

"Then they'll miss the best day of my life. Their loss."

"I wouldn't want anything to spoil it for you, Gracie."

"I'll be marrying you, right?"

"Damn straight."

"Then nothing, and I do mean *nothing*, could spoil it for me."

"You're the best thing that ever happened to me. I can't wait to put another ring on your finger and make it official."

"I can't wait either. January eighteenth."

"Be there or be square."

"I wouldn't be anywhere else."

Evan stifled a yawn. He didn't want to sleep yet. Running two thriving businesses, they got so little time to spend together, especially this time of year when the island was so busy. He hated to waste a minute of their time sleeping, especially now that they'd taken this huge step toward the next stage in their life together.

"You can't get out of it now that we've got it booked," she said in a teasing tone.

"Getting out of it isn't the goal."

"I really can't wait." Her arms tightened around him, keeping him close as she drifted off to sleep.

"Me either, baby." Evan lay awake for a long time, thinking about the news Jack had relayed earlier. What the hell was he going to do about that?

BEFORE SIX O'CLOCK THE next morning, Alex was back at work, driving one of the company trucks to the new home of Island Breeze Studios. The idea of a recording studio on Gansett Island had struck Alex as odd at first, until he heard his old friend Evan McCarthy was behind it. From the time they were in middle school, Evan had been obsessed with music, and Alex firmly believed the studio would be a huge success in Evan's hands.

Evan had called the office weeks ago asking for someone to come deal with the overgrown vegetation on both sides of the driveway that led to the studio. As he pulled up to the address Evan had given them, Alex groaned at the sight of the jungle that needed to be tamed.

"That'll take all damned day," he muttered, sending a text to Paul to let him know that the job was bigger than they'd thought.

Sorry, Paul replied. *I'm already fucking roasting.*

The heat was as killer as it had been the day before, beating down on him with vicious intensity. Today Alex had actually worn sunscreen, which he normally didn't bother with as his complexion was so dark he rarely had to worry about burning. But this heat wave was something else altogether, thus the sunscreen. Before he started on the bushes, he also applied a healthy dose of bug spray.

"Here goes nothing," he said as he got busy with a chain saw. He was working out months of frustration on Evan's brush when the man himself appeared on an old Honda motorcycle that looked like it had seen better days.

"Am I hallucinating?" Evan said after Alex cut the motor to greet his friend.

"I know I deserve that, but it's probably not wise to harass a man with a chain saw, especially in this heat."

Evan held up his hands and laughed. "Stand down. I come in peace."

"Sorry it took so long to get here. Things have been…complicated."

"How's your mom?"

Alex was prepared for the question, as he answered it often enough in the course of each day. "She's declined rapidly, but we're coping, thanks to the generosity of a lot of people."

"If there's *anything* we can do, please don't hesitate to ask. I mean it, Al. Anything."

"Thanks. Your mom and the other ladies from church have been incredible. They're propping us up."

"If you can bust loose tonight, Owen and I are playing at the Tiki. Everyone's coming, so it should be a good time."

"I'll have to see what the situation is at home, but if I can get there, I will."

"Call me if I can help."

"I will. Appreciate it." Alex eyed the brush. "Better get back to it. This is going to take a while."

"My family and friends will be grateful for your efforts. Lots of bitching about scratched cars and trucks when they come to visit."

"I'll get you fixed up."

"Thanks, man. Come up to the studio if you need to cool off."

"I might take you up on that."

"See you later." Evan started the bike and took off down the lane toward the studio.

Alex fired up the chain saw and got back to work. The mindless task gave him plenty of time to think about what had happened the night before with Jenny. He'd spent a lot of hours staring up at the ceiling when he got home, reliving every exquisite minute he'd spent wrapped up in her.

She'd claimed she didn't do things like what they'd done together, but he'd known that before she told him. She might as well have the words *good girl* tattooed on her forehead. Despite her reservations, she'd responded to him like a bad girl—a very bad girl—and he'd loved it.

He'd responded to her, too. In fact, he hadn't responded to anyone the way he had with her in a long time. Even Aimee, the woman he'd dated for two years in DC, hadn't stirred him the way Jenny had. She was an intriguing paradox—part innocent, part vixen—and he couldn't wait to see her again. Even though she'd told him theirs was a one-time interlude, he didn't believe for a minute that she'd honestly meant it. She'd been embarrassed by how far she'd let him go and had been reacting to that.

How could she not be curious when they'd ignited like a powder keg together? He was pretty damned curious about what it would be like to actually have sex with her, but he couldn't think about that right now, because a raging boner would only add to his extreme discomfort in the heat.

Frustrated, roasting and exhausted after the sleepless night, Alex turned off the chain saw and went to the truck to grab one of the bottles of water he'd frozen in anticipation of another scorcher. He'd left them to melt in the truck while he worked. As he chugged the cold water and dumped another bottle over his head, Alex knew with absolute certainty that he'd be visiting the lighthouse again—as soon as he possibly could.

CHAPTER 6

*A*rriving home after another twelve-hour day, Alex wanted a shower, a cold beer and some food—in that order. What he found, however, was a gathering of employees outside the greenhouses, where his brother was arguing with their mother, who was naked as a jaybird.

Standing before her, Paul held her bathrobe in his hands and had obviously been trying to get her to put it on.

"Oh my God," Alex whispered as he exited the truck and took off at a run to help Paul, who brightened when he saw Alex heading toward them.

Marion's back was turned, so she didn't see Alex approach, but he could hear her sobs.

"I want you to get your father right now and bring him to me, do you understand?"

"I can't do that," Paul said, looking imploringly at Alex.

"I'm not asking you. I'm telling you. You'll do what you're told."

Ignoring the crowd of employees that watched their sad drama unfold, Alex approached his mother and wrapped his arms around her shoulders. "I'm here, Marion," Alex said gently in a voice not all that different from his father's. "I'm right here, and I've got you."

She reached up to grasp his hands. "Oh, George. I've been waiting for you to get home. The boys have been unmanageable this afternoon."

Paul approached them tentatively.

"I'm here now." Alex took the robe from Paul and put it around their mother's shoulders.

"Why are we outside?" she asked Paul, anger replaced now with confusion.

Paul's face was lined with exhaustion and despair unlike anything Alex had ever seen, except for when their father was dying. "You wanted to come find Dad after your shower."

"But Daddy died, didn't he?" she asked in a small voice that made Alex want to sob with the utter injustice of this horrific illness.

"Yeah, he did," Alex said, saving Paul from having to say the words. "Let's go home and have some ice cream, Mom."

"Not before dinner," she said in a scolding tone that reminded Alex of the mother he used to know.

Paul turned to the employees who'd come out of the store and greenhouses to see what was going on. "Show's over," he said somewhat harshly. "Get back to work."

"I think I'd like to take a nap," Marion said when they got back to the house.

"The ladies are coming to take you to bridge night at church," Paul said. "You want to go, right?"

"Of course I do. I've been looking forward to that. Wake me up in time to get ready, will you?"

The moments of lucidity were almost harder to bear than the departures from reality.

"Sure, Mom," Paul said.

Alex walked her into the master bedroom and helped her into bed. He lowered the blinds and returned to the bed to adjust the covers over her. Bending, he kissed her cheek. "Sleep well, Mom."

"Was I naked in front of all those people, Alex?"

"Just for a second. They understood you forgot your robe. Don't give it another thought."

"I'm sorry."

"Don't be sorry. You couldn't help it. They know that."

"You and Paul shouldn't have to deal with this. You should be off having families of your own and instead—"

"We're right where we want to be, Mom. We love you, and we're happy to take care of you. Now don't fret. Get some rest so you can enjoy the night out with the ladies."

"I love you, too, Alex. And your brother. Tell him, will you?"

"I will." Alex left her to sleep, wishing he were alone so he could indulge the need to howl with rage at the entire situation. In the family room, he found Paul sitting in one of the easy chairs, elbows on his knees, head in his hands. "She told me to tell you she loves you and she's sorry for putting us through this."

Paul's head whipped up, his tearful eyes widening with surprise.

"Totally lucid," Alex said.

"Son of a bitch," Paul said through clenched teeth.

"What happened?"

"Mrs. Connor called to tell me she had to leave because her grandson got sick at summer camp, and she had to go pick him up. She locked up before she left, and Mom was here alone for maybe twenty minutes. When I got here and found her standing naked in the yard, I ran into the house to get her robe. In the time I was inside, she went down the driveway toward the greenhouse, calling for Dad.

"I chased after her, and when she saw me coming, she started shrieking at me to leave her alone and go get Dad. People came out of the store and the greenhouse to see what all the noise was about. You know the rest."

Alex got them each a cold beer, opened them both and handed one to Paul before he sat in one of the other chairs.

"How long had you been there when I got home?"

"About fifteen minutes."

"Shit…"

"Yeah. Exactly."

"I'm sorry I didn't get here sooner."

Paul waved off the apology. "You had no idea what was going on."

"Where do we stand with the nurse candidates?"

"We set up a Skype interview in an hour with one of them, Hope Russell. She's the one who has the young son. The other candidate bailed out because she doesn't think island life would suit her. So it's down to Hope."

"Her name is ironic, huh?"

"No kidding. I said that to David. He'll be by around six to sit in on the conversation."

"Will Mom be here?"

"Mrs. Feeny is due to pick her up a little before six for bridge night." Though Marion could no longer play the game, her friends were faithful about making sure she got to attend anyway. "We planned the interview for a time when she wouldn't be here. Can you make it then?"

"Yeah, sure. I'd like to hear what she has to say, too." He thought of Jenny and how badly he could use another hour or two wrapped up in her softness, but the despair on his brother's face took priority at the moment. "After that—you and me? We're going to eat a couple of gigantic, artery-clogging steaks and then go see Evan and Owen play at the Tiki."

"Oh, we are?"

"We are. Mom will be out until at least eleven, so we're going out, too. Maybe we'll even get totally fucking hammered." As much as he couldn't wait to see Jenny again, Paul needed him more.

"You're on," Paul said grimly, raising his beer bottle in Alex's direction.

GRACE RAN up the stairs from the pharmacy, determined to shower before Evan got home. The air-conditioning in the store had been no match for the oppressive temperature, and she felt disgusting after the long day in the swampy heat. On the way upstairs, she noticed the motorcycle parked under the stairs and groaned.

"Hope he doesn't get too close," she muttered as she opened the door and stepped into their place, where she found him sitting on the bed, head in his hands. Forgetting all about how she might smell, Grace dropped her bag and keys on the floor and went directly to him. "Evan."

He looked up, seeming startled to see her there. "I didn't hear you come in."

"What's wrong?"

Shaking his head, he held out a hand to her. "Nothing, honey."

She sat next to him. "Please don't lie to me. Whatever is wrong, we'll figure it out, but if you lie to me, we have a much bigger problem."

He leaned his chin on their joined hands. "Apparently, Buddy Longstreet has managed to wrestle my album from the Starlight bankruptcy proceedings."

"Wait. So what does that mean?"

"It means it's going to be released under the Long Road Records label."

"Oh." An astounding array of implications cycled through her mind in about thirty seconds of stunned silence. "When did you hear about this?"

"First heard it might happen last night, and Jack called today to confirm it's a done deal. The judge ruled today that Buddy can take ownership of the album by paying the court for the rights."

"You'll have to promote it."

"Probably."

"Which means you'll be gone for weeks at a time."

"Possibly."

"What about the studio?"

"I don't know. That's one of many things I'm sitting here trying to figure out, when I should be heading for the marina to meet Owen."

Grace noticed his guitar cases lined up like soldiers next to the wall by the door. He'd brought them home from the studio for the gig tonight. What would her home be like without him and his guitars and his oversized shoes all over the place? Her stomach ached and her chest felt tight as she tried to get air to her lungs. "This is really good news, Ev. You worked so hard on it, and for no one to ever get to hear it would be horrible."

With his head still propped on his hand, he glanced at her, smiling. "You always see the bright side, don't you?"

"What's the point of seeing any other side? It's happening, so we have to deal with it."

Evan caressed her face. "You're amazing. My amazing Grace."

She knew he'd written a song with that title, but he hadn't played it for her yet. He'd said he was saving it for a special occasion.

"I don't want to be away from you for one day," he said, "let alone weeks on end."

"You'll do one tour to promote the record and then come home and pick up your life here. That's what you'll do."

"I might be gone for months, Grace. And then what if it takes off?" He shook his head. "I don't know if I can do it. Buddy will want me to tour with him, which means huge arenas."

"You're worried about the stage fright."

"Yeah. Despite how insanely hot it is, I break into a cold sweat every time I think about performing in front of that many people."

"Could you maybe refuse to do it?"

"After Buddy paid God knows what for the rights? You think he's going to just let me get away with doing nothing to promote it?" He ran his hand over the stubble on his jaw. "I hate to say it, but I've got to go meet Owen. We're on in an hour, and I need to set up."

"We'll talk about it later. Go have a good time tonight. Nothing's going to happen immediately, so we've got time to figure things out."

"True." He leaned in to kiss her. "Try not to worry, okay? It doesn't change anything that truly matters. I promise you that."

Grace smiled and ran her fingers through his hair. "Take the car. I'll get a ride from Laura."

"Are you sure?"

"You can't take all those guitars on the bike, Evan."

"How do you think I got them home?"

Her mouth fell open.

"Psych," he said with a laugh. "Owen picked them up at the studio and brought them here earlier. I didn't want them exposed to the heat, so he didn't take them to the marina."

"I wouldn't put it past you to try to bring them on the bike."

Smiling, he kissed her one more time. "I'll admit to giving it some serious thought." He got up and went into the bathroom. As he brushed his teeth, he said, "Make sure you hydrate before you drink tonight. It's hot as snot."

"Believe me, I know. It was crazy hot in the store today. Will you be okay playing in the heat?"

"I'll probably sweat my balls off, but I'll be fine."

"Don't do that. I have plans for them."

He froze, toothbrush in his mouth, eyes wide with shock. "What?"

Removing the toothbrush, he said, "You never would've said that a year ago. I've been a terrible influence on you."

"Nah, you've loosened me up. I'm a better version of my old self thanks to you."

He spit out the toothpaste, splashed water on his face and combed his hair. Emerging from the bathroom, he came over to her and gave her hand a gentle tug until she stood before him. Wrapping his arms around her, he kissed her again. "I'm a much better version of my old self thanks to you, too."

"Love you," she whispered as she took a moment to wallow in the overwhelming love she felt for him.

"Love you more."

"No way."

"Yes way."

"We'll fight about that later. Go to work."

"See you there?"

"Wouldn't miss it."

"Good, because I never have stage fright when you're there."

Grace hid her surprise at hearing something he'd never told her before. Watching him pick up all the guitars and somehow get them through the door, she felt a crushing sense of fear that everything they'd managed to achieve together could be threatened by this unexpected change of plans.

Jenny's day had been dreadfully unproductive thanks to the nagging guilt and shame over her behavior with Alex. Everything she'd attempted to accomplish had been derailed by her lack of attention as much as the blistering heat that was literally sucking the life out of her.

At three o'clock she'd surrendered to the heat-induced exhaustion and gone upstairs to her bedroom to lie down for a while. She'd dozed off and slept fitfully, plagued by odd dreams that had her tossing and turning only to wake up throbbing with unfulfilled desire.

That was when she realized she'd been dreaming about Alex. "Oh God," she whispered through dry lips. Every cell in her body was on full alert, the way it had been last night when he'd driven her out of her mind with desire so potent she'd been unable to shake off the sex-induced stupor all day.

Glancing at the clock, she gasped at the late hour, then dashed out of bed and ran for the shower with only twenty minutes until Linc Mercier was due to arrive. After a quick and very cold shower intended to cool her body temperature as well as her suddenly ravenous libido, she kept one eye on the driveway watching for Linc and another on the bathroom mirror as she attempted to do something with her hair.

But the heat and humidity had other ideas, and she gave up on trying to tame the curls that had formed around her face in the heat since she was a little girl. Toby had called them her banana curls for some strange reason, she recalled with a pang of nostalgia. She hadn't thought of that in years.

Her face was so shiny with perspiration that she decided not to bother with makeup but applied some powder to combat the shine. This date was doomed to disaster status before she even left her own bathroom, and it was all Alex's fault. He'd fried her circuit board with a gruff voice, sexy body and incendiary kisses.

"Stop thinking about him and focus on the guy your friends were good enough to fix you up with," she said as she threw her cell phone, keys, some cash and lipstick into a small purse and stomped down the stairs, wearing the lightest-weight dress she owned and not bothering with a sweater because she knew she wouldn't need it.

She was far too out of sorts for a first date tonight, but it was too late to cancel. Besides, she had no desire to cancel. It was time to get back out there and meet people—men in particular—unless she wanted to spend the rest of her life alone. And that wasn't what she wanted. She'd loved being half of a couple during the years she'd spent with Toby and hoped to experience that kind of special bond again someday.

The only thing she knew for sure was if she stayed holed up in her own little safe zone, she'd never achieve that goal, and she'd sacrifice any remaining chance she had of being a mother.

While the lighthouse was a popular tourist destination, single men weren't lining up outside her door. Except for the one who'd come to cut the grass…

"You're not thinking about him, remember?" Right… Easier said than done after the most explosive sexual experience she'd had in twelve long years. She would never forget the first time she'd had sex after Toby died. It had taken more than five years to even consider the possibility of doing that with someone else. The guy, Drew, had been nice enough. They'd gone out a few times, and he'd known her story, so he was patient and considerate, which had only made the whole thing more excruciating.

Afterward, she'd cried uncontrollably. He'd said and done all the right things, such as they were, before taking her home and promising to call. She'd never heard from him again, not that she could blame him. That was one of the reasons why she'd appreciated the anonymity with Alex. He had no idea he was supposed to

be careful or patient with her, which was exactly the way she
wanted it.

When she'd gone out with Mason Johns last week, her past had
never come up, but she knew he was aware of it. Her friends would've
prepared him to ensure he navigated her emotional battlefield with
the utmost care. In truth, she hated being "tragedy girl," and for a brief
—albeit mortifyingly out-of-character—moment last night, she'd been
"Just Jenny" for the first time in a dozen years. She'd rather liked being
"Just Jenny" again.

She hadn't seen "Just Jenny" in a very long time, and apparently
she'd changed quite a bit over the years, if her behavior with Alex was
any indication.

You are not thinking about him!

A sharp rap on the mudroom door startled her, and she took a
deep breath in through her nose and blew it out of her mouth before
she went down the spiral staircase to greet Linc. He was a good friend
of Tiff's new husband, Blaine Taylor. As Blaine was the Gansett Island
police chief, Jenny took Blaine's approval as a ringing endorsement.

She opened the door and absorbed the wave of heat that smacked
her in the face. *Oh, he looks good.* Wearing madras plaid shorts with a
pink polo, Linc directed an appreciative smile at her. Tall and broad-
shouldered, he had close-cropped blond hair and friendly blue eyes.
He was more than man enough to pull off the pink shirt. "Hot enough
for you?" he asked.

"It's brutal."

"You look gorgeous."

"Thank you, but I feel like a wilted flower."

"Heat getting to you?"

"Big-time. No AC in the lighthouse, which is normally fine, but not
this week."

Executing a gallant bow, he extended his arm to her. "Right this
way, madam. I promise you an icy blast of air-conditioning to go with
dinner."

"You had me at icy blast." The instant she said the words, she began
to second-guess them. Did saying he'd "had her" make her sound

loose or easy? After her unprecedented behavior last night, she had cause to question everything.

But Linc just laughed at her comment and led her to a royal blue two-seater BMW and held the passenger-side door open for her.

"Nice car," she said as he slid into the driver's seat.

True to his word, he set the air conditioner to blast. "Thanks. It's my one major indulgence."

Jenny closed her eyes and let the cool air wash over her. "I suppose everyone has one."

"What's yours?"

"At the moment, it's your air-conditioning."

"Very funny." Shifting the car into gear, he left a cloud of dust in his wake as he pulled away from the lighthouse. "What is it the rest of the time?"

"I've moved around a lot, so I don't have all that much stuff I can't live without, but I do love my e-reader." She glanced over at him, appreciating his attractive profile and the scent of subtle but appealing cologne coming from him. He was exactly the type of guy she had always gravitated toward—handsome, a bit preppy, successful, confident, obviously witty and intelligent.

She made up her mind to give him a fair chance tonight, and the best way she could do that was to forget all about the moment of madness with Alex. It was in the past where it belonged, never to be repeated. There was no point giving it any more attention, especially when the perfect guy had just appeared at her door possessing all the qualities she looked for in a partner.

"So you're a big reader?" he asked.

"I love to read."

"What do you like to read?"

"Anything and everything. Mostly mysteries and suspense, some memoirs." She didn't mention that she'd recently been devouring the memoirs of 9/11 widows and widowers. Enough time had passed that she was able to read about the partners others had lost on that horrible day.

"I figured you were a romance type of gal."

"I used to read a lot of romance, but not so much anymore." He was only making conversation, and she didn't want him to be uncomfortable, so she didn't elaborate. The truth of it was she'd gravitated away from the genre she used to enjoy, because reading about fictional characters ending up happily ever after made her yearn for her lost love.

Linc took her to dinner at the Lobster House and regaled her with stories about the Coast Guard, including some amazing tales of his tenure with the search-and-rescue teams, and had her laughing about life as the older brother to four conniving younger sisters.

"I'm being a total bore talking about myself," he said as he poured the last of their bottle of chardonnay into her glass.

"Not at all. I enjoy your stories."

"I wouldn't mind hearing some of yours, too."

"My life is nowhere near as interesting as yours. No searches, no rescues, but I do have two younger sisters, so I feel your pain there." She made a joke, but her sisters were her best friends. "Yours sound a bit more spirited than mine, who married their high school sweethearts and have made me an aunt five times over."

"I bet you have pictures."

Charmed that he would ask, she withdrew her phone from her purse and found the latest pictures of her nieces and nephews. "Matter of fact, I do. Meet Michael, Lacey, Brent, Tyler and Mackenzie."

He flipped through the pictures with genuine interest. "They're incredibly cute, and clearly, blond hair runs in your family."

"Yep. We're all blondes." She found another picture of the entire family taken last Christmas and showed it to him. "Here's one with all of us. My dad, the one with the dark hair and eyes, is king of the blonde joke."

Linc cocked a brow that only added to his rakish good looks. "You let him get away with that?"

"In a house full of women, he put up with a lot more than we did. He deserves to take his fun wherever he can get it."

"Beautiful family. Where do they live?"

"They're all in North Carolina."

"How'd you end up so far from home?"

She suspected he already knew but was hoping to hear it from her. "That is a very long story."

"I don't have anywhere to be. Do you?"

He was charming and easy to talk to and funny. It would be too easy to share her story with him, but she wasn't in the mood for a trip down memory lane. "If it's all right with you, I'd like to pass on telling you that very long story, for now anyway. I'm having fun tonight, and it's not a fun story."

"Fair enough," he said, running his fingers over the stem of his wineglass. "As long as you know I'm interested."

She couldn't miss the double meaning in his words and smiled at him, grateful for his kindness, his interest and the fact that he didn't try to cajole the story out of her despite her obvious reluctance. That had happened before, and it was an instant turnoff for her. Anxious to change the subject, she said, "Some friends of mine are playing at the Tiki Bar at McCarthy's Marina. How do you feel about live music?"

"I love it, especially when Evan and Owen are playing together. I was going to ask if you wanted to go."

"Great," Jenny said, excited to continue the date and see their mutual friends.

He paid the check and casually reached for her hand on the way out of the restaurant.

Jenny curled her fingers around his much bigger hand, marveling at the strange twenty-four hours she'd had. Last night Alex had been arriving at the lighthouse right around this time, and... Well, there was no need to go over all that again.

And here she was tonight, holding hands with Linc Mercier during what was turning out to be one of the better dates she'd had since Toby died. As much as she liked Linc, though, he didn't inspire the same level of edgy, gut-wrenching desire she'd experienced with Alex.

Oh for God's sake! Give the guy a chance, will you? She admonished herself all the way back to the car, where Linc once again held the door for her and waited until she was safely settled before he closed the door and walked around to the driver's side.

On the drive from South Harbor to the marina in North Harbor, it occurred to her that she'd already known Linc for longer than she'd known Alex, and still, she wasn't climbing all over him the way she had Alex.

That thought made her mad—at Alex. If she'd never met him, she wouldn't be sitting here comparing him to Linc, who was exactly the kind of guy she needed in her life. Unlike Alex's man-of-mystery act, Linc was straightforward, forthcoming and handsome as hell. Not that Alex wasn't handsome… That was hardly an issue where he was concerned.

Determined to push all thoughts of him to the far corners of her mind, she recommitted to enjoying her evening with Linc.

He reached across the center console for her hand. When they pulled into a parking space near the marina, he turned off the car but didn't let go of her hand. Sitting in the waning daylight a couple of blocks from the marina, she was acutely aware of him and the fact that he intended to kiss her.

If he made the move, she decided, she would let him. She glanced over to find him watching her.

"You're incredibly beautiful, but you probably hear that all the time."

What might've been a cheesy line from another guy actually sounded sincere coming from him. "No, I don't."

"Well, someone should tell you that every day, because it's true."

Once upon a time, a wonderful young man had told her she was beautiful every day.

"Did I say something to upset you?"

Jenny shook off the moment of melancholy. "Not at all."

Turning toward her, he raised his hand to her face and leaned in to kiss her. While it was happening, Jenny felt removed from the situation, as if she were watching someone else kiss the sexy Coast Guard officer. The kiss was nice. He moved slowly and didn't go for broke at the first sign of interest from her. He showed restraint that she appreciated.

And when he pulled away and smiled at her, she smiled back.

Walking hand in hand with him to the Tiki Bar, it occurred to her that she'd felt absolutely nothing during that perfectly lovely kiss.

That, too, was Alex's fault.

CHAPTER 7

$\mathcal{M}$ ac, Maddie, Abby, Adam, Luke, Sydney, Grant, Stephanie, Tiffany, Blaine, Grace and Laura had commandeered a large table at the Tiki Bar.

Laura nudged Jenny's arm as she sat down next to her. "Having a good time?"

"Very good."

"Oh yay."

"Shush," Jenny said. "Don't let him hear you."

They introduced Jenny and Linc to Grant's friend Dan Torrington and his girlfriend, Kara Ballard, when they joined the group. Jenny had met Dan but not Kara.

Evan and Owen were playing "Home" by Phillip Phillips. The combination of the awesome music, the glorious sunset over the Salt Pond, the table full of good friends and the handsome man sitting next to her had Jenny relaxing a bit. She was determined to enjoy the perfect evening despite the lingering disquiet over last night's events.

The conversation flowed easily, as did the laughs. Mac and Grant grilled Adam about his trip with Abby to the mainland to visit Janey, Joe and baby P.J. in the hospital.

"The baby is *so* cute," Abby said.

"I think he looks just like me," Adam said. "He's got my strong, handsome jaw."

"Grant, will you please punch him in his strong, handsome jaw?" Mac said from the other end of the table.

"Oh, I'd love to," Grant said, "but I can't endanger the tools of my profession." He wiggled his fingers dramatically.

Adam snorted and nearly choked on a mouthful of beer. "He doesn't dare risk his digits on this jaw."

Abby made a fist and playfully landed it against her boyfriend's jaw.

"You'll pay for that," he said meaningfully as the others groaned.

Up on the stage, Evan picked up a banjo and gave it a quick tune.

"He plays the banjo, too?" Jenny asked, incredulous.

"He plays *everything*," Grace replied, watching her fiancé with pride. "He's so talented."

"Always has been," Mac said. "He used to drive us crazy when he was learning how to play the guitar and the piano. He didn't always sound as good as he does now."

"Haven't played the banjo in a while, so here goes nothing," Evan said into the microphone as he launched into the complicated banjo intro to "I Will Wait" by Mumford & Sons.

"They haven't played this before," Mac said.

"It's new," Laura said. "They've been working on it."

"They're so good," Maddie said.

All eyes were fixed on Evan and Owen, which was how Jenny didn't immediately notice when Alex walked into the bar. It took Grace calling out his name for Jenny to realize he'd come in with another guy who looked an awful lot like him.

"Over here," Grace said, gesturing for them to pull up chairs at their table. "You guys all know AM and PM, right?"

"Can't say I do," Linc said.

"Alex and Paul Martinez," Grace said. "Evan's friends from high school."

Alex Martinez. So he was at least a co-owner of the business… Jenny registered a pang of disappointment at losing the anonymity she'd shared with him and then just as quickly chastised herself for caring. She couldn't deny he looked really good in a slightly rumpled white shirt that was rolled up over his tanned forearms along with olive green cargo shorts. His dark hair shone in the late-day sunshine, but his eyes bore signs of disquiet, which had her wondering if something was wrong. Of course, she instantly hated herself for caring.

Linc stood to shake hands with the brothers. "Do you know Jenny?" he asked, gesturing to her.

Jenny wanted to curl up in a ball and dive under the table. But she calmly met the intense gaze Alex directed her way and even managed to shake his hand when he said, "Can't say I've had the pleasure."

She wanted to smack him when he gave her hand an extra squeeze, but she wouldn't give him the satisfaction.

"My brother, Paul."

"Hey, Jenny." Paul leaned across Alex to shake her hand. "Nice to meet you."

"Same to you." He was every bit as handsome as his brother but seemed to lack Alex's rough edges.

"We need some beverages," Alex said. "Another round for the table?"

"I won't say no to that," Mac said. "We've got a tab going. Buy yourself one on us."

"Thanks."

Was it her imagination, or was he staring right at her? And why did Linc choose that moment to put his arm around her? Alex directed his dark-eyed gaze at the hand that cupped her shoulder before continuing on to the bar, waving hello to Evan and Owen as he went by the stage.

Her gaze riveted to him, she watched his every move as he approached the bar and exchanged greetings with the bartender, a young blonde who lit up at the sight of him and seemed to know him well. Of course she did. Jenny would bet most of the young, single women on the island had made his acquaintance. A guy like him probably got around.

"How's your mom doing, Paul?" Maddie asked with a kind, concerned smile.

"Good days, bad days. Mostly bad days. Today was brutal, which is why we're out drinking."

"I'm so sorry," Maddie said. "If there's ever anything I can do to help, I hope you won't hesitate to call."

"I appreciate that. Everyone has been so great. We just had a promising interview with a potential nurse who we're hoping to hire to help us out."

"I so hope that works out for you," Grace said. "I don't know how the two of you have managed this long without professional help."

"Thanks to the generosity of many, many friends and Dr. David, who has been a rock."

Jenny's mind was spinning as she listened to the conversation while Evan and Owen played "Cool Change" by Little River Band. What was wrong with his mother? Was that what he'd meant by female problems, but not the kind she thought? She startled when she realized Linc was talking to her.

"Excuse me. What did you say?"

"I was asking where you'd gone off to."

"Sorry, just daydreaming."

Alex sent the round of drinks to the table with one of the waitresses, but he remained at the bar, his back to it, as he stared at her across the crowded venue.

Jenny felt his stare on her as intimately as she'd felt his fingers on her and in her the night before. She shifted in her seat, suddenly aware of a deep throb between her legs. How was that possible? How was he able to do that to her with merely a look, when a perfectly wonderful guy sat next to her, actually *touching her*, and she didn't feel a damned thing?

The worst part was the small, satisfied smile on his handsome face that told her he knew exactly what he was doing to her. So she decided to ignore him. She focused her attention on Evan and Owen, who were now playing "Ho Hey" by the Lumineers. As usual, their performance was full of energy and awesome music.

Half an hour later, she was still focused intently on the stage as well as the friends at their table, but she desperately needed to use the restroom, which would mean walking past Alex's post at the bar. Which was worse? Walking by him or wetting her pants? Right then, she couldn't say.

"I'm going to hit the restroom," Jenny said to Linc, charmed when he rose to help her from her chair. "Be right back."

Focused on not actually wetting her pants, she made a beeline for the bathroom and was proud of herself for not so much as glancing in Alex's direction as she went by him. She took care of business—with tremendous relief—and then gave herself a minute to calm down and get control of her ridiculous emotions.

Why did she react so strongly to him? What was it about him that made him different from other guys? Why couldn't she garner the same level of interest in Linc, who was a great guy?

Laura, Sydney and Tiffany came into the bathroom, looking for her.

"Okay, girlfriend, spill the beans!" Tiffany said. "Linc seems really into you! Are you into him?"

"He's a really nice guy," Jenny said, frantically trying to offer the level of enthusiasm they were hoping for.

Sydney took a closer look. "Oh no."

"What?" Grace asked, looking at Jenny for insight.

"She doesn't like him," Syd said.

"I never said that!"

"You didn't have to. I've seen you more excited to pick strawberries than you were when you called him a 'nice guy.'"

"I love strawberries," Jenny said, crossing her arms in annoyance. "I only met him tonight. I'm not rendering any verdicts. Yet."

"Are there sparks?" Tiffany said. "You've either got sparks or you don't. Take it from me—I've had both, and there's no mistaking sparks and no sparks."

"Thank you for that sage wisdom, Obi-Wan, but the jury is still out on the sparks."

Tiffany shook her head. "This isn't good at all."

"It's just one guy," Laura said, as if Jenny wasn't standing right in front of her. "We'll keep trying until we get it right."

"No," Jenny said. The word came out more forcefully than she'd intended. "No more fix-ups. For now anyway. I'll probably see Linc again, and my parents are talking about coming to visit. I'll let you know when I'm ready for more."

"Fair enough," Tiffany said, eyeing her shrewdly. "But we're not giving up until you're as happy as we are."

"You've been warned," Laura said with mock menace.

SHE'S IGNORING ME... *As if that'll get me to stop staring at her.*

After sending the drinks, Alex had stayed at the bar, trying to give them both a bit of space after the shock of running into each other and realizing they had mutual friends. And she was here with a date. Awesome.

She told you she's been dating here and there.

Nothing serious, she'd said. The blond dude in the pink shirt was awfully touchy-feely to say there was nothing serious going on between them. And how stupid did he look in a *pink* shirt anyway? What kind of self-respecting guy wore pink?

And you're jealous.

I'm not jealous.

Yes, you are.

Caught in the middle of an argument with himself, he almost missed the conversation taking place two barstools from where he leaned against the bar.

"She was bare-ass naked," a female voice said, "and running around the yard screaming at her son like he was twelve or something. It was hilarious. The woman is batshit crazy."

Seeing red with rage, Alex pushed himself off the bar and took two steps to confront the woman, gasping when he realized it was Sharon, the manager of the retail store.

Her face went slack with shock when she saw him standing there.

82

He could only imagine how furious he looked. "Mr. Martinez... I didn't see you there."

"Clearly."

"I...um..."

"My mother is not 'batshit crazy.' She has dementia, which is a disease that affects her behavior and her memory."

"I'm so sorry. I didn't know."

"Which is exactly why you should've kept your mouth shut."

Her mouth fell open and then closed just as quickly.

Silence had fallen around them, and Alex was aware that everyone nearby was tuned in to what was going on. "Get your things and get out. Tonight. You're fired."

"You can't fire me!"

"I just did. Now get your stuff off our property tonight, or I'll send my friend Chief Taylor over to help you along." As the manager, she lived in an apartment behind the store.

"You're as crazy as she is! Who are you going to get at this point in the season to take my place?"

"I don't care if we have to shut down the store. I'm not giving you one more red cent of my money."

She grabbed her purse and, with her wide-eyed friend in tow, vacated the bar.

As they walked away, Alex noticed that Jenny had witnessed the entire exchange when she'd emerged from the restroom. She stared at him with big doe eyes full of confusion and compassion. The last thing he wanted from her was compassion. He put his unfinished beer on the bar, dropped some cash to cover his beer, Sharon's unpaid tab and a tip for his bartender friend, and walked out without another word to anyone.

Paul chased after him. "Alex! What the hell just happened? What did you say to Sharon? Why did she tell me I'd better have a good lawyer?"

Fueled by rage, Alex kept walking until Paul caught up to him, grabbed his arm and spun him around.

"What the fuck happened?"

"I heard her talking shit about Mom to her friend. She said she was bare-ass naked and batshit crazy, so I fired her."

"Oh God, you fired her."

"I fired her."

"Okay." Paul combed all ten fingers through his hair repeatedly, a gesture that indicated his brain was racing.

Alex could certainly relate. "I'm sorry, Paul. I know the hiring and firing decisions are yours, and this is the last fucking thing we need right now, but I refuse to pay someone who's going to talk trash about our family in public."

"I'm with you, brother. Hundred and ten percent."

"But you're freaking out."

"Little bit." He dropped his hands from his hair, looking wearier than Alex had ever seen him. "We'll figure something out. Let's go home before she has a chance to screw things up on her way out."

Alex glanced back at the bar, wishing he had the balls to march in there and demand that Jenny come with him. But he didn't have the balls or the right to ruin her date with a guy who probably came with a heck of a lot less emotional baggage than Alex was dragging around behind him.

Fittingly, Evan and Owen were playing "Let Her Go" by Passenger. Jenny was a nice girl who had a nice guy interested in her. He would leave well enough alone, but damn, he wished he had the balls…

AFTER WITNESSING ANGRY ALEX, Jenny was more attracted than ever and devastated to learn his mother was suffering from dementia. With sons in their mid-thirties, Mrs. Martinez couldn't be that old. Jenny's grandmother had had dementia as an older woman, so she was familiar with how difficult it could be to manage and how devastating it was to family members.

She was proud of him for standing up to his rude employee and firing her on the spot, even if Jenny had noticed the hint of panic in his eyes when he'd calmly told the woman off.

As she rejoined Linc at the table, Jenny's brain whirled with everything she'd learned about Alex during the brief confrontation with his employee. He was loyal—fiercely so—to his family, willing to stand up on their behalf, unwilling to tolerate anyone making fun of his mother's infirmity and sexy as all hell when he was pissed.

But the agonizing pain she'd sensed in him overrode all the other thoughts that filed through her busy mind.

"Everything okay?" Linc asked.

Jenny started to assure him that she was fine, but she wasn't. Her skin was prickling with awareness and the need to do something, *anything* to ease the pain of a man she barely knew. "My stomach is a bit upset. Would you mind terribly if we called it a night?" She hated herself for lying to him, but she needed to get out of there. Immediately. Before she gave in to the urge to run after Alex.

"Not at all." Linc handed a twenty to Mac to cover their portion of the tab and stood.

"See you all," Jenny said.

Tiffany winked and gave her a thumbs-up.

Jenny rolled her eyes at her irascible friend.

Linc placed a proprietary hand on the small of her back that made Jenny feel uncomfortable. She didn't belong to him and didn't want anyone to think she did, especially a certain dark-eyed man who'd turned her whole life upside down in the span of two days.

He was just outside the marina gates, talking intently to his brother, when Jenny and Linc walked past on the other side of the street.

She glanced at him, and his gaze smacked into hers, nearly making her gasp with the yearning she felt coming from him. Like shards of metal drawn to a high-powered magnet, Jenny felt the pull from twenty feet away and had to fight her way through it when all she wanted was to run to him.

"Are you okay?" Linc asked, thankfully oblivious to the sizzling connection with Alex that she finally broke when she looked away.

"Yes, thank you." No, she wasn't okay. While on a date with one man, her mind was full of thoughts about another. That was certainly unprecedented. "Sorry to cut our evening short."

"It's okay. I have PT at zero-six-thirty anyway."

After a silent ride through town, they arrived at the lighthouse. Jenny hadn't locked the gate for the night yet, so Linc headed down the long, dark driveway. "It's kind of creepy out here at night. Are you ever afraid?"

"Not really. I usually lock the gate before sunset, so I have the place to myself." Except, she thought, when men on motorcycles drove around the gate.

"I had a really nice time tonight, Jenny. I'd like to see you again."

How to say this diplomatically? "I had a nice time, too." That much was true. "Things are a bit…unsettled in my life right now."

"Is that a polite way of saying you don't want to go out again?"

Jenny winced, thankful for the cover of darkness. "That's a polite way of saying my life is unsettled, and this isn't the best time."

He pondered that for a minute. "All right, then. How about I call you in a week or two to see if things have settled down?"

"That'd be great," she said with a sigh of relief that he wasn't going to push her to commit to a second date.

Leaning toward her, he spared her further embarrassment and awkwardness by kissing her cheek.

"Thank you for dinner," Jenny said.

"Thank you for the pleasure of your company."

Jenny got out of the car and appreciated that he waited until she was inside before he drove off. She ran up the stairs to the kitchen as she tried to figure out what to do. Should she go to Alex? And do what, exactly? Push him to talk about something he didn't want to talk about?

In the drawer under the microwave, she found the phone book the previous lighthouse keeper had left behind and thumbed through it, looking for the address of Martinez Lawn & Garden. She found the address and even knew where it was. But how did she know if he lived there?

Below the listing for the business, she found separate listings for

George & Marion Martinez and Paul Martinez, all at the same address as the business. So they lived on the grounds.

Jenny still didn't know what she was going to do with this information when she went up one more level to her bedroom and changed into shorts and a tank top, tossing the dress she'd worn on her date across the foot of her bed. She slid her feet into comfortable flip-flops and went back downstairs, grabbing her purse and keys in the kitchen and running for the stairs to the mudroom.

She threw open the door and screamed with fright at the sight of a large person standing in the dark outside her door.

"It's me," Alex said. "I knocked."

"I...I was upstairs. I didn't hear you."

"I hear keys. Going somewhere?"

"I...um, I was going to find you."

"Were you now?" He took a step forward and then another.

Out of self-preservation, Jenny backed away from him until her backside bumped against the far wall of the mudroom, right where one of their previous encounters had taken place. Her purse and keys dropped to the floor with a clatter.

"What happened to pretty boy?"

"Who?"

"The pink shirt you were with earlier."

"He went home."

"Did you send him home with a smile on his face?"

A bead of sweat slid between her breasts, and she wasn't sure if it was the heat or his nearness that had caused it. Probably both. "How is that any of your business?"

His hands found her hips in the darkness. "I'm making it my business."

He nuzzled her neck and made her melt. How did he do that so easily? She wanted to object to what he'd said, but her brain cells were as fried as her nerve endings.

"Did you send him away smiling?" he asked, more insistently this time.

"I sent him away confused about where exactly our great date went wrong."

"Where exactly did it go wrong?" His lips and breath against her neck made her nipples tighten.

"You know exactly where it went wrong."

"I want you to tell me."

"It went wrong the minute you walked into the Tiki Bar."

"Why's that?"

As her frustration with the conversation mounted, so did the throbbing need between her legs. "You know why!"

"If I knew for sure, I wouldn't be asking."

"Yes, you would, because you enjoy tormenting me."

His rough chuckle against her neck gave her goose bumps on her arms. "Is that what I'm doing?"

"How did you get here anyway? I didn't hear the bike."

"My brother dropped me off."

"Did you tell him about me?"

"Nope. I told him I was going for a walk in one of my favorite places. I've always loved it out here." His hands slid from her hips to cup her breasts. "Now I love it even more than I used to."

Jenny arched into his hands, needing to get closer.

"So what happened when I walked into the Tiki Bar?"

She'd hoped he had forgotten that she'd never answered his question. "I thought about what happened last night."

"I thought about it, too. All damned day." He pushed his erection into her belly. "I walked around like this all day, which is your fault."

"How is that my fault?"

"Because all I could think about is how damned sexy you are, and how badly I want another taste of you."

His words made her lips burn for another taste of him.

"Alex?"

"Hmm?"

"Do you want to talk about what happened earlier with your mom?"

"Fuck no."

His adamant reply made her sorry she'd asked.

"This is what I need." His hands were big and rough against her face as he held her still for his almost violent possession of her mouth. Lips and tongue and teeth and needy moans combined in an explosive wave of desire. "Take me upstairs."

CHAPTER 8

*J*enny was moving toward the stairs before the words were fully out of his mouth. With her hand wrapped around his, she led him up two flights of stairs to her bedroom.

"This is awesome," he said reverently as he went to the window to check out the glow of the moon over the water.

Jenny took advantage of the opportunity to stash the picture of Toby in her bedside drawer. Before the guilt could set in, Alex held out a hand.

She went to him.

"I'm sorry I was rude downstairs when you asked about my mom. It was nice of you to ask, but it's the last thing I want to talk about."

"I understand." And she did. How could she not? She had her own list of things she'd rather not talk about.

He looked at her, seeming to see all the way inside her. "Somehow I think you do." Glancing at the bed and then at her again, he said, "Is this what you want?"

"Yes," she said without hesitation. For the first time since she lost Toby, she felt like she was exactly where she belonged, and even if nothing came of the intense attraction between them, she was determined to enjoy it while it lasted.

"I don't share. If we're doing this, and I hope we'll be doing a lot of it, you're not doing it with anyone else at the same time."

"Neither are you."

"Done. I haven't been with anyone in the year since I moved back here. I'm healthy, and I can prove it. Do we need protection?"

After she'd made the decision to start dating again, she'd seen Victoria, the island's midwife, about birth control. "No."

"Jesus, I think I just died for a second there."

"Please don't do that."

"Figuratively speaking." He drew the tank top up and over her head.

Jenny's heart beat so hard she could feel it in her temples and between her legs and the bottoms of her feet in a steady drumbeat of desire and adrenaline. She stood perfectly still while he unbuttoned and unzipped her shorts, inserting his hands into the back to push them down. The heat of his hands branded her bottom through the silk of her panties.

She fumbled with the button to his shorts and nearly wept with relief when it broke free. The zipper followed, and she imitated his move when she used her hands on his finely shaped ass to push his shorts down. Only he wore nothing underneath them. "Commando?"

"Is there any other way to go in this blistering heat?" He raised his hand and pulled the rumpled white cotton button-down she'd admired earlier over his head, leaving him naked before her. In the faint moonlight, she could see the fine contours of his muscles, his dark tan, the paler skin below his waist, dark chest hair and the trail of hair that led to a darker patch around the erection that hung long and thick between his legs. "See anything you like?"

Since all the saliva in Jenny's mouth had dried up as she looked at him, she could only nod.

"Me, too. I see all kinds of things I like. Starting right here." He twisted his fingers against her back and freed her breasts from the tight constraint of her bra.

She whimpered in relief as he peeled the lace from her body and rubbed his chest hair over her tight nipples. Something inside her snapped at the rush of desire that came with the friction. Fisting his hair, she dragged him into a deep, searching kiss. She couldn't wait for the second taste he'd promised her downstairs.

When the backs of her legs bumped against the bed, she realized he'd been walking them backward. He came down on top of her, arms and legs entangled, his erection hard and hot against her belly as his tongue thrust into her mouth.

"As sweet as your kisses are, that's not the taste I've been yearning for since last night." He kissed a path from her throat to her chest, teasing her nipples on the way to her belly button.

Jenny was burning up from the inside. After not having a man do this to her in a dozen years, to have Alex do it twice in two days was overwhelming, to say the least.

He slid down on the bed, pushed her legs apart and opened her to his tongue. "Mmm, that's what I was thinking about all day." The flutter of his breath against her sensitive tissue and the scrape of his whiskers over her inner thighs drove her crazy as she arched her back, trying to get closer to the heat of his mouth. "Easy." His arm across her abdomen kept her anchored to the bed as he kept up the sensual torture. He licked and sucked and teased, making her scream from the pleasure. And then he added his fingers, driving two of them into her as he rolled her clit between his lips. He kept it up until she was on the verge of climax, then backed off, slowing the strokes of his tongue and fingers.

Jenny sagged into the bed, breathing hard and sweating profusely from the heat and the desire that thrummed through her in a relentless rhythm. She was about to beg him when he started all over again, slower this time. Grasping a handful of his hair, she tried to hurry him, but he wouldn't be hurried.

She groaned in frustration, which made him laugh.

"Patience."

"I have none."

"Get some."

Her hands fell to her sides, gripping the sheet as he continued to torture her with his tongue and deep strokes of his fingers. Jenny's hips surged against his mouth, and he took the hint, sucking her clit and running his tongue back and forth over it.

She detonated, screaming from the overpowering pleasure that ripped through her.

He stayed with her through the whole thing before moving up to cover her with his big, muscular body. "That was amazing," he whispered as he took himself in hand and pushed into her. "God, that feels incredible." He flexed his hips. "Oh, you're so *tight*."

Jenny dug her fingers into the muscles on his back as she struggled to accommodate him. Despite how primed she was after the powerful release, he was big, and she hadn't done this in years. A slight whimper escaped from her clenched teeth.

"Does it hurt?"

"A little."

"We'll have to go slow, then." He bent over her and drew her nipple into his mouth, sucking and tugging as he eased the pace of his entry. Little by little, he worked his way in, moving carefully and watching her closely with those dark-chocolate eyes. "Better?"

She nodded, sliding her hands from his shoulders down his back to his tight, muscular ass, which she gripped to keep him from moving until she was ready.

He released a tortured groan. "Gotta move."

"Not yet."

Throbbing and lengthening inside her, he dropped his head to her shoulder, his perspiration melding with hers to make their bodies slick. Between the heat outside and the heat they were generating together, Jenny was about to implode. She gradually lightened her hold on his ass and wriggled under him.

"Ready?" he muttered against her ear.

"Think so."

"Hold on to me."

She grasped his shoulders as he began to move, slowly at first, until he was sure she was with him.

"So fucking hot," he whispered. "And I'm talking about you, not the weather."

Jenny moaned as he picked up the pace, clutching her bottom in his big hands as he pounded into her. He took her on a wild ride, giving her no chance to think about anything or anyone other than him. Apparently, his patience extended to intercourse as well, because he kept up the ruthless pace for far longer than he should've been able to.

All at once, he slowed again, pushing hard into her and staying there as he gazed down at her. He brushed the hair back from her face and kissed her softly, lingering at her lips as he throbbed inside her. "Hold on tight."

Before she could ask him why, he had turned them over and positioned her on top of him, all without losing their connection.

"Speaking of fucking hot," he whispered as he reached up to cup her breasts, running his thumbs back and forth over her nipples.

Jenny flattened her hands on his chest, adjusting to the new position and the tight squeeze of his cock inside her.

"Ride me," he said gruffly, his hands finding her hips to guide her movements.

She swiveled her hips, and he groaned, surging into her. His thumb pressed against her clit, making her stagger and lose her rhythm until he helped her find it again.

His eyes closed and his lips parted. "Yeah, like that. *God*... So good."

Jenny had never been hotter in her life, and only part of that heat could be blamed on the weather.

He kept up the pressure on her clit as she moved over him, drawing a keening release from her that ripped through her body like a wildfire. She came back to reality to find him over her, hammering into her as he found his own release, surging into her again and again until he finally collapsed on top of her.

"Christ, I'm burning up." He withdrew from her and took her hand. "Let's go swim."

"You expect me to move right now?"

"Come on. It's so fucking hot I can't breathe. We need to cool off."

She'd never been with a guy who dropped the F bomb as often as he did, but somehow it suited him—a little rough, a little gruff, a whole lot sexy.

He coaxed her out of bed but stopped her when she reached for a T-shirt. "Just like this," he said, cupping her breasts and teasing her sore nipples.

"I'm not going out there naked."

"Yes, you are. Come on." He tugged her along behind him, heading for the stairs.

"You're crazy! I work here. People come out here all the time."

"There's no one here at this hour." As he argued with her, he continued down the stairs, keeping a tight grip on her hand.

Jenny made one last futile attempt to stop him before he marched through the mudroom door in all his glory, bringing her along with him in all her glory. She'd never been naked outside before last night, and here she was doing it again.

As they took the stairs to the beach and hit the sand, Jenny decided to stop worrying about getting caught and enjoy the most insane thing she'd ever done. They splashed into the cool water together, and she had to admit it was the first time all day she hadn't felt like she was roasting over an open fire.

"Now that's what I'm talking about," he said as he fell backward into the water, completely submerging himself.

Jenny had begun to wonder where he'd gone when she felt his hands cupping her ass and his lips on her back.

He drew her into his lap, settling his erection into the cleft of her bottom.

"How can you be ready to go again after what just happened up there?" She gestured to the lighthouse.

"It's all you, baby. You turn me on like no one ever has."

The revealing statement went straight to her heart, where it was firmly rejected. This relationship was not about hearts or flowers or even relating in any way other than physical. She'd do well to remember that before she got too involved. He didn't even know her last name or anything about her other than where she lived and who some of her friends were.

Linc Mercier knew more about her than the man who was currently playing with her nipples as his hot, wet lips tortured her neck. Jenny couldn't believe the way her sex tightened in anticipation of more. She wouldn't be able to move tomorrow.

"Bend forward a little bit," he whispered in that gruff voice that got to her every time.

"Why?"

"Just do it." He kept a firm grasp of her hips as she hesitantly did as he directed. When he had her positioned the way he wanted her, he slid into her from behind, driving all the way to the hilt in one long stroke that made her cry out from the impact as well as the cool rush of water inside her. "Hurt?"

She swallowed frantically, trying to form words. "No."

He settled her back against him, spreading her legs wide so they were on either side of his and working her clit and nipple from behind. "I told you a swim was what we needed to cool off."

Her shaky laugh drew one from him, too. *This is utter insanity!* Then he flexed his thighs, opening her farther so he could cup her sex where they were joined. He barely moved, and yet he managed to take her to the brink with just the angle of his penetration, the press of his fingers and the brush of his whiskers on the back of her neck.

She covered his hand to keep him from removing it and directed his attention to the place that throbbed for him. Impossibly, he opened her even farther, stretching her nearly to the point of pain as he drove deeper into her, making her come hard against their joined hands.

His arms banded tight around her as he followed her, groaning against her ear as he heated her from the inside. He lifted her off him and turned her to face him, sliding his arms around her and sinking into a deep kiss that had her tingling all over again.

She turned away from the kiss.

"What?"

"That's it, buster. All you're getting tonight."

"We're just getting started."

"No, we're just getting finished."

"Come on…" He tweaked her nipples and surged to life under her.

"Oh my God, you're a freaking machine!"

"Not usually."

"Stop pretending like this is something special when we both know we're just scratching an itch." The words came out more harshly than she'd intended, and judging from the way his muscles tightened with tension she'd scored a direct hit. "Sorry, but come on… We both know what this is. And what it isn't."

"So you have this kind of chemistry with everyone? That pink-shirt dude… He turns you on the way I do?"

He had her there, Jenny thought. "No, but—"

Alex's lips stifled her words. "No buts. We're hot together, and there's no denying that."

"Maybe so, but you don't even know my last name or where I come from."

"Your last name is Wilks, and you come from the South, judging by the accent you slip into whenever you're annoyed, which is often when I'm around."

"How do you know my last name?"

"I asked someone."

"Who did you ask?"

"None of your business."

Jenny struggled to get free of him, but she was no match for the tight band of his muscular arms.

"Stop," he said, laughing softly as he caught her earlobe between his teeth. "I asked Owen earlier, and he told me your name."

"*Great*," she said with a groan. "He'll go home and tell Laura you were asking about me, and they'll be on me like bees on honey tomorrow."

"No, they won't. I told him you were pissed at me for showing up so early to mow the grass out here."

"You did?"

Nodding, he nibbled on her bottom lip and managed to scramble her brain until she nearly forgot the sort-of argument they were having. "Hold on." With his hands cupping her ass, he stood and walked them to the beach.

Jenny kept her arms and legs tight around him as he went directly to the stairs and carried her all the way to her bedroom. By the time they got there, they were dry again. "Is it always this hot here in the summer?"

"Never like this." He came down on top of her, settling into the V of her legs and pinning her hands over her head.

"No more," she said in a tone that barely convinced her, and judging from the grin that lit up his face, he wasn't convinced either. "I mean it."

"Okay." His lips moved on her neck as his big body kept her pinned to the mattress, surrounding her with his strength, the musky scent of sex and salt water and his obvious desire for her that pulsed against her belly.

"Turn over," she said.

"Don't want to."

"My turn to be in charge."

"I thought we were done."

"Are you saying no?"

"Definitely not." He released her hands and did as she asked, flopping onto his back, knees raised and arms curled above his head.

Jenny licked her lips as she eyed the sexy man laid out before her. She could touch him and kiss him anywhere she wanted to, which filled her with a sense of her own power, especially when his eyes heated with obvious desire. His erection lengthened, stretching to above his navel. Being the devil that he was, he let his legs fall open, almost daring her to put her focus where he wanted it most.

Recalling the way he'd tortured her, she ran her hands up the insides of his legs, taking her time and making him wait for what he wanted, the same way she'd had to. She let her hair drag over his erection, making him groan as he lifted his hips.

"Patience," she said mockingly.

He barked out a laugh. "Ain't got none."

"Get some."

The more he tried to control her, the longer she made him wait. Despite the recent swim, he broke out in a sweat when she dragged her breasts over his chest and groin.

"Motherfucker," he whispered fiercely, making her smile. He did have a way with a swear word.

"My mother would wash your mouth out with soap if she heard you talking that way," Jenny said in a prim, scolding tone.

"My mother tried to wash the dirty words out of my mouth, but they haven't invented a soap strong enough." He slid his hands into her hair, pressing on the back of her head to tell her what he wanted. "I want to wash your mouth out with something other than soap."

"Oh my God, you're so fresh!"

His laughter made his abs quiver, which caught her attention.

She licked and nibbled his eight-pack until his laughter morphed into a groan and the pressure of his fingers in her hair became almost painful. That was when she decided to have mercy on him and ran her tongue over the rigid length of his arousal.

He released a sharp gasp that became yet another groan. "*Jenny.*"

She lifted her head to meet his gaze. "Yes?"

"For Christ's sake, don't *stop*."

"Then be quiet and let me concentrate."

"Yes, please concentrate. You wouldn't want to miss anything."

He was really quite irreverent but also enormously entertaining. "Shhh." This was said against his straining shaft. She wrapped her hand around the base and squeezed. How could he be so hard after coming the way he had—twice? As she stroked him, she ran her tongue over the tip, dipping into the slit and then under to tease the sensitive skin below the head.

"Oh my fucking *God*, that's good."

Jenny held back a laugh as she took him into her mouth while keeping a firm grip on the base. This was another thing she hadn't done since she'd lost Toby, and she hoped she remembered how. She didn't want to think about Toby right now, not when Alex was so vibrant and alive under her, begging her with the subtle movement of his hips to take him deeper.

She opened her mouth wider and let him slide toward her throat as she cupped his balls.

He fisted handfuls of her hair and arched his back, swearing softly under his breath as she licked and sucked and applied gentle pressure to his most sensitive area.

Her lips were stretched almost to the point of pain as he got impossibly harder.

"*Stop*," he cried.

She knew he was warning her that he was on the brink, so she gave him a taste of his own medicine and backed off, leaving him sweating and panting for the release she'd denied him.

He fell back to the mattress and released a harsh laugh as he continued to breathe heavily and throb in her hand. "So mean."

"Revenge is a bitch, and so am I," Jenny teased, continuing to stroke him with her tongue.

"No, you're not," he said, tucking a strand of her hair behind her ear and running his finger over her cheek. "However, I wouldn't be opposed to some more of that."

With only her lips touching him, she said, "Hmmm, let me think about that."

He startled from the electric connection of her vibrating lips. "You're out to kill me, aren't you?"

"Most definitely not."

He gave her a curious look that quickly became something else entirely when she took him into her mouth, lashing him with her tongue as she applied gentle suction. His entire body trembled and his grip on her hair tightened.

"Jenny…" he said on a long sigh as his back arched. "*Jenny.*" The second time he said her name more urgently, which was the only warning she got before he came in her mouth. "God*damn*."

She wiped her hand across her tingling lips.

"Come here." He held out his arms to her and brought her to lie on top of him. "That was incredible. *You're* incredible."

"Good to know I haven't forgotten how to do that," she said and instantly regretted the telling statement.

"You've definitely not forgotten. You made me crazy, but I suspect that was your goal."

"Turnabout is fair play." She loved the way he held her. She loved the way he smelled of soap and clean sweat and salt water. She loved a lot of things about the way she felt when she was with him. Despite all this love she was feeling, she reminded herself what this was about—and what it wasn't.

There was no reason that she could think of why a woman her age couldn't have a hot summer affair that was all about sex. People did it all the time, right? Just because she'd never done it didn't mean she couldn't start now with something new and different. She'd certainly had enough of the status quo. Maybe a hot summer affair was just what she needed to shake things up before she moved on to a more significant relationship.

"I can almost hear you thinking," he said as he ran his fingers through her hair, making her scalp tingle along with her lips. He tapped a finger on her forehead. "What goes on in there?"

"Nothing much. You've managed to fry most of my brain cells tonight."

"You fried most of mine, too."

As his chest hair tickled her nose, Jenny smiled. It was good to know they were equally affected by what had transpired between them.

"Could I ask you something?"

"Sure," she said tentatively.

"You said it's been a long time since you did this, which leads me to wonder why a gorgeous, sexy woman like yourself would choose to live alone in a lighthouse."

Her brain was stuck on the words "gorgeous, sexy woman."

"Living in this lighthouse, on this island, has been very good for me, believe it or not."

"Have you ever been married?"

The question as well as his curiosity took her by surprise. "No.

You?"

"Nope. Engaged?"

Jenny closed her eyes tight. "Once."

"What happened?"

"It… He, um…"

"It's okay. You don't have to tell me. We've all got stuff we'd rather not talk about."

While she was relieved that he wasn't going to push her for answers, she suddenly wanted to know what he'd rather not talk about. It wasn't that she didn't want to tell him about Toby, but she knew how that story changed things. It made people look at her differently, and she didn't want Alex looking at her differently. Not yet anyway. If this continued, eventually he'd ask again and she'd have to tell him. But for now, she liked the fact that he didn't know about her awful tragedy.

"Are you roasting with me on top of you?" she asked.

"Not too bad."

As much as she didn't want to move, it was way too hot to stay pressed together sharing body heat. "How do you feel about a very cold shower?"

"That sounds like heaven." He released her, and Jenny stood, acutely aware of her nudity, which was rather foolish in light of what they'd done together.

She bit back a groan when her already sore muscles protested the movement. *Tomorrow—or I guess it's today now—will be fun.* With him following her, she went into the adjoining bathroom, where the small shower stall had just enough space for both of them. Jenny turned on the water, set it to cool and retrieved towels from under the sink.

"This place is so awesome," Alex said as he took in the bathroom.

"It's got everything I need, along with the most amazing view."

Standing pressed together in the shower, they rinsed off salt water, sand and sex, taking turns washing each other. He even massaged shampoo into her hair. His tenderness was somehow harder to process than the raw erotic side he'd shown her earlier.

"I should go," he said when they were clean, dry and wrapped up in towels.

"You don't have to go yet. Unless you want to."

"I don't really want to." He ran his fingers down her arm, took her hand and led her back to bed.

"We should change the sheets. They're all sandy and gross." She crossed the room to the trunk where she kept extra linens and retrieved clean sheets.

"Did you paint that?" he asked of the painting of her view propped on an easel.

"Yes, that's my masterpiece."

He took a closer look. "It's really good."

"Thanks. Maybe someday I'll actually finish it."

Working together, they changed the sheets.

When the bed was made, he came over to her side and tugged at the towel she'd knotted above her breasts. "It's too hot to sleep in anything other than the altogether."

She let him remove her towel and watched as he dropped his into a pile on the floor next to hers. "As long as you know we're not getting these clean sheets dirty."

Laughing, he followed her into bed. "That sounds like a challenge."

"It's not."

He turned on his side to face her. "You're pretty far away over there."

She turned on her side. "Better?"

"Still too far away."

She slid a bit closer. "It's too hot for much more than this."

He placed a hand on her hip over the sheet. "Is it too hot for this?"

"I suppose that would be okay."

Lifting himself on one arm, he leaned in to kiss her softly. "I had a really, really good time tonight after a really, *really* shitty day. Thank you for that."

She caressed his face, running her thumb over the stubble on his jaw. "I had a really good time, too."

Alex smiled and kissed her again before he settled on the pillow next to hers. "Are you sure it's okay if I stay? You won't get in light-house-keeper trouble or anything?"

"It's fine," she said with a chuckle.

"I should go home, but my brother is there, and I'm so damned comfortable here."

"Relax and get some sleep while you can."

He brought their joined hands to his chest, where Jenny could feel the strong, steady beat of his heart. Long after he fell asleep, she was awake thinking about how much she liked him and how strangely connected she felt to him despite her plans to keep her emotional distance from a man who'd initially seemed all wrong for her.

The more time she spent with him, the more she began to suspect he could actually be all right for her.

CHAPTER 9

$\mathcal{E}$van and Owen played the last notes of "Ring of Fire," played in homage to the heat, and stepped back from the microphones to guzzle the bottled water they'd been drinking all night.

Grace was glad to see Evan taking his own advice about hydrating between beers.

"Damn, it's a hot one on Gansett," Owen said to cheers from the crowd. "We've got a special treat for you tonight. As you know, my buddy Evan is the owner of the new Island Breeze recording studio right here on Gansett. He's recorded the first single on the Island Breeze label, and he's going to debut it here tonight. How lucky are we?"

More cheers from the crowd at the Tiki Bar.

"Oh and Grace," Owen said, "you're going to want to come up here, if you would."

It took a second for Owen's request to sink in. She glanced left at Laura and right at Stephanie.

"Go," Steph said, giving her a push. "He's waiting for you."

Evan nodded at her, gesturing for her to come to him.

Grace's heart beat hard and fast as she stood and walked on wobbly legs to the stage.

"Ladies and gentlemen," Owen said, "let's have a round of applause for Evan's fiancée, Grace Ryan."

The hooting and hollering from the table full of friends and family as well as everyone else in the bar had Grace burning with embarrassment. She hated being the center of attention, which her fiancé certainly knew.

Owen took her hand and helped her up the stairs.

"I'll get you for this," she said under her breath.

"He made me do it," Owen said as he went down the stairs, leaving Grace alone on stage with Evan.

"Isn't she gorgeous?" Evan asked, setting off another round of cheers and whistles.

"You're a dead man," she hissed at him.

As if he didn't have a care in the world, Evan tossed his head back and laughed. "Have a seat in my office, baby."

When she was settled on the stool Owen had abandoned, Grace folded her hands and tried to ignore the sensation of sweat rolling down her back. So much for the cool shower she'd enjoyed after Evan left earlier.

"I've been saving this for a special occasion." As he spoke into the microphone, he never took his eyes off her. "We met right here just over a year ago, and my lady and I have been making some wedding plans, so I'd say this counts as a special occasion, wouldn't you?"

More cheers and whistles. She really was going to have to kill him for embarrassing her this way. And then he started to strum his guitar, and everything faded away except for him and the music and the words and the love as he sang "My Amazing Grace" to her. They might've been completely alone for the way he focused entirely on her.

My amazing Grace, how sweet she is,
She took a wretch and made him a man
When I was lost, she was there
When I was blind, she led me home

'Twas Grace who taught me how to love
And Grace who took away my fear
How precious is my darling Grace
She gives me hope to carry on

Amazing Grace, how lucky I am
To be the guy she loves
To be the one she chose
To be the one to take her home

My amazing Grace, how sweet she is,
She took a wretch and made him a man
When I was lost, she was there
When I was blind, she led me home

When we've had ten thousand days together
I'll still want more
A lifetime with my amazing Grace
Will never be enough

My amazing Grace, how sweet she is,
She took a wretch and made him a man
When I was lost, she was there
When I was blind, she led me home

By the time he played the final notes, Grace had tears running down her face, and all she could think about was what she'd do when he left. She couldn't picture a day without him, let alone weeks on end.

Pushing the guitar to his back, Evan put his arms around her as the crowd went wild cheering and stomping their approval of the beautiful song.

Grace couldn't seem to stop crying.

"Good tears?" Evan asked.

She nodded.

"Are you mad I did this here?"

She shook her head.

"Can you talk?"

She shook her head again, making him laugh. It took a few minutes for Grace to recover her composure, wipe her face and pull back from his embrace. "That was incredible. Thank you so much."

He kissed her right there in front of everyone. "We'll be back in a few," Evan said to the crowd.

Canned music blasted through the speakers.

Evan held out a hand to help her off the stool.

Owen appeared to assist her down the stairs.

She heard Evan say, "I'll be right back," to Owen.

"Take your time. I can handle things here for a minute."

With his hand on the small of her back, Evan escorted her to the table, where their friends and his brothers greeted them with applause.

Grace fanned her face, certain it was bright red from the emotional wallop as much as the heat.

"That was incredible, Ev," Maddie said.

"It's gonna be a smash hit," Grant added.

"Let me know if you need an entertainment lawyer," Dan said. "I know people."

"Thanks, everyone. Glad you liked it." Evan accepted the beer that Mac handed him and offered it to Grace.

She took a long drink before she handed it back to him. "Thank you," she said softly, hoping he knew she wasn't talking about the beer.

"Thank *you*." He kissed her forehead and leaned in close to whisper in her ear, "I can't wait to marry you. I know you're freaking out about what I told you earlier, but when I think about the next year, that's the number one thing on my agenda. No matter what else happens, we've got a date to keep in January."

"Will you play the song again at the wedding?" she asked, looking up at him, fortified by his assurances.

"You bet I will."

~

A RINGING PHONE jarred Jenny out of a deep sleep. Movement next to her startled her for a second until she remembered that Alex had stayed.

"What's up?" he asked in a gruff, sleepy-sounding voice. Suddenly wide awake, he sat up straight. "I'll be right there." He got up and started looking around for his clothes.

Jenny turned on the light for him. "What's wrong?" she asked, blinking him into focus.

With his back to her, he stepped into his shorts. "My mom. Paul thinks she might be having a heart attack."

"Oh my God." Jenny got up and went to her dresser for clothes.

"What're you doing?"

"I'll drive you so you can get there quicker."

"You don't have to do that."

"I know I don't." She got dressed as fast as she could, which wasn't easy with hands that didn't want to work the way they were supposed to and a body full of sore muscles. When they were dressed, they rushed down the spiral stairs to the kitchen, where Jenny looked for her purse and keys before remembering she'd left them in the mudroom earlier.

In the car, she blasted the air-conditioning, taking the relief from the heat where she could get it. She glanced over to find Alex staring straight out the windshield, his jaw rigid with tension. "Has she had heart trouble before?"

"No."

"Am I taking you home?"

"Would you mind going to the clinic? Paul called rescue, and they're on their way there."

"Of course." Jenny drove as fast as she dared on the winding road to town and pulled up to the clinic's emergency entrance ten minutes later. "Do you want me to come in with you?"

For a second, he seemed torn with indecision. "No, you don't have to. Thanks for the ride."

"I hope she's okay."

"So do I." He got out of the car to meet the ambulance as it turned into the parking lot.

Jenny moved her car out of the way but couldn't seem to make herself leave. She parked and watched from a distance as Paul emerged from the back of the ambulance. He and Alex stood together to watch the paramedics remove the stretcher from the back. David Lawrence came out of the clinic to meet them, and Alex and Paul rushed inside with him.

She knew she ought to leave. His family crisis was none of her business. But that second of indecision she'd seen on his face had her shutting off the car. It had her reclining the seat ever so slightly. And it had her watching the clinic door for the rest of the night.

ALEX EMERGED into the soft dawn light feeling like he'd been assaulted after the long night without sleep—and the sexual marathon that had proved he wasn't as young as he used to be. The relentless heat smacked him in the face as he left the cool interior of the clinic. He did a double take when he saw Jenny's car in the lot. Other than David's car, it was the only one there, so it was hard to miss.

Approaching the car, he saw that she was asleep with all the windows open. Seeing her there, obviously waiting for him, hit him square in the chest, making him ache for much more from her than what they'd already shared. He knew it was stupid to feel that way. After all, what did he have to give her besides a family and business in disarray? But he couldn't deny the ache in the vicinity of his heart as he touched her shoulder gently, trying not to scare her.

She came awake, blinking her eyes. "How is she?"

"She had a bad case of heartburn from something she ate at bridge night."

"Oh thank goodness."

"David is keeping her for observation for a few more hours. I'm going home to get my truck and coming back to get them."

"I'll give you a lift."

"You didn't have to wait for me, Jenny."

"I know."

He looked at her for a long time, drinking in the sight of big brown eyes, kiss-swollen pink lips and soft blonde hair and trying to decide what it was about her that had him so undone. She'd waited all night for him, even after he'd told her she didn't have to. Why had she done that?

"Are you coming?"

Realizing he'd been staring at her, he nodded and walked around the car to the passenger seat.

Without asking him where she was going, she drove him home. As they went through the entrance to Martinez Lawn & Garden, he directed her around the greenhouses.

"Home sweet home," he said, looking to break the silence—and the tension.

"It's nice," she said as they approached the ranch house where he'd grown up.

"It was nice of you to wait."

She shrugged as if it had been no big deal to sacrifice a good night's sleep for him. "I had a lot of time to think while I waited."

Oh please don't let her say she doesn't want to see me again. He really would lose his will to live if he couldn't lose himself in her once in a while. Or every day. Every day would definitely be preferred to once in a while. He held his breath while he waited to hear what she had to say.

"You fired the woman who runs the retail business."

He released a deep sigh of relief that she wasn't telling him they were over. "You heard that, huh?"

"I think the whole bar heard it."

The reminder of the new challenge facing them made Alex feel even more exhausted than he already was.

"I'd like to help you."

He was shaking his head before the words were even completely out of her mouth.

Her hand on his arm stopped him cold. "Hear me out. I have an MBA from Wharton, and I have extensive retail experience. I put myself through college managing a clothing store. I don't know a thing about plants or greenhouses or horticulture, but I could probably fake it well enough to lend a hand. If it would help you."

Touched by her offer and her sincerity, he said, "You may not know much about horticulture, but you grow—and throw—a mean tomato."

Jenny's laughter filled him with an unreasonable amount of happiness. Similar to a limb reawakening, the feeling bounced through his body like a bad case of pins and needles. It'd been so long since he'd felt anything resembling happiness. "It's really nice of you to offer."

"I want to help."

Those four simple words packed one hell of an emotional punch. He was a fucking mess this morning if that was all it took to unravel him.

"And for what it's worth," she added. "This," she said, gesturing to the greenhouses and retail store in front of them, "has nothing to do with what happened last night."

"Sure, it does."

"Well, that's not why I offered. You and your brother are going through a tough thing. My grandmother had dementia, so I know how difficult it is. I'd like to think that while we were frying each other's brain cells, we might've formed the start of what some people call friendship. That's what I'm offering you—friendship and professional assistance. No strings, no ties, no obligations. If it would help."

He took her hand and gave it a squeeze. "It would help tremendously. Sharon came to us with management experience. The rest of the staff is made up of college kids, so it's not like there's someone else who could easily take her place." Glancing at her, he said, "If you're serious, I gratefully accept your offer, but only temporarily until we can get someone permanent. I don't expect you to upend your life to help me."

"I'm not upending anything, but I'm happy to help you in the interim."

"I'll need to run it past Paul. The hiring and firing are usually his department."

"Of course, that's fine. Let me give you my number, and you can call me if you want my help. If you don't, no worries." She recited her number, which he programmed into his phone.

"Isn't that a New York area code?"

"I used to live there."

"I'll talk to Paul this morning and give you a call later." He leaned across the console to kiss her. "Thank you."

She cupped his cheek. "Try to get some sleep."

"Not seeing that on the day's agenda." Because she was so gorgeous and sweet, he took one more kiss. "It means a lot to me that you waited and that you offered to help. Thank you."

Her smile was lovely and potent. "That's what friends are for."

"I'll call you later."

"Okay."

As he walked into the house to shower and change before going back to the clinic, Alex's thoughts were full of Jenny. He couldn't deny their amazing physical connection, which was unlike anything he'd ever had with another woman, but more significant all of a sudden was the emotional connection. She'd touched him deeply this morning, and he couldn't wait to see her again.

JENNY DROVE HOME IN A DAZE, stunned by the way Alex had looked at her when he told her it meant a lot to him that she'd waited for him and offered to help. She'd be a fool to deny that something powerful was happening between them. What started off as a purely physical thing had taken a turn toward something far more significant in the last twenty-four hours.

If she were being honest, what she'd found with him was exactly what she'd been hoping for when she told her friends she was ready to start dating again. The connection she felt with him was one she'd experienced only one other time, and it had been just as immediate with Toby. They'd met in an accounting class and commiserated over the relentless pace of the class and grad school in general.

She'd talked to him exactly once and had known he was someone special. It hadn't taken long for them to be inseparable. They'd stayed that way for three incredible years until they were forced apart by horrible tragedy.

For a long time after Toby died, she'd expected never to feel that way again, and she hadn't until she met Alex and knew right away there was something different about him. At first she'd thought it might only be physical, but now she knew it could go beyond that—if they wanted it to.

Did she want it to? *Yes,* she thought without a doubt. *Yes, I want it to go beyond the physical.* Seeing him in pain over his mother's condition had made her hurt, too. She'd felt elated when she had the idea in the middle of the night to help him and his brother at the store. It might not be much, but it was something she could do to relieve their over-whelming burden.

Jenny returned to the lighthouse and went straight up to bed. Every muscle in her body was sore and stiff from the sexual gymnas-tics of the night before. Despite the merciless heat, she slept for a couple of hours and actually felt worse when she woke up.

"If I was looking for proof that I'm not cut out for nonstop sex, here it is," she said to herself as she sat on the edge of the bed. Shuf-fling to the bathroom, she decided it wasn't possible to feel this bad from having too much sex. This felt more like the flu—with an over-dose of sex thrown in to make it worse.

She swallowed some painkillers, took a long, cool shower and emerged feeling barely human. The thought of eating made her want to vomit, so she went downstairs for some water and returned to bed.

Lying in bed, looking up at the ceiling, Jenny could only hope that Alex didn't get whatever she seemed to have. That was about the last thing he needed at the moment. Her cell phone rang, and she checked the caller ID, delighted to see her mom's number.

"Hi there."

"Hi, honey. How's it going?"

"I'm actually lying in bed wondering if I might have the flu."

"Oh, too bad. What're your symptoms?"

"Achy all over and nauseated." She didn't mention the unreasonably sore muscles or the reason for them, even though her mother would probably be delighted to hear that Jenny had found someone special to spend time with.

"That doesn't sound good. Is it still hot?"

"Crazy hot."

"I wish I was there to take your temperature and bring you ginger ale the way I used to."

"I wish you were, too." Jenny missed her family in North Carolina, but the opportunity to go somewhere new, where no one knew what'd happened to her, had been greatly appealing when she'd read about the Gansett Island lighthouse-keeper job in the newspaper. "What's going on there?"

Her mom regaled her with news about her sisters and their families, including a funny story about her nephew Tyler being scolded at preschool for kicking his friends with his new boots. "Needless to say, Emma took the boots away from him until he can play nice with his friends," her mom said of the younger of Jenny's two sisters.

"Poor Tyler. He loves those boots."

"I know, but as Emma said, who knew they came with attitude?"

Jenny smiled as she pictured her pint-size nephew with hair so blond it was nearly white. She and Toby had planned to eventually move back to North Carolina after they got their careers off the ground. They'd also hoped to wait a few years to start a family, so their children should've been growing up alongside her nieces and nephews.

The sheer unfairness of what had happened to him—and to her—was never far from her mind, especially when she was around her sisters and their families.

"Are you and Dad still hoping to come visit?"

"We'd love to. He's trying to figure out a few things at work, and then I'll email you some dates."

"Sounds good."

"Let me know how you're feeling, okay?"

"I will. I'll text you tomorrow."

"Love you, honey."

"Love you, too."

Jenny put down the phone and toyed with the idea of getting up and trying to eat something, but her stomach turned from the idea alone, so she stayed put, dozing intermittently until Syd called later that afternoon.

"Were you sleeping?" Sydney asked.

"I hate to admit that I was. Not feeling too hot. Well, that's not true. I feel like I'm going to implode I'm so hot, but I might have a fever on top of this miserable heat wave."

"Ugh, that doesn't sound like fun."

"I'm sure it's nothing to worry about. I just feel like shit. But how are you? It was good to see you out last night."

"It was good to be out. I'm sick of looking at my own four walls."

"You're feeling better?"

"Still a little tired and sore, but much better than I was."

"Glad to hear it. How long do you have to wait to test out the new plumbing?"

Sydney laughed. "Another two weeks, not that Luke is counting down or anything."

"Aww, poor guy."

"Poor guy will survive. We've been...improvising."

"I'm sure you have," Jenny said, amused by her friend. "You know... You two, you give me hope."

"How so?"

"Seeing you so happy with Luke after all you've been through, it makes me believe it could happen to me, too."

"It will happen for you. I know it will."

Jenny thought of Alex and what they'd shared the night before. She wanted to tell Sydney about it but hesitated, because if she did, it wouldn't belong just to them anymore. For now, she wanted to keep it private.

"Speaking of things happening for you, Luke ran into Mason

yesterday. He said he had a really nice time with you, and he'd like to see you again."

Jenny cringed and was grateful Sydney couldn't see her expression. "He's a great guy, but he's not the great guy for me."

"I know you said the jury was still out on Linc—"

"He's not the great guy for me either."

"Oh, I was so hoping… You seemed to be having a good time together last night."

"We did. It's just, you know, no spark." Jenny sighed. "I must sound like the biggest princess. You guys have gone to all this trouble to arrange dates for me—"

"Stop," Syd said gently. "If it's not there, it's not there. You're not eighteen anymore. You know yourself and what you're looking for. Please don't feel like you owe us any explanations."

"Still, I hope you know I appreciate the fix-ups, even if they haven't worked out the way we hoped."

"We know that. Let us know when you're ready to try again. We've got other guys in the stable."

Jenny laughed at the vision of hot guys lined up next to each other in stalls waiting to be found by the right woman. If only it were that easy. "Did I miss anything after I left last night?"

"Oh, you should've seen it! Evan played the song he recorded for release from the studio—'My Amazing Grace.' He brought Grace up on the stage and sang it to her. I swear, we were all bawling our heads off—no one more so than her."

"I'm sorry I missed that."

"It was quite something, and apparently they've set a wedding date. January eighteenth in Turks and Caicos."

"A destination wedding," Jenny said with a sigh. "How nice."

"They thought it would be fun to get everyone out of here in the dead of winter."

"It's a great idea."

"We're getting together here this afternoon to go over the details of Tiffany's shower. If you feel better, come on over."

"I will as long as I'm not communicable."

"Sounds good. Hope to see you."

"Syd… I just want to say… You and the others have been such a godsend to me. You have no idea."

"Oh, honey, yes, I do. The people here saved my life in every way that matters, and we love having you as part of our group."

"Thank you. I hope to see you later."

"We'll be here."

Jenny ended the call and turned on her side, snuggling into her pillow, counting her many blessings. Before she'd come to Gansett, she'd been floundering at home in North Carolina, working for a PR firm and surrounded by well-meaning people who watched her all the time for cracks in the armor.

Here, no one had known her before the great tragedy. No one had known Toby. No one had known them together. Though her friends on Gansett knew what had happened, her tragedy didn't define her relationships here the way it had at home.

She could breathe here, and at some point during her time at the lighthouse, she'd finally healed. The night she'd spent with Alex had shown her she was still capable of emotions she'd thought buried forever. Part of her heart would always be broken over the loss of such a wonderful, beautiful man in the prime of his life. But her life wasn't over, and her time with Alex had reawakened her desire and her passion and her hope for a second chance. Whether her second chance would be with him or not was yet to be seen, but he'd shown her it was possible to find that connection again.

And she couldn't wait to see him.

CHAPTER 10

*A*t times, Maddie McCarthy hated living on an island where she couldn't get exactly what she wanted when she wanted it. Both the pharmacy and grocery store had been completely sold out of pregnancy tests, so she'd had no choice but to make an appointment with the island's midwife, Victoria Stevens, to figure out whether or not she was pregnant.

Annoying, right?

If she lived anywhere else, she'd already know by now. But if she lived anywhere else, she wouldn't have met Mac and found the perfect life with the perfect man. Well, he was mostly perfect. He'd been driving her nuts for two days as they waited for her appointment time to arrive.

She'd flat-out refused to allow him to accompany her to the appointment, which had sparked a rather intense argument that she had won. *If* she was pregnant, he'd get to attend enough of the appointments. She was doing this one on her own. And Victoria was running late, which was only adding to Maddie's annoyance.

David Lawrence emerged from the swinging double doors that led to the exam rooms, escorting an elderly patient to the registration desk. When he'd finished with his patient, he turned and saw her sitting there.

"Hey, Maddie. How are you?"

"I'm good, and you?" She would be eternally and forever grateful to him for saving the life of her darling Hailey, not to mention what he'd done for Janey and P.J.

"Busy as hell, but I wouldn't have it any other way. What's the latest on Janey and the baby?"

"P.J. is off the vent and breathing on his own. Janey is feeling stronger every day. They're hoping to come home in another couple of weeks."

"That's great to hear."

"How's my friend Daisy?" Maddie asked with a sly grin.

"She's fantastic. I've finally convinced her to move in with me."

"Oh, that's so great, David. I'm happy for both of you."

"I'm pretty happy for us, too."

"You both deserve every good thing."

"That's nice of you to say in light of what you know about me."

"You and Janey weren't meant to be," Maddie said with a shrug. "She was meant for Joe, and I'm starting to believe you were meant for Daisy."

"I think you might be right."

Victoria came rushing through the double doors. "Hi, Maddie. I'm so sorry I'm running late. Come on in."

"I'll see you later, David."

"Bye, Maddie."

As she followed Victoria to an exam room, Maddie could feel the beat of her heart in her throat. It was hilarious to realize that a few short weeks ago, the idea of being pregnant again had been horrifying to her and Mac. But now that the possibility had been dangled before them, all they wanted to hear was that she was pregnant.

"What's going on? Your appointment was tagged as urgent."

"I feel silly, but I think I might be pregnant, and there's not a test to be found on this godforsaken island, so you were my only option."

"What're your symptoms?"

"A very brief, less than one-day period that might not have actually been a period, sore boobs, emotions all over the place, cranky as hell, horny as all get-out. Same as the last two times."

"When was your last real period?"

Maddie rattled off the date.

"And you've had unprotected sex since then?"

"Yes. Quite by accident and due to far too many glasses of wine."

"Ahh," Victoria said, her eyes lighting up. "I was going to say... I thought you'd decided to wait awhile before you talked about another baby."

"We had decided to wait, but..." Maddie shrugged and grinned at the pretty midwife. "Shit happens."

"Yes, it does, and it keeps me very busy."

They shared a laugh as Victoria made some notes in her laptop. "Let's do a urine test and a quick exam and see what's what. Good?"

"Yes, sounds good." Well, except for the part about the exam, but after two pregnancies, she'd gotten used to the indignities associated with childbearing. Victoria took her to the lab for the urine test and then left her in the exam room to undress. Riddled with nerves, Maddie donned the gown that barely covered her copious breasts and sat on the edge of the exam table.

While she desperately wanted the baby she might not be carrying, the thought of three children under the age of five was daunting, to say the least. Thomas and Hailey were well-behaved, good sleepers and relatively easy kids, but parenthood was a lot of work. It was an all-consuming proposition.

Mac had said if they were going to have three kids, they may as well have them close in age so they could all grow up together the way he had with his siblings and she had with her sister. While she bought into that rationale, she hoped she could handle two babies in diapers at the same time.

"You're getting a bit ahead of yourself," she whispered. She didn't even know for sure that she was pregnant, and she was already making plans. By the time Victoria knocked on the door, Maddie was practically trembling from the bout of nerves.

"All righty," Victoria said with her usual peppy enthusiasm for all things reproductive, "let's see what we've got. You know the drill." She pulled on gloves and settled Maddie's feet into the stirrups that magically appeared at the end of the table.

While Victoria poked and prodded from the inside and outside, Maddie stared up at the ceiling, trying to prepare herself for the possibility of a false alarm.

"Your uterus is slightly enlarged, but that could be left over from Hailey, so I don't want to say anything for certain until we get the test results back. You can go ahead and sit up. If you want to get dressed and meet me in my office, I'll go move the lab along."

"Thanks, Vic." Disappointed to not yet have a definitive verdict, Maddie got dressed and went to Victoria's office at the end of the hall.

"They need a few more minutes, so have a seat. Can I get you some coffee or anything?"

"No, thank you."

Victoria's cell phone rang, and she glanced at it longingly.

"Go ahead," Maddie said with a laugh. "It's just me."

Victoria grinned. "I'll be quick." She picked up the phone. "Hey there. No, I'm at work. Where are you?" She listened for a few minutes. "Sure, that sounds good. Meet me here at five? All right, see you then." After another pause that turned her face bright red, Victoria said, "I'm hanging up now." She put down the phone and seemed embarrassed to look at Maddie. "Sorry about that."

"So who is he?" Maddie asked with a teasing smile.

"Um, well… Do you know Seamus O'Grady?"

"Sure. I love Seamus."

"It's his cousin, Shannon. We've been seeing each other."

"If he's anything like Seamus…"

"He's just like Seamus, only younger and even hotter, if that's possible."

Maddie fanned her face. "Hot damn, girl. Good for you."

"It's been *very* good for me, if you catch my drift."

They shared a laugh that descended quickly into hysterics that went a long way toward relieving Maddie's tension. "Thank you," Maddie said as she wiped up laughter tears. "I needed that."

"Happy to help, even if it's frightfully unprofessional to be dishing about my sex life with my patients."

"Oh please, we've been through two pregnancies together, and you had your hand up my hoo-ha five minutes ago. I think it's safe to say we're friends by now."

Maddie's statement set Victoria off again, and the two of them were mopping up more tears when someone knocked on the door.

"Enter," Victoria called.

"Test results you're waiting for," the receptionist said, eyeing the two of them with curiosity.

Maddie figured they probably were red-faced and silly looking after their laughing fit.

"Thank you," Victoria said, scanning the page and then smiling. "Congrats, Mom. Looks like we're going for three."

Maddie promptly burst into tears that had nothing to do with laughter. She wasn't sure if it was relief or fear that had her sobbing like a fool.

Victoria got up and came around her desk. "What's this? I thought you'd be thrilled."

"I am," Maddie said between sobs. "I'm thrilled."

"Um, you don't look thrilled."

"I've been on this roller-coaster ride of emotions this week, thinking I was pregnant and then being convinced I wasn't and now finding out I am when my friend Syd is dying to be pregnant, and it's not fair that I'm having a 'whoops' baby when she wants one so badly."

"Wow, that's a whole lot of hormones in one sentence."

"See? I'm a wreck. How will I handle *three kids* under the age of *five?*"

"As beautifully as you handle two of them. If anyone can do it, you can. Think of it this way, at least yours are coming one at a time, unlike your friend Laura, who's having twins."

"That's true," Maddie said, wiping her tears.

"It's all going to be fine. I promise. You'll have a couple of crazy years, and then you'll be on to the easy stuff like school and teenagers and driving."

Maddie sobbed anew at the thought of those unimaginable worries.

"Too far?" Victoria asked.

"Maybe just a bit."

Victoria started laughing again, and before she knew it, Maddie was laughing while she cried.

"My husband is going to leave me," Maddie said.

Victoria's face went flat with shock. "No… No way."

Seized by sobs and tears and laughter, Maddie waved a hand. "He doesn't have any plans to leave right now. That I know of, anyway. But if I'm going to be like this for nine months, he's going to be long gone before this baby arrives."

"He will not. That guy is crazy about you."

"Let's hope so, because he hasn't seen crazy yet."

"Go take a nice bath and pamper yourself."

Maddie took the tissues Victoria offered and wiped her face. "Sorry to be such a spaz. I've been a mess all week."

"You're not a mess, Maddie. You're pregnant."

"I'm a pregnant mess."

"It'll feel better when the shock wears off. I promise."

Nodding, Maddie picked up her purse, stood and gave Victoria a hug. "Thanks for putting up with me."

"No problem. Set up an appointment for an ultrasound, and we'll get you a due date on your next visit, and confirm there's only one in there."

Maddie blanched at the very idea of more than one. "Too far again."

Victoria covered her mouth to hold in the laughter.

"Good luck with your sexy Irishman."

"Why, thank you," Victoria said with a wink. "I hope to get very lucky later."

Shaking her head at Victoria's irreverence, Maddie went to the reception desk to make an appointment for a follow-up visit. She'd be hard-pressed to keep Mac away from that one. Here she was with a three-year-old and a nine-month-old and another on the way. Her already too large breasts would be explosive again in no time, the stretch marks from the last time had finally begun to fade, and she'd only recently been able to fit into her regular clothes again.

And now she was going to do it all again. Maddie trudged out of the clinic into the sweltering heat, blinded by bright sunshine, despite the sunglasses she pulled from the top of her head to cover her raw eyes. She headed for her SUV, stopping short at the sight of her husband leaning against the vehicle, arms folded and blue-eyed gaze pinned on her.

"What're you doing here?" she asked, less surprised to see him than she probably should've been.

"Waiting for you."

Maddie took a few more steps that brought her to within inches of him. He never failed to take her breath away when he looked at her as if his every hope and dream were tied up with her, which they were. And hers were just as tied up with him.

"Where else was I supposed to be when you were finding out whether we're having another baby?" He reached out and flipped her sunglasses up, making her wince from the shock of the sunlight on her aching eyes. "You've been crying. So it's a no?" Before she had a chance to respond, she was wrapped in his strong arms, sobbing all over again. "I'm so sorry, honey. We'll try again next month. We'll try every month until we get it right."

She shook her head.

"You don't want to try again?"

"We don't have to."

"I'm confused."

"I'm pregnant."

As long as she lived, she'd never forget the expression on his face when her words registered with him. Shock, amazement, awe, love... And then his eyes filled with tears, and she fell in love with him all over again. "You are? Really?"

"Really."

He crushed her to him, holding her so tight she could barely breathe.

She held on just as tightly to him, her rock, her love, her life.

"If the news was good, why were you crying?" he asked after he held her for several minutes.

"Because I can't not cry. It seems to be all I do lately."

"Have I told you today how much I love you?" he asked.

"Don't be nice to me. It makes me cry."

His hands on her face made her feel loved and treasured. "I love you more than anything. You have no idea how happy you've made me—today and every day."

"So you're happy about the baby? Even though we didn't plan him? Or her?"

"How could I not be thrilled about a baby we're having together, no matter how he or she came to be? It's *our* baby, Maddie. Yours and mine, and I'll love him—or her—as much as I love you and Thomas and Hailey."

Maddie held on tight to him, fortified as always by his love.

"But you'll be having this one in the biggest, safest hospital I can find—on the mainland. You got me?"

"Yes, Mac. I've got you." And she was never, ever letting go.

DAVID DISCHARGED Marion Martinez at two o'clock with instructions to follow a bland diet for a couple of days. Paul had left to deal with the store and its employees while Alex waited with their mother, who'd been asking every two minutes when his father was coming to get her. The same question, repeated over and over again, had worn on Alex's already frayed nerves.

"I'll just wait for Daddy," she said when Alex told her it was time to go home.

"Dad isn't coming," Alex said.

"Of course he is. He always comes for me."

"He died, Mom. Ten years ago. You know this."

"Why would you say such an awful thing?" she asked, horrified. "What have we ever done to you to deserve such behavior? We've loved you and cared for you and put up with your nonsense."

Nonsense, he wanted to ask. *What nonsense?* As far as he knew, he and his brother had been model sons. But if he asked the question, it would only further agitate her, and that was the last thing he wanted to do.

"I'm waiting for your father, and that's the end of it."

"Marion," David said as he came into the room. "I just heard from George, and he said he got tied up at a job. He wants you to go home with Alex, and he'll meet you there."

Alex waited breathlessly to hear what she'd say.

"Well, let's go, Alex. I don't want to keep your father waiting."

As Alex pushed the wheelchair out of the room, he looked at David. "I could kiss you right now," Alex said under his breath.

"That's a lovely offer, but I think I'll pass."

David walked alongside Alex as he pushed the chair to the main door of the clinic. "You're a lifesaver, David. In more ways than one."

"Happy to help. Call me if you need anything—day or night."

"We'll never be able to properly thank you."

"You don't need to. This is why I spent all those years in school. I wanted to be able to help people."

"You're making one hell of a difference for our family. Don't ever doubt that."

"That's nice to hear. I'll wait with your mom while you get the truck."

Alex jogged across the parking lot, taking note of a few aches and pains he couldn't attribute entirely to the hard work he did every day. He'd been dying to call Jenny, just to hear her voice if nothing else, but he'd held off until he could focus entirely on her.

With the air-conditioning blasting, he drove up to the clinic entrance and got out to help his mother into the truck.

"Turn down that horrible air-conditioning, Alex. I'm freezing."

"You have to be the only person in the state of Rhode Island who's freezing today."

David laughed at their banter as he waved them off and went back inside with the wheelchair.

"You're driving too fast," his mother said when Alex pulled out of the clinic onto Ocean Road.

"I'm barely moving."

"Don't talk back to your mother."

Alex bit the inside of his cheek to keep from snapping at her. She couldn't help it. Maybe if he kept telling himself that, he'd eventually believe it. He drove home as slowly as he possibly could. By the time he turned into the driveway to Martinez Lawn & Garden, a line of cars was piled up behind him, but at least his mother wasn't angry with him.

Before the illness, she'd hardly said a cross word to him or Paul in their entire lives. She'd been a strict mother who set high expectations for her sons, but she'd also been kind and sweet and generous. He missed those qualities the most. The dementia made her angry, suspicious and impulsive, among other things that were hard to live with.

An hour later, he had his mother settled in her bed for a nap before dinner. Alex wandered into the living room and stretched out on the sofa. The workday was a total bust, and he couldn't leave his mother alone anyway. He withdrew his cell phone from his pocket and went through the text messages from clients as well as a couple of friends who'd checked in to see how he was doing.

And how was he doing? Depended on when he was asked. Other than the unpleasantness with Sharon, last night had been awesome, from the moment he got to Jenny's until Paul had called about their mom's chest pains. Today had mostly sucked, except for when Jenny had driven him home and offered to help. That had been great. Being around her made him feel good, which was more than enough to keep him going back for more time with her.

The ups and downs of his daily life lately were nausea inducing, a thought that reminded him he needed to eat. But getting up to find food would take energy he just didn't have, so he stayed on the sofa and called Jenny. He wanted to hear her voice. No, he *needed* to hear it, which was a thought that should've scared the shit out of him. But it didn't. The thought of her soothed him.

"Mmm, hello?"

"Hey, it's me. Were you sleeping?"

"Yeah. I conked out. How's your mom?"

Alex pictured her in her bed, her face rosy from sleep. "Home and resting in her own bed."

"Glad to hear it," she said. "And how are you?"

"I feel like someone beat the shit out of me."

"Funny, I feel the same way. I've been wondering if it might be more than a night without sleep and other stuff…"

"*Other stuff?*" he asked with a laugh. "Is that what we're calling it?"

"What would you call it? No, wait, don't answer that. I'm afraid of what you'll say."

He'd been on the phone with her for five minutes, and he was already grinning like a loon. "Can I come over later?"

"Sure, but I'll warn you, I may have the flu, and there's not going to be any 'other stuff.'"

"Are you sore?"

"That might not be a good enough word for what I am."

"I know just the thing to fix you right up."

"Not. Happening."

Chuckling, he said, "What're your flu symptoms?"

"Complete lack of interest in anything resembling food, general lethargy and a possible fever."

"Ugh, a fever in this heat?"

"I know. It's a drag."

"I'll come over when I can bust free here. Not sure what time it'll be."

"I'm not going anywhere. I was supposed to get together with my friends, but I already called to tell them I'm staying home. If it is the flu, they don't need it—and neither do you, for that matter."

"The way I see it, I've already been extremely well exposed to whatever's ailing you, so there's no reason for you to be miserable alone."

"I suppose you have a point."

"Mmm, yes, I do, and he'd really like to see you again."

"Alex! Oh my God! You're like a fifteen-year-old boy!"

"I know, right? I didn't hear you complaining about my stamina last night."

"I'm hanging up now."

"I'll be over when I can."

"I'll leave the door unlocked for you."

"Jenny…"

"Yes?"

"I can't wait to see you." He ended the call before she could reply. Let her think about that until he saw her again. As he closed his eyes to take a quick nap, he smiled at the thought of seeing her soon. He really couldn't wait.

MADDIE WAS FRIGHTFULLY late to the gathering at Syd's house to plan Tiffany's shower, but she had a good excuse. She and Mac had run away together for the afternoon, since his parents had the kids, and they had a rare opportunity to spend some time alone. Hours after she'd gotten the happy news from Victoria, Maddie still wasn't sure if she should tell her friends or hold off because of Sydney's situation.

She hadn't resolved the internal debate when she gave a quick knock on Syd's door and stepped into the house. "Hello?"

"Out here," Sydney called from the back deck.

Maddie went through the kitchen to the sliding door.

"Grab a glass of wine and come on out," Sydney said. "We found a breeze."

"If you can call it that," Stephanie muttered. She was fanning herself with the latest issue of the *Gansett Gazette*.

Since there'd be no more wine for the foreseeable future, Maddie fixed a glass of ice water and went outside, where the heat hung low and heavy over the island. The word "incinerator" came to mind. "How much longer is this grossness supposed to last anyway?" she asked as she ran the glass over her face, looking for relief anywhere she could find it.

"I heard on the news that it's here to stay for a couple more days," Laura said.

"*Days?*" Abby asked. "As in more than one?"

"Afraid so," Laura said. "They're predicting thunderstorms later in the week."

"Can't happen soon enough for me," Maddie said. "Hey, where's Jenny?"

"Sick," Sydney said. "She has a fever."

"Ugh, that's too bad." Maddie sat next to her mother on a lounge chair. "Hi, Mama." She leaned in to kiss Francine's flushed cheek. "Glad you could make it."

"Why have you been crying?" Francine asked, taking a long perusing look at her eldest daughter.

"What? I have not."

"Yes, you have. What's wrong?"

Everything stopped as the others stared at her, and Maddie wilted as much from the heat of their stares as the thick humidity. "Um, well, so it's kind of funny, actually."

"What's so funny?" Grace asked.

Maddie glanced at Sydney and saw that her old friend was waiting to hear what she had to say. "It seems that, despite my histrionics the other day, I'm pregnant after all."

The girls went wild screaming and hugging Maddie until she was in tears all over again.

"I knew it," Francine said smugly. "You had that look about you. Same as the last two times."

"I'm glad you knew it, because I had myself convinced I wasn't."

Sydney came over to hug her. "Congratulations, Maddie. I'm so happy for you."

"I've got my fingers and toes crossed for you, too."

"If it's meant to be, it'll happen. Don't let my situation take anything away from your excitement. Do you hear me?"

Sydney's kind words had Maddie bawling her head off all over again. "You can't be nice to me, or this happens. Don't anyone be nice to me for the next nine months."

"All right, bitch," Stephanie said. "Stop your damned blubbering, and let's plan this shower for your sister."

"Much better," Maddie said, laughing as she mopped up her tears with a tissue her mother handed her.

"How's Mac handling the news?" Francine asked.

"Surprisingly well. He's very excited but also very determined to move to the mainland in plenty of time to ensure there're no more train-wreck deliveries."

"I bet he won't have to twist your arm on that one," Abby said.

"Not at all. I learned my lesson with Hailey. There's no way that's happening again." Despite the seemingly never-ending need to bawl her head off over every little thing, Maddie forced a watery smile for her friends. "I talked to Patty today," she said of Tiffany's assistant at the store. "She gave me the schedule for this week so we'll know when Tiffany is off. Looks like Tuesday is our shopping day and Saturday is our party day."

"Have you mentioned this idea to Blaine?" Francine asked. "They might have plans on Saturday if that's their only day off."

"I was thinking we should make the party for both of them so it'll be super embarrassing when she's opening presents from the store," Maddie said.

"Oh, I love that idea," Abby said. "We'll invite all the guys and tell them they have to come to support Blaine. They don't need to know what kind of party it is."

The others howled with laughter at the thought of the guys at a sex-toy-and-lingerie party.

"It's the least of what they deserve after the number of times they've crashed our girls' night out," Maddie said.

"Absolutely," Grace said. "But if you guys do this to me, I'll kill you all. You hear me?"

"I see a new tradition in the making," Stephanie said, rubbing her hands together as she directed a diabolical smile at Grace.

"No way," Laura said. "I'm next, and they haven't invented a naughty nightie that'll fit this body."

"Is that a challenge?" Maddie asked her husband's cousin.

"Oh God," Laura groaned. "Me and my big mouth!"

"This is perfect for Tiffany," Francine said. "She'll love it."

"So will Blaine—but he won't love it until they get home with the goods," Sydney said.

"This is going to be awesome," Maddie said. "What's the plan for getting them to the lighthouse?"

"I have the perfect idea," Sydney said. "Here's what I think we ought to do."

CHAPTER 11

She waited until the five o'clock ferry cleared the South Harbor breakwater before she approached the Gansett Island Ferry Company ticket window.

"Mrs. Cantrell." The young woman working the car reservation line seemed surprised to see her. "How are you?"

"I'm great. Thanks for asking. I'd like to book my car on the nine o'clock ferry in the morning."

"Oh, um, could you hold on for just one minute?"

"What's your name, honey?"

"Kristen."

"No, Kristen, I will *not* hold on while you call your boss and tell him I'm here trying to get my car on the boat." Carolina kept her voice calm and friendly, even if her words were anything but. "My son and I *own* this company, and I'm asking you to make me a reservation."

"Ye-yes, ma'am." Kristen's hands trembled as she typed on the computer and then reached for a slip of paper from a printer. "Here you are. I'm sure you know to be here an hour before the boat leaves."

"I sure do. Thanks for your help, Kristen." Carolina picked up a pen, wrote her phone number on a slip of paper and slid it across the counter. "If your *boss* gives you any trouble over this, you call me, honey, okay?"

Kristen took the paper and tucked it into her pocket. "I will."

Satisfied that she'd taken care of business, Carolina turned away from the ticket window to find her fiancé, Seamus O'Grady, standing with his legs parted and his arms crossed over his broad chest. Even with his brows narrowed in displeasure, he was one sexy devil. "What're you about, love?"

"Taking care of a little business, which is none of yours."

"What business of yours isn't mine?"

Carolina poked her index finger into his chest. "The business of my *grandson*, who I am going to see tomorrow."

"But you've been so sick—"

"Past tense. I'm fine now. The fever is gone. The congestion is gone. If I don't see that baby, my son and daughter-in-law, I'm going to kill someone. And since you're handy, it'd be in your best interest to stay out of the way of these plans."

"I'll make some calls."

"What calls? If you cancel my reservation or give that very nice girl Kristen a hard time for helping me—"

"I was going to call in one of our part-time captains to cover for me tomorrow so I can go with you."

Chastened, Carolina said, "Oh."

He ran his thumb over her cheek, making her want to lean into him even when she was sort of fighting with him. "I want to see them, too, love. It's been killing me that you were too sick to go, because I knew it was breaking your heart to be kept from them."

"I can't go one more day without seeing them."

"I understand."

"You understand, yet you're the one who's been telling me I can't go."

He tossed his hands up in frustration. "Because you were *contagious*. You couldn't take that around a premature baby."

"I know that! I just wanted to…" She shook her head, filled with frustration that fizzled as she looked up at his gorgeous, sincere face.

"You're right. I know you're right, but I'm going crazy stuck on this island while they're in Providence. I've already missed so much with my grandson."

His warm smile softened his demeanor, and his delicious Irish accent had the same effect on her as it always did. "Caro, love... You haven't missed any of the good stuff. That boy is going to love you so damned much." He put his arms around her and kissed her forehead. "I'm sorry I was a hard-ass about keeping you from him, but I knew you'd never forgive yourself if you passed along a germ that did him harm."

"It wasn't enough that I shredded myself in the thorn bush. Then I had to get the flu on top of it."

"It was very unfair indeed."

She looked up at him. "Are you done working?"

"Yes, thank God. I'm exhausted, overheated and starving."

"Let's go to the Beachcomber for dinner and then straight home to bed." While she was no longer contagious, her energy level still wasn't what it could've been. "We've got an early morning tomorrow."

"Sounds like heaven to me, love." He kept his arm around her as they strolled up the hill toward the iconic white hotel that anchored downtown Gansett. "While we're on the mainland, how about we do a little shopping?"

"For what?"

He brought her ring finger to his lips. "Something sparkly for this lovely finger."

"I don't need that, Seamus."

"What if I do?"

"There're so many better things you could spend your money on."

"Name one."

"Surely there's something you want that you don't have."

His arm tightened around her as his lips slid over her hair. "Now that you've agreed to marry me, there's not one damned thing I want that I don't have, and you're getting a ring. That's all there is to it."

Carolina had learned over the last year to choose her battles wisely with him. She suspected this was one she couldn't win. "If you say so, dear."

His bark of laughter over her unusually easy capitulation had other people on the street looking at them, probably wondering what a hot young guy like him was doing with an old fool like her. *Let them wonder*, she thought as she slid her hand into the back pocket of his khaki uniform shorts. Every sexy, bossy, overbearing inch of him was all hers.

A SLAMMING door and a loud voice woke Alex from a sound sleep. He rubbed his face as Paul came in from work, talking on the phone. Alex checked his watch, which indicated that two hours had passed. He was up and heading for the hallway to check on his mother before he was even completely awake.

Thankfully, she was resting comfortably in her bed and hadn't escaped while he was dead to the world. He went back to the kitchen, where Paul had cracked open a beer and was leaning against the counter with his cell phone wedged between his ear and shoulder.

"That sounds good," he said. "I'll meet your ferry. We'll look forward to seeing you on Saturday." Paul ended the call and put his phone on the charger. "That was the nurse, Hope, who we talked to the other night. She and her son will be out on Saturday to check out the place."

"And us."

"And us."

So much was riding on this, and they both knew it. The only hope they had of keeping their mother at home was if they could persuade a qualified medical professional to come to work for them, and they had exactly one person interested in the position.

"Kinda funny that her name is Hope, right?" Alex said.

"Seriously."

"So listen... A friend of mine has offered to help out at the store. She has an MBA from Wharton and a lot of retail experience—not in horticulture, but she'd probably figure out what she needs to know. What do you think?"

"A *friend*, huh? And does this *friend* have anything to do with the fact that you didn't come home last night?"

"I called you to tell you I was staying out, and you said it was fine, so don't bust my balls. Do you want her help or don't you?"

"Will your Wharton MBA be satisfied with twelve bucks an hour?"

"She's not in it for the money. She heard we're in a tight spot, and she offered to help. Nothing more than that."

Paul eyed him skeptically. "Nothing more than that?"

"Paul… Will you shut the fuck up and answer the question? Do you want her help or not?"

"Sure," Paul said with a calculating smile. "I'd love to have your *friend's* help at the store. Tell her to call me in the morning, and we'll set up a meeting."

"You're such an asshole."

"That's why you love me."

"Right, keep telling yourself that. I'm taking a shower. Are you going to be home tonight?"

"Where else would I be?"

"Do you care if I go out for a while?"

"I don't care, but when you say a *while*, do you mean a couple of hours or all night?"

"Ugh," Alex said, grunting with aggravation as he left Paul laughing in the kitchen and went to take a shower. Even though he wanted to punch his brother for being such an asshole, he couldn't deny that if the situation had been reversed, he would've done the same thing.

They'd been busting each other's balls for as long as they could talk. In fact, ball busting had been at the heart of their relationship until they were forced to come together to care for their mother. It was kind of nice to know that underneath all the drama and despair of their mother's illness, his relationship with his brother remained intact.

Dressed in shorts and a T-shirt, Alex entered the kitchen, where

Paul was eating dinner with his laptop open on the table next to him. "This computer is giving me heartburn."

"Take some of Mom's stuff."

"Seriously. I might need to get a new one. It's running so slow."

"Call Adam McCarthy to look at it before you spend the money on a new one."

"Good idea. I keep forgetting he moved home."

Alex picked up the keys and tucked his wallet into his back pocket. "How about I help you get Mom up and changed and everything before I go?"

"Nah, I can handle it. She's apt to stay asleep at this point anyway."

"Call me if you need me."

"I wouldn't want to interrupt anything."

"Shut the fuck up."

Paul was still laughing as Alex walked out the door, letting it slam behind him. As annoying as his brother could be, it was nice to hear some laughter in their house for a change of pace.

In the barn, he got on the Harley and headed for town, where he stopped at three different places before he found what he was looking for and then headed for the lighthouse, his body humming with anticipation. It was amazing how quickly she'd become a bright spot in a life full of mundane routine.

Alex parked the bike and removed the bag he'd stored in the compartment under the seat. As promised, she'd left the door unlocked for him. He took the stairs two at a time, eager to see her.

In the kitchen, he put the bag he'd brought on the table. "Jenny?"

No answer. Damn, was she still sleeping? He went up the flight that led to her bedroom on the top floor. She was curled up on her side, her hand under her face, blonde hair spread out on the pillow. Alex sat on the edge of the bed and leaned over to kiss her bare shoulder. The blazing heat of her skin seared his lips. *Uh-oh.*

Her eyes fluttered open. "Hey," she said, her voice gravelly and sleepy sounding.

That was all it took to get his cock pressing insistently against his zipper. *Down, boy. She's sick, and we're not here for that.* "How you feeling?"

"Not so great. I'm hot."

He rested a hand on her forehead. "You've got one hell of a fever. Have you taken anything for that?"

"Earlier. Didn't help much."

"I brought you some soup."

Her eyes widened in surprise. "You did?"

Nodding, he said, "I couldn't find chicken noodle, but they had chicken with rice at the deli."

Her stomach growled, making them laugh.

"I'll take that as a yes to the soup."

"It does sound good."

"Stay right there. I'll bring it to you." Alex went downstairs to the kitchen to set her up with a tray that he found in a drawer under the stove. Opening doors and drawers in the tiny galley kitchen, he located a bowl and spoon. He added a stack of crackers and an icy glass of ginger ale to the tray and carried it upstairs.

Jenny was sitting up against a pile of pillows. She'd turned on a light, and he could see that her cheeks were red from the fever. "I can't believe you brought me soup."

"Why not? You're sick, right?"

"I know, but still… It was really nice of you."

"I got some for me, too. Be right back." He went down to get the container of minestrone and the Coke he'd brought for himself and carried it upstairs to join her.

Propped against his own pile of pillows, he devoured the soup and the baguette that had come with it. They ate in companionable silence, which he enjoyed tremendously. Being around her calmed him and settled his racing mind.

"How's the belly?" he asked.

"Happier than it's been all day. This is great. Thanks again."

"It was no problem."

"It was *nice* of you."

"If you say so."

"I do. How's your mom?"

"Sleeping a lot."

She took a long perusing look at him that made his skin tingle with awareness of her. "Did you get some sleep?"

"A couple of hours."

"I hope you don't get whatever it is I have."

"I never get sick. Don't worry about me."

"I never get sick either, and I am worried about you. You're burning the candle at both ends. I'd hate to see that catch up to you."

Her kind concern touched him deeply. Despite living at home with his mother and brother and the compassion of the Gansett Island community all around them, Alex had felt very alone in the midst of the chaos. He felt less alone when he was with her.

"Are you done?" he asked when she put down her spoon.

"Yes, thanks. It was great."

"Glad you enjoyed it." He took the tray downstairs and washed the dishes before returning to the bedroom. "Do you want me to go and let you sleep?"

"I'd much rather you stayed for a while, if you don't have anything you need to do."

"I don't have anything I need to do, and I'd love to stay."

"I'm going to hit the bathroom. Make yourself comfortable." She got up slowly, the covers falling away to reveal a skimpy tank and a skimpier pair of lacy panties.

Alex bit back a groan as he took in miles of gorgeous leg and toned buttocks. She half walked, half hobbled to the bathroom, and he fell back against the pillows, praying for deliverance from the desire that pounded through him at the sight of her bare skin. He'd never had a stronger physical reaction to a woman. From the first time he touched her, she'd affected him on every possible level, and he was starting to realize the need for her had only gotten greater since he'd had her.

Propped up on one hand, he watched her return, noting how gingerly she moved as she got back into bed.

"You're pretty sore, huh?"

"Extremely."

"I'm sorry."

"It's not your fault. I hadn't done...that...in a really long time."

"You should've told me I was being too rough with you."

"I was too busy having multiple orgasms to tell you anything."

Alex laughed and put his arm around her, bringing her in close to him. "Next time, I'll be more careful."

She rested her arm on top of his. "I liked you exactly the way you were."

He breathed in the fresh, sweet scent of her hair, content to be close to her even if another part of him wasn't content at all. That part of him needed to stand down, but damn if he could keep the desire he felt for her at bay. When she was close to him like this, he wanted her. If she was in the room, he wanted her. "I talked to Paul, and he gratefully accepts your offer. He said to call him to set up a time to get together."

"I will as soon as I can move again."

"I'll let him know you're under the weather. We can handle things for a couple of days, so don't worry about it until you feel better. You're doing us a huge favor, and we're on your schedule."

"I'm glad there's something I can do to help you guys."

"It's nice of you to want to help."

"Tell me about your mom. What was she like before this happened?"

"She was awesome," he said with a sigh. "Fun and funny and clever. She loved to read and knit and do needlepoint and play bridge with her friends. She can't do any of those things anymore. My dad died ten years ago, and even though she was shattered to lose him, she stepped right in to take over the business. It's hard to believe she was still in charge only a year or so ago. The illness has progressed rapidly."

"Wow," Jenny said. "What happened to your dad?"

Alex normally hated to talk about one of the darkest times in his life, but it was so easy to tell her because he sensed her genuine interest. "He battled cancer for about seven years and died ten years ago."

"I'm so sorry."

"He was a good guy, and they were great together. Still dancing in the living room after twenty-five years of marriage. The hardest part of my mother's illness is she keeps forgetting he's gone. She asks for him all the time."

"God, that must be so hard for you and Paul."

"It sucks. It's like she has to lose him all over again every time we tell her he's gone. I hate that so much."

She turned toward him, her arm curling around his waist as she snuggled up to him. "She's very lucky to have two such devoted sons."

"She was very devoted to us. The other day, after the incident in the yard, she was totally lucid. She told me how sorry she is to be doing this to us, that we should be married with families of our own by now." All at once, he caught himself and realized he might be over-sharing. He kissed her forehead. "Sorry. I didn't come over here to dump all my shit on you."

"That's not what you're doing, Alex."

"I sort of liked it better when you didn't know."

"I'm glad I know, and I hope you'll never hesitate to talk to me about what you're going through."

"It's not fair to you that I'm getting so involved with you when I don't have a damned thing to offer you. But I can't seem to stay away."

"I'm glad you're here, and you don't need to offer me anything other than your company."

"You and I both know it doesn't take long for things like this to become far more complicated than that."

"It doesn't have to be complicated. I'm not looking to add to your stress level or give you one more thing to worry about every day."

"You're too good to be true."

"No, I'm not," she said with a laugh that became a yawn.

He stroked her hair and back. "Go to sleep."

"Don't you have to get home?"

"No, Paul is there. I'll be right here."

She exhaled a deep breath and relaxed against him.

Holding her while she slept was the best part of what had been a long, shitty day.

He'd dozed off, too, waking when she became restless, her lips moving and her hand clutching his arm. Alex couldn't tell if she was in pain or dreaming, and he hated to wake her when she was feeling so lousy.

"Toby, wait… Don't go. Please don't go."

"Jenny," he whispered, kissing her cheek and then her lips. "Wake up, honey. You're dreaming."

Her eyes were full of tears that spilled down her cheeks when she opened them, seeming disoriented as she stared at him.

Undone by her tears, Alex brushed them away. "Are you okay?"

She nodded, but he could tell she wasn't okay, especially when the tears kept on coming.

He rubbed her back, trying to soothe her.

"I'm sorry," she said after a long period of quiet. "The dream… It was upsetting."

"You don't have to apologize for being upset." He continued to rub her back, wishing he could do something to make her feel better.

"I'll be right back," she said as she got up and went into the bathroom.

Moved by her obvious sorrow, Alex fell back against the pillow, running his hands through his hair while he waited for her. He had so many questions, but he wasn't sure if he dared to ask any of them.

The water ran in the bathroom for several minutes before she emerged, free of tears, and slid back into bed.

"Do you want me to go?"

She turned on her side to face him. "No."

He took her hand and flattened his palm against hers. "Could I ask you something?"

Nodding, she focused on their joined hands.

"Who's Toby?"

CHAPTER 12

*J*enny held back a gasp at his gently worded question. She'd had the dream again, twice in the same week, which hadn't happened since Toby first died. What did it mean that she'd had it again now, right when she'd started something new with Alex?

And she'd obviously spoken in her sleep. What had she said? Did she want to know?

"He… He was my fiancé."

"Oh." Alex continued to stroke her hand, his touch sending electric currents up her arm and through her body. "It ended badly?"

"You could say that." *Tell him! Tell him what happened so it's out there. I don't want to tell him. I don't want him to know. I want to enjoy being with him without my overwhelming tragedy standing between us.*

"I'm sorry."

"Thanks." She forced herself to look at his face. "Will you tell me what I said when I was sleeping?"

"I don't want to upset you."

"I want to know."

"You said his name and asked him not to go."

Jenny closed her eyes tight against the unreasonable blast of pain. That it still could hurt so badly after all this time…

"Do you want to talk about it?"

"Not really."

"Okay."

Jenny immediately felt guilty for holding back when he'd shared so much of his story with her. But she'd seen it happen before. The minute she told him how and when she lost Toby, he would look at her differently. It would color the way he talked to her, the way he touched her, the way he thought of her.

Alex put his arm around her and snuggled her into his chest.

She closed her eyes and breathed in the appealing scent of soap and deodorant, trying to relax even as her mind raced with questions about why she'd had the dream—twice—recently. What did it mean? Would it happen again? Would she finally get to relive the final moments she'd spent with Toby? Did she need the answers to those questions before she could move forward with Alex?

"I can almost hear you thinking," he said, his lips curving into a smile against her forehead.

"Sorry."

"Stop apologizing."

"Stop being so nice to me."

"Why wouldn't I be nice to you?"

"Because you've told me all about yourself, and I've shared very little of me with you."

"You don't need to apologize for that. I understand better than most people would."

"It's not fair, though."

"I'm not keeping score. Are you?"

"No, but—"

He kissed her softly and gently. "No buts, no worries. We're enjoying some time together. That doesn't mean you have to tell me your deepest, darkest secrets."

He'd said exactly what she needed to hear, and yet she still felt guilty for holding out on him. Maybe it was because she'd felt an honest, genuine connection to him that she hadn't had with any of the other men she'd dated since Toby died. Her thoughts wandered to the first man she'd had sex with, years after she lost Toby, and how her overly emotional response had scared him off. That experience had taught her to be wary of how much she shared with potential partners.

Yes, she thought, *it's better if he doesn't know.* Then he won't feel like he has to be extra careful with her. Besides, he had enough on his plate without being burdened with her stuff, too.

While she was comfortable with her decision, she knew she'd bought herself only a little bit of time. When people learned they were seeing each other—if it came to that—there'd be a risk of him hearing her story from someone else.

No matter what, she couldn't let that happen.

THE ALARM on Alex's phone went off when it was still dark outside. For a moment, he couldn't remember where he was. Then he breathed in the scent of Jenny's hair, which calmed and settled him. Amazing... How did she do that simply by sleeping close to him?

He moved carefully, hoping she would stay asleep for a while longer, but with their arms and legs curled around each other, he couldn't help but wake her.

"Do you have to go?" she asked in that sleepy, sexy voice that got to him every time he heard it.

"Yeah. I lost all day yesterday, so I need to hit it hard today."

"Drink lots of water."

"Yes, ma'am. How do you feel?"

"Better."

"Good." He bent to kiss her. "Tonight, if I can get away, I want to take you on a date."

"Oh..."

"Is that all right?"

"I...um, I thought you wanted to just...you know...have sex."

"I want that, too."

"I thought that was all you wanted."

Alex wished it wasn't still dark. He'd like to see her face for this conversation. "I'm not going to deny it started out that way. And I'm not going to deny I have my reservations about getting involved with anyone when my life is so unsettled. Despite all that, I like being with you." He took her hand. "I like how I feel when I'm around you."

She wrapped both her hands around his in a gesture that comforted him and reinforced his desire to spend more time with her. "How do you feel when you're with me?" she asked, sounding a bit breathless.

"Calm. When I'm close to you like this, my mind stops racing for a little while, which is a very welcome relief." He kissed her forehead and then her lips. "And then, other times, I feel anything but calm, but I like that, too. I like that a lot. So… Date? Yes?"

"Okay."

"You aren't convincing me it's what you want."

"Don't get me wrong. I'd love to go out with you, but part of me enjoys the fact that no one knows about us. The minute we step foot in town together, people will know."

"I don't mind that if you don't."

"The thing I didn't want to tell you last night… I'll need to tell you about that before we go out, before someone else does."

She sounded so sad and resigned that he almost regretted asking her to go out with him. Almost…

"Before we go anywhere, we'll talk. You can tell me anything you think I need to know. Will that work?"

She released a soft but audible sigh. "Yes."

"Whatever it is, I don't want you to worry about telling me. Do you promise you won't worry all day?"

"I promise I'll try not to worry."

"I suppose that'll have to do. I'll call you later."

"Tell Paul I'll check in with him at some point today to get started at the store."

Alex sat on the edge of the bed and put on the boots he wore on the bike. "Don't do that until you're sure you feel better."

"I feel much better. Good enough to work." She raised herself up on one elbow. In the faint early morning light, he could make out her silhouette as she watched him get ready to go. "So when we go on this date of yours, do you think we could take the bike?"

He turned to face her. "Is that what you want?"

"Uh-huh."

"You gotta wear jeans or long pants, and it's awfully hot."

"You don't wear jeans when you're on the bike."

"That's because I'm an idiot, but I don't take chances with passengers."

"So you have a lot of passengers?"

He cuffed her chin playfully. "Not one since I moved home." Leaning over, propped on his hands, he kissed her one last time. "See you later."

"Have a good day at the office."

"Pray for rain."

"I'm praying. Enough already with this heat. If it's sucking the life out of me, I can't imagine what it's like for you working outside in it."

"It sucks." He kissed her again and then one more time, lingering with his lips barely touching hers. "Okay, this time I'm really going."

"This time I'm really letting you."

Even though her sweet kisses had him hard as a rock, he bounded down the spiral stairs with a smile on his face. How many hours until he could see her again?

FOR A LONG TIME after she heard his motorcycle start and drive away, Jenny lay in bed, staring up at the ceiling. She'd told Alex she felt better, and physically she was less sore and achy than the day before. But emotionally... She felt battered by the reoccurrence of a dream that always had the power to crush her with the reminder of what she'd lost.

And that she'd said Toby's name out loud while Alex was with her… God, what he must've thought. He'd been kind and understanding, but Jenny knew the time had come to tell him the truth about her past. It wasn't fair to keep such a thing from him, especially when they had mutual friends who knew. If she didn't want him to hear about it from someone else, she needed to find the courage to tell him herself.

It occurred to her that it hadn't been all that difficult to divulge the details of her past with the other men she'd dated in the years since she lost Toby. This was different, she acknowledged. Alex was different. Their connection was more significant, which made it that much harder to tell him what he needed to hear.

It wasn't like her past was some big awful secret. But she'd told the story often enough to know that it changed how people viewed her, and she sort of liked the way Alex looked at her now. Would he look at her the same way after he knew? Or would his gaze be tinged by that hint of sorrow others had directed her way once they knew the truth?

She hadn't missed that since she moved away from home. She hadn't missed the overwhelming care and concern of the well-meaning people who loved her. Her life was divided solidly in half—before the great tragedy and after. Those who'd known her before had been deeply affected by her loss, so much so that she found it painful at times to be around people she'd known all her life, including her parents and sisters.

That was why it was such a relief to be here on Gansett, where no one had known her before. While her close friends were aware of what she'd lost and had provided tremendous comfort, support and friendship, they didn't look at her the way her family and friends at home did. They didn't watch her vigilantly for the slightest sign of crisis or despair.

She didn't want Alex watching her for those things. She wanted to move past the despair, and being with him made her feel hopeful again. Somehow, she had to tell him the story and make it clear to him that as much as she missed Toby and would mourn his loss forever, she was ready to move on and to take a chance on something new.

And that, right there, was a rather major development after having been stuck for a dozen years.

With the sun rising on the horizon, Jenny got up and walked to the bathroom on legs that were slightly less sore than the day before. She wasn't ready to run a marathon or anything, but she didn't feel like she'd been hit by a bus either. Her stomach growled, and the thought of coffee had her mouth watering—also good signs.

She showered, got dressed in another lightweight dress, had breakfast and two cups of coffee. And then she decided she needed to see Syd. Despite the rapid beat of her heart, Jenny moved slowly, washing her breakfast dishes before going upstairs to brush her teeth and make the bed. She came down the stairs, grabbed her purse and keys, went down one more level and out into the swampy heat.

Gripping the steering wheel, she drove to the gate and got out to unlock the lighthouse property for the day before continuing on toward Syd's house. She obeyed the speed limit, even though she wanted to push the accelerator to the floor so she could get there faster. When she pulled into Syd's driveway, she was relieved to see her friend's Volvo parked in the driveway but Luke's truck gone.

As much as she loved Sydney's wonderful husband, she wanted some time alone with her friend. Jenny got out of the car, walked around the house to the door and knocked.

Buddy's loud howl made Jenny smile. He sounded so fierce but was a total love.

"Hush, Buddy," Sydney said as she pulled open the door. "Hey! Come in! Are you feeling better?"

Sydney's cheerful welcome and her bright smile broke the fragile hold Jenny had on her composure. She didn't cry, but it took everything she had to keep the tears at bay.

Syd grabbed her hand and tugged her to the sofa. "Oh my God, Jenny. What's wrong?"

"I...I've met someone."

"Wait, what? Who?"

"Alex Martinez."

Sydney's eyes widened with surprise and delight. "Do tell. And don't leave out a single detail."

"He came to cut the grass, and he woke me up with the mower, so I threw tomatoes at him."

"You threw tomatoes at him. For real?"

"I was pretty mad. He interrupted the Toby dream with the mower."

"Oh shit. Is that why you asked me the other day about whether I dream about Seth and the kids?"

Jenny nodded.

"So what happened when you threw the tomatoes at him?"

"I hit him in the back with one of them. Then we argued about the proper time to cut grass, and he promised he wouldn't come that early again, so I let him finish. Did I mention I was wearing next to nothing when I stormed out of the lighthouse to throw tomatoes at him?"

Syd held two fingers to lips that curled into a smile.

"Anyway, I got dressed and was going out to open the gate for the day when I caught him taking a shower under the hose. He... Well, he's quite hot."

"I've noticed."

"I'm only human, and it had been a while, so I couldn't help but stare. The next thing I knew, he was standing right in front of me, dripping water all over me and staring at me with intense brown eyes."

Sydney hung on her every word, hardly seeming to breathe while she waited for Jenny to continue.

"Then he kissed me."

"He just swooped in?"

"He told me to say no if I didn't want it. I couldn't breathe, let alone speak, so I didn't say no."

"Damn straight you didn't say no. What happened then?"

"It was a good kiss. I mean an A-plus, plus, *plus* kiss that went on and on and on until we were inside the lighthouse and I was pressed against a wall."

"Holy shit."

"Exactly. He came back later that night, and we went swimming. And stuff."

"What stuff?"

"Stuff I haven't done with anyone in twelve years."

"Jenny…"

"I've had sex since Toby died. A couple of times. But I haven't allowed some things that were just too…"

"Intimate?"

"Yes, exactly."

"And you allowed that with Alex?"

"Allowed," Jenny said with a laugh. "It was so out of control that it wasn't really about allowing anything. It was happening before I caught up."

Sydney fanned her face. "I need a drink—or a cigarette."

"You don't smoke," Jenny said, laughing. The laughter helped to ease some of the tension she'd brought with her. Telling Sydney was helping, as she'd known it would.

"I wish I did. So what happened then?"

"He's very good at certain things—so good I didn't have a chance to dwell on the past or anything other than what was happening right in that moment."

"That's so great," Sydney said with a sigh.

"It was great, and extremely overwhelming, too."

"In a good way?"

"I think so. He's very sexy."

"Yes, he is, and so is his brother."

"When we saw Alex at the Tiki, that's when I heard about what's been going on with his mom and met his brother and figured out his last name."

"Wait, so you hadn't even exchanged last names?"

"No," Jenny said, her face burning with embarrassment. "I think we were both taking some comfort in the anonymity. He didn't know my shit, and I didn't know his. It was a relief, you know?"

"I can definitely understand that."

"You know the look people give you, as if they're watching you and waiting for you to crumble."

"I know that look."

"I hate that look. I liked being with someone who doesn't know anything more about me than my first name and where I live. It was comforting in a way."

"Sounds like it also took care of some inhibitions."

"You could say that again. After the incident at the Tiki with Alex and his employee, I could tell he was really upset. I had to remind myself I was there with Linc, and I couldn't go chasing after Alex in front of everyone I know. But I wanted to. I told Linc I wasn't feeling well and asked him to take me home."

"No wonder you said there was no connection with him when you were all kinds of connected to someone else."

"I know! I felt so bad about that. I never should've gone out with Linc when this was happening with Alex. I'd only met him the day before, and you guys had gone to the trouble of fixing me up with Linc, so I didn't want to cancel."

"What did Linc say when he took you home?"

"That he'd had a good time and wanted to see me again."

"Ouch."

"I told him things were complicated at the moment, and it wasn't the best time for me to be starting something. I'm a bad person."

"Stop it," Syd said. "You had the plans with Linc long before you threw tomatoes at Alex. How were you supposed to know that was going to happen?"

"True, but still… I probably should've canceled the date with Linc after I rolled around naked in the sand with Alex."

Sydney fanned her face again. "This is so hot."

"It got hotter when I decided to go after Alex and found him standing in my doorway. We were all over each other. We…you know…had sex. Lots and lots of sex, so much sex I couldn't move yesterday. I think he might've sexed me into a fever."

Sydney lost it laughing. "Girlfriend, if anyone deserves to be sexed into a fever, it's you."

"I haven't told him about Toby," Jenny said, getting to the heart of the matter. "Before this goes any further, I have to tell him. Especially since I had the dream again last night, and I said Toby's name. Alex asked me who he was. I said he was my fiancé. I couldn't bring myself to tell him the rest."

"Because you're afraid of the look."

"Yes! I like the way he treats me now—not like I'm fragile and breakable, but like I'm strong and sexy. I don't want that to change, but I also don't want him to hear about it from someone else."

"That is a predicament." Sydney got up and headed for the kitchen. "We need beverages."

Jenny followed her and gratefully accepted the tall glass of icy lemonade that Sydney poured for her.

Sydney leaned against the counter, eyeing Jenny shrewdly. "You really like this guy?"

"I do. I feel a connection with him that I've only ever had with one other person. He's told me it's a terrible time for him to be starting something, that he has nothing to offer me, but that doesn't keep me from wanting to be with him. And it hasn't kept him from coming back to me either."

"Then I think you tell him the story, but you also say what you don't want. Put it right out there. Tell him it would hurt you if he treated you differently in the future because of what he knows about you."

"You think that'll work?"

"I think he'll get it better than some guys would. He's in the thick of it with his mother, and he probably enjoys the respite he finds with you as much as you do."

"Why does my stomach ache every time I imagine telling him my story?"

"Because it still hurts to talk about it all these years later, and you haven't had to tell the story in a long time."

"I knew you'd understand."

"Of course I do, honey. I've lived it. I know exactly what you're going through, trying to move forward while continuing to honor the past. Neither of us asked for what happened to us, and the only choice we've had is to go on with our lives. That's not always the easiest thing to do."

"No, it isn't. But for the first time since I lost Toby, I want to take a chance again. I'm worried that he won't want the same thing, but I can't deny the connection I feel with him—and not just physically. It's more than that."

"Does he feel it, too?"

"I think so."

"Then you've got to have some faith in him, Jenny. Tell him the story, tell him what you want and don't want from him, and try to enjoy yourself. You've waited a long time for this."

"I'm also afraid that if I get all wrapped up in him and it doesn't work out for whatever reason…" She shrugged.

"That would suck, but that's always a risk where these things are concerned."

"It's more of a risk for me than it would be for most people."

"That's true, but the alternative is to remain alone for the rest of your life, and I don't think you want that either."

"I'm sick of being alone, and I like how I feel when he's around. It's exciting."

Sydney put down her glass and crossed the kitchen to hug Jenny. "That's the most wonderful thing I've heard in a very long time. I've been so hoping you'd find someone special."

"Don't jinx me," Jenny said, returning the embrace. "It's still very new."

Sydney released her but kept her hands on Jenny's shoulders. "But there's a connection. That doesn't happen every day."

"No, it doesn't." She looked up at Sydney. "Do you ever worry about something happening to Luke and having to go through the whole nightmare again?"

"I worried about that every day when we were first together, especially after the accident at the marina when he was hurt. I was a wreck for weeks after that. I obsessed about what could've happened."

"How did you get past that?"

MEANT FOR LOVE

"Luke got me past it. He told me I was worrying needlessly, that in all the years he's worked at the marina, that was the first time he'd ever been seriously injured or seen anyone else seriously injured. He said his daily life isn't particularly risky, and I replied that neither was Seth's. Over time he's helped me to see that what happened to Seth and the kids was a terrible tragedy, but I have no particular reason to worry that it'll happen again."

Jenny thought about what Syd had said and had to admit it made a lot of sense.

"It comes down to a choice, really," Syd continued. "Do I miss out on the most wonderful second chance with Luke because I'm afraid to love and lose again? Or do I take the risk that everything might just be fine?"

"No regrets on choosing option B?"

"Not one. Luke has helped me to see that while Seth's life is over, and my children's lives are over, mine is not. You and I were both dealt a shitty hand, but we honor the people we lost by loving again. At least that's what I believe."

"That's a lovely thing to believe. The last time I talked to Toby, after the plane hit the building and he knew what was going to happen… He told me he wanted me to be happy, that my happiness was the most important thing in the world to him. Imagine… He was aware that he was probably going to die, and all he was thinking about was me."

"He knew what you most needed to hear, and he knew that when the time came to truly move forward, those words would mean every-thing to you."

Jenny brushed at the tears that fell despite her desire to get through this without them. She'd cried more than enough over the last twelve years. You'd think she'd be all cried out by now.

"For what it's worth, I think you'll feel better after you tell Alex about Toby. It's weighing you down at a time when you should be feeling happy at having found someone you want to be with. Tell him sooner rather than later so you can put the past where it belongs and start to enjoy the future."

157

"That's very good advice."

"He works for himself, doesn't he?"

"Yes."

"Do you have his number?"

Jenny nodded. She'd programmed it into her phone after he called her last night.

"Text him and ask him where he's working and whether he might be interested in a lunch delivery."

"I can't bother him in the middle of his workday."

"Why not?"

Jenny couldn't think of any good reason why not.

Sydney's smug smile made her laugh. "Get your phone before you lose your nerve."

Still not convinced this was a good idea, she retrieved the phone from her purse.

"Ready to take dictation?" Syd asked.

"Are you always this bossy?"

"Only when it serves a good purpose. Get the text ready."

Jenny typed his name into the text screen. "It's ready."

"Ask him if he's interested in a lunch delivery."

Shaking her head, Jenny sighed. *Any interest in a lunch delivery?*

Her phone chimed almost immediately in response. *I'm already starving so that sounds awesome. I'm working at the Chesterfield estate today. You know where that is?*

I know where it is. Any special requests?

Surprise me.

Ok. See you soon.

Can't wait.

Sydney was standing next to Jenny, reading the texts as they were sent and received. "I think I might be in love with this guy, too."

"Hands off. You've got your own hot guy to love."

"Yes, I do, and Alex is all yours." She gave Jenny a tight one-armed hug. "I'm so happy this is happening for you."

"Stop jinxing me."

Sydney laughed. "Thanks for telling me about him."

"Thanks for listening. I've been dying to tell someone for days now."

"You should invite him to the shower on Saturday. We're inviting the guys to pay them back for all the times they've crashed girls' night out. We figured making them attend a sex-toy-and-lingerie party was the very least of what they deserve."

"Oh my God, I love that! But I don't know if I'm ready to expose Alex to a sex-toy party *and* our crowd at the same time."

"It'll be a good test," Sydney said with a smirk.

"I'll think about it." She gave her friend a hug. "Thank you so much for listening."

"Any time. You and I share an unfortunate bond, so I'm glad you came to me."

"There was no one else I could've gone to. I knew you'd tell me exactly what to do."

"Of course I want to hear every detail of how lunch goes." Sydney walked her to the door. "It'll be hard to tell him the story, but once you do, you'll feel better. I promise."

"I hope you're right."

"I'm always right. Ask Luke."

"I'll do that," Jenny said on her way out the door. "Next time I see him." Sydney's laughter followed her down the sidewalk. Bolstered by her friend's support, Jenny drove into town and picked up sandwiches, drinks, chips, cookies and fruit at the grocery store. In deference to the heat, she also got him two bottles of water and a bag of ice to keep everything cold.

Giddy with excitement at the thought of seeing him, she set off for the Chesterfield estate, determined to tell him what he needed to know about her and then get back to enjoying what was happening between them.

CHAPTER 13

*T*he ferry ride was endless, and the drive to Providence even worse. Carolina felt like she was coming out of her skin as they sat in traffic on Interstate 95. She strained to see what was causing the delay.

"Relax, love," Seamus said for the ten thousandth time since they left the house.

"I don't want to relax. I want to see my kids."

"And you will. Very soon. Looks like an accident up ahead. Once we get past that, it'll be smooth sailing."

"This trip has been anything but smooth sailing."

"I told you it was going to be rough out there today."

"And I told you I didn't care." The bumpy ferry ride had made her queasy, but thankfully, she hadn't gotten sick. Even if she had, she'd still be on her way to see Joe, Janey and baby P.J. Judging by the phone call she'd received from her son earlier, he was equally elated that she was finally able to come see them.

They were in Seamus's company truck because he wanted to bring back some lumber for a project he planned to do at the house. Carolina had barely heard him when he outlined the improvements he wanted to make to their house. What did she care about a leaky roof and other such things when she was about to meet her grandson?

Inching along in bumper-to-bumper traffic, she felt as if the universe was conspiring to keep her away from her loved ones, but she refrained from sharing that thought with Seamus. He would tell her she was being foolish, which she was. Nothing other than a series of regrettable events had kept her from her grandson.

First, there'd been the thorn bush she'd fallen into when she made the mistake of playfully running away from Seamus after they'd made up from one of their regular arguments. Then came the virus that had hung on through Seamus's mother's entire visit, which led Carolina to joke to the good-natured Nora O'Grady that her son had taken on an invalid. And today, rough seas and lousy traffic had made for a tedious morning.

After about thirty minutes of inching along at less than five miles per hour, they finally broke free of the accident that had snarled traffic on the interstate.

"Drive like you're being chased," she said to Seamus.

"What good will you be to baby P.J. if you arrive at the hospital through the emergency room?"

"Don't talk. Drive."

He laughed, which made her want to punch him—except for the fact that he was driving her to see her grandson.

When he parked at the hospital a short time later, Carolina was out of the car before he'd even turned off the engine.

"Hold your horses, woman, will you?"

"I will not hold my horses. You need to hurry up."

They bickered about their differing senses of urgency all the way to the elevator, where he punched the number for the neonatal intensive care unit. At the reception desk, she asked for directions to their room.

"They aren't here anymore," the nurse said. "They got moved to a regular room on the pediatrics floor an hour ago."

"That's great news," Seamus said.

"Yes, it is," the nurse agreed.

While Carolina knew it was great news, it was also another delay. Back in the elevator, she kept her arms folded tight across her chest as if that would contain the overwhelming anxiety that beat through her. Thankfully, Seamus seemed to get that touching her right then would not be in his best interests.

On the pediatrics ward, they were directed to a room at the far end of the hallway—naturally. Standing outside the door, she was suddenly frozen as weeks' worth of anxiety rendered her limbs useless.

Seamus's arm came around her shoulders. "It's okay, love. Everything's good. Let's go see them."

Apparently mute as well as frozen, Carolina nodded and let him lead her into the room. And there was her tall, handsome son, his beautiful wife and their newborn son. Caro nearly swooned from the relief she felt at finally laying eyes on the three of them. Joe and Janey looked exhausted and pale, but their smiles were radiant as they welcomed Carolina and Seamus.

Carolina hugged her son far longer than she had in years. "I'm so happy to see you."

He clung to her the way he had as a little boy, and she loved it. "Same here, Mom."

"You have no idea how happy I am that she's finally getting to see you," Seamus said drolly, making them laugh.

"Come hold your grandson, Carolina," Janey said.

Caro wiped tears she hadn't realized were there until they blinded her as she hugged her daughter-in-law around the baby. "Oh, can I? Are you sure it's okay?"

"I'm positive. He's been waiting to meet you. We've told him all about you."

"Luckily, he won't remember that it took his silly Grammy two weeks to get here after he was born." Carolina sat in a rocking chair and accepted the swaddled bundle from Janey.

"Through no fault of yours," Joe reminded her.

"I think she would've swum to the mainland through shark-infested waters today if that's what it took," Seamus said.

"You're absolutely right, I would've," Caro said, dazzled by the little face, the perfect lips, the tiny nose, the feathery eyebrows, the dusting of golden-blond hair. How could he be anything but blond with Joe and Janey as his parents? "Oh, he looks just like you did, Joseph!"

"Poor bugger," Joe said. "I was so hoping he'd look like his gorgeous mother."

"Oh hush," Janey said. "He'll be every bit as handsome as his daddy is."

Caro ran a finger over the sweet softness of the baby's cheek. "When can he come home?"

"They're going to release him in the next couple of days," Joe said, "but they want us close by for a week or two after that, so we're going to stay at Janey's Uncle Frank's house until they release us to take him to the island."

"We don't want to be too far from here if he needs something," Janey said.

"He graduated from the NICU this morning," Joe said proudly as he sat next to his wife on a small sofa next to a window that over-looked downtown Providence. "It all happened so fast, I didn't have time to text you."

"That's all right." Caro had yet to take her eyes off the baby. "We found you." Holding Peter Joseph Cantrell, who'd been named in honor of her late husband and Joe's father, Carolina took the first deep breath she'd taken in two weeks. They were fine. They were all fine, and her baby grandson was absolutely perfect despite his chaotic birth. "P.J., I have someone I want you to meet. Now, I don't want you to listen to too much of his baloney, but he's vowed to be a very good grandpa to you."

Seamus squatted in front of her and leaned in to kiss the baby's cheek. "Hi there, P.J. I'm your handsome and charming Grandpa Seamus, but you can call me Da, because that's what my nieces and nephews call my dad. I promise to spoil you rotten."

"If you want to stay out of trouble, don't listen to a word that Irish charmer says." Carolina finally peeled her eyes off the baby to give her fiancé a warm smile. "He'll lead you astray every time."

"Look, love," Seamus said, grinning as he nodded toward the baby's parents.

Janey had her head on Joe's chest, and his arm was tight around her. The two of them were fast asleep.

Carolina smiled down at her grandson. "Looks like Grammy and Da are in charge for a little while." She wouldn't have it any other way.

ON THE DRIVE to the Chesterfield estate, Jenny thought about what she needed to tell Alex and hoped she could make it through the conversation without getting emotional. She didn't want to scare him off like the first guy she'd slept with after Toby. He'd run for his life from her emotional firestorm, not that she blamed him. It was a lot to take in. She couldn't deny that, and she couldn't deny that by the time she pulled into the long driveway that led to the late Mrs. Chesterfield's estate, she felt sick again.

Alex was trimming hedges, but he was watching for her and stopped what he was doing when he saw her car enter the circular driveway.

As she got out of the car, holding the bags from the grocery store in one hand, he came toward her, his stride eating up the grass.

Jenny's entire body stood up to take notice.

Alex wore his usual work "uniform," consisting of a deliciously bare chest, khaki cargo shorts and work boots with white socks peeking out the top. His skin shone with perspiration that dampened his chest hair and made his abdominal muscles glisten.

He was gorgeous, sexy and, judging by the wide smile on his face, very happy to see her. "This is such a nice surprise," he said as he approached her, bending his head to kiss her cheek and then her lips.

Jenny wanted to cling to him and lose herself in one of his unforgettable kisses. But that wasn't why she was here, so she reluctantly pulled back from him.

"Sorry, I'm all sweaty, and you're so pretty and perfect."

"I don't care if you're sweaty." To prove her point, she ran her index finger over the moisture on his chest, stopping when she reached his belly button and noticed the hard ridge of his erection.

She looked up at him. "Are you hungry?"

"Starving," he said, his tone rife with double meaning that had the full attention of all her most sensitive places. "Let's find some shade." He took her hand and led her to his truck, where he retrieved a beach towel that he flung over his shoulder. "Glad this was still in the truck from the last time I went surfing."

"You surf?"

"Yep. I could teach you if you want."

"I'd love to learn."

"We'll do that sometime." He strolled toward a grove of trees on the far-right side of the area where he'd been working. "You've got to see this." Parting a curtain of willow tree branches, he gestured for her to go ahead of him into a garden in full bloom, surrounded on all four sides by tall hedges.

"Oh my goodness!" Jenny turned in a complete circle, taking in the incredible sight of thousands of blooms: lilies and roses and sunflowers, and those were just the flowers she could easily identify. "It's incredible. And the scent…"

"Isn't it crazy? The Chesterfield estate pays us to take care of it, even though no one lives here anymore. It was Mrs. Chesterfield's pride and joy."

"I can see why. It's amazing."

He gave her a quick tour of the garden, dazzling her with his in-depth knowledge of every type of rose and how they were germinated as well as the Latin name for every plant in the garden.

"How do you know all this?"

"It was my job in another life." The far-right corner was tucked in the shade, so Alex guided her that way with his hand on her lower back. He spread the towel and said, "After you."

Jenny moved carefully to settle on the ground, her legs protesting the movement.

"Still sore?" he asked as he settled next to her.

"Not like yesterday."

MARIE FORCE

"I feel bad about that."

"You shouldn't. It was fun." She smiled, hoping to reassure him. "A lot of fun."

"So much fun I've thought of little else since then."

"Is that so?"

"Yep." He poked his nose into the bag that was closest to him. "What's for lunch?"

"I got turkey and chicken salad. I'll eat either, so you can pick."

"Half of each?"

"That sounds good."

Jenny unwrapped the sandwiches, handed him half of the turkey, along with a Coke. She opened a bag of chips and put them close to him as she reached for the grapes while he devoured an entire sandwich before she'd had her first bite.

He guzzled a bottle of Coke as Jenny watched him, fascinated.

"Sorry, totally dehydrated from the heat," he said. "Thank you for this."

"My pleasure."

"Um, no, it's definitely my pleasure. My long, boring day just got a whole lot more interesting."

He made her burn when he said things like that, but she couldn't get so caught up in being with him that she forgot why she'd come.

"I have a bit of an ulterior motive."

"Yes, I'll do you right here in the garden. You didn't have to bring me lunch to butter me up. I'm kinda easy where you're concerned."

Jenny laughed—hard. "You should've been spanked more as a child."

"I'm happy to let you discipline me any time you'd like."

"Alex. Stop."

"Why? If I stop embarrassing you, I won't get to see your sweet blush every time I say something outrageous."

"I don't blush."

"Um, yeah, you do, and it's fucking hot."

Jenny blew out a deep breath. He was far too much for her, and yet

166

he was just enough, too. "If you can be serious for a minute, I'd like to talk to you about something."

"I can be serious, as long as you aren't going to tell me all the reasons why we can't possibly keep doing what we've been doing."

"I'm not going to say that," she said, touched by his concern.

"Oh good." He popped a grape into his mouth and reclined on one elbow. "The time I've spent with you lately is directly related to my will to live."

"No pressure or anything."

He smiled widely at her. "None at all."

Did he have any idea how sexy he was? And he wasn't even trying to be.

"So what do you want to talk about?"

Jenny took a deep breath, summoning the calm and the courage she needed to get through this. "I want to tell you about Toby."

He stared at her, not a muscle in his body moving for a long moment. "Okay."

"It's important that you hear it from me, and enough people on the island know my story that I was worried about someone else telling you. I feel bad about interrupting your workday, but I couldn't wait until later to get this off my chest."

"You haven't interrupted anything, and I want to hear anything you want to tell me. But I don't like seeing you so nervous about talking to me."

"It's kind of a big deal."

"I figured it had to be, or you wouldn't have been dreaming about him and asking him not to go."

Closing her eyes, she took a deep breath in through her nose. "I rarely have the dream anymore, and I've had it twice recently. I'm trying to figure out what that means."

His hand on her knee was warm, heavy and comforting. "Start at the beginning. Take all the time you need."

Jenny forced herself to say words she'd prefer to never say again. "Toby was killed on 9/11. He was in the South Tower of the World Trade Center, above where the plane hit."

Alex blew out a long deep breath. "Oh God. I'm so sorry. I don't know what to say."

"You don't have to say anything. Just listen, if you would, and then I'd like to tell you how to successfully navigate this situation, if that's okay."

"I'd love to hear that."

Jenny focused on a cluster of pink rose bushes. "We'd been together three years, from almost the beginning of grad school at Wharton, through the first year of new jobs in New York. We were due to be married just over a month after the attacks." Jenny rolled a cold bottle of water between her hands. "I've been on a very difficult journey since then, to say the least. I've been better, much better since I moved here more than a year ago now. The island has given me the fresh start that I desperately needed."

"Could I ask you something?"

"Anything."

"The other night, with me. Was that the first time?"

"No, but it was the first time in a long time and the first time it's mattered, and that's why I wanted to tell you about this."

"I'm glad you told me, but I hate that you had to go through such an awful thing."

"Thank you. I hate it, too. I hate it for everyone who loved him and all the others who were lost that day. I hate it for him because his life was just getting started, and it was snuffed out by people with no regard for what a gift life is to all of us. I hate a lot of things about it, but more than anything, I hate when people look at me and only see my tragedy."

He thought about that for several quiet minutes.

Jenny took a sip of her Diet Coke and waited to hear what he would say.

"You said it was the first time that mattered. Why do you suppose that is?"

"I don't know, but it's been different from the beginning with you. I'm almost afraid to say that, because it's awfully revealing. And the last thing I want to do is put more pressure on you at a time when you have more than enough to contend with."

"I don't feel pressured. I feel honored that you care enough to tell me yourself before I heard it from someone else. I appreciate that you told me what you don't want, and I get that, too. I hate that everyone here thinks of me as the guy whose mother has dementia. Those things have a way of defining a person."

"Yes," she said with a sigh of relief. "Exactly."

"It was why I liked that you didn't know who I was at first or what I was dealing with. There was comfort in the anonymity."

"For me, too. My friends have been fixing me up on dates, and I know the guys are fully prepped, and it's sweet of my friends to see to that. But I liked it so much better that you didn't know."

"I was rough with you."

"No, you weren't. You were perfect. If the next time is different, I won't be happy with you."

That drew a short laugh from him. "I stand warned." He looked up at her. "You're amazing."

"No, I'm not."

"Yes, you are. You've survived the worst possible thing, and you're still able to laugh and joke and tease and smile so brightly you make me ache. If I say you're amazing, you're amazing."

Deeply touched by his kind words, she said, "It took a really, really long time to be able to do any of those things."

"I'm sure it did." He kissed her hand, setting off a firestorm on the surface of her skin with only the rough brush of his whiskers. "Do you feel better after telling me about it?"

"I do. I felt bad last night that I didn't tell you when you asked me about him. You told me about your family and your mom. It didn't seem fair that I was unwilling to do the same."

"You weren't unwilling. You weren't ready." He reached up to caress her face and then wrapped his hand around her nape, giving a gentle tug to bring her down to him, pillowing her head on his arm. "What you said about this being the first time it mattered?"

She nodded, breathless as she waited to hear what he would say.

"It's the first time it's mattered for me in a very long time, too. I had a girlfriend in DC when I lived there. I thought she was the one, until she let me know she wasn't going to wait around for me to work out my family issues."

"She actually said that?"

"In so many words. But the funny thing was, I barely gave her a thought after we broke up. I guess it wasn't what I thought it was."

"She hurt you."

"She disappointed me more than anything."

"I heard what you said about this being a bad time for you to start anything—"

"It is a bad time. Probably the worst possible time, but as far as I'm concerned, it's already started."

Jenny rested her hand on his face. "For me, too."

He curled his arm and brought her in close enough to kiss her.

"Don't you want to finish your lunch?" she asked over the racing beat of her heart.

"I'm ready to move on to dessert."

"How about I put the rest of this away and then we talk about dessert?"

"Hurry up about it. Dessert is my favorite part of the meal."

He made her laugh when she'd expected to cry. He made her smile all the time. He embarrassed the hell out of her sometimes, but even that was charming. Most important, he made her *feel* again after twelve years of numbness that she'd once thought was permanent.

With the remnants of the picnic back in the bags and set off to the side, Jenny said, "We've got cookies for dessert."

He held out his arms to her. "I had something sweeter in mind."

Jenny snuggled into his embrace.

"I don't want to get you all dirty."

"I don't care. I'm going home after this."

"That sounds like a green light for dirty," he said with a sexy grin.

"Wait. What did I just agree to?"

"I'll show you." He kissed her long and hard, his tongue demanding and persuasive.

That he now knew her story but still wanted her and still kissed her the same way he always had was a huge relief that had her relaxing in his arms. His lips and hands were everywhere, or so it seemed, and then he was on top of her, their bodies aligned for sensual pleasure. "I want you right here," he whispered, his lips soft and his whiskers rough against her neck.

Jenny shivered from desire as much as the need she heard in his voice. "What if someone comes?"

"We'll both come. That's the point."

"*Alex!* You know what I mean."

Laughing at her outrage, he pressed his hard cock against her, letting her know how badly he wanted her. "There's no one around. We won't get caught."

"I don't know…"

"Come on, live dangerously." As he said the words, his hand traveled up her leg, taking her skirt with it as it went.

While she was still formulating her objections, he had her dress completely off.

"Alex…"

"Shhh, relax. Trust me." His lips on her neck were almost as persuasive as his gruffly spoken words.

Powerless to resist the desire that thrummed through her like a live wire connected directly to an electrical source, Jenny decided to trust him and forced her rigid muscles to relax.

"That's it," he whispered as he kissed his way to the tops of her breasts. He reached under her to release her bra with one-handed skill that indicated lots of practice. She'd have to ask him about that sometime. With her breasts bared to his intense gaze, she couldn't have found the words just then.

He bent his head and ran his tongue in teasing circles around her straining nipple.

Jenny grabbed his head and tried to direct him where she wanted him, but he wouldn't be rushed. By the time he finally sucked the tip into the heat of his mouth, she was prepared to beg. He made it well worth the wait with a combination of tugging, sucking, biting and swipes of his tongue that had her pressing her sex against his shamelessly.

And then he switched sides and did the whole thing over again.

The sweltering heat made her skin slick with perspiration as he slid down the front of her, forcing her legs apart with his broad shoulders.

"Alex, no. Not that. Not here."

"Yes that. Yes here." He pulled her panties down and tossed them aside, using his hands to open her to his questing tongue.

Jenny couldn't believe this was happening, right out in the open in broad daylight when anyone could come upon them and find his face buried between her legs. She also couldn't deny it was the hottest, sexiest thing she'd ever done. And when he sucked on her clitoris and pushed two fingers slowly and carefully into her, she ceased to think of anything other than the exquisite pleasure that accompanied the slight bite of pain.

She wasn't entirely recovered from the last time, but he took it easy on her, seeming to sense she was still sore.

"Hurt?" he asked.

"No."

"Tell me if it does." He went back for more, his tongue relentless as he took her up, up, up to the straining edge of completion, and then backed off, leaving her hanging and desperate. "I want to be inside you when you come." He knelt before her, wiped his face with the back of his hand and pulled open his shorts.

With all her earlier reservations about where this was happening forgotten, Jenny held out her arms to him, welcoming him as he came down on top of her, kissing her with broad sweeps of his tongue, which bore her flavor. The blunt nudge of his cock between her legs required her full attention until he moved ever so slightly, abrading her nipples with his chest hair.

God, he was nonstop sensory overload—and sex on a stick. Let's not forget that part. The thought made her giggle at the worst possible moment.

"What the hell is so funny?"

His indignant tone only fueled her laughter.

"Don't you know how crushing it is to a guy's ego to have a woman dissolve into laughter when he's trying to make love to her?"

"There's nothing wrong with your ego."

"Tell me what's so funny?"

"My nickname for you."

"Do I want to hear this?"

Jenny started laughing again.

He took advantage of her preoccupation to nibble on her neck, which turned her laughter into moans of pleasure. At the same time, he teased her with the slide of his erection over her sex as his fingers tweaked her nipples.

Suddenly, nothing was funny anymore. She arched her back, seeking him. "Alex... *Please*."

"Not until I hear my nickname."

"Sex on a stick."

He stopped moving to look down at her. "Are you for real?"

She bit her bottom lip to keep from laughing again at the incredulous look on his face. "Um, if the stick fits…"

Alex slid into her slowly but surely. "The stick definitely fits."

Jenny sighed with relief and pleasure. "Yes, it definitely does."

"Sex on a stick," he said with a disdainful laugh. "I should spank your ass until it's hot pink for that."

"You wouldn't dare."

"Wouldn't I?" He looked down at her, watching her intently. "Anything hurt?"

"No."

"Will you tell me if it does?"

"Mmm." She closed her eyes and concentrated on the delicious sensations traveling from her core to every sensitive place on her body. She tingled everywhere, from her scalp to her lips to her nipples to the soles of her feet. His slow possession was every bit as overwhelming as the fast and furious coupling the other night.

Jenny forgot all about where they were, the emotionally fraught conversation they'd just had and everything other than the sublime pleasure they generated together.

"So fucking good," he whispered gruffly against her neck as he hooked his arm under her leg, opening her wider to his possession.

Jenny cried out when he went deeper, igniting a fire inside her. "Don't stop," she said, grasping his backside.

He groaned and pressed harder into her, which was all she needed.

Her cries of completion melded with his as they strained together, lost in a moment of perfect harmony.

"Holy shit," he said as he gasped for breath.

"We're a sweaty mess."

"I know." He throbbed inside her as she twitched with aftershocks. "Isn't it awesome? Stick with me, kid. I'll get you dirty any time you want."

"I'm starting to want pretty much all the time."

He raised his head off her chest and touched his lips to hers. "Is that right?"

Jenny nodded, unable to look away from the dark-chocolate gaze that had captivated her from the very beginning.

"I'm right there with you. It's a good thing you can't know how often I think about you while I'm working. You'd want to get a restraining order."

His words weren't flowery or romantic, but they went straight to her heart just the same.

She reached up to push his hair back from his sweaty forehead. "You need to get back to work."

"I know," he said with a sigh. "But not yet. A few more minutes in paradise, please?"

When he asked so nicely, how could she deny him anything? Despite the outrageous heat that was multiplied by his nearness, she wrapped her arms around him and held him close.

CHAPTER 14

*G*rant McCarthy tried to meet his friend Dan Torrington at least once a week so they could read each other's work and offer critiques. While Dan was a lawyer and not a writer by trade, he'd had some excellent suggestions for the screenplay Grant was writing about Stephanie's efforts to free her stepfather from prison after he was wrongfully accused of abusing her.

The writing of the screenplay had been more emotionally exacting than he'd expected it to be, as he relived the horror of Stephanie's childhood through interviews with her and her stepfather, Charlie Grandchamp. It had taken some time for Charlie to open up to Grant about the details of the abuse and neglect Stephanie had withstood at the hands of her mother, some of which he'd heard for the first time from Charlie.

That left him with a dilemma—did he tell Stephanie what he'd learned from Charlie or let her read about it in the screenplay? He was still mulling over that question when Dan came bounding into the South Harbor Diner, looking woefully out of place on Gansett with his wrinkled dress shirt and the loafers he insisted on wearing with shorts, even though he looked like a total fool.

Dan stopped to chat with Rebecca, who owned the diner, which was jammed for a weekday morning.

From what all the women said, Dan could wear anything he wanted, because he was so good-looking he could get away with it. Whatever. Grant loved to bust on him about how out of place his West Coast style was on their East Coast island, but his opinion on such things didn't matter to Dan. No, Dan was far more interested these days in Grant's opinion of the book he was laboring to write about the unjust convictions he'd helped to overturn.

Ever since the day they'd spent in freezing-cold water together after a sailboat accident, Dan had felt more like a brother than a friend, and Grant was thrilled to have him around—not that he'd ever tell Dan that. His ego was big enough without that kind of validation.

Dan slid into the booth across from Grant. "Sorry I'm late. My mom called right when I was leaving, and she's full of questions about me and Kara." Dan rolled his eyes. "She's like a dog with a bone."

"Nice. Comparing your mother to a dog. How did she find out about the 'bone,' as you call it?"

"I refuse to refer to the woman I love as 'the bone.'"

"Why? Does it give you a *boner?*"

"Jesus. Shut up, will you? I might've made the huge mistake of mentioning that I'd met someone here. You should know how mothers of sons in their mid-thirties get *hopeful* at the first sign of commitment of any kind."

"So it's your own fault that she's planning the wedding."

"Yes, I guess it is."

"Speaking of weddings, is there going to be one?"

"Not you, too! We're not talking about weddings or other such foolishness. We're enjoying our time together. Why isn't that enough for everyone?"

"Because you're no longer in your mid-thirties. You're thirty-six now, which is that side of forty rather than this side of thirty. You ain't getting any younger."

Dan picked up the bread knife and ran it over his wrist.

"Not sharp enough," Grant said. "And I didn't waste an entire day

176

saving your sorry life so you could end it with a dull butter knife just because your mom wants you to get married."

"Wasted? I'm hurt."

"Not anymore you aren't. So what's stopping you from popping the question? You know you don't want to let her get away."

"What's stopping *you* from getting married? Seems to me you popped the question quite some time ago, but I don't hear any bells ringing in your neighborhood either."

Grant kept his expression impassive as Dan's question struck at the heart of his insecurities. Despite frequent attempts on his part, Stephanie had dodged all conversations about setting a date for their wedding. But Grant would never admit that to anyone, so he went with the obvious excuse. "We're both so busy. We haven't had time to breathe, let alone plan a wedding. We're not in any rush."

"Need I remind you that you're thirty-six now, too? Just in case you'd forgotten."

"I haven't forgotten." That was one of his many concerns. He wanted a family, and he also wasn't getting any younger. At some point he'd have to sit Stephanie down and force the issue, but he was reluctant to do that during her busy season at the restaurant, when she had more than enough going on. Timing was everything in these matters, so he planned to wait until October, after the season ended, to try to get her to set a date.

After hearing last night that Evan and Grace were getting married in January, he felt a greater sense of urgency to nail down his plans with Stephanie. They'd been engaged longer than Evan and Grace. Shouldn't they have plans by now? Even after more than a year together, he still worried from time to time that they weren't as solid as they could be. Part of that went back to her upbringing and her constant fear of the floor falling out from under her without any warning.

That was one reason why he'd proposed when he did. He wanted to assure her that he was in it for keeps, but every time she dodged talk of their wedding, he had reason to wonder if she was in it for keeps, too. The very thought that she might not be was enough to give him heart failure, so he tried not to think about it. Much… Absorbed as he was in writing about her fourteen-year effort to free her beloved stepfather from prison, it was hard not to think about her all the time.

This was especially true in light of the crisis they'd withstood following the sailboat accident, when he'd been so riddled with guilt over his inability to save both Dan and the boat captain, Steve, who'd died.

"What planet did you just visit?" Dan asked.

Jarred from his musings, Grant realized Dan had been talking to him and he hadn't heard a word. "Sorry. Just thinking about some stuff."

"Is everything okay?"

"Sure. A lot going on as always. Did you hear the plan the girls have for surprising Blaine and Tiffany with a shower this weekend?"

"I heard some rumblings about that. What I'd like to know is why we have to be part of it. Why can't we take him out and get him drunk the way men are supposed to?"

"Because as much as we'd like to think otherwise, the girls are in charge, and we do what we're told."

"I don't like it."

"You'd better get used to it if you're planning to keep Kara around."

"I'm planning to keep her around, but she's not the boss of me."

Grant howled with laughter. "Keep telling yourself that. Let me know how that works out for you."

"Are we going to get some work done, or do I have to continue listening to you talk shit?"

"Both." Grant slid his latest pages across the table to Dan, who handed over his.

"Go easy on me with that red pen of yours, will you?" Dan said.

"My red pen is making this a better book."

"No doubt, but you're ruining my self-esteem."

"Good thing you've got plenty to spare. Now shut up and read."

Grant thought he heard Dan utter "fuck off and die" under his breath, but he chose not to engage, because he did want to get some feedback on the latest scenes, and Dan had proved to be an able critique partner. His expertise was more in the storytelling than the writing, while Grant was helping to polish the writing in Dan's book. It had turned out to be an unlikely yet productive partnership.

Grant was completely absorbed in the story of how Dan and his team of law students had helped to free a man who'd been on death row in California for thirty years. He almost missed it… A conversation taking place in the booth behind him. They were speaking loudly enough to be heard over the din of voices in the diner.

"I don't care if Kara wants to see me or not," the woman said. "Connor is her nephew. She can't refuse to acknowledge him."

"I've gone along with this mission of yours, but I want to reiterate my objections to blindsiding her," the man said. "She's not going to be happy to see either one of us."

"I don't care if she's happy to see me. She won't be rude to us with the baby there."

"Don't be too sure."

Grant reached across the table to nudge Dan with his pen.

Dan grunted in reply.

"Dan."

"What?"

"Listen. Behind me."

"This whole thing has gone on long enough," the woman was saying. "I mean I didn't *steal* you from her. What man in his thirties can be *stolen* from a woman if he doesn't actually want to go?"

"That's not how she sees it, and you know it. She had no idea that we'd begun seeing each other when I was still seeing her, too."

The baby let out a squawk that had both his parents focusing on him for a minute.

"She'll be happy to meet Connor, even if she wants nothing to do with us. I promised my mother I'd try to fix things with her, and that's what I'm doing."

Dan's eyes got very wide as a look of utter distress overtook his face.

"Don't come crying to me when the whole thing blows up in your face," the man said.

"Sometimes I think you still care about her more than you care about me."

"Honestly, Kelly, which one of you did I marry?"

"Go," Grant whispered to Dan, who seemed frozen with shock. "Go to her."

Dan pushed the pages he'd been reading across the table to Grant and was out of the booth like he'd been shot from a cannon. During their long day together in the water, Dan had told Grant about Kara's sister Kelly, who'd married the man Kara had once expected to marry and how hurt Kara had been. Dan had been lucid for probably an hour all day, but he'd talked about Kara the entire time. They'd both been afraid they'd never again see the women they loved.

"Let's get going," the woman behind him said. "I want to get this over with."

As he gathered up the papers Dan had abandoned, Grant could only hope that Dan got to Kara before her sister and brother-in-law could blindside her.

DAN HAD NEVER DRIVEN SO FAST on the island's winding roads, but he'd never been more frantic to get to Kara. Well, except for the day he'd spent fighting for his life in freezing water, thinking he'd totally blown it with her before he left on the ill-fated sailboat trip.

Flashing lights behind him made him groan with impatience and despair as he pulled his Porsche to the side of the road. He gave thanks when he saw his friend Blaine Taylor approach the car.

"In a rush, Counselor?"

"A big rush. I need to get to Kara. It's a bit of an emergency."

"What kind of emergency?"

"The kind that will hurt her badly unless I can get to her and warn her before it happens."

Blaine took a step back. "Slow down, all right?"

"Yeah, sorry about that."

"Go."

"I owe you one." Dan didn't need to be told twice. He took off toward the McCarthy's Marina in North Harbor, adhering more closely to the speed limit after his friend cut him a break. As he drove, he thought about the absolute audacity of her sister showing up out of the blue, expecting Kara to forgive and forget because there was now a baby involved.

He felt kind of sorry for baby Connor. It wasn't his fault his parents were jerks. But Dan would be goddamned if he'd let Kelly and Matt do any further damage to Kara. She'd worked hard enough to overcome the betrayal of two people she'd loved. They weren't going to get another chance at her. Not if he had anything to say about it.

As he drove, he scrolled through his contacts, looking for the number for Kara's backup driver, Tim. He and Dan had gone out for beers a few times and had exchanged numbers, for which he was now extremely grateful.

"It's too early to drink, Torrington," Tim said when he answered the phone, sounding as if he'd just woken up.

"I need you to relieve Kara."

"Why? I'm working tonight."

"It's urgent. Will you get down to the dock and use the backup boat?"

"What's wrong with the main boat?"

"Nothing. I'll explain later. Please. I wouldn't ask you if it wasn't urgent."

"I'll be there in twenty."

"I don't care who asks, you have no idea where Kara is. Got me?"

"Yeah, sure. Is she okay?"

"She will be. I'll make sure of it. Thanks, Tim."

"No problem."

Dan found a parking space on the street that led to the marina and grabbed it, knowing it might be as close as he'd get. He locked the car and took off running, which was still rather painful in the vicinity of his ribs, which had been broken in the accident. The pain was of no consequence, however, when it came to reaching Kara before her sister did.

He flew past the marina restaurant, oblivious to shouts from Grant's brother Mac, who asked him where the fire was.

Dan took the ramp to the floating dock that housed Kara's launch. Giving thanks to every god in the universe that she was just pulling in with a boatload of passengers, Dan waited until every one of them had disembarked before he jumped on the boat. As always, his loafers slid precariously on the deck, which made Kara laugh.

"Where the heck did you come from?" she asked, flashing the smile that made him weak in the knees. Her long hair was contained in a ponytail pulled through the back of a Ballard Boat Builders ball cap that protected her fair complexion from the sun.

"Go," he said, tossing off the stern line.

"What're you doing? I have customers."

The bench on the dock where people waited for rides to their boats in the anchorage was empty at the moment.

"Drive the boat. I'll explain on the way."

"On the way to where?"

"Anywhere but here. Please. Drive the boat."

Giving him a puzzled look, she tossed off the spring line and backed the boat out of the slip.

When she turned it toward the Salt Pond, Dan exhaled a deep breath that made his ribs burn like a mother.

"What's gotten into you?" Kara asked.

He moved to her at the helm, wrapped his arms around her waist and brought her back to rest against him, his head dropping to her shoulder.

"You're kind of freaking me out."

Since there was no easy way to say what he needed to tell her, he went with quick and dirty. "Kelly and Matt are here with the baby."

Her entire body went rigid with shock. "What? How do you know?"

"Grant and I were in the diner for our weekly meeting, and we heard them talking about you and how they'd come to clear the air and to introduce you to the baby."

"Are you kidding me?"

"I wish I was. Their plan was to force you to deal with them by showing up with the baby."

Because he was holding her so close to him, he felt her begin to tremble, which enraged him. Hadn't they gotten enough from her already? "I called Tim. He's coming in to drive the other boat."

"Wait... You called Tim?"

"If they can't find you, they can't force you to do anything."

"We can't stay out here all day."

"I don't have anything else to do. Do you?"

"You do have other things—such as a book that's due after Labor Day and is still not finished."

"I'll get it done. This is far more important."

"What about food?"

"I'll call Mario and have him deliver to us in the pond."

"He only does that at nine, noon and six. We missed the noon run."

"If I pay him enough, he'll do it."

"So we're really going to hide out for the day?"

"Either that or we can go back to the dock and let Kelly try to blindside you."

"Won't I have to face her eventually?"

"Possibly, but this way you give her a very long and miserable day of waiting for you in the broiling sun with a newborn and a reluctant husband along for the ride."

"Why do you say he's reluctant?"

"Because I heard him tell her he thought it was a bad idea to show up unannounced and force you to deal with them."

"I'm glad for Connor's sake that one of them has a bit of sense left." Clearing the anchorage, Kara slowed the boat, shifted into neutral and turned to him, sliding her arms around his neck. "My hero."

"Hardly."

"Did you or did you not come running, with broken ribs that aren't entirely healed, when you heard what my sister planned to do? And did you or did you not have the foresight to call in another driver so I could actually run away for the day?"

"I might've done those things."

"Then you're absolutely my hero."

"I absolutely love you, and I couldn't let them do that to you. When I think about how they might've succeeded if Grant and I hadn't heard them…"

"Well, they didn't, and it's all thanks to you."

"And Grant. He heard them first."

"How did he know about them?"

"That day in the water. I told him what you'd been through. He was as mad about it as I am. He heard Kelly say your name and some other stuff, so he knew they were talking about you."

"You're both my heroes. Thank you so much for coming running. I would've hated to give her that moment of my utter shock at seeing them."

"I'm happy to deny her that. So, how do you feel about running away with me today?"

"There's nothing else I'd rather do. Where should we go?"

Dan took a good look around and pointed to a free mooring. "Let's grab that and hang here for a while and see if we can entertain ourselves."

Kara directed the launch toward the mooring and pulled up next to it, picking up the stick attached to the rope that she looped around a cleat on the bow. Turning back, she found him removing the pads from the bench seats and tossing them onto the floor of the open launch.

"You got any extra sunscreen?"

"Do I have sunscreen? I bathe in it hourly." She tossed him a can and watched him remove his shirt and kick off the ridiculous loafers he insisted on wearing in the heat of summer.

He covered his chest, belly and arms in sunscreen, wincing as he ran his hand over his ribs, which were still colored by yellowing bruises.

"Let me do your back."

"Only if I can do yours."

"I have a shirt on."

"You won't for long."

"Oh, so it's going to be that kind of field trip, is it?"

"Of course it is. Have you met me?"

"My delicates can't handle this sun."

"I'll keep you covered so the sun won't find your delicates."

She raised her hands to his face and brought him down for a kiss that blew the top off his head.

He dropped the can of sunscreen and wrapped an arm around her.

"I love you, too," she said. "Thank you so much for this."

"While my approval ratings are at an all-time high, I've got something I need to ask you."

"What's that?"

"When are you going to marry me?" The words were out of his mouth before his brain had time to catch up. But when his brain joined the party, he discovered he had absolutely no regrets about blurting out a somewhat major question without having given it his usual deliberation. Who was he kidding? He'd been deliberating on how to make her a permanent part of his life for as long as he'd known her. "Your mouth is hanging open. Not that I mind that, because it gives me all kinds of ideas, but I was sort of hoping you might say something at this juncture."

"What am I supposed to say when you throw that out there like a live grenade?"

"How about yes?"

"You didn't ask me a yes-or-no question."

"Pardon the error." He fell gracelessly to his knees before her, grimacing at the flash of pain that radiated through ribs that refused to fucking heal. "Kara Ballard, center of my universe, love of my life, future mother of my children, will you do me the humongous and probably undeserved honor of being my wife?"

Once again she stared at him with the flabbergasted look on her face that only made him love her more, if that was possible. "That was a yes-or-no question, in case you didn't notice."

"I noticed."

"And? Are you planning to make me suffer?"

Apparently she wasn't, because she dropped to her knees in front of him, wrapped her arms around him and held him. "Yes. But—"

He had no interest in any buts, so he kissed the words right off her sweet lips.

Kara, being Kara, turned away from the kiss, determined to be heard despite his intense desire to avoid anything that sounded like a qualification of her acceptance. "Tell me you're not asking me because of Kelly and Matt showing up here."

"That's not why I'm asking you."

"The timing is a bit curious."

"Perhaps, but that's not why."

"Then why?"

"Um, other than the fact that I love you to the point of madness, and the thought of you leaving me gives me nightmares?"

"Other than that."

Damn, she was a worthy adversary for a man who prided himself on out-arguing just about anyone. "My mom laid into me about when I planned to marry you."

"I knew it!"

"There's only one other woman who scares me more than my mom does."

"Who is she?"

"You, stupid," he said, kissing her nose and then her lips. "It scares the hell out of me when I consider all the many ways I'm capable of messing up the best thing to ever happen to me. It's in my best interests to get a ring on your finger before you wise up and figure me out."

"I've got you figured out, Torrington, and you're not getting rid of me that easily."

"I'll get you a ring, as soon as we can get to the mainland. You can pick any ring you want. Sky's the limit."

"I don't need the sky when I've already got the sun and the moon."

Didn't she know exactly how to stop his heart? "You know what the best day of my life was?" he asked.

"The day you met me?"

"That was second best. You know what the first one was?"

"The day I let you sleep with me?"

"That's tied for second."

"*Second?*"

"Stay with me here, and remember my propensity for messing things up. The very best day of my entire life was the day I caught my fiancée in bed with my best man."

Kara's brows furrowed with confusion. "*That* was the best day of your life?"

"It certainly was. If that hadn't happened, I might've married the wrong woman, and that would've ruined my life, because I never would've met you on the second-best day of my life."

"Your logic needs some work, Counselor, but your point is well taken. I guess the best day of my life was the day I found out that Kelly and Matt had been fooling around behind my back, because it sent me out here, where I found you—or where you found me and drove me crazy until I had mercy on you and went out with you."

"Is that the story our grandchildren are going to hear?"

"Is there any other version of that story?"

"I guess there isn't. Luckily, my persistence is as legendary as my argumentativeness."

"How lucky for me."

"So if your sister and her husband did you a favor by stabbing you in the back, maybe we should return to the dock so you can introduce them to your extremely handsome and very, *very* successful—as well as famous, did I mention I'm famous?—fiancé, and you can have the last laugh."

Kara's silent laughter filled him with unreasonable joy. "You are so freaking full of yourself."

"Is anything I said a lie? Am I handsome?"

"You're not ugly."

"Am I successful?"

"You're not a total loser."

"Am I famous?"

"In your own mind, for sure."

He cupped her bottom and pulled her in tight against him. "Let's go face them and show them they've got no power over you anymore."

"Yes, let's do that, but not until she's had a few hours to broil in the hot sun."

"What about the baby?"

"She'll keep him in the shade with Matt while she paces the dock waiting for me to return after someone tells her we're out on the boat. If I know Kelly, she won't be satisfied until she gets her moment of drama."

"What do you propose we do in the meantime?"

She gave him a gentle nudge toward the pads he'd put on the floor of the boat. "Lie down."

Intrigued by the sexy glimmer in her eye, he did as he was told. Never let it be said that he couldn't be trained.

Still kneeling, Kara took her shirt off and then her shorts before she stretched out next to him, wearing only her bra and panties. "We're going to celebrate our engagement."

He turned on his side to face her and put his arm around her. "That's the best idea you've ever had."

CHAPTER 15

*S*till processing the phone call he'd received right before
leaving the studio, Evan turned the motorcycle into the
pharmacy parking lot at one o'clock as planned. He stashed the bike
under the stairs and sat to wait for Grace.

Running his fingers through his hair, Evan tried to stop his mind
from repeatedly racing through the conversation he'd had with Buddy
Longstreet. The king of country music had called him to celebrate the
freeing of his album from the Starlight Records bankruptcy proceedings. Buddy had plans for him—big plans that were in sharp conflict
with the plans Evan had been making for himself lately.

After the tremendous amount of time and attention he'd poured
into the studio—not to mention the huge investment Ned Saunders
had made to get the place off the ground—how in the world would
Evan walk away from that to pursue the performing and recording
career he'd once thought he wanted?

And then he thought of Josh Harrelson, the sound engineer he'd
wooed to Gansett and Island Breeze Records with the promise of a
steady paycheck. Didn't he owe it to Josh to follow through on the
plans they'd made?

Finally, he thought of Grace and their amazing life together, which would be totally turned upside down if he went out on tour for God only knew how long. To hear Buddy talk, he'd be on tour for the rest of his natural life if things went according to the grand plan. And things mostly went according to Buddy's plans. He was a star maker. There was no denying that.

At one time, not all that long ago, Evan had wanted the kind of stardom Buddy had promised him today. He wanted the big time, and nothing else would do. But now he knew a different kind of life, a simpler life that suited him far more than life as a performer ever had.

Never once, in all the gigs he'd played on Gansett Island with Owen and on his own, had Evan ever experienced the crippling stage fright that plagued him at almost every other venue he'd played. The stage fright was one of the reasons he'd been secretly relieved to hear that his record had been taken down by Starlight's bankruptcy.

That news had forced him to go in a different direction, and that direction had been far more satisfying than anything else ever had. Buddy had put up a lot of money to bail him out of the bankruptcy. Evan didn't know just how much, but his manager, Jack, had inferred it was no small amount. So Buddy would be looking for some return on that investment, which would require months on the road promoting the album Evan had worked so hard on.

Recording the album now seemed like it'd happened in another lifetime. That was how far removed he was from the years he'd spent in Nashville chasing the dream, only to watch it all go to shit when his record company went bankrupt. He'd had reason to think in the last year that the bankruptcy was actually the luckiest thing that had happened to him in show business.

What the hell am I going to do?

He'd no sooner had the thought when Grace stepped out of the pharmacy, looking pretty and put together in her work clothes, which today consisted of a lightweight dress and a sweater she immediately shed when she encountered the blast of heat in the parking lot.

Evan got up to meet her.

As she studied him, her smile faded. "What's wrong?"

"How can you take one look at me and know something is wrong?"

"Because your hair is standing on end, and that only happens when you run your fingers through it over and over, which you only do when something is wrong."

He stared at her, amazed. Had anyone ever known him better or paid closer attention to his every mood, want and need? No, never. "It's nothing that won't keep until after lunch. Are you ready?"

They were meeting his parents for lunch at the Oar Bar at the Gansett Boat Works Marina, or, as his father had said, *"Lunch with the enemy."* Not that Big Mac McCarthy had enemies. No, he had competitors who were as much his friends as anyone on the island. Evan had chosen the so-called enemy over lunch at their own marina, because he didn't want interruptions while he and Grace shared their wedding plans with his parents.

Evan took her keys and held the passenger door to her car until she was settled. He got in the driver's side and adjusted the seat to his much longer legs.

"You're not going to tell me?"

He blew out a deep breath. "I don't want to."

"Great," she said with a testy edge to her voice.

"Buddy Longstreet called me."

"As in he called you himself or one of his people called you?"

"He called me himself."

"Wow."

"Yeah. He's got some pretty big plans for me now that he's gotten me free of Starlight."

"What kind of big plans?"

"Six months on tour when the album drops to begin with, followed by getting me back in the studio to record my second album."

"I assume he means for that to happen in his studio in Nashville."

"You assume correctly."

She didn't say anything, but he could see her fingers linking and unlinking.

He reached over and put his hand on top of hers, feeling the bite of the engagement ring he'd given her against his palm. "I haven't said yes to any of it. He did all the talking."

"But he expects you to say yes."

"I believe Buddy Longstreet is quite accustomed to people saying yes to him, so it doesn't occur to him that I wouldn't say yes."

"God, Evan, what're we going to do?"

"See that, right there, what you said?"

"What did I say?"

"You asked what *we're* going to do. *We.* This involves both of us, and we're going to figure it out together. No matter what happens, we're getting married on January eighteenth. That is non-negotiable."

"But what happens on January nineteenth?"

"That's the part we've got to figure out."

"I can't go anywhere. I'm up to my eyeballs in the pharmacy. Even if I wanted to walk away, I can't afford to. Not for a couple of years anyway."

"I know, baby. I need a little time to think about how to handle this. I've got to play it right, because if I turn down Buddy's offer the wrong way, he could squash Island Breeze like a bug if he wanted to. I don't want that to happen, so I've got to figure out the best way to play it."

"You're going to say no to him?"

"Yeah," Evan said, surprising himself as much as her. "I think I am."

"Can you do that?"

"I don't know. I've got to talk to Jack and figure it out."

"You're really going to say no to Buddy Longstreet."

"My life is here. *Our* life is here. I want to make a go of the studio, and I want to make babies with you. I can't do that if I'm on the road for half the year."

A sniffle from the passenger seat had him looking over to find tears rolling down her cheeks. Evan pulled the car off the road and put it in park. He held out his arms to her. "Gracie... I'm so sorry. Please don't cry. You know I can't stand it when you cry." He held her until she got it all out, stroking her silky hair and breathing in the scent of home.

No matter how great the offer or how great the superstar making it, Evan couldn't leave her to chase a dream he'd given up on since he met her and found a whole new set of dreams.

"I've been so scared about what was going to happen," she said after a long period of silence.

"You gotta have some faith in me, baby. That I want the same things you do."

She looked up at him with a tearstained face that broke his heart. "I do have faith in you, but I also have faith in your amazing talent. I don't want to be responsible for holding you back from where you should be."

"You're not doing that. I promise you I'd stopped wanting the big dream long before I met you."

"So if you'd never met me, you'd still be saying no to Buddy?"

Evan mulled that over just long enough that she looked away.

"You wouldn't have said no."

"Only because I wouldn't have had a good reason to say no—the best possible reason."

"I don't think you ought to do anything rash that you might regret later. Buddy has a wife and kids and a family life. If he can make it work, you can, too."

"Buddy makes it work because his wife is as big of a star as he is and they tour together—with their kids. You have your own life and your own business that's every bit as important as mine is. Our situation is very different from theirs, and we can't compare the two."

"We're going to be late to meet your parents," Grace said as she found a tissue in her purse to wipe her face and blow her nose. She pulled down the visor to check the damage. "Great, I'm a wreck."

"You are not. You're as gorgeous as ever."

"You have to say that. You love me."

"You bet I do, and don't you forget it." He pulled the car back onto the road and turned into the long driveway that led to Gansett Boat Works. The Oar Bar was situated off to the side of the main dock and boasted about ten thousand oars painted by people who'd come through the island on boats, for Race Week, bachelor and bachelorette parties, for weddings and other major events. They hung from the roof, on the walls and on every available space in the cluttered bar. Evan loved the place and never got tired of reading all the messages on the oars, some of them dating back more than forty years.

His parents were already seated at a table inside when he escorted Grace into the bar. He kept a tight grip on her hand, hoping to reassure her after their emotional conversation.

"Hi, honey," Linda said, embracing Grace and then Evan.

Big Mac stood to greet Grace with a kiss to the cheek.

"Um, excuse me for one second," Grace said.

Evan released her hand and watched her scurry toward the stairs that led to the bathroom.

"Everything okay?" Linda asked, giving him the Voodoo Mama stare that saw right through her adult children.

"It will be." Evan sat with them, and while they waited for Grace to return, he brought them up to date on the goings-on with Buddy and the album once lost to bankruptcy.

"Oh my goodness," Linda said. "No wonder Grace is so upset."

"That's a tough spot you're in, son," Big Mac said.

"No kidding. There's a lot to think about to be sure. Listen, before Grace comes back, this isn't why we invited you to lunch. We have some other news we wanted to share with you—good news, or at least I hope you'll think so."

"Am I going to be a grandmother again?"

"No," Evan said, laughing. "At least not because of me."

"I still haven't recovered from the latest delivery," Big Mac said.

"Because it was so hard on you?" Evan asked, amused as always by his dad.

"Exactly."

"We heard earlier today that Mac and Maddie are expecting again," Linda said. "Your father is upset enough about that news."

"Only because of what happened the last time," Big Mac said, "but Mac assured me there's no chance of that again."

"I sure hope not. Once was enough." Evan was about to go check on Grace when she appeared at the top of the stairs and made her way across the room to them. He stood to hold her chair and waited until she was settled and then bent to place his lips against her ear. "Okay?"

She nodded and smiled up at him.

When Evan was seated again, he took her hand. "You want to share the good news?"

"You don't want to?"

"You can."

"Someone needs to tell us what's going on," Linda said.

"Evan and I have set a wedding date."

"Yes!" Big Mac said. "That'll be twenty bucks, please, my love."

"Wait, you guys *bet* on what we had to tell you?" Evan asked his parents.

"Your mother had twenty on a baby."

"Well, I'm glad I could help you score an easy twenty," Evan said, amused.

"And I get to gloat, too."

"Of course you do."

"Shush and let them talk," Linda said to her husband. "When and where?"

"January eighteenth in Turks and Caicos."

"Ohhh, how fun! A destination wedding with beach time in the dead of winter!"

"We were hoping you'd approve." Though she seemed pleased by his mother's reaction, Grace's smile wasn't as potent as usual.

"Everyone's going," Big Mac announced. "I'm paying. Get tickets and rooms for all of them, and I'll take it from there."

"Really, Dad, no one expects you to do that."

"So what? I can do what I want. Just try to stop me."

"Don't try, honey," Linda said, patting Evan's hand across the table. "You know how he can be when he gets something in his head."

"Yes, you know how I can be," Big Mac said with a satisfied smile.

Grace laughed, and the sound filled Evan's heart to overflowing. He loved to hear her laugh as much as he hated to see her cry. He took hold of her hand. "See what you're marrying into?"

"I know exactly what I'm marrying into, and I couldn't be happier about it."

"We couldn't be happier either," Linda assured her future daughter-in-law. "You two are a perfect fit, and we have no doubt that you're going to have a long and happy life together."

Evan would do everything within his power to make sure they had exactly that and nothing less.

ELATED after her lunch date with Alex, Jenny went back to the lighthouse to shower and change. When she'd offered to bring him lunch, she hadn't pictured an enchanted garden or sex outside in broad daylight. Earlier in the summer, when she told her friends she was ready to shake things up a bit, she'd never imagined shaking things up to the extent she had since she met Alex.

Part of her—the part concerned with self-preservation—wanted to take a step back and slow things down a bit. But the other part—the part that had missed being half of a couple, the part that had missed the connection she'd had with Toby—wanted to dive into what she was feeling for Alex without reservation.

Being with him was exciting, and Jenny felt more alive with him than she had since her life was shattered. And he'd said and done all the right things when she told him about Toby. He'd reacted with the perfect amount of distress on her behalf but hadn't overreacted the way so many people had before him. Jenny appreciated that and would tell him so when she saw him later for their date.

She couldn't wait. She felt like a teenager in the throes of first love, a thought that made her giggle, since she was hardly a teenager and this was hardly first love. Hell, she'd be hard-pressed to call it love, but it was definitely something. Her entire body tingled with awareness every time he was close by. All he had to do to get her motor running was look at her with eyes full of sexy intent, and she was his. Completely and absolutely his. She wondered if he had any idea how ridiculously gone over him she was.

"Probably better that he doesn't know, or he'll run for his life from the crazy lady in the lighthouse," she said to her reflection in the bathroom mirror.

Her cell phone rang in the bedroom, and she ran to answer the call from Sydney.

"How'd it go? Tell me everything and leave out nothing."

Jenny laughed. She so enjoyed her Gansett friends and the way they talked about *everything*. "It was a smashing success. Thanks for the brilliant idea."

"It was a rather brilliant idea, wasn't it?"

"You have no idea how brilliant."

"Jenny Wilks! Did you have sex outside?"

"I'm not telling."

"Oh my God! You did!"

"Well, there was this garden, you see, surrounded on four sides by very tall hedges. And then there was this hot gardener with abs like you read about. What was a girl to do?"

"I love it! Did this happen before or after you told him about Toby?"

"After."

"So I take that to mean the conversation went well?"

"It went as well as I could've hoped for. He was perfect, and he wasn't different or weird afterward, because I told him not to be. He seemed to appreciate the guidance."

"You live and you learn, don't you? What's wrong with saying, 'After I tell you this huge thing, this is what I need from you'?"

"Nothing at all. When you think about it, how would anyone know what the right thing to say or do is after hearing that story unless I tell them?"

"When Linda first told us about you, we talked about how best to approach you out there all by yourself in the lighthouse. I remember thinking about what I would want before I went to see you. I volunteered to go because I understood what not to do better than the others could have."

"I'm so glad it was you who came, and that you shared your

story with me. Right away I felt comforted to know that I wasn't alone with that kind of pain—not that I'd wish it on anyone. But that you understood so well made it easier to accept your offer of friendship."

"We're all thankful you accepted the offer."

"No one more so than me."

"Awww, shucks. You're a perfect fit with us, kiddo. We'd have badgered you until you had no choice but to join our happy clan."

"It is a happy clan, and I'm thrilled to be part of it." Her phone beeped. "Oh, that's my mom."

"I'll let you go. Glad it all went well."

"Thanks again for today, Syd."

"Any time. Talk soon."

Jenny pushed the button to end her call with Syd and accept her mother's call. "Hi, Mom."

"Hi, honey. Hope I'm not catching you at a bad time."

Jenny thought about where she'd been forty-five minutes earlier and held back a nervous giggle at the thought of her mother calling then. "Nope. Good time. What's up?"

"Dad was able to score three full days off next week—Tuesday through Thursday. We were thinking of flying up Monday afternoon and leaving on Thursday. Would that be okay?"

Guilt flooded through her, because her very first thought was *three days with no Alex.* "Of course," she said to her mother. "That's absolutely fine."

"I looked on a map and I saw that the McCarthy's hotel is fairly close to the lighthouse, so I booked a room there hoping you'd say yes to a visit."

"You can stay here."

"That's very sweet of you, but we'll be very happy at the hotel, and you won't have us around your neck the whole time. I'm sure you've got your own things to do."

Images of what she'd done with Alex in the garden chose that moment to pass through her mind like an erotic movie. Jenny cleared her throat. "A few things here and there."

"So we'll be on the eight p.m. ferry on Monday. Should I try to get the rental car on the boat?"

"No need. I'll pick you up at the ferry, and you can use my car while you're here."

"I can't wait to see you and your lighthouse and meet your friends."

"I can't wait either. I'm really glad you're coming, Mom."

"So are we. See you soon, hon."

Jenny tucked the phone in her purse, grabbed her keys and headed out to check in with Paul Martinez, who was working at the retail store today. She wished she'd asked Alex what his brother knew about the two of them, but she hesitated to interrupt his work again with a phone call.

"I guess I'll find out soon enough," she said as she drove down the long driveway from the lighthouse to the road. A short time later, she pulled onto the grounds of Martinez Lawn & Garden and realized she was strangely nervous about meeting with Alex's brother. "You're offering to help him. What do you have to be nervous about?"

Not knowing if Alex had told his brother that he was seeing her fueled her anxiety as she grabbed her purse and headed inside. Paul was at the counter, huddled around a computer terminal with Adam McCarthy.

Both men looked up at her as she came in the door.

"Hey, Jenny," Adam said.

"Hi, Adam." She shifted her gaze to Paul, who was every bit as handsome as his brother. "Paul."

"Hi, Jenny. Good to see you again. Thanks for the offer of help."

"Sure. Happy to do whatever I can."

"It all depends on Adam, the computer magician. Sharon's parting shot was to password-protect the system, and naturally we can't reach her to find out what it is."

Incensed on his behalf, Jenny said, "Have you reported that to Blaine?"

"Filed a report this morning. He's issuing a warrant for her arrest on charges of malicious mischief. We won't actually press charges if she gives us the damned password."

The poor guy seemed exhausted, stressed out and frustrated, but who could blame him? Like he didn't have enough to deal with without a spiteful ex-employee tampering with his business.

"I hope you're also withholding her final paycheck," Jenny said.

"Haven't done that yet, but you're absolutely right. I'll call the payroll company and get that done. Thanks for the reminder."

Jenny didn't know him at all, but she suspected the computer situation was about to take him over the edge. "While Adam does his thing, maybe you could show me around and give me a sense of the routine so I can get to it as soon as we have access to the computer again."

"You're going to work here, Jenny?" Adam asked, his gaze never wandering from the computer terminal.

"I'm helping out until things settle down."

"And we're extremely grateful for the help," Paul said. "Come on, I'll give you the tour and introduce you to some of the employees."

CHAPTER 16

*A*fter a truly wonderful and relaxing afternoon with her new fiancé, Kara brought the launch to a smooth landing at the dock. She wasn't at all surprised to see her sister sitting on the bench where customers waited for a ride to their boats.

Fortified by her time with Dan and the things he'd said to her when he proposed, Kara busied herself tying up the boat and shutting down the engine, all the while pretending that Kelly wasn't watching her every move. A petite blonde, Kelly had always attracted lots of male attention. Kara, who'd felt like an amazon next to her younger sister, realized Kelly no longer had the power to hurt her. At some point over the last two years—well, mostly since she met and fell in love with Dan—she'd moved past what'd had happened with Kelly and Matt.

She wished she was a more forgiving person, but some things couldn't be forgiven. The last time she saw her sister, nearly two years ago now, they'd had a screaming fight and both had said things that could never be taken back. Not that Kara regretted a word of what she'd said that day. Nor did she regret the two years that had passed since then with nary a word between them. She had no earthly idea what her sister was trying to accomplish by showing up like this and thinking she could force Kara to deal with her and her husband.

"I'm right here," Dan said quietly, his hand warm on her back.

Kara nodded, grateful for what he'd done earlier and for his presence beside her now. She took a deep breath, grabbed her bag and got off the launch.

As she stood, Kelly appeared wilted from the heat, and there was no sign of Matt or the baby, for which Kara was thankful. "It took you long enough to come back," Kelly said.

"I didn't realize I answered to you."

"Your employee had no idea where you were. Shouldn't he know how to get in touch with you?"

"He knew exactly where I was. He chose not to tell you." First two points were hers, Kara thought smugly. "Is there something I can do for you? I have plans."

"You know why I'm here. You don't have to act so surprised to see me."

"Why wouldn't I be surprised to see you? I don't want you here, and you know that, which is why you tried to blindside me with your visit. You thought you could force me to deal with you and your darling little family." Kara leaned in closer, and Kelly took a step back. "Sorry your plan failed so dismally."

"You're so hard and bitter. I pity you."

Kara laughed, which she could see infuriated her sister. "*You* pity *me*? Whatever. I really ought to take this opportunity to thank you for stealing Matt from me. You truly did me a favor." Kara glanced at Dan, appreciating the pride she saw in his gaze. "I'm engaged to someone who's ten times the man Matt will ever be, and the sex… *Whoa.*" Kara fanned her face. "I had no idea what I was missing out on, so thanks for that, too."

Next to her, Dan made a sound that was half grunt, half laugh. No doubt, her comment had pumped up his already overinflated ego.

Kelly's face got very red, and Kara wasn't sure if she was embarrassed or enraged. Probably the latter. She'd never wanted anyone to have something better than what she had. "Wait, so you're *engaged*? Since when?"

"Why do you sound so stunned? Were you under the illusion that I was hiding under a rock, licking my wounds while you two rode off together into the sunset? Sorry to disappoint you, Sis, but I've been *just* fine."

Kelly's eyes darted between Kara and Dan. "Where have I seen him?"

"Probably on TV. He's a famous lawyer. He saves people's lives. What does Matt do again? Oh right, he attempts to make money for people. Last I heard, he's not all that good at it, unlike my fiancé, who is very, *very* good at making money. Aren't you, honey?"

"Yeah, that's one of several things I'm pretty good at," Dan said suggestively, earning major points with Kara.

"So again I say thank you," Kara said with a wide smile that seemed to further ruffle her sister. "Who wants a man who's all talk and no action in more ways than one?" High on her own success, Kara winced dramatically. "Oh sorry, I guess you want that guy. Well, congratulations. He's all yours. My fiancé and I have somewhere to be, so enjoy your visit."

Kara took Dan's hand and started for the ramp that led to the main dock.

"*Burn*," Dan whispered under his breath, making Kara laugh.

"Kara! Wait! I want to talk to you! I waited all day."

Kara spun around and pointed a finger sharply at her sister. "No, you wait. When I told you two years ago that you were dead to me, I wasn't spouting off. I have nothing to say to you or your husband. Go home, Kelly. There's no reason for you to be here."

"You have no interest in your nephew?"

"Sure, I do, and I expect to have a very meaningful relationship with him—as soon as he's old enough to see me when his parents aren't around. Until then..." Kara shrugged. "Nothing to say." She smiled at Dan. "Let's go, babe."

"What about Mom and Dad?" Kelly asked, sounding more

desperate by the second. "Don't you care at all about what this is doing to them?"

"How dare you try to lay that on me? If you were worried about how a rift between us would affect Mom and Dad, you should've kept your hands off my boyfriend. But you didn't, so that, too, is your problem—not mine. I hope he was worth it, Kel. I really, really do."

Since Kara had already given her sister far more time than she deserved, she hooked her hand through Dan's arm and headed for the parking lot.

"Oh my God," he whispered. "I'm so hot for you right now, I'm about to implode."

Kara laughed. "I never could've done that if I hadn't had a couple of hours to prepare myself. I owe you big for that."

"No, you don't." He put his arm around her. "But remind me to never get on your bad side. It's a pretty darned scary place. The litigator in me is extremely impressed."

"Goddamn, that felt good."

"I bet it did."

"I mean really, really *good.*"

Dan laughed. "You honestly don't plan to speak to her again? Ever?"

"I'll probably get around to forgiving her. Eventually." Arm in arm, they walked toward her apartment in a building that abutted the marina property. "But not today."

"No, not today. You'll be too busy having hot sex with your rich fiancé."

"Didn't take long for that to go straight to your head."

"It was actually pretty instantaneous."

"In case I failed to mention it earlier, I love you, Torrington."

"Love you right back, Ballard. Now, about that hot sex…"

By the time Alex arrived home after six o'clock, Paul, Adam and Jenny had moved from the store to the house, where Adam was working on Paul's laptop. He'd had the idea to log in to the system from the laptop and try to change the password that way. He was seated at the table with Paul and Jenny standing behind him, offering suggestions and moral support.

Watching Adam operate behind the scenes in the guts of the computer had been nothing short of fascinating for Jenny. The guy was clearly brilliant, and she had full faith that if anyone could get them into the system, he could.

Marion had left a short time ago for a ride with one of her friends but would be returning soon.

"Hey," Alex said when he came in, looking tired and dirty. "Are we having a party and I wasn't invited?"

"Goddamned Sharon," Paul said. "She password-protected the system before she rode out of town on her broomstick. We've been working all day to try to get in."

Alex's dark eyes flashed with rage. "Are you freaking kidding me?"

"I wish, and I've already reported it to Blaine. He's issued a warrant for her arrest."

"Good. Tell him we're pressing charges."

"I just want the damned password."

Jenny sent Alex an empathetic smile, wishing she could go to him and hug him, but she quelled the urge until a more appropriate time.

"I'm going to hit the shower," he said as he cracked open a beer to take with him. Looking directly at her, he added, "I'll be right back."

The message couldn't have been clearer—*don't leave*. As if there was anywhere she'd rather be. Adam and Paul continued to converse about the system, and Jenny pretended like she was paying attention, but all she could think about was Alex and the despair she'd sensed in him at the thought of yet another challenge to contend with. She wanted to wrap her arms around him and provide all the comfort she was capable of. Hopefully, he'd let her.

Before Alex emerged from the shower, Marion returned home with her friend.

Paul left Adam to work on the computer alone and got busy putting dinner together for his mother.

Jenny eyed the pan of lasagna Paul had pulled from the fridge. "Could I help with that so you can keep working with Adam?"

"You don't have to do that."

"I know I don't. I'm offering anyway."

His smile was warm and full of gratitude, but it couldn't hide the exhaustion. "Thanks. That'd be great."

"No problem." Jenny cut a piece of lasagna, heated it in the microwave and served it to Marion, who was seated at the bar.

"Who are you?" she asked.

"I'm Jenny."

"I don't know you."

"We met earlier, before you went for a ride with your friend."

"I went for a ride?"

"Yes, you went to look at the sunset."

"I do love a good sunset."

"You should come to the Southeast Light sometime. It's the best place for a sunset."

"What's your name again?"

"Jenny. I'm a friend of Alex's and Paul's."

Marion took a small bite of her lasagna. "My boys always had nice friends and lots of pretty girls around. The girls have always liked them."

Jenny bit her bottom lip to keep from laughing.

"Mom, what're you telling her?" Paul asked.

"None of your business," Marion said with a wink for Jenny that made her laugh. "It's girl talk." She stared at Jenny for a long moment. "Tell me your name again. I have trouble remembering."

"Jenny."

"And you're friends with my boys?"

"Yes, I am."

"Are you dating one of them?"

"I, um…" Where was Alex when she needed him?

"She's dating me, Mom," Alex said as he came into the kitchen, wearing a pair of plaid shorts with a navy polo shirt. His wet hair had been combed into submission, his face was freshly shaved, and he smelled amazing as he joined her at the counter.

When he declared their relationship in front of his mother, brother and Adam, Jenny's heart tripped into double time. His hand on her lower back was reassuring and arousing at the same time. She had to remind herself to breathe.

"She's very pretty," Marion said.

"I think so, too," Alex said with a smile for Jenny that made her melt.

She couldn't believe the effect he had on her just by walking into the room fresh from the shower. She'd spent the entire afternoon with Paul and Adam, two exceptionally good-looking men in their own right, and hadn't experienced so much as a flutter of interest for either of them. But the second Alex walked in the door, her entire body had woken up to take notice. The powerful reactions he inspired in her were exciting and frightening at the same time.

Adam checked his watch. "I hate to say it, but I've got somewhere to be. Can we continue this tomorrow?"

"Sure," Paul said, defeat radiating from him. "I have a town council meeting tonight anyway, so I've got to get going."

Alex's hand curled around Jenny's hip as he uttered one word. "Damn."

It occurred to her that Alex hadn't known about Paul's meeting when he made plans for their date.

"You'll be home tonight, right?" Paul asked Alex after he saw Adam out.

"Yep. No problem."

"I'll be home by ten if you want to go out later," Paul said with a teasing wink for Jenny and Alex as he headed for the hallway.

"Bite me," Alex said, making Jenny laugh.

"Don't be mean to your brother, Alexander," Marion said.

"Why not? He's mean to me."

"Be nice," Marion said, pointing her fork at Alex. "Your friend didn't come over to listen to you bicker with your brother."

"That's right," Jenny said. "You tell him, Marion."

"I like this girl, Alex. What did you say your name was again?"

"Jenny."

"That's a nice name. I like it."

"Thank you. Marion is a nice name, too."

"It's an old-lady name."

"No, it isn't," Jenny said with a smile.

"Want some more lasagna, Mom?" Alex asked.

"No, I'm full. Thank you."

"Don't thank me. Thank Mrs. Upton. She made it."

"That's very nice of Verna."

"Yes, it is."

"Is Daisy coming tonight?"

"Probably. Do you want to sit in the rocking chair and watch for her?"

"That would be very nice," Marion said. "It's freezing in here."

Alex walked her to the door and got her settled in one of the rockers. He came back inside and opened the blinds so he could keep an eye on her. "I'm sorry our plans got screwed up," he said when they were alone.

"It's no problem."

"How do you feel about Verna Upton's lasagna and a movie on TV?"

"That sounds lovely. Verna's lasagna comes highly recommended."

Alex approached her with intent in his dark eyes, and Jenny took a couple of steps backward until she bumped up against the counter. He surrounded her, with a hand on either side of her. "You were really great with her. Thank you."

"She's very sweet."

"I'm glad you got to see the sweetness. Her moods run the gamut these days. At times, like just now, she's almost lucid, like her old self. But then she disappears into the confusion again, which is particularly crushing for us."

"I'm sure it is." Jenny reached up to corral a wayward strand of damp hair from his forehead. "You get a reminder of who she used to be, and then it's snatched away from you."

"Yes," he said. "That's it exactly."

Jenny placed her hands on his hips and drew him toward her.

Alex put his arms around her, and they stood that way for a long time while he kept a vigilant eye on his mother.

There was nothing sexual about their embrace. It was all about comfort, which he seemed to need badly.

"You're so good for me," he whispered gruffly against her ear, sending a cascade of shivers down her arm. "I was so damned happy to see you when I came in from work."

"I was happy to see you, too."

His arms tightened around her. "I thought about our 'picnic' all afternoon."

"So did I."

The sound of car doors closing outside had them pulling away from each other. But Alex took hold of her hand as they went outside into the still-sweltering heat to greet the new arrivals. A row of dark clouds hung ominously over the island, giving Jenny hope that relief from the heat might be in sight.

Dr. David Lawrence's girlfriend, Daisy Babson, came up to the porch to hug and kiss Marion, who seemed delighted to see the pretty blonde woman. Another man was with them, and Jenny knew him from somewhere but couldn't immediately come up with his name. She felt like it was on the tip of her tongue.

David came up the stairs and shook hands with Alex.

"You know Jenny, right?" Alex said, his arm now around her shoulders. Apparently, they were going fully public with their relationship, which pleased her greatly.

"Sure, nice to see you again, Jenny."

"You, too."

David turned to the other man who'd come with them. "Get up here, will you?"

When he joined them on the porch, Jenny tried desperately to remember how she knew him.

"This is my landlord and friend, Jared James," David said.

Alex and Jared shook hands.

209

"Yes!" Jenny said. "That's how I know you. You're Jared James." He was tanned, with dark blond hair, piercing blue eyes and a few age lines around his eyes that hadn't been there the last time Jenny saw him.

"I'm afraid you have me at a disadvantage…"

"I'm Jenny Wilks. I was a year behind you at Wharton."

"Oh, of course. You were Toby's girlfriend."

"Yes."

"I was so very sorry to hear he'd died."

"Thank you."

"I knew him quite well. He was a great guy."

"Yes, he was. So, you've been all kinds of successful since we left school. What do they call you, the new king of Wall Street?"

He shrugged off the praise. "I had a few good years despite the crap economy. Anyone who did well during that time got a lot of attention."

"Well, from what I've read, it was well deserved."

While Alex talked to David, Jenny visited with Jared, comparing notes on people they'd known at school and who they kept in touch with.

"So what are you doing out here?" he asked.

"I'm the lighthouse keeper at the Southeast Light."

"Wow, that's cool. How'd you get that gig?"

"Saw an ad and applied. I was in need of a change of pace, and the move has been good for me. What about you?"

"I have a house out here. David rents my garage apartment."

"So you're here for the summer?"

"I'm taking a little time off after a particularly rough breakup."

"Ouch, I'm sorry. That sucks."

"Sure does."

"You should come out to the lighthouse sometime. I'll give you a tour."

"I'd love to. I'll definitely take you up on that."

David, Daisy and Jared stayed for another half hour, drinking the beers Alex had provided, before Marion began to visibly tire.

Daisy kissed the older woman's cheek. "I'll see you tomorrow, Marion."

"I'll look forward to it."

"I can't thank you enough for coming by every evening," Alex said quietly to Daisy. "I'm sure you have other things you need to be doing."

"I'm very happy to give her an hour of my day." Daisy patted Alex's arm. "I've begun to look forward to seeing her, too."

"Thank you again," Alex said gruffly.

"It's my pleasure." Daisy looked at Jenny. "Will I see you guys at Blaine and Tiffany's shower?"

"I haven't told Alex about it yet, but I'll be there."

"Not sure I want to hear about this," Alex said, making the others laugh.

"Looking forward to it." Daisy leaned in to hug Jenny, whispering, "Good going, girlfriend. He's adorable."

Jenny smiled at Daisy. "I agree."

"It was good to see you again, Jenny," Jared said. "I'll be by to check out your lighthouse."

"Any time."

They waved to their friends as they drove off, and then Alex turned to his mother, his face set in a grim expression Jenny hadn't seen before. "Come on, Mom. Let's get ready for bed."

"Could I help?" Jenny asked.

"No, thanks."

"Why not?" Marion asked. "I like her. She's a nice girl. She can help me get ready for bed."

"You really don't have to," Alex said, looking less strained than he had a few minutes earlier but no less concerned about what she was offering to do.

Jenny placed two fingers on his lips to quiet him and because she felt the need to touch him. "I know I don't. If I didn't want to, I wouldn't have offered."

"Thank you," he said in the same gruff tone he'd used to thank Daisy.

"How about it, Marion?" Jenny held out a hand to her. "Shall we get you ready for bed?"

Marion reached up to take Jenny's hand. "Tell me your name again."

"It's Jenny."

"You're very pretty."

"Thank you. So are you."

"My George thinks I'm pretty."

"Tell me about him. What's he like?"

"Oh, he's so handsome. You know how handsome Alex and Paul are?"

Jenny gave Alex a saucy smile over her shoulder as he held the door for her and his mother. "I sure do."

Alex pinched her rear playfully.

"Well, they get that from my George. He has dark hair like they have and eyes so brown they remind me of dark chocolate."

"You know, it's funny, I've thought of Alex's eyes as dark chocolate."

Marion's bedroom was at the end of a long hallway. She looked around at the room as if nothing in it was familiar, and then she looked at Jenny, seeming baffled. "Who are you?"

"I'm Alex's friend Jenny. I'm here to help you get ready for bed. What can I do to help?"

"I…I don't know."

"She has trouble with buttons and snaps," Alex said from the door. "Nightgowns are in the third drawer. She needs to use the bathroom and brush her teeth, and then she has to take these pills." He put a medicine cup and a glass of water on the desk inside the door. "Sure you don't want me to do it?"

"We've got this, don't we, Marion?"

"Of course we do." She shooed her son from the room with a wave of her hand.

As Jenny helped her to unbutton her blouse and unhook her bra, her heart broke at the thought of her sons handling these tasks on most evenings. How difficult it must be for all of them. It took about twenty minutes to guide Marion through her nightly routine. At least once per minute, she had to remind Marion of who she was.

"He's a very nice boy," Marion said, taking Jenny's hand after she tucked the older woman into bed. "My Alex."

"Yes, he is."

"He watches you. Every minute, his eyes are on you."

Astounded by Marion's moment of utter clarity, Jenny said, "Are they?"

Marion nodded. "Will you take care of him for me? I wish I could, but I can't anymore."

"I will. Of course I will."

"Thank you. Jenny. Did I get your name right?"

Her uncertainty brought tears to Jenny's eyes. "You sure did." Jenny leaned in to kiss Marion's lined cheek. "I'll see you again soon, okay?"

"Okay."

"Good night, Marion." Jenny closed the bedroom door and took a moment to get her emotions under control before she joined Alex in the kitchen.

He stood when he saw her coming. "Everything okay?"

"Everything is fine."

"I don't even know how to properly thank you. That was way above and beyond… Well… Thank you."

Jenny went to him and put her arms around him.

He hesitated for a second, as if he thought he might not deserve the comfort she offered so willingly, before he sagged against her and held her so tightly she could barely breathe. And then he raised his head and captured her mouth in a ravaging kiss, full of all the emotion he normally kept bottled up inside. It poured forth in passionate strokes of his tongue that had Jenny on tiptoes trying to get closer to him.

"Christ," he whispered when he finally broke the kiss. "I'm all over the place tonight."

"That's okay. Kissing you is certainly no hardship."

He ran his fingers through her hair and down her neck, his touch making her tremble. "You must be hungry." He placed strategic kisses on her neck that had her wishing they were alone so she could touch him all over.

"You must be hungrier. You worked hard all day."

"Not all day," he said with a smile that she felt against her neck. "There was this one part, right in the middle… Mmm, pure pleasure. No hard work required."

Jenny let her hands slide down to his backside. "There was a little bit of hard work involved. It was awfully hot out there."

"It was some kind of hot," he said suggestively as his lips traveled from her throat to her ear, capturing her earlobe between his teeth. "Let's eat, and then we can pick up this conversation while we watch a movie."

They enjoyed Mrs. Upton's tasty lasagna, as well as salad and garlic bread that Jenny said she would only eat if he did, too.

"Sounds like you want to make out with me after dinner."

"If you're lucky," she said with a nonchalant shrug.

He covered her hand with his much larger, work-roughened hand. "I'm sorry our plans for tonight got messed up."

"Did they? I hadn't noticed."

"You are far too kind."

Jenny swirled the merlot he'd opened to go with dinner around in her glass. "Do you think I'd ever blame you because you needed to be at home with your mother when we had other plans?"

"Some women would."

"Well, I'm not some women."

"No, you certainly aren't."

"I understand what you're dealing with, Alex. I saw my mother and her sisters go through it for years with their mother. I helped where I could. I answered the same questions over and over. My heart broke when I had to identify myself to the grandmother who'd once doted on me. I get it."

"Was this before or after you lost Toby?"

"After."

"I thought about that, about him and what happened, all afternoon. I wondered…" He shook his head as if he'd reconsidered the question.

"It's okay to ask about it."

"Are you sure?"

She nodded, but her stomach knotted with nerves. Even though she'd said it was okay, it was never an easy topic for her.

"I wondered where you were that day and how you found out."

"I was at work in Midtown, and he called my cell phone. We texted but didn't call each other during the day, so I took the call even though I was in a meeting and got the stink eye from my boss. It was the hardest call I've ever received, but I'm so glad I didn't ignore it."

"Did he know how bad it was?"

"Yes," Jenny said, transported back to that horrible day and the panic she'd heard in Toby's normally calm voice. "He knew. The plane hit below his floor."

"God," Alex said with a sigh.

"Where were you that day?" she asked, turning her hand so her palm was flat against his.

"I was in California visiting a friend from college. I was supposed to fly back to Boston that day, but everything was canceled for days afterward."

"I suppose it was. The first few weeks were a bit of a blur for me. I don't remember much about it." She forced a smile for his benefit. "So how about that movie you promised me?"

"You got it. I'll even let you pick."

"Ohhh, I see a chick flick in your future."

"You wouldn't do that to me, would you?"

"Oh yes, I definitely would." Their playful banter was a welcome relief after the conversation about the worst day of her life. She appreciated that he had questions and was happy to answer them, but she also appreciated that he knew when not to linger on that topic.

They worked together to clean up from dinner, and Jenny teased Alex about his poor dishwasher-loading skills.

"Don't tell me you're one of those who sorts the silverware."

"Okay, I won't tell you that," Jenny said as she arranged the forks, knives and spoons into separate compartments.

"That's just so wrong. Throw it all in there." He reached for the knives, clearly intending to mess them up, and Jenny grabbed his arm to stop him.

"Don't even think about it. I won't be able to sleep tonight if they aren't sorted."

"I'm going to mess them up after you leave."

"You wouldn't dare."

The gleam in his eye was positively sinister as he came toward her. "Wouldn't I?"

Jenny dodged him and took off out of the kitchen, squealing with laughter.

He was right behind her and grabbed her around the waist. Somehow they landed in a mess of arms and legs on the sofa, their lips perfectly aligned.

"Wait," Jenny said, turning her head before he could kiss her. "Your mother. What if she comes out?"

"She won't. She sleeps pretty soundly."

"Still…"

Groaning, he dropped his head to her shoulder. "Come on. You don't expect me to actually *watch* the movie, do you?"

"Yes, I do," Jenny said primly, pushing at his shoulders to dislodge him.

Alex sat up, complaining all the way. "You're absolutely no fun."

"I'll remember you said that the next time we're alone. Now what are my choices for movies?"

He sighed—deeply—and then reached for the remote.

Jenny hid a smile she knew he wouldn't appreciate. How could any woman not be crazy about a man who wanted her the way Alex seemed to want her? And she was crazy about him. To deny that would be foolish. "This is one of my favorites," she said when she found *Notting Hill* playing on one of the movie channels.

"Shoot me now," Alex grumbled.

"'I'm just a girl, standing before a boy, asking him to love her,'"

Jenny said in breathy imitation of Julia Roberts's famous line in the movie.

"Are you now?" Alex said, staring intently at her.

Undone by the way he looked at her, she said, "I was quoting the movie."

He didn't look away when he smiled and said, "Uh-huh."

While they watched Hugh Grant bumble through the romancing of Julia's international-movie-star character, Alex moved subtly closer to her until he was right next to her, his arm around her.

"You didn't say no snuggling."

"Mmm," she said as she curled up to him.

He reclined against some pillows, his arms around her as Jenny used his chest as a pillow.

A wave of contentment flowed through her, and she realized, right in that moment, that she hadn't felt this content since before her world imploded. "This is nice," she said softly.

"It could be nicer."

"This is as nice as it's getting while your mother is here."

"If you say so." He didn't try to kiss her again, but his hands were busy, moving up and down her back in a soothing pattern that made her feel relaxed and sleepy even as a buzz of desire kept her very much awake.

The movie was almost over when they heard a car door close outside.

"That'll be Paul."

Jenny reluctantly sat up and ran her fingers through her hair to bring order to it. "I should go."

"You don't have to."

"I know I don't, but you need to get some sleep."

"That's not what I need."

"Alex…"

"Jenny…"

They were engaged in a visual standoff when Paul came in, stomping his feet on the mat inside the door. "It's pouring out there," Paul said. "Relief is in sight."

Jenny had been so wrapped up in Alex that she hadn't noticed it was raining. A flash of lightning and the rumble of thunder made her startle. "I'm going to head out."

"Will you be okay to drive in the rain?" Alex asked.

"I'll be fine."

"What about the gate?"

"I'll leave it open tonight. No one will be out there in this weather, and it's not worth getting soaked to close it."

"I don't like the thought of you out there alone in this weather."

"You're very sweet to worry, but I'll be fine."

"You could stay here if you wanted to."

Jenny leaned in to kiss his cheek, whispering, "Nice try." She got up to collect her purse, keys and phone from the counter. "I'll be at the store in the morning, Paul."

"Thanks, Jenny. See you then. Hopefully we can get this computer situation resolved."

"I hope so, too. If not, we'll go the old-school pen-and-paper route until we work it out."

"Sounds good."

Alex walked with her to the porch.

Jenny stopped him before he followed her down the stairs. "No sense both of us getting wet."

He hooked an arm around her waist. "There's so much I could say to that."

"You're such a brat."

"You love it."

"Yes, I do." With her hands on his shoulders, she went up on tiptoes to kiss him. "Thank you for a lovely evening."

"Thank *you*. See you tomorrow?"

"Hope so."

"Text me to let me know you got home okay."

"I will."

He kissed her again, lingering this time and groaning when he reluctantly released her.

Jenny dashed down the stairs into the pouring rain and was soaked through by the time she got into her car. The cool rain was a welcome relief from the staggering heat, but it left her shivering from the chill.

All the way home to the lighthouse, thoughts of Alex and the evening they'd spent together kept her warm and smiling. It occurred to her as she navigated dark, wet roads that she was falling fast for him. While she ought to be afraid of how strong her feelings for him had become, she wasn't scared at all. Rather, she was exhilarated and looking forward to the next time she'd get to see him.

CHAPTER 17

"It's really coming down out there," Alex said to Paul. He locked the door and shut off the outside lights.

"Supposed to last into tomorrow night."

"Great," Alex said. "Right when we're starting to get caught up a bit, we could lose an entire day to weather."

"A day off won't kill either of us, but the schedule we've been keeping just might."

"True. How was your meeting?"

"Oh, you know, the usual bullshit. Mayor Upton has all kinds of grandiose ideas, and we spend most of our meetings keeping him in line."

"I don't know how you can stand to sit through those meetings." Alex had teased Paul endlessly about his decision to run for town council in the last election, but he was proud of his brother. Not that he'd ever tell Paul that.

"How was Mom tonight?" Paul asked.

"Fine. No problems."

"Glad to hear it." Paul sat across from him in one of the chairs. "So you and Jenny, huh?"

"Yeah, so?"

"Do you know about her?"

"What does that mean? I know her quite well, in fact."

Paul rolled his eyes at the double meaning he detected in his brother's comment. "You know about her fiancé and what happened to him?"

Nodding, Alex said, "How do you know?"

"The council hired her. Hang on a minute." Paul went into the bedroom they used as an office and returned a couple of minutes later holding papers folded in thirds. He handed them to Alex. "We asked applicants to write us a letter telling us why they wanted to be the lighthouse keeper. This was her letter. It was one of the most powerful and haunting things I've ever read. I've never forgotten it."

With a sinking feeling in his belly, Alex took the letter from his brother. "Are you allowed to show it to me?"

"She's a town employee, so technically it's public record."

"And it's not wrong of me to read this when she didn't show it to me herself?"

"Did she tell you what happened?"

"Earlier today. Not all the details, but the gist."

"Then she doesn't mind if you know, right?"

"I guess not."

"I'm going to hit the hay. I'm tapped out after this incredibly long and frustrating day."

"I'm sorry I caused you a ton of shit by firing Sharon."

"You didn't. She did, and clearly you did the right thing if she's capable of this kind of maliciousness. Don't sweat it."

Though Paul gave him a pass, Alex still felt bad for his role in the entire mess. But he didn't regret firing Sharon.

"See you in the morning," Paul said.

"Night."

For a long time after his brother left the room, Alex stared at the folded pages Paul had given him, trying to decide if it was the right thing to read them. He'd understood after their discussion tonight that she was willing to talk about her loss—to a point. It had been clear to him that it was difficult for her, even after all this time, and that it had been a relief to her to change the subject.

It would be better, he decided, to get the details this way than to force her to share things she'd rather forget. Since he found himself thinking about her pretty much all the time, he couldn't help being curious to know more about her and what she'd been through. And, he reasoned, if she'd been willing to share such personal memories with people she didn't know, surely she wouldn't mind if he read the letter. At least he hoped she wouldn't mind.

Alex's fingers trembled ever so slightly as he unfolded the pages and began to read.

My name is Jenny Wilks,
and I'm applying for the lighthouse keeper's position on Gansett Island. I currently reside in Charlotte, North Carolina, and the reason for my interest in the position dates back almost eleven years.

The morning of September 11, 2001, began like any other Tuesday for my fiancé, Toby, and me. We woke up in our Greenwich Village apartment, had breakfast, got dressed and left for work—me at an ad agency in Midtown, and he as a financial services advisor at the World Trade Center's South Tower. I don't remember what we said to each other that morning. Probably the usual stuff about our plans for the day, what time we might be home, what we'd do for dinner. I so wish I could remember our exact words. I had no idea then how very precious they would be.

We met at Wharton, survived the MBA program together and were due to be married that October. Toby was quiet and studious and destined for big things in his career. I used to call him my sexy nerd. While he tended to be shy with other people, with me he was easygoing, fun to be around and always making plans for our future. As we grappled with the stress of managing new jobs in New York while planning a wedding in North Carolina (where I'm from), his easygoing nature kept me sane.

I was in a meeting when Toby called my cell phone that morning. We often sent texts back and forth but rarely called each other during the day. I was worried he might be sick or something, so I took the call despite the look of

*disapproval I received from my supervisor. I vividly recall getting up and
starting to walk out of the room. I was about halfway to the door when the
fear and panic in Toby's voice registered. He was saying things I couldn't
comprehend. An airplane had hit the building, there was a fire, and they were
trapped. He told me they were going up on the roof, hoping to be rescued, but
if it all went bad, he wanted me to know how much he loved me.*

*Right around then, people in the office heard what was going on, and
everyone ran to the windows, where we could see plumes of smoke coming
from Lower Manhattan. I started to scream. It couldn't be happening. I heard
the words* terrorists *and* Pentagon *and* hijacking *and all sorts of things
that didn't seem real. Toby was yelling at me over the phone. "Jenny," he said,
"are you there?" I snapped out of it and realized my entire body was cold. I
was shivering uncontrollably. Toby needed me, and I had to pull it together
for him.*

*Somehow I managed to form words. I managed to tell him how very much I
loved him, how certain I was that everything would be fine and we'd have a
long and happy life together the way we'd always planned. Even though I was
utterly terrified, I held it together until he started to cry. He told me he didn't
want to leave me and that he was so sorry to do this to me. He said he wanted
me to be happy no matter what, that my happiness was the most important
thing to him.*

ALEX SWIPED at tears that rolled unchecked down his cheeks. His
entire body ached as he read about the utter agony she'd endured.

*You all know what happened, so I won't belabor the point. His body was
never recovered. It was like he went to work one morning and disappeared off
the face of the earth, which is essentially what happened. For days, weeks,
months afterward, I was a total zombie. My parents came to get me, and I
went home with them to North Carolina. Toby's parents had a funeral in
Pennsylvania that my parents took me to. I barely remember being there. My
sisters quietly canceled the wedding I'd planned down to the last detail.
Everyone was so very nice. Our money was refunded. People wanted to help
in any way they could, but all the kind gestures in the world couldn't replace*

what I'd lost. The oddest part was I never cried. I didn't shed a single tear, even though every part of me hurt.

I had nightmares for months over how Toby's life might've ended. It's a terrible thing to hope the person you loved most in the world had suffocated from the smoke before other more horrific things could happen to him. I went to therapy and grief groups and all the things my family thought might help. A year went by without my knowledge, and it suddenly became critically important that I attend the anniversary ceremonies. My parents were adamantly opposed, but I needed to see it. I needed to see where he had died. Minutes after I arrived at the place they call Ground Zero, a name I've always hated, I broke down into the kind of heartbroken tears you see in the movies. Apparently, I made quite a scene. It's another thing I barely remember. My parents carted me out of there, and I'm told I cried for days. Once the tears stopped, I was finally, somehow, a little better. I didn't feel quite so numb, which was a good and bad thing because that's when the pain set in. I won't bore you with the details of that stage. Suffice to say it was ugly.

"God," Alex whispered, barely able to see through his own tears.

After two years of barely functioning, I wanted my old life back—or as much of it as still remained. For all that time, my company held my job for me. Can you believe that? I still can't. That was a bright spot in a sea of gray. They welcomed me back with open arms. I found out my parents had paid the rent on our place in Greenwich Village, which was another bright spot. I went back to our home and wallowed in the comfort of being surrounded by Toby's things. After four years, I asked his parents to come take what they wanted and packed up the rest because it was no longer a comfort to be surrounded by his belongings.

In the fifth year, I started dating again. That was a comedy of errors with one disaster following another. I felt sorry for the very nice guys my well-meaning friends fixed me up with. They didn't stand a chance against the fiancé I'd lost so tragically. Still, I went through the motions, mostly because it made the people around me more comfortable with my unending grief. I did what I could to make it better for them, because nothing could make it better for me.

I became involved in the planning for the memorial, which was somehow cathartic when my rational self knew it probably shouldn't be. New York slowly recovered, the debris was cleared away, and new construction began. Against all odds, life went on. I still had nightmares about how Toby died. I dreamed about the wedding we'd so looked forward to that hadn't happened. I went to work, I came home, I went to bed, I got up and did it all again the next day.

As the tenth anniversary approached, I couldn't do it anymore. I couldn't stay in that city, in our apartment, in the job I'd had that day, with the well-meaning people who went out of their way to try to fix the unfixable. I started looking around for something to do that would get me out of the city, something that would get me off the treadmill my life had become. Two weeks before the tenth anniversary, I moved out of our apartment and went home to North Carolina. I couldn't stay for the dedication of the memorial or all the hoopla that would surround the anniversary. Leaving our apartment and our city for the last time was one of the most difficult moments in a decade of difficult moments.

I've worked for the last year at a small PR firm in Charlotte. I saw your advertisement for the lighthouse keeper's position in The New York Times *last weekend, and everything about it appealed to me. I have absolutely no experience running a lighthouse, although where one would get such experience, I couldn't begin to imagine! I'm thirty-six years old, well educated in both the classroom and the school of hard knocks. I'm a reliable person looking for the opportunity to start over in a new place. I'd be honored to be considered for this position. Thank you for "listening" to my story. I look forward to hearing from you.*

Sincerely, Jenny Wilks.

ALEX HELD the pages in both hands, his head bowed as he absorbed her incredibly moving words. He already admired her more than he'd admired anyone in a long time. But after reading her heartfelt words, he suspected he might also be on his way to falling in love with her. That she'd suffered such an unimaginable loss and could still be so positive and upbeat and fun was a testament to who she was underneath it all.

It was suddenly imperative that he see her. He tucked her letter into a nook in the kitchen to return to Paul in the morning and went to his room to grab a jacket. In the bathroom, he splashed cold water on his face and brushed his teeth. Then he tapped lightly on Paul's door and opened it.

"What?" Paul muttered.

"I'm going out."

"Are you okay?"

"Yeah… I just… I need to see her."

"Go ahead. I'll be here."

"Thanks, Paul. For showing me the letter and for everything else, too." In the midst of the daily struggle with their mother, he and his brother didn't often get into emotional topics if they could avoid them. But Jenny's letter was a reminder that life could be short, and there was no time like the present to tell people how you felt about them.

"You, too. Thanks for coming home when I asked you to. I never could've done this by myself."

"I never would've let you."

"Don't take the bike out in the rain."

"I won't."

"I like her, Al."

He knew his brother meant Jenny. "I like her, too. Get some sleep." On the way out the door, he sent Jenny a text. *Coming over. Didn't want to scare you.*

Didn't I just see you?

Wasn't enough.

Alex ran through the rain to his company truck and headed toward the Southeast Light. On the way, the story she'd told in her letter ran through his mind like a horror movie. How did anyone survive a loss like that? He'd thought it traumatic to lose his dad to cancer, but at least his dad had lived a good long life.

And what was his plan when he got there? Would he tell her what he'd learned about her in the hour since they were last together? At some point, he'd tell her. Maybe not right away, but he'd let her know that he'd read the letter and admired her even more than he had before.

He had to keep in mind what she'd said about not treating her differently after he knew the truth of her past. She didn't want that and had been very clear on that point. So he had to make an effort to compartmentalize what he'd learned about her past and put it aside to give the woman she was today what she wanted and needed.

As she hadn't bothered to lock the gate at the lighthouse, he was able to drive right up to her door. When he cut the engine and the headlights, he noticed the total darkness surrounding the lighthouse. The place was downright spooky.

Holding a flashlight, Jenny met him at the door.

"Did you lose power?"

"Yes, and it's scary. Is it okay to say I'm really glad to see you?"

He smiled at her as he shut the door and kicked off his shoes in the mudroom. "Yeah, babe, it's okay to say that."

"To what do I owe this very nice surprise?"

"I told you. I didn't get enough of you earlier."

"You had all of me earlier," she reminded him as she led him up the spiral stairs to the first level.

The view of her sweet ass in sexy boy shorts on the way up the stairs made his mouth water. At the top of the stairs, she turned abruptly and caught him staring. Alex smiled sheepishly at her. "I'm only human, and that's a very nice ass you've got there."

"Glad to know all my yoga has been good for something."

The thought of her bent into all sorts of intriguing positions had him widening his eyes. "Yoga? Could I get a demonstration?"

She set the flashlight on the table, and the small circle of light made the room seem smaller and cozier than usual. "Maybe. If you're good."

With his hands on her hips, he brought her in tight against him to ensure she knew how badly he wanted her. "How good do I have to be?"

"Very, very good."

"I can do that." He closed his eyes and leaned his forehead against hers, absorbing her alluring scent and the peaceful calm that came over him whenever he was near her.

"What's wrong?"

"Nothing's wrong."

"Are you sure?"

When she looked up at him with those bottomless brown eyes, Alex decided he couldn't keep what he knew from her. It wouldn't be right. "Paul showed me the letter you wrote to the council when you applied for the job."

Her face lost all expression. "Oh."

"I hope you're not mad that I read it."

"Why would I be mad? You already knew a lot of it."

"Still… I want to say that if I didn't already admire you as much as it was possible to admire anyone, I would after reading that. I know you don't want to talk about it or dwell on it, and I promise not to treat you differently, but I need you to know I think you're amazing and resilient and…" His throat closed around a tight knot of emotion. "And I'm very honored that you choose to spend time with me."

"Alex…" She put her arms around his neck and rested her head on his chest. "That's very sweet of you to say."

"I mean it."

"So I might be forgiven for the tomato incident?"

He smiled as her soft hair brushed against his lips. "I wouldn't go that far."

"Can you sleep over?"

"I was hoping you'd ask me to."

"Good, because I'm a little creeped out by the dark."

Relieved that they'd successfully navigated yet another emotional minefield, he said, "So that's all I'm good for? Keeping the boogeyman at bay?"

She took his hand, picked up the flashlight and aimed it toward the set of stairs that led to her bedroom. "You might be good for a few other things, too."

"That sounds very promising."

Lightning zigzagged in the sky as Jenny propped the flashlight on her bedside table, which drew Alex's attention to a framed picture.

He picked it up and took a closer look. "Is this Toby?"

"Yes."

"He was a good-looking guy."

"Yes, he was."

"Where was this the other night when I was here?"

"In the drawer. I didn't think you needed another guy watching us while we did...you know...*that*."

Smiling, Alex returned the frame to the table and ran a finger over the blush that flamed her cheek. "I don't want you to feel like you ever have to hide him or pictures of him or the life you shared with him from me. He's part of you, and I'm falling very deeply into serious like with you."

"Serious like," she said with a grin. "That's a good thing?"

"That's a very good—and very unexpected—thing."

"For me, too. It's very good and very unexpected. And it means a lot to me that I don't have to hide what I shared with Toby from you."

"I'd never want or expect that. However, we do need to talk about your shameless flirtation with Jared James earlier. Right in front me, too!"

Jenny's mouth fell open in shock. "I wasn't flirting with him!"

"Oh *Jared*," Alex said in a phony female voice, "come see my lighthouse. *Any time*."

"You've lost your mind. I was *not* flirting with him. I knew him years ago at school."

"Whatever you say. I know flirting when I see it." Deciding to give her a break, he put his arms around her.

"Get away. You're being a jerk."

"I'm teasing you."

"I wasn't flirting with him. I wouldn't do that right in front of you."

"So you'd do it when I'm not looking?"

"You are an extremely exasperating person sometimes. Has anyone ever told you that?"

"Me? Exasperating? I don't know what you're talking about." He caught her by surprise with a kiss. "And I know you weren't flirting with him, but you charmed him nonetheless."

"That wasn't my intention. I felt sorry for him when he said he's nursing a broken heart."

"That is too bad, but he's not going to make you his private-duty nurse."

"Honestly, Alex! What part of *I'm not interested in him* didn't you get? For some reason, which is escaping me at the moment, I seem to be interested in you."

"You are? Really?"

Her eyes narrowed with suspicion. "Was this whole thing a round-about way to get me to admit something you already knew?"

"It worked, didn't it?"

She shocked the living shit out of him when she gave him a hard shove that landed him on his back on the bed. She further shocked him when she removed her T-shirt to reveal bare breasts and a tight belly. Wearing only the boy shorts that had fascinated him earlier, she came down on top of him.

"That was hot. Seriously hot."

"Don't they teach you boys up here in the North not to mess with GRITS?"

"Um, GRITS?"

"Girls Raised in the South."

Alex cracked up laughing, but his laughter became a moan when she straddled his lap, letting the heat between her legs settle above his erection. "I'm very sorry I messed with you, and I apologize for tricking you into admitting you're digging me."

She poked him in the belly. "I don't think you're one bit sorry for either of those things."

"I am! I swear I am!" He held out his arms to her. "Come down here, and I'll show you how very sorry I am."

With her hands flat on his chest, she bent at the waist until she hovered just above his lips. "I'm here."

"So I see." He framed her face with his hands and kissed her softly yet persuasively.

A split of thunder, crashing directly over the lighthouse, made Jenny gasp. The rain beat down upon the metal roof, and lightning continued to zip across the sky that was visible through the windows she'd left uncovered.

"I hate thunderstorms."

"Don't worry. I'll keep you safe, and I'll take your mind off it."

"And how exactly will you do that?"

He reached up to cup her breasts. "Leave that to me."

She gently but insistently removed his hands. "Not yet. Hands to yourself until I say otherwise."

His raised brow was the only indication that he wondered what she was up to.

Starting at the hem, she lifted his shirt up and over his head, dazzled as always by the rippling muscles on his chest and belly. She wanted to kiss every one of them and scooted down so she was straddling his legs.

Using her tongue, she traced the outline of his eight-pack, taking her time to make sure she didn't miss anything. An occasional sharp inhale and the quiver of skin let her know her efforts were having the desired effect on him. As she worked her way down, his breathing became harsher, especially when she traced the sharp outline of the V-cut over his hips.

"Jenny, that's enough."

"Nowhere near enough."

Air hissed from between his clenched teeth as she tugged on the button to his shorts and unzipped him. She worked his shorts and boxer briefs down his legs, her gaze fixed on the sight of his impressive erection. She arranged his legs so they were bent at the knees and pushed them open with the gentle press of her hands against his inner thighs.

"Jenny… Jesus. You're killing me here. Let me touch you."

"Not yet."

She tipped her head and let her hair fall over him before she added her tongue to the mix, traveling the length of him and circling the tip, marveling as he got longer and harder. Then she took him into her mouth, stroking the base with her hand tight around him. With her free hand, she cupped his balls in a gentle caress.

"*Fuck*," he groaned, his hands grasping her hair. "Don't stop."

She loved that she could give him such pleasure, that she could take his mind off the litany of troubles he faced every day, even if only for a short time.

"Jenny…"

Aware that he was warning her of his impending release, she took him deeper and stroked him harder. And when he came with a shout, she was ready.

"Holy shit," he gasped when he sagged into the mattress.

Jenny licked him clean as he twitched with aftershocks from the powerful release. She kissed her way from his belly to his chest to his lips.

His arms came around her, tight and fierce. "Is it my turn yet?"

"If you insist."

"I do. Give me a minute to recover, and then it's all about you."

"Mmm," she said, smiling at the sensual promise in his tone.

"Jenny?"

"Yes?"

"I haven't felt this good in a really long time, and it's not just because of the sex, which is amazing. It's everything. It's you."

She raised her head to look at him. "Me, too. I'd started to wonder if…" Catching herself before she could make an overly revealing statement, Jenny shook her head.

With his hands on her face, he compelled her to meet his gaze. "What were you wondering?"

"I can't say it."

"Yes, you can. I want to hear it."

Jenny licked her lips and watched his eyes zero in on the movement of her tongue. "I wondered if I'd ever feel this way again."

"And how do you feel exactly?"

"Hopeful." She said the first word that came to mind, but it summed things up rather well.

"I do, too. Except… The situation with my mom and everything… The timing is a bit tough for me. Nothing about the life I'm living now was part of my grand plan."

"What was your grand plan? Before your mom got sick."

He sighed and combed the fingers of his right hand through his hair. "I had an incredible job working at the U.S. Botanic Garden. My degree is in horticulture, and I've had some success with breeding rare orchids. It was satisfying work that I enjoyed."

"Is there any reason why you couldn't do that here? I mean, maybe it wouldn't be the same exact thing you were doing before, but do you have to be in Washington to do whatever you did with the orchids?"

"I was working under a grant, so that was a big part of it, but the grant was mine, not the Garden's."

"Maybe you could reapply and relocate your program? Just thinking out loud."

"Maybe," he said, seeming intrigued by the idea.

"From what I know about dementia, your mom could live in this condition for a long time, and I already know you won't want to be far from her. I bet she'd hate to be responsible for you and Paul putting your lives on hold indefinitely because of her."

"I know she'd hate that, because in her rare moments of clarity, she's said as much."

"Why are you cutting grass in the broiling heat if you have a degree in horticulture?"

"Because it's what's needed at the moment. We had a rough couple of weeks with my mom earlier in the season and fell behind on everything. My dad used to say when you own the place, there's no such thing as too good for any job. He'd say that when my brother and I would bitch about the owner's sons having to cut grass."

"I like his attitude."

"The business has been successful, but he was always humble. He never forgot where he came from."

"I think I would've liked him."

"You would have. Everyone did."

"He'd be proud of you and Paul and the way you've stepped up for your mom."

"I hope so."

"What father wouldn't be proud of sons like you two?"

"Thank you for that. I like to think he'd be proud of us. When he was sick, he asked us over and over to take good care of our mother. She was foremost on his mind."

"And he's still foremost on hers."

"I want that," Alex said. "I want what they had."

"So do I. That's all I've ever wanted. My parents have it, too. They're amazing together, even after all these years." She propped her chin on her hands. "Speaking of my parents… They're coming for a visit this week. I'd like for you to meet them."

"I'd love to meet them. Are they staying here?"

"No, they're staying at the McCarthy's hotel."

"Oh thank God," he said as he rolled them so he was above her, looking down at her with those dark-chocolate eyes. "I was already trying to figure out if I could scale the lighthouse from the outside to get to you while they're here."

Laughing, Jenny said, "You're downright incorrigible."

"I'm downright smitten."

His sweet words went straight to her overcommitted heart, flooding the empty corners with warmth and excitement. "So am I." It was the truth. Why not say so?

He looked at her for a long time before he kissed her. At first, it was just his lips, soft and persuasive.

Her arms tight around his neck, she squirmed under him, needing more.

"Easy, honey. Let me take my time."

Jenny forced air into her lungs, trying to relax when his every touch set her on fire. He wasn't kidding when he said he planned to take his time. Everything happened in slow motion as he paid homage to her lips, neck, breasts and belly, working his way down slowly, so slowly that by the time he was settled between her legs, all he had to do was touch her with his tongue, and she came.

"I love how responsive you are," he whispered against her sex, making her tremble.

She didn't have the words to tell him that she wasn't usually so responsive. In fact, only one other man had ever been able to coax such responses from her.

Alex was the reason she was so responsive. It was him and the incredible energy they created together.

He kissed his way back up just as slowly, capturing her lips as his cock pressed against her slickness. Keeping up the slow theme, he entered her in tiny increments.

Jenny dug her fingers into his back, trying to encourage him to move faster, but he was determined to take his time.

"So hot," he whispered in her ear. "So tight. I can't get enough of you."

She bent her knees and arched into him, trying to move things along.

"Patience."

"I'm fresh out. You're driving me crazy."

"That's the whole idea." Flexing his hips, he drove the rest of the way into her. "Is that what you wanted?"

Gasping, Jenny gripped his backside as she struggled to adjust and accommodate him.

A deep groan rumbled through his chest as he took hold of her hands, raised them above her head and began to move, all the while looking down at her, his eyes dark and intense with longing that he didn't try to hide from her.

Jenny couldn't look away as he took them on an incredible ride. The deep sense of connection was undeniable as was the realization that this was no longer sex. This was lovemaking at its very finest.

He released her hands and wrapped his arms around her, whispering in her ear, "Come with me, baby." His gruff words, fierce possession and incredible tenderness combined to send her soaring. "Ah God, yes. *Yes*," he said with a groan. He was right behind her, surging forth inside her over and over again until he collapsed on top of her.

"I'm too heavy," he muttered after a long period of contented silence.

"No, you're not." She wrapped her legs around him to keep him right there for a little while longer.

"Jenny."

"Hmm?"

"That was incredible."

"Yes, it was." Jenny stroked his hair, enjoying the slide of silky strands through her fingers. She no longer wondered if she was falling in love with him. She had fallen and fallen hard.

As he withdrew from her and turned on his side, bringing her with him, Jenny snuggled into his embrace. She hoped they could find a way to make this work. It hadn't taken long, but she already couldn't imagine a day without him in it.

CHAPTER 18

*W*hen Jenny's alarm went off in the morning, she knew right away that she was alone. She must've slept rather deeply if she hadn't heard Alex's alarm. A quick look outside indicated the rain had stopped, but the sky was still overcast with dark clouds. A cool, refreshing breeze came through the open window. The thunderstorm had done its job, and the heat wave from hell appeared to be over. Thank goodness. On the bedside table, she found a note from him.

Working at the Chesterfield's place again today if you want to come for another visit to the secret garden... Tonight. Date night. Be ready at 7. Wear jeans. Thanks for giving me a reason to smile again.
Alex

His note put a smile on her face that stayed there while she showered, dried her hair, got dressed and had breakfast. It stayed with her until her cell phone rang with a local number she didn't recognize.

"Hello?"

"Hi, Jenny, it's Linc Mercier."

Oh jeez... "Hi, Linc. How are you?"

237

"I'm good. I've been crazy busy, though. I meant to call you before now. How are you?"

"Same. Busy. Lots going on." Jenny's face heated when the sensual memories resurfaced to remind her that she had no business talking to Linc when she was sleeping with Alex.

"So I know you said things are kind of weird right now, but I haven't stopped thinking about what a good time I had on our date. I was hoping to see you again."

"I…ah… That's really nice of you to say." She grimaced at how stupid she sounded. "But I, um…"

"Not going to happen?" he asked softly.

"No, I'm sorry. Some things have happened, and… Well, it's complicated." She couldn't very well tell him she'd met someone else before she first went out with him, which had been a mistake. So much for doing what she thought was the right thing. Damned hindsight.

"No worries. I figured it was worth a shot. I hope I'll see you around."

"I hope so, too."

"Take care, Jenny."

"You, too." As she put the phone in her purse and grabbed her keys to head to the store, she felt like total shit. Her reasons for keeping the date with Linc had been noble—her friends had gone to some trouble to arrange the evening with him, and she'd only just met Alex the day before. She hadn't yet realized that he might be someone special.

"Now you're just lying to yourself, girl," she said out loud. "You knew the first time you kissed him that he was different." *But I didn't know then that he felt the same way or that he'd be back for more or that we would form such a deep bond. I didn't know any of those things then.* While Jenny knew there was no sense rehashing the past, she truly wished she hadn't gone on the date with Linc. She hated to think that something she might've done could've hurt someone who didn't deserve it.

He was a nice guy, and he'd be fine. It wasn't like she'd gone out with him and made promises that she was now reneging on. It wasn't like that at all.

Still, the lingering sense of having done the wrong thing stayed with her all morning as she worked side by side with Alex's brother at the store until he felt she was adequately prepared to handle things on her own.

Paul was getting ready to head out to a job site when Blaine Taylor came into the store.

"Tell me you have good news for us," Paul said to the police chief.

"In fact, I do. Your friend Sharon was apprehended in Massachusetts, and when she was told she faced malicious mischief charges as well as a potential civil suit, garnishment of wages and other unpleasant things thrown in to ensure her cooperation, she ponied up the password." Blaine laid a slip of paper on the counter.

"Yes!" Paul said as he picked up the paper.

Standing next to him, Jenny laughed when she saw the password Sharon had chosen: AlexMartinezIsADick.

"Well, shit," Paul said. "Why didn't I think of that?"

The three of them shared a laugh that was interrupted when Adam McCarthy came into the store. "What's so funny?"

When they filled him in, Adam joined in the laughter. "So much for my code-cracking skills. We should've started with that."

"I can't wait to tell my brother this one," Paul said. "Please oh please don't anyone tell him so I can fully enjoy it."

"It's all yours," Jenny said.

"So I guess my services are no longer required?" Adam asked.

"If you could figure out if my laptop is salvageable, that would be a huge help," Paul said. "I'd hate to buy a new one if I don't need to."

"Sure thing. Is it up at the house?"

"Yeah, I'll take you up there." To Jenny, Paul said, "Ready to fly solo?"

"I assume one of the others can show me the system."

"Hey, Carly," Paul called to one of the young women who was watering plants. "Can you please come give Jenny the 411 on the system for me?"

"Sure," Carly said. "No problem."

"All right, then." Paul wrote something on a piece of paper and handed it to Jenny. "My cell number. Call me if you need anything."

"I will. Don't worry. We can handle things here."

"Thanks again for this. You're saving our lives."

"Happy to do it." And she was, Jenny realized. It felt good to put her skills and experience to work for people who truly needed the help. Not to mention, it felt doubly good to be doing something that would relieve just a tiny bit of the burden Alex carried. She knew he felt responsible for the debacle with Sharon, even if it wasn't his fault. He'd done the right thing getting rid of her, and now Jenny would ensure this portion of their business was in good hands while they took care of the rest.

The morning flew by as Jenny familiarized herself with the routine at the store and got to know the young but enthusiastic employees. She took a break in the office and discovered a message light flashing on the phone. After debating for a minute about whether listening to their messages fell under her purview as the temporary store manager, she pushed the button and discovered thirty-six new messages.

Grabbing a pad and pen, she recorded every one of them, and then called Paul to update him on four of the more urgent messages, including the woman on Shore Point Road who had a family reunion this coming weekend and was still waiting for someone from Martinez Lawn & Garden to do the early-season cleanup of her yard that she'd scheduled in May.

"Shit," Paul muttered. "I can't remember the last time I listened to those messages. I'll get someone out there."

"We need to triage the rest of these," Jenny said. "You've got a few more irate customers to deal with."

Over the next thirty minutes, they worked together to come up with a plan to deal with all of the most urgent jobs.

"Can you please call Alex about the situation at the Gregory house?" Paul asked. "He can leave the Chesterfield place for another day, since no one lives there."

Jenny's skin tingled at the mention of Alex's name and the anticipation that came with knowing she'd get to talk to him soon. "Sure. I'll tell him. Would you like me to return the other calls and let them know we've got them on the schedule for the next week or so?"

"That'd be awesome. Thanks, Jenny."

"Sure, no problem." She programmed Paul's number into her phone in recognition that she'd be talking to him frequently. And then she hit Alex's number and waited for him to pick up.

"Hey, baby. How are you?"

She wanted to sigh with pleasure at the sound of his gruff, sexy voice. "I'm very busy at my new job. How are you?"

"I'm hoping you're going to visit my secret garden again today."

"No such luck, I'm afraid." She told him about the call from Mrs. Gregory and Paul's request that Alex get over there today to get their yard ready for the family reunion. "Be prepared for them to be pretty pissed. They've been waiting since May."

"Shit," Alex said with a groan. "Well, at least I've got tonight to look forward to and last night to think about while I work."

"Are you thinking about last night?" Jenny asked as a smile spread across her face.

"Nonstop. I think about you all the time."

She'd never been with a man who was so free about how he felt. Even Toby had been less forthcoming at the beginning of their relationship, to the point that she had to drag everything out of him. Not Alex. If he thought it or felt it, he said it, which she appreciated. That quality made it easy for her to know where she stood with him.

"Still there?"

"Yes."

"Am I overwhelming you with my bluntness?"

"Not at all. I was just thinking that I rather like knowing where I stand with you."

"You're right up at the top of my list, babe. We're good for tonight?"

"We're good."

"I'm literally counting the minutes."

"So am I. I'll see you at seven."

"See you then, and tell Paul I'll take care of the Gregorys."

"I will." Jenny waited for him to end the call. "You're supposed to hang up now."

"I don't want to."

He made her melt when he said things like that. "You have work to do, and so do I."

"I know." Still he didn't hang up.

"I'm going now."

"Not yet."

"Alex…"

"Jenny…"

She sighed with pleasure and exasperation and anticipation—so many things she hadn't felt in such a long time. "The store phone is ringing. I've got to go, or I'll get in trouble with my bosses."

"All right. If you're going to be that way about it. Talk to you later."

"Yes, you will." Jenny ended the call with him and grabbed the ringing phone on the desk. "Martinez Lawn & Garden."

"Finally, a *person* answers the phone there."

That was the first of many calls she handled from disgruntled customers. She apologized to each of them for the delay in hearing back from the company, assured them they were on the schedule and promised to call in the next couple of days with more definite times to expect the landscapers.

She talked to Paul at least six times about some of the unhappier situations and helped him to come up with a schedule for their work force that addressed the angriest customers first. By the time Paul arrived at six to help her close the store, Jenny had a splitting headache and was in bad need of a drink, but at least she felt she'd made a worthwhile contribution.

"Did you have a good day, dear?" Paul asked with a smile and eye roll.

"It was positively awesome."

"Sorry you got hit with a pile of shit on your first official day. I've been avoiding the voice mail for a while now."

"No, really?" Jenny said, grinning. "I never would've guessed that."

"You were a very good sport, and I greatly appreciate it."

"No problem. But you offer hazardous duty pay, right?"

"Does beer count as hazardous duty pay?"

"Tonight it does."

"Stand by." Paul went out to the greenhouse and returned with two cold bottles. He opened them and handed one to Jenny. "Here's to shit days."

"I'll drink to that. So you've got a secret stash, huh?"

"Shhh, the college kids haven't found it yet." He walked her through the procedure for closing the store, accounting for the money and preparing for the next morning.

At six-thirty, Alex came in looking filthy and worn out and annoyed to find her alone in the store with his brother, or at least that was how it seemed to her.

"What're you still doing here?" Alex asked her.

"Finishing a couple of things."

"Let her go home, Paul. She's got plans."

"We're almost done."

"She's done now."

As the brothers engaged in a visual standoff, Jenny held up her hands, hoping to diffuse the tension. "Alex, go take a shower. Paul, finish your sentence, and then I'll go home."

"It's okay," Paul said. "He's right. It'll keep until the morning. Thanks again for everything today. You moved mountains, and I appreciate it."

"I'll see you tomorrow."

"I'll be shocked if you show up."

"I'll be here just so I can shock you."

Paul smiled and downed the rest of his beer. "I'll look forward to that."

To Alex, Jenny said, "I'll be ready at seven."

His face set in an angry-looking expression, he nodded but didn't say anything. He kept his gaze fixed firmly on his brother.

As she drove out of the parking lot, thinking about the stormy way he'd looked at his brother, she hoped she hadn't done more harm than good.

∼

"WHAT THE HELL was that all about?" Alex asked Paul the minute they were alone.

"What was what about?"

"You and Jenny and a cozy after-work beverage while you breathe down her neck."

"What the fuck are you talking about? We were *working*! And if you'll recall, it was *your* big idea for her to work here. Am I not allowed to talk to her because you're banging her on the side?"

Alex saw red and moved before he took a moment to consider what he was about to do. He grabbed his brother by the T-shirt and jacked him up against the wall, smashing two vases in the process.

"What the fuck is wrong with you?" Paul asked as he twisted his way out of Alex's grasp. The bastard was a lot stronger than he used to be.

"She is *mine*. You got me? *Mine*."

"I never said otherwise! You've lost your mind if you think there was anything more to what you saw than two colleagues enjoying a beer after a particularly hideous day."

"You were standing right next to her."

"Because I was helping her with the fucking computer, you asshole."

"That's not how it looked to me."

"Are you listening to how ridiculous you sound? I never laid a hand on her, and I wouldn't, because I know you're into her." Paul ran both hands through his hair. "I don't need this shit after the day I've had. You can take your accusations and go straight to hell."

Oblivious to the mess they'd made with their brief altercation, Paul headed for the door.

"Wait," Alex said.

Paul slowed, but he didn't stop.

"Paul, wait."

His brother stopped at the door but kept his back to Alex.

"I'm sorry. I was out of line. I saw you standing next to her, joking around and drinking beers, and I fucking lost it. I should've known you'd never do that to me."

"You're goddamned right I wouldn't."

"I'm really sorry," Alex said again, hoping this time his brother would believe him.

Paul turned to face him. "So you're in love with her, huh?"

Alex felt like his brother had gut-punched him. "No, it's not that."

"Isn't it?"

Alex sagged against the counter. "I don't know. It might be."

Paul, that bastard, cracked up laughing. "You're such a jackass, you know that?"

"Yeah, I know. I already said I was sorry. Twice."

"For what it's worth, I think she's awesome. You should've seen what she got done around here in one day. It's more than Sharon did in two months."

"I'm not surprised." Alex glanced at his watch. "I'm supposed to pick her up in like twenty minutes. Are you going to be home tonight? I should've checked with you before now."

"Yeah, I'm home. No worries."

"I owe you for all the time I've been spending with her."

Paul waved him off. "No, you don't. I'd never begrudge you the chance for some happiness in the midst of all the chaos. Just don't forget we've got that meeting with Hope tomorrow at noon."

"I haven't forgotten. You're meeting her boat?"

"Yeah." Paul straightened out of the slouch he'd slipped into as he leaned against the door. "Oh my God, I almost forgot. The cops found Sharon and got the password. You'll never guess what it was."

"Do I want to hear this?"

Paul laughed—hard. "Probably not as much as I want to tell you. It's AlexMartinezIsADick."

Alex tossed his head back and laughed. "You gotta be fucking kidding me."

"Nope, not kidding. I only wish I'd thought to try that. Should've been my first attempt."

"You're enjoying this a little too much."

"I gotta get my jollies where I can."

"Glad I was able to help." Alex went behind the desk, grabbed a broom from the corner and started sweeping up the broken glass. He couldn't believe the way he'd reacted to seeing Paul alone with Jenny.

"Hey, Al?"

"Yeah?"

"If you love this girl, don't let her get away. She's special."

"I know." While it pleased him that his brother could see that Jenny was special, it also infuriated him. However, he wisely kept that last part to himself. "Do you think it's fair of me to be getting so involved with her?"

"What do you mean?"

"Mom and everything. It's a lot to ask of anyone."

"If she were the kind of person who couldn't handle what you've got going on, you wouldn't care about her as much as you do."

"That's true, but still…"

"I get where you're coming from, but how long are we expected to put our lives on hold? For the rest of Mom's life? There's no right or wrong answer here. For what it's worth, I say go for it. We'll figure it out the way we have already." Paul pushed open the door. "See you back at the ranch?"

"I'll be right there."

"Don't forget to lock up."

"Yes, Dad."

Paul's raised middle finger was the only indication that he'd heard Alex's snide comment.

Alex swept up the glass, turned off the lights, shut down the computer and locked the main door. As he walked up the hill to the house, he thought about what Paul had said about timing and also tried to figure out why he'd gone so ballistic on his brother. He was about halfway home when it dawned on him. He was jealous—jealous of his own brother and the easy rapport he'd found with the woman Alex considered his.

"When was the last time you were jealous because of a woman?" If he were being truthful with himself, he'd never experienced that particular emotion before. He'd felt the same way the other night when he heard her invite her old friend Jared James to visit her at the lighthouse. Alex had felt then like someone was peeling back his skin to reveal a rather ugly interior.

Jealous.

As he showered off the grime of the day and shaved, he thought about the other thing his brother had said, the part about Alex being in love with Jenny. Was that even possible so soon after meeting her? Yes, it was more than possible, he decided. That realization had him questioning whether she felt the same way and what he'd do if she didn't.

"Christ, you've got it so bad for her," he whispered as the water cascaded down upon him. Was it too soon to tell her how he felt? Probably. The last thing he wanted was to scare her off by pushing her for more than she was ready to give. But maybe she was ready, too.

He had no earthly idea how to approach this latest dilemma as he wrapped a towel around his waist and reached for his phone to text her.

Running a little late. Will be there soon.

No worries, she replied. *I'm running late, too.*

No worries, he thought. That was an apt description of their relationship. It was easy and peaceful and calming and somewhat effortless. All of those things were exactly what he needed when he had so much else to contend with. Since the heat had finally broken, he pulled on faded jeans and a cotton button-down shirt that could use some time with an iron. Hopefully, Jenny wouldn't care that he hadn't taken the time to iron his shirt for her. He could always say he was in too big of a rush to get to her to bother ironing, which wasn't far from the truth.

Alex combed his hair, brushed his teeth and splashed on a bit of cologne. Then he went out to the living room to spend a few minutes with his mother before he left.

When she looked him over from top to bottom, he could tell she was in one of her more lucid periods. "You look nice."

"Thank you."

"You should've ironed your shirt." Marion Martinez had made sure both of her boys could do their own laundry and knew how to handle an iron before they left her house. She'd tried and failed to impart some basic kitchen skills, however.

"I know. I'm already running late, though."

"That's no excuse to go out looking rumpled." She surprised him when she stood. "Take it off. I'll do it for you."

"Oh," he said, stunned by the offer as much as the lucidity. "You don't have to."

She looked at him with the eyes of the mother he used to know. "Please let me."

Overwhelmed by her request, Alex unbuttoned the shirt and took it off, following her to the laundry room off the kitchen to keep an eye on her while she operated the iron. But he needn't have bothered. She ironed the shirt with the kind of skill that came from a lifetime of doing such things for the men she loved. When she was finished, she held it for him while he slid his arms into the cooling sleeves.

He turned to face her and watched in stunned amazement as she buttoned it and then patted his chest.

"Much better."

"Yes, it is. Thanks, Mom."

"My pleasure."

He could see that doing something for him had indeed brought her pleasure.

"Are you seeing that nice girl who was here the other day? I can't recall her name."

Alex saw to putting the iron away and stashing the ironing board. "Yes, I'm seeing Jenny."

"I like her."

"So do I."

"Bring her to see me again soon, will you?"

"I will." As tears stung his eyes, Alex hugged her. "Love you, Mom."

"Love you, too, honey. Now don't stay out too late. You know how Daddy and I worry when you boys drive at night."

Alex wasn't sure what hurt more—the stark reminder of who she'd once been or the sudden return to dementia. "I know, Mom. I won't be out too late." He pulled back from her and looked down at her. "Thanks again for ironing my shirt."

"Your shirt? What about your shirt?"

"Never mind."

She might not remember, but he'd never forget.

CHAPTER 19

*W*hen she heard the rumbling roar of the motorcycle coming down the lane that led to the lighthouse, Jenny grabbed her jacket and put it on, slung her purse over her shoulder and headed down the stairs to meet him.

Filled with anticipation, she stepped outside as he brought the bike to a stop and cut the engine. While he took a good long look at her, she did the same, enjoying the sight of him in a freshly ironed cotton shirt that was rolled up to reveal his tanned forearms, well-faded jeans and the boots he always wore on the bike. His dark hair was messed up from the ride, but the messy look—like everything else—only added to his over-the-top sex appeal. Or maybe it was the fact that she thought everything about him was sexy.

He got off the bike and held out a hand to her. "Those jeans are hot, babe."

Feeling the now-familiar magnetic pull, she went to him and was thrilled when he wrapped her up in a tight hug. She put her arms around him and held on just as tightly to him.

"You have no idea how badly I needed this," he said after a long moment of quiet.

"Everything okay?"

He released a deep sigh. "It is now."

Jenny loved that he seemed to feel better when he was with her, that they brought each other comfort as well as passion and companionship and all the other things they'd found together. But the comfort seemed to be what he needed right now. "You want to talk about it?"

"Later." He drew back from her so he could kiss her. "I want to enjoy being with you, because I've been looking forward to it all day."

"I've been looking forward to it just as much."

"Well, I promised you a date, so let's get to it."

"If it's not a good night for it, we don't have to go anywhere."

"It's a good night, and it's going to get even better before it's over."

The playful wiggle of his brows was much more in keeping with the Alex she'd come to know. He helped her into the helmet he'd brought for her and showed her where to put her feet.

"It's probably best if you hold on really tight to me," he said when she was settled behind him on the bike. "Then there's no chance you'll fall off."

"You're just saying that about me falling off to get my hands on you."

"Well, *yeah*. What's the point otherwise?"

It was her very great pleasure to put her arms around him and to feel the press of his most-excellent ass against her spread thighs. She was already hot and bothered, and they hadn't even left yet.

"Ready?" he asked over his shoulder.

"I think so."

"All kidding aside, hold on tight and follow my lead." He fired up the engine, and they took off like a shot down the dirt lane that led to the main road.

She'd had very limited experience with motorcycles. A high school boyfriend had had one, but her parents freaked out when they heard she'd been on it and forbade her from ever going with him again. Being the good girl that she'd been at the time, she'd obeyed their directive, which wasn't hard, because that guy was a moron, and he'd scared the crap out of her with his crazy antics on the bike.

251

As Alex took her on a thrilling ride on the island's winding roads, Jenny was glad her parents didn't know what she was doing, because she absolutely loved everything about it—especially being pressed up against him as he drove. This was nothing like the last time, when she'd been too scared to enjoy the ride. This time was exhilarating and freeing and extremely exciting. But that probably had more to do with the man than the motorcycle.

When they pulled into the parking lot at the Sand & Surf Hotel, Jenny was almost disappointed that the ride was over. Alex got off first, helped her remove the helmet and kept his hands on her shoulders until she got her legs under her.

"How does dinner at Stephanie's and a movie at the theater sound?"

"It sounds perfect."

He took her hand and led her inside, where Sarah Lowry was working at the hotel's front desk.

Owen's mom noticed their joined hands but thankfully offered only a welcoming smile. "Hi there, Jenny, Alex. How are you?"

"We're good," Jenny said. "How are you?"

"Keeping busy," Sarah said. "Are you having dinner?"

"We were hoping to," Alex said.

"Go on in," Sarah said. "I think Steph still has some tables."

"Great, thanks."

"I'm looking forward to the shower tomorrow," Sarah said to Jenny.

"So am I. See you there."

"Wouldn't miss it."

"What's all this about a shower?" Alex asked as they waited for Stephanie to seat another party.

"I keep meaning to ask you if you want to come. Tiffany and Blaine got married so quickly that we never got a chance to give them a shower, so we're doing it late tomorrow afternoon at the lighthouse."

"That sounds like fun for you, but why would I want to go? Isn't that a chick thing?"

"Usually it is, but here on Gansett, we like to include the guys."

"You mean you like to torture the guys."

"Trust me when I tell you, they give as good as they get."

"I haven't done anything to deserve that level of torture."

"You haven't yet, but you will," she said with a saucy smile that made him laugh. "There'll be plenty of other guys, lots of food and beer. What more do you need?"

"Well, when you put it that way... I guess I could *try* to make it."

"Yay."

"I never made any promises." He gave her a sideways glance. "So you're ready to take this public with all your friends?"

"I believe I am. Is that okay with you?"

He put his arm around her shoulders and kissed her forehead. "That's more than okay with me."

Stephanie approached them, stopping a couple of feet from them to stare when she realized they were on a date. "Okay, so what did I miss?"

"A few things here and there," Jenny said mysteriously.

"Apparently. Am I allowed to spread this rumor far and wide?"

"Since it's no longer a rumor, have at it," Jenny said with a smile for Alex.

"This is the biggest news since Tiffany and Blaine's three-day engagement." Stephanie seated them at a table with a view of the sunset and within earshot of the music Owen was making on the deck. "Is this okay?"

"It's perfect," Alex said. "Thanks, Stephanie."

She gave them a rundown of the specials and then left them to peruse the menu after giving Jenny's shoulder an affectionate squeeze. A waitress appeared at their table a few minutes later with a bottle of champagne. "Compliments of Stephanie," she said.

Touched by the gesture, Jenny said, "Please tell her thanks from us."

"I sure will." The waitress poured the bubbly into crystal flutes and took their order.

When they were alone, Alex raised his glass to her. "Here's to going public."

Jenny touched her glass to his. "To going public."

"You sure you're feeling okay about that?"

"I'm feeling extremely okay about a lot of things that haven't been okay for me in a very long time."

"It makes me happy to hear you say that."

"You look really nice tonight," she said. "Not that you don't always look nice."

Alex looked down at his shirt. "My mom ironed for me."

"She did? Really?"

"Yeah. Ten minutes of complete lucidity, during which I got back my mom and then lost her again almost as quickly."

"I'm sorry. That's got to be awful."

"It sucks so bad." He looked down at the table and then at her. "I acted like an ass with my brother earlier."

"How so?"

"I…um, well… I was pissed off about what I witnessed when I came into the store after work."

Genuinely baffled, Jenny said, "What did you witness?"

"You, him, the beers, the nearness."

Her mouth fell open in shock.

"Before you can assure me there was nothing to be pissed off about, I already know that."

"But still, that you even thought it…"

"I know. I was way out of line, and the only reason I'm even telling you is because I thought you might like to know that you have the power to make me insanely jealous."

She stared at him, incredulous. "Because I was talking to your brother and having a beer with him after a long and extremely awful day?"

"Uh-huh. Pretty sad, huh?"

"It's actually rather adorable, if I can get past the fact that you thought you needed to worry about me messing around with your own brother."

"I know I don't need to worry about that with either of you, so let's get back to the adorable part."

Jenny laughed and shook her head in amazement. "You were really jealous?"

"Insanely."

"Huh."

"What does that mean? *Huh.*"

"Nothing. I'm just enjoying this for a minute."

"I never should've told you."

Jenny reached for his hand across the table. "I'm glad you did. I like knowing how you feel."

"If that's the case, I've got other stuff to tell you."

"Good stuff?"

"I hope you'll think so. It feels good to me."

Jenny wondered if he was hinting at what she thought he was and tried to determine how she felt about that. It didn't take long for her to decide she felt very good about it, because she was definitely on the same page.

Without exchanging words, they decided to table that discussion for later, and Jenny told him about her day at the store.

"I feel bad that you had to deal with all our irate customers."

"Someone had to do it, and I think I smoothed some ruffled feathers."

"Again, that's above and beyond the call of duty."

"I don't mind, Alex. It makes me feel good to think there's something I can do to help you and Paul."

"Do you think maybe…" He shook his head. "Never mind."

"Tell me. Do I think what?"

He blew out a ragged deep breath. "Paul, David and I are interviewing a nurse tomorrow, hoping she'll agree to move out here to help us manage Mom's care. I was wondering if you might have time to sit in on the meeting. I'd love to get your take on her."

"I'd be happy to."

"You would? Really? I know it's a lot to ask—"

She tightened her grasp on his hand. "It's not a lot to ask. I'm honored that you want my opinion."

"I just want to do the right thing for my mom, but I have no idea what that is."

"For what it's worth, I think that getting a qualified professional to be part of her daily life at this point is the right thing to do. You and Paul can't continue like this forever, or your health is going to be affected, too. Hopefully this woman will be who you need."

"Her name is Hope," he said with a small smile.

"And how perfect is that? My fingers are crossed for you."

"Thanks, and thank you for coming to the interview."

"Well, you're coming to a wedding shower with me…"

He laughed, as she'd hoped he would. "That's blackmail."

"I prefer to think of it as quid pro quo. I scratch your back, you scratch mine."

"I can't wait for you to scratch my back, but not until after the movie. You'll just have to keep your hands off me until then."

She rolled her eyes at him. "I'll see if I can control myself."

"Don't try too hard."

ALEX WAS in love with her. He'd more or less acknowledged that fact earlier when he nearly took off his brother's head for daring to have an after-work beer with her. But sitting across from her as she offered care and concern and support along with incredible sweetness and hot sexiness, Alex knew she was the whole package. She was exactly the woman he'd nearly given up on ever finding, and to think he'd found her on Gansett Island. The irony wasn't lost on him. If he hadn't come home to Gansett to help care for his mother, he never would've met Jenny.

Now that he had met her and fallen for her, he hoped he could find a way to keep her when his life was in such turmoil at the moment. The addition of full-time nursing assistance to their situation would offer a measure of relief, but he and Paul would still be responsible for their mother—not that either of them would have it any other way.

Still, it was a lot to ask any woman to take on, especially a woman like Jenny, who'd already been through so much in her life. He wanted to make things easy and simple for her, but his life was hardly easy or simple.

After a fantastic dinner at Stephanie's, they walked to the movie theater at the other end of town. Alex loved walking through the busy downtown area with her hand tucked into the crook of his elbow. He loved the sense of connection he felt to her. He loved that she was easy to talk to, compassionate and understanding of the challenges he faced. He also loved how hot her ass looked in those jeans.

At the theater, they shared a laugh over the one-man show as Alex paid the man in the ticket booth for the tickets, and then the same man moved to the other side of the counter to serve them popcorn. Then he collected their tickets at the door to the theater.

"This place hasn't changed one bit since I was a kid," Alex said. "It even smells the same—mildew and popcorn."

"Folding chairs?" Jenny asked as she took in the ramshackle theater.

"I take it this is your first time at Island Cinemas?"

"Plural? I see one cinema, and calling it that is being very generous. And yes, it's my first time."

"Oh, you're in for a very special treat. Shall we make ourselves comfortable in the folding chairs?"

"That's an oxymoron."

"Are you calling me a moron?"

She elbowed his ribs, making him grunt with laughter as he strategically led her to the back row.

"What're we doing way back here?"

"You'll see."

More people filtered into the theater and took seats closer to the screen, leaving Alex and Jenny with the back mostly to themselves.

"I'm beginning to see the method to your madness."

"Just wait." He offered the popcorn to her and took a huge handful for himself.

"Didn't you just eat?"

"I'm a growing boy, and you can't go to the movies and not get popcorn. It's un-American."

"If you say so."

"I say so."

The lights in the theater went off, plunging them into darkness. Alex put his arm around her and dragged her metal chair closer to his. At the top of the far-left wall, windows allowed in the sweeping headlights of cars coming down a hill into town. The lights illuminated almost everyone in the theater, except for those in the back row.

"You didn't tell me this was a drive-in theater."

"That's part of the charm of the place."

"It would appear to me that you might've done this before."

"Done what?"

"Commandeered the back row with a date."

"Are you accusing me of something?"

"Yes, I'm accusing you of being an opportunist."

"I'm really hurt by that."

Her laughter delighted him. He enjoyed every second he got to spend with her, no matter what they were doing. She was easy to talk to and quick to laugh, which brought lightness to his life that had been sorely lacking before he met her. Alex was beginning to think that the instant her tomato connected with his back would turn out to be the most fortuitous second of his life.

The movie was a comedy that had been released on the mainland months ago.

Jenny's eyes were fixed on the screen, while his were on her. He was like a lovesick fool hoping the girl would turn her attention to him rather than the movie. After a particularly funny exchange between the characters, she glanced at him, smiling at the joke, and found him staring at her like a crazy stalker. But he couldn't help it. If she was close by, he'd much rather look at her than watch a movie he had no interest in.

"Pay attention," she whispered.

"I am paying attention."

"To the movie."

"You're much more interesting than the movie." He gave her shoulder a gentle tug and brought her close enough to kiss. Her lips were salty and sweet from the popcorn, and one taste was nowhere near enough.

"Now I know why you wanted to sit back here."

"May as well make the most of our dark corner," he said as he went back for more of her.

Her hand on his face was all the encouragement he needed to drop the nearly empty popcorn box to the floor and dive into the tongue-tangling kiss he'd been dying for all night. It only took about fifteen seconds for the kiss to spiral almost completely out of control.

Alex drew back from her, dragged in a deep breath and buried his face in her hair. "Can we please get out of here?"

"But you paid for the movie."

"I don't give a fuck about that."

Because he was holding her so tightly, he felt the shudder ripple through her. She was so sweet and her responses to him so genuine. She made him wish he were a better man, someone more worthy of her—someone more refined than he'd ever be. But she didn't seem to care that he could be rough around the edges. If anything, his coarse language seemed to turn her on.

"Let's go."

Alex launched out of his seat and led her by the hand from the theater, cursing his lack of foresight in leaving the bike parked at the Surf. On the sidewalk, he put his arm around her and steered her back the way they'd come through town. He was so into her that he didn't notice they were about to slam into someone coming the other way until it was nearly too late.

"Well, isn't this cozy," a male voice said.

Alex and Jenny looked up at the same second to see her pink-shirted date from the other night taking a hard look at the two of them together and apparently not liking what he was seeing.

"Linc," Jenny said. "I... How are you?"

"Not as good as you are, apparently. Is this why you aren't interested in seeing me again? Because you met him the night you were with me?"

"I knew him before I went out with you, not that it's any of your business."

"What kind of game are you playing, Jenny?"

"Wait a minute," Alex said as his blood began to boil. If he thought he'd been jealous earlier with Paul, that paled in comparison to the rage he felt at Linc's apparent sense of entitlement where she was concerned. "Am I confused? Does she owe you anything more than a thank-you and goodnight after a date?"

"I never said she did, but—"

"Here's a big idea," Alex said. "Don't finish that thought. We met the day before she went out with you. It was no big deal then. It is now. Let it go, okay?"

"I'm sorry," Jenny said softly, making Alex want to roar with outrage. What did she have to be sorry about?

"Yeah," Linc said as he stepped aside to let them pass. "Me, too."

Alex propelled them forward, more anxious than ever to get back to the bike and get the hell out of town. He desperately needed to be alone with her.

"Sorry about that," Jenny said.

"Don't you dare apologize to me." His unusually harsh words had her stiffening under his arm. He made an effort to soften his tone when he added, "You didn't do anything wrong."

"Are you jealous?"

"What do you think?"

"Alex—"

"We'll talk about it when we're alone." Annoyed by the other people on the sidewalk, the cars and mopeds that slowed them down at intersections and everything that stood in the way of what he wanted and needed, he quickened his pace.

"Slow down. I can't keep up with you."

"Sorry," he muttered.

Back at the Surf, he had the helmet strapped on her so fast she didn't have a chance to protest before he was helping her onto the back of the bike. He was hovering on the edge of control, and he knew it, so he focused all his thoughts on the safe operation of the bike as they headed out of town. Thankfully, it wasn't far to the lighthouse, and they pulled onto the dirt lane about ten minutes later.

He was off the bike as soon as he parked it outside her door and practically lifted her off the back.

"You're in a big rush," she said when he'd removed her helmet.

He took hold of her hand. "You have no idea."

Inside, they went up the first flight of stairs single file, with Alex in the back, his eyes fixed on the sway of her denim-covered ass. He decided one more flight was too far and directed her to the sofa.

"Wait," she said. "Where are we going?"

"Right here." His patience was officially gone, and the need for her in that moment was unlike anything he'd ever felt before. "Right now." He began pulling at clothes—his and hers.

"Alex—"

"Now," he said against her lips. "Right now." He was acting like a lunatic. He knew that, but knowing it didn't stop him from taking what he needed more than the next breath. Her soft skin and sexy curves made his mouth water with lust as he came down on top of her on the sofa. "Jenny... I can't wait. I need you."

Her arms encircled his neck and her knees hugged his hips, providing all the encouragement he needed to sink into her wet heat. With their bodies connected, Alex felt like he could finally breathe again. Even with desire beating through him relentlessly, a sense of calm came over him at knowing she wanted him every bit as much as he wanted her.

He looked down to find her watching him closely, probably trying to decide when he'd turned into a sex-crazed madman. "Are you okay?"

Nodding, she smoothed her hands from his shoulders, down his back to cup his ass and keep him lodged deep inside her. "More than okay."

"You make me crazy."

"I like you that way."

He huffed out a harsh laugh at her unexpected comment. "I like you every way, but this way is becoming a particular favorite of mine."

"It's been a favorite of mine for a while now."

After that, there were no words. There was no need for words. Their bodies did the talking for them. What started out urgent became slow and sensual, their hands linked, their eyes locked on each other, their movements perfectly choreographed, as if they'd been lovers for years rather than days.

"Jenny," he said on a gasp when the pleasure became almost too much to bear. "I can't…" He couldn't breathe, he couldn't talk, he couldn't think of anything other than the need for completion.

And then she blew his mind when she pulled her right hand free of his grasp and reached down to help herself along. Christ alive, he'd never seen or felt anything hotter in his life.

"Now," she whispered, her body arching into his deep stroke.

Alex didn't need to be told twice. He gave himself over to the powerful release, losing himself in her, in her sweetness, her sexiness, her incredible kindness. As if they, too, could no longer be contained, the words poured forth. "I love you," he uttered gruffly against her ear. "It's too soon, and it's too much, but it's true."

Jenny turned her face into his deep, searching kiss.

He wanted to show her everything he felt for her. He wanted to show her how essential she'd become to him. He wanted to offer her everything, which was when he remembered how little he actually had to give anyone at a time when his family needed him so greatly. The thought was like a pinprick to his euphoria, a deflating reminder of his reality.

"What's wrong?" she asked. "Why did you just go rigid?"

"I shouldn't have said what I did."

"Why? Is it not true?"

"It's true, but it also puts a ton of pressure on you when this is so new."

She looked up at him with incredibly expressive eyes. "Why does it put pressure on me?"

"Because... It's just... I still have nothing much to offer you beyond that."

"*That* is a lot in and of itself, and you have plenty to offer."

"I don't want you to feel pressured or weighted down by me."

She pressed her hips against his, reminding him he was still lodged deep inside her—as if he needed the reminder. "I like feeling weighted down by you—in case you hadn't noticed."

He gave her a small smile, because he knew she was trying to make him feel better.

"I love you, too."

As if he hadn't heard her correctly, he stared down at her. "You don't have to say that—"

Her fingers on his lips quieted him. "I'm not saying it because you did. I'm saying it because I feel it. I know what it feels like to be in love. It feels just like this."

"Jenny," he said with a sigh, his forehead dropping to her chest.

She combed her fingers through his hair. "You told me you were jealous because I was having a beer with Paul after work."

"That was stupid. I know that."

"Hush up and listen to me. Yesterday, I spent most of the afternoon with him and Adam, both of them exceptionally good-looking guys who also happen to be very nice, too."

"I'll have to take your word on the good-looking part."

"You can trust me and all of womankind on that. Anyway, as I was saying, I was with them all afternoon and never once in all that time did I look at either of them and think, '*Whoa*, I want him.'"

"That's very comforting," he said sarcastically. "Thanks for sharing."

"Will you shut up and let me finish?"

He laughed at her sauciness, delighted and amused by her. "If I must."

"When you came in after work, the second you walked in the door, everything female in me woke up to take notice of you."

Touched by what she'd said, he raised his head to kiss her softly. "Everything in me noticed you, too. It noticed you were alone with my brother and Adam, and I wanted to drag you out of there and claim you in the barn."

"Oh for God's sake," she said with a laugh. "What am I going to do with you? You're nothing more than a caveman in disguise."

"Guilty as charged."

"I feel bad about what happened with Linc before."

"Why should you?"

"It's not my way to go around hurting people on the way to getting what I want."

"He's not hurt, Jenny. His pride is wounded because a woman he's interested in isn't interested in him. There's a difference between actual hurt and a damaged ego."

"I suppose that's true."

"I didn't like the way he looked at you, as if he had some sort of claim on you. The whole time we were standing there, I wanted to chant mine, mine, *mine*."

"You are a caveman."

"And judging by the heat I'm feeling down below, you like me that way." His comment made her blush furiously, which had him laughing.

"Stop it."

Rather than stop anything, he began to move again, wrapping his arms around her legs to open her to his fierce possession. "Mine," he whispered. "Mine, mine, *mine*."

"*Yes*." She pulled so hard on his hair that it hurt, but the bite of pain only made him want her more than he already did—if that was possible. "I'm yours."

CHAPTER 20

*E*arly the next morning, Evan left Grace sleeping on the one morning off she allowed herself in the summer, and headed for the marina on the motorcycle. He hoped to catch his dad before the rush of the day began. At the picnic table outside the restaurant where Big Mac and his friends held their morning meeting, Evan found his dad and Ned enjoying a cup of coffee and a plate of sugar doughnuts.

Evan's mouth watered at the sight of the doughnuts. "Can you spare one of those for me?" he asked when he took a seat at the table.

Though his father sent him a delighted smile, he moved the plate out of Evan's reach. "These are all accounted for."

"He can have one a mine," Ned said, handing a doughnut to Evan and sending a disgusted look to his best friend.

"Thanks, Ned. Nice to know where I stand with my dear old dad."

Ned guffawed with laughter that made Big Mac smile.

"Don't get in the way of me and my morning sugar fix," Big Mac said.

"My apologies."

"What brings you out and about so early?" Big Mac asked around a huge mouthful of doughnut.

"I'm looking for a little advice, so I decided to come to the brain trust."

"Yer a wise man," Ned said gravely. "Right here's where all the world's problems get solved. What can we do fer ya this fine morning?"

And it was a fine morning indeed. The sultry heat was gone, the sky was clear and blue, the breeze warm but not oppressive. A perfect Gansett Island day.

"Did my dad tell you about the situation with the album?"

The two men exchanged guilty glances.

"Oh, come on," Evan said, laughing. "I know he told you. You two are more married than he and my mother are."

"Not sure how I feel 'bout that," Ned said.

"It's kinda true," Big Mac said. "I told him because I knew you wouldn't care if I did."

"And I was comin' to see ya today," Ned said. "So ya saved me a trip."

"Coming to see me about what?" Evan asked, eyeing the doughnut plate and trying to decide if he dared to steal a second one.

"I don't wantcha ta think that just cuz I gave ya the money ta start the studio, I expect ya ta pass up a golden opportunity with Buddy Longstreet. There ain't no strings attached ta that money. You shoulda damned well known that."

"I do," Evan said, moved by Ned's impassioned speech. He'd been a beloved second dad to Evan and his siblings all their lives, and none of them had any doubt about where they stood with him. The studio had been Ned's idea in the first place, and he'd financed the purchase of the equipment. Ensuring Ned's investment was well protected had been foremost on Evan's mind in the last few days. "Of course I know there were no strings, but I appreciate the reminder."

"What're you thinking, son?" Big Mac asked. "Air it out with us, and let's figure this out together."

Since there were no two men he'd rather air it out with, Evan took a deep breath and spilled his guts. "The kicker is," he said when he had explained the situation from every angle, "I no longer want what I once would've given everything for."

"Then that's what you need to tell Buddy," Big Mac said. "I don't know the guy at all, but it seems to me he'd probably understand that plans change. Goals change. Dreams change. What did he expect you to do for the last year while the bankruptcy was hashed out? Twiddle your thumbs?"

"Yer daddy's right," Ned said. "I've read about this Longstreet fellow. He's known fer being a straight-up kinda guy. I'm sure he'd appreciate ya being straight up with him, too."

"I suppose he would," Evan said, even though the thought of being straight up with Buddy Longstreet made his stomach hurt.

"Why don't you give him a call right now," Big Mac suggested. "Get this off your chest so you can get on with your life."

"Right now as in *right now?*"

Big Mac leaned across the table. "Right. Now."

Evan wasn't sure what was more intimidating—the thought of calling Buddy, or his father when he had his mind set on something. Evan pulled his cell phone from his pocket, found the Nashville number from when Buddy had called him the other day and put through the call. Since he fully expected to leave a message with an assistant or one of the many people who worked for the superstar, Evan's heart nearly stopped beating when he heard Buddy's distinctive drawl.

"Longstreet."

"Um, hi," Evan said haltingly. "This is Evan McCarthy."

"Oh hey, how's it going?"

"Um, pretty well. Do you have a minute?"

"Sure thing. What's up?"

"I wanted to talk to you about the album and the tour and…everything."

"What about it?"

Evan looked up to find his father and Ned hanging on his every word. His father nodded in encouragement. Evan took a deep breath and dove in. "When the whole thing happened with Starlight, it forced me to make some changes to my plans."

"I imagine it did."

"A close friend of my family's put up the cash for me to start my own recording studio. We've recently opened our doors, and we've got artists booked through October. I'm also engaged to a woman who owns a business here on the island where I live, so she's unable to move right now. I guess what I'm saying is…"

"You're saying you don't want the same things you wanted a year ago."

"Yes. Exactly."

"Well, this puts me in a bit of a bind. I shelled out a hefty sum to free your album from the bankruptcy proceedings."

Evan winced. "I know. That's been keeping me awake at night."

Buddy was silent for a long time, and Evan could almost hear him thinking.

"Could you give me six weeks spread out over the next year?"

Six weeks… Evan's mind spun with the implications of six full weeks away from Grace. At least they wouldn't be all at the same time… "I think I could make that work." As miserable as it would be, they could do it. Couldn't they?

"Excellent."

"I'm sorry about this, Buddy."

"Don't be sorry. I think you have an incredible talent, which is why I pursued the project. But if you don't have the drive to go along with the talent, then there's no point in putting us all through the paces."

"It's not that I don't have the drive. It's more that my drive was forced to go in a different direction, and I'm too far along with the studio to abandon it now."

"Believe it or not, I understand that. I'll get with Jack, and we'll figure out a plan. I'd like to recoup my investment, and I think we can make that happen with a smaller time commitment from you."

"I really appreciate that."

"When's the wedding?" Buddy asked, surprising Evan with the personal question in the midst of business.

"January eighteenth in Turks and Caicos."

"Congratulations. Married life is the best thing to ever happen to me. I hope it will be for you, too."

"I have no doubt whatsoever that it will be."

"We'll be in touch. Don't lose any more sleep, Evan. It's business. It works itself out."

If he hadn't already respected Buddy Longstreet more than just about anyone in the music industry, he would now. "Thanks, Buddy."

"Everything okay?" Big Mac asked when Evan had stashed the phone in his pocket.

"I think it's going to be."

"Excellent. Now have another doughnut."

Evan laughed and snagged the doughnut while his dad was feeling generous. He felt like a hundred tons had been lifted off his chest with one phone call. It was going to be okay. He could survive six separate weeks away from Grace. Sure he could. If he kept telling himself that, maybe he'd actually believe it by the time he had to go.

AT NOON, Jenny left two of the college students in charge of the store and walked up the driveway to the Martinez house for the interview Alex had asked her to attend. All morning, Jenny had walked around in a stunned state of disbelief over the amazing events of the previous evening.

I love you. You're mine. Mine, mine, mine.

She shivered, thinking about the way he'd looked at her, their intense lovemaking and sleeping in his arms after they finally wore each other out and went upstairs to bed.

Alex must've been watching for her, because he came out to the porch to meet her. He wore a black polo shirt with plaid shorts and looked serious and sexy and thrilled to see her.

I love you. You're mine. Mine, mine, mine.

As she recalled his words from the night before, her heart gave a happy leap of joy at the sight of him, and she walked a little faster up the stairs and right into his outstretched arms.

"I just saw you a couple of hours ago." His lips against her ear and his nearness sent a shiver down her spine, as did the memory of him pressing her against the wall of the shower earlier as he thrust into her. "And it seems like forever."

She held on tight to him, amazed and overwhelmed by how strongly she felt in such a short amount of time. If she hadn't experienced similarly powerful emotions once before, she never would've trusted them now. But like she'd told him the night before, she knew what this was, and she wasn't about to deny it.

"I missed you, too."

"Thanks for doing this."

"No problem. How does she seem so far?"

"Pretty cool. She's talking to Mom right now, and she seems to have the sort of patience required for the position."

The door opened behind them, and a dark-haired boy shot past them, down the stairs toward the tire swing hanging from a large maple tree in the yard.

"That'd be Ethan, Hope's son. He's seven and apparently full of energy."

"He's cute."

"I suppose he is if you can get past the incessant talking and endless questions. My mom took an instant shine to him. She said he reminded her of us when we were that age."

"Awww, I bet you were so cute."

Before he could respond to that, David and Daisy arrived. Alex had told her David would attend the interview while Daisy took Marion for a drive and out to lunch.

A short time later, they had sent Marion and Daisy off in David's car. Paul suggested they sit outside on the porch since it was such a nice day. When they were all settled, Jenny took a closer look at Hope, who was probably in her late twenties. She had long brown hair with red highlights, a creamy white complexion and brown eyes. Alex had introduced her to Hope as his girlfriend, which had given

Jenny another reason to glow from the inside. He was racking up the points.

Jenny decided that Ethan must take after his father, which led her to wonder if the father was in their lives.

"Hopefully, you got a good chance to evaluate our mom and to get a sense of what she needs," Paul said.

Nodding, Hope said, "I'm terribly sorry she's so afflicted at such a young age."

"It's very unfortunate indeed," Paul said. "Our goal is to keep her at home for as long as we can, but that's becoming increasingly more difficult with only the two of us and a litany of friends helping out when they can. We need more reliable help."

"It's amazing you've gotten this far on your own," Hope said.

"I've been trying to tell them that," David said, "but they don't listen to me."

David's comment cut through any remaining tension, and they all relaxed into laughter.

"At this point," Alex said, "we know you're well qualified or you wouldn't be here. I guess it's only fair to ask what questions you have for us."

"I do have one concern that's keeping me from leaping at the opportunity, and that's the idea of living on an island year-round. Not just for me, but for Ethan, too."

"Would you mind if I took that one?" Jenny asked.

Alex and Paul gestured for her to go ahead.

"I worried about that when I came here, too. I took the lighthouse keeper's job just over a year ago. Even though it looked like a fun adventure, I had the same fear of what it would truly be like to live here all the time."

"And how has it been?"

"It's been incredible. After a while, you forget you're on an island." Jenny glanced at Alex. "Because everything you need is right here."

Hope tipped her head to look at Ethan, who was entertaining himself on the swing. "How about socially? Are there a lot of people here in the winter?"

"About seven hundred live here year-round, a lot of them our age with young families," Paul said.

"I've found an amazing circle of friends," Jenny said. "I'd be happy to introduce you to my group if you decide to come."

"That's very kind of you. Thank you so much."

"We don't want to twist your arm," Alex said. "We know it's a huge decision, and there's a lot to consider."

"Actually," Hope said, taking a long gaze around the yard and the greenhouses, "it's not that big of a decision. Ethan and I are in bad need of a change of pace, and I think this'll work out great for us. It's such a beautiful place, and the guesthouse is ideal for what we need. If the offer is still good, I'd be honored to help with your mother."

Jenny experienced a sudden rush of relief at knowing Alex and Paul would be getting some qualified help—soon. She glanced at Alex and smiled as he blew out a deep breath and seemed to visibly sag with relief.

"The offer is definitely still good," Paul said. "How soon could you get here?"

"The first week in August?"

That was in a few short weeks.

"That'd be great," Paul said.

"That'll give Ethan some time to acclimate before school starts."

"If you want to come inside," Paul said, "we can go over all the details, and you can review the medical information with David."

"Don't go too far, Ethan," Hope said to her son, who waved from his perch on the swing. She went inside with David and Paul, leaving Jenny and Alex alone on the porch.

He bent at the waist, propping his head on his hands.

Jenny put her hand on his back, wanting to offer comfort. "I'm so happy it worked out for you guys. For what it's worth, I think she's terrific."

"It's worth a lot. Thank you."

"Are you okay?"

"Yeah, sorry. It's just knowing that help is on the way…"

"I know." Jenny gave him a gentle tug, urging him to lean on her, which he did. She put both arms around him and slid her lips over the silk of his hair.

His arm encircled her waist. "Let's go surfing."

"What? Where did that come from?"

He sat up to kiss her. "It came from me wanting to spend the afternoon with my hands all over you."

"I have to work, and so do you."

"We're taking the afternoon off. I'm the boss. I can make up the rules as I go along."

"Um, Paul is my boss, so…"

"If he messes with me, I'll pound on him."

"If you do that, Hope will see that you're nothing more than a caveman, and she'll quit her new job before she starts."

"You do make a good point. Perhaps I won't pound on him. I'll just kidnap you and let him wonder what became of you."

"That's not happening either."

"The surfing? That's happening, so go square it with the boss man before I forget I have to be on my best behavior today."

"Only because an afternoon with your hands all over me doesn't sound awful, I'll do what I'm told. But don't get used to my obedience."

Alex smiled and raised an eyebrow.

Jenny got up and went inside to talk to Paul before Alex could say something outrageous.

David and Hope were going over Marion's medical records, so Jenny signaled to Paul. "Your brother has a big idea about playing hooky this afternoon. Any objections?"

"Not at all. Hope is here for the day, and she's going to spend some time here with Mom this afternoon when she gets back with Daisy, so we're covered."

"What about the store?"

"They can handle things for a couple of hours. We need you for the big-picture management stuff."

"I've got you covered there."

"Go have some fun. You both deserve it."

273

"So do you, Paul. There's a party at the lighthouse later with the McCarthys and other friends. We'd love to have you join us, if you can get away."

"I'll see what I can do."

"Great."

Paul glanced at the window to the porch where Alex was waiting for her. "You're really good for him."

"We're good for each other."

"I'm happy for you guys," Paul said, his expression wistful. "Maybe I'll see you later."

"I hope so." If only she had a single friend to fix up with Paul. He was a great guy—smart, funny, almost as handsome as his brother and genuinely devoted to his family. But all her friends were happily settled now, except for Toby's sister, Erin.

"I've got the afternoon off," Jenny said to Alex when she returned to the porch, "but I have to be back at the lighthouse by four to help set up for the party late this afternoon."

"I need to talk to Paul and spend a few more minutes with Hope. I'll be over shortly with my board." He hooked an arm around her waist and kissed her. "Wear that pink bikini."

"Yes, sir. Anything else?"

His eyes did that dark-chocolate thing that happened when he was aroused. "That'll do for now, but I reserve the right to add to the list later."

"So noted. See you soon."

"I won't be long. No more than an hour."

Over her shoulder, she said, "Thanks for the warning."

Jenny drove home to the lighthouse, thinking of him and how dramatically he'd changed her life since the day he and his lawn mower showed up and blasted her out of bed. Their connection had been instantaneous and intense. Her feelings for him seemed to grow exponentially with every passing day.

Jenny couldn't wait to go public with him in front of her friends later and to introduce him to her parents next week. It was moving so quickly, but after years of marching in place, she was ready to move forward, especially if moving forward meant a future full of days like this one.

She'd forgotten how it felt to be newly in love. She'd forgotten the giddiness, the excitement, the endless possibilities, the constant hum of arousal and the need to make plans that included him. Jenny hadn't made a lot of plans since she lost Toby. Rather, she'd coasted from one day to the next, focused on getting through and getting by.

She wasn't yet to the point where she was practicing writing Jenny Martinez on her notebook covers or anything like that, but she was beginning to picture a future that included him, his brother and their mother in her life to stay.

Back at the lighthouse, she went upstairs to change into the requested bikini. After slathering on sunscreen, she found a beach cover-up and slid her feet into flip-flops. She was brushing her teeth when her cell phone rang, so she took the call without checking the caller ID.

"Hey, it's Erin. Are you busy?"

Erin was Toby's twin sister, and they'd kept in close touch in the years since their devastating loss. "Never too busy for you. How are you?"

"I'm okay. You?"

"I'm doing great, actually."

"That's really nice to hear. You sound happy."

"I am." Jenny hadn't given the first thought to how she might break the news to Toby's family that she was in love again. She sat on her bed when her legs began to tremble under her.

"Any particular reason?"

Jenny fixed her gaze on the picture of the fiancé she'd lost. Then she closed her eyes against the sharp bite of pain. "I've met someone."

"Well, you have to tell me more than that!"

In for a penny, in for a pound, Jenny thought, remembering the grandmother who'd loved that saying. "His name is Alex Martinez. He and his brother own a landscaping company here on the island. He came to cut the grass at the lighthouse at five o'clock in the morning. I threw tomatoes at him, and that was the start of a lovely friendship that has become more. Much more. And now I feel sick because I have to tell you this, and… And, well… It's hard."

"Don't feel sick, Jenny. Who knows better than I do what you've been through? I'd never begrudge you the happiness you so deserve."

"Thank you for that. It means a lot. You have no idea how much."

"So you really threw tomatoes at him?"

"I really did," Jenny said with a laugh. "He woke me up!" She didn't mention that he'd woken her out of a dream about Toby.

"Then I suppose he deserved it."

"I hit him smack in the middle of his back."

Erin's laughter was a welcome sound. "I love it."

"Luckily, he decided to forgive me. We're having fun together."

"It's great to hear you sounding so happy."

"How about you? Any new prospects?"

"No one worth throwing tomatoes at."

"Are you trying, Er? Do you get out?"

"Sometimes. Other times, it's just too much trouble."

"I know that feeling," Jenny said. She knew it all too well. "But you can't jumpstart your life if you spend most of it hiding out."

"You're right. I know you're right. It's just knowing and doing can be two different things."

"You should come out here for a visit. Alex has a very handsome and very single brother you might like to meet."

"Subtle, Jenny," Erin said with a laugh. "Very subtle."

"Will you think about coming to visit? It's been too long since we've seen each other."

"I'll try. I'd love to see your island and your lighthouse."

They chatted for another few minutes about the news in Toby's family before Erin said she had to run to a birthday party for her best friend's son.

"Thanks for calling," Jenny said. "It's always so great to hear from you."

"I'm so glad to hear about your Alex. I hope he makes you very happy for a very long time."

"Thank you," Jenny said softly. "Love you."

"Love you, too."

Following the conversation with Erin, Jenny was filled with restless energy and decided to go outside to check on her garden while she waited for Alex. It had been great to hear from Erin, as always. The two of them had been close friends since the day Toby first introduced them, and had supported each other through the darkness after they lost him.

While she treasured her friendship with Erin and her close relationship with Toby's entire family, hearing from Erin was always a reminder of what had been lost. It took her back to that awful day and the frantic calls from his family in Pennsylvania. Having to tell them he'd called, that he was in the building, that he was above where the plane had hit... She'd never forget their anguish or how it had added to hers.

Jenny hated to admit that she'd put a tiny bit of distance between herself and her old friend since she moved to Gansett. In bad need of a fresh start, she'd tried to put the past where it belonged, but doing that meant seeing less of the people she loved.

It was probably time to bridge that gap, and she hoped Erin would take her up on the invitation to come visit.

In the mudroom, she grabbed a metal bucket and headed out to harvest her tomatoes and the bumper crop of cucumbers. As usual on bright summer weekend days, the lighthouse grounds were crawling with tourists checking out the cliffs and the beach down below.

Sometimes she interacted with the visitors, other times she kept to herself. Today, she wasn't in the mood to answer a million questions about the lighthouse and what it was like to live there, so she went about her work in the garden until someone called out her name.

She turned to find Jared James approaching her. Behind him, she noticed a black Porsche parked in the lot. He wore dark sunglasses along with shorts and a T-shirt. Other than the car, nothing about his appearance indicated his extreme wealth.

"Hi, Jared. Nice to see you."

"You, too. Great place you've got here."

His teasing grin made her smile. "It's the best view in the world."

With her bucket full to overflowing with tomatoes and cucumbers, she gestured to the door to the mudroom. "Want a tour?"

"I'd love one."

She took him inside and up to the first level, where he marveled at how compact and cozy the living space was. Upstairs in the combined bedroom and bathroom, he couldn't get enough of her view.

"Did you paint this?" he asked of the canvas on an easel.

"I dabble. I haven't worked on it in weeks. There's so much other stuff to do here in the summer."

"What's it like in the winter?"

"Desolate and quiet. I actually welcome the change of pace after the craziness of the summer. My friends keep me busy and engaged, but I like coming back to my quiet lighthouse."

"I wondered about you," Jared said, glancing at the photo of Toby on the bedside table. "I didn't know you well in school, but I knew Toby was engaged, and I wondered what had become of you."

"Nothing worth writing home about. It's been a very long and difficult journey."

"Toby and I were acquaintances more than friends, and his death hit me very hard, so I can't begin to know what it must've been like for you."

"Did you know anyone else who died that day?"

"A couple of people I knew through work. Even all these years later, sometimes it's hard to believe that it actually happened. It was so surreal, and New York afterward was such a different place for a very long time."

"I'll have to take your word for it. The first year is a bit of a blur for me. I was home in North Carolina for most of it."

"I'm sorry. I don't mean to dredge up unhappy memories."

"It's fine. It's easier to talk about than it used to be, and I always enjoy meeting people who remember Toby fondly."

"He was an awesome guy. I enjoyed him very much."

"Me, too." Mindful of the fact that Alex would be arriving soon and wouldn't appreciate finding Jared in her bedroom, she led the way downstairs and offered him a cold drink.

"I'd love some water."

"Coming right up." She fixed glasses of ice water for both of them and joined him on the sofa. "So you said you were taking some time off this summer?"

He nodded, his gaze fixed on the icy glass. "Very bad and very unexpected breakup."

"I'm sorry." She looked over at him. "If you want to talk about it, I'm a pretty good listener." The poor guy looked like he could use a friend. She no sooner had that thought when she chuckled to herself at the characterization of Jared James the billionaire being a poor anything. But even billionaires could get their hearts broken.

"It's pretty simple, actually. She couldn't handle the money or the lifestyle that goes along with it."

As his words registered, Jenny stared at him. "She couldn't handle the money."

"That's what she said when I proposed and she turned me down."

"Wow." Jenny blew out a deep breath.

"I knew she could be a bit squirrely about the luxury, the gifts, the benefits, the largeness of my life, but I thought she loved me enough to get past all that. I've spent the last few weeks trying to figure out a way to get rid of all the money."

"You shouldn't have to do that. If someone loves you, truly loves you, they love everything about you. If you have to change who you are to accommodate her, then she's not the one for you."

"So I've been told, and intellectually, I agree. Emotionally, however..."

"You grieve."

"More so than I ever have over anything, which may sound sort of melodramatic to someone who's been through what you have."

"A loss is a loss no matter how it happens. Does she know you're so crushed over this?"

"I haven't talked to her since she ended it. She's texted a few times, but I haven't replied."

"Maybe if she knew how upset you are it would make a difference."

"I'm sure she knows. She was fully aware of how totally in love with her I was. I am."

"I'm so sorry, Jared. That's just such an awful situation."

"Isn't it ironic?" he said with a small smile. "And here I thought money bought happiness."

Jenny smiled at his attempt at levity, and her heart gave a happy leap when she heard Alex's heavy footsteps on the metal stairs.

"Hey, baby," he was saying as he arrived at the landing. "Are you ready?" He took one look at Jenny sitting on the sofa with Jared, and his smile became a scowl. "Am I interrupting something?"

"Nothing more than a visit with an old friend," Jenny said with a pointed look. She wanted to say, *Stand down, tiger.*

"I should get going," Jared said, probably sensing the tension pouring off Alex in nearly visible waves. "Thanks for the tour and the ear. I appreciate it."

"We're having a party out here later," she said. "You should come. I'll introduce you to some fun people and get your mind off your troubles for a little while."

"Are you sure no one would mind?"

"Of course not. Our motto is the more the merrier."

"That sounds like fun. I'll stop by."

"Great." She walked him to the stairs, all the while ignoring Alex's glare.

"Alex," Jared said, extending a hand. "Nice to see you again."

"Yeah, you, too." He shook Jared's hand reluctantly, or so it seemed to Jenny.

"I can see myself out," Jared said. "Thanks again, Jenny."

A heavy silence hung over the room until they heard the mudroom door close behind Jared.

CHAPTER 21

*a*s soon as the door closed, Jenny turned to face Alex. "Ready to go?"

"Was he in your bedroom?"

Stunned by the angry tone of his voice, she said, "What?"

"You heard me. Did you take him upstairs?"

"I showed him the lighthouse, which includes the upstairs. We talked about Toby and the girlfriend who dumped Jared because she couldn't deal with his wealth. That was about the extent of it. Should I have recorded the conversation so you could hear the full playback?"

"I can't believe you took him into your bedroom."

"I can't believe you're acting like a jealous fool when nothing happened."

His shoulders slumped, and he shook his head. "I can't believe it either. I don't know what the hell is wrong with me where you're concerned, but seeing you sitting there with another guy… I wanted to beat the shit out of him."

"I'm really glad you didn't do that."

"Sorry." He ran his hands through his hair, his frustration nearly palpable.

Jenny went to him and flattened her hands on his chest. "What are we going to do about this little problem of yours? I'm not going to stand for you flipping out every time I talk to another guy."

"I know."

"Soooo…"

"I'm crazy about you," he said gruffly, his hands falling from his hair to her shoulders. "And that's making me crazy. If that makes any sense at all."

Touched by the worry she heard in his voice, she said, "It does, but you have to know you're the only one I want. You're the only one I've truly wanted since I lost Toby. There's no one else but you."

"Will you keep telling me that and forgive me when I act like a jealous ass?"

"Sure. I can do that. It's kind of cute when your dark-chocolate eyes go green, but make no mistake, it won't be cute if you make a scene over me having guy friends. I had a nice time with Jared just now. He's going through a tough time, and I plan to follow up with him in a few days to see how he's doing. I enjoyed talking to someone who knew Toby and remembers him with affection. I refuse to apologize for that."

"I get it. You shouldn't have to apologize."

"And I'm also not going to be happy if you can't be nice to my friends because you think they shouldn't be allowed to talk to me."

"I won't do that. I don't know where this is coming from. I've never felt this way before. About all of it—you, other guys paying attention to you, the way I want to be with you all the time, the crazy way you make me feel. It's new to me. I'm out of sorts over you."

"I don't want you out of sorts. I want you comfortable and secure that what we have is special and that I feel the same way you do."

His hands traveled from her shoulders, down her back and below the hem of her cover-up. He cupped her bottom, drawing a sharp gasp from her.

"I thought we were going surfing."

Tipping his head, he made her shiver with the light brush of his lips on her neck. "We are. Eventually. I need you so bad. So fucking bad. You have no idea. And not just like this." He squeezed her ass for emphasis. "Everywhere. All the time. I need you."

"Alex," she said on a sigh. "You have me. I'm right here, and I'm all yours."

"Yes, you're mine." He tugged on the ties to her bikini bottoms, and the fabric dropped between her feet. His fingers caressed her sex, sliding through the dampness, teasing and tormenting as his mouth came down on hers, hard and demanding.

In no time at all, he had her clinging to the edge of sanity as he completely dominated her senses. When he removed his fingers, she cried out from the loss until he freed himself from the board shorts he'd worn for the beach and lifted her onto his erection.

Jenny slid down on him, taking him in one deep thrust that made her head fall back and her mouth open in a silent scream. The pleasure was nearly unbearable. And then he leaned her against the wall and began to thrust into her.

"I was with someone," he said against her ear without missing a beat on the pace of his possession. "For two years. She had guy friends. Lots of them, and I didn't give a shit. I was never jealous, because I didn't love her. I know that now. I didn't love her."

His words and actions made for a powerful combination.

"I love you," he whispered.

Overcome with the emotion and swept away by desire, Jenny could barely think, let alone speak. But she knew he needed the words from her. "I love you, too."

He pushed hard into her, coaxing her with his fingers. "Come with me."

Jenny was so close that all he had to do was touch her once. She held on tight to him as he rode wave after wave of her release and then let himself go, too. It went on forever, or so it seemed.

"I'm sorry for being an ass." His lips and whiskers rubbing on her collarbone ignited her all over again.

"I forgive you."

"It's your fault anyway."

"How do you figure?"

"I was never this way until I met you."

Laughing, Jenny tightened her arms around him, wanting to hold on to him forever. Was he perfect? Far from it, but it seemed he might be perfect for her. "How about this surfing you promised me?"

He withdrew from her slowly and settled her on her feet. Cupping her face in his big hands, he kissed her and gazed into her eyes for a long moment, seeming as dazed as she felt. "Let's go."

GRACE WAS RUNNING LATE. The pharmacy had been unusually busy on that Saturday afternoon, and there went her plans to scoot out early to go help set up for the party.

She ran up the stairs to the apartment, planning to shower, change and get to the lighthouse. She'd been distracted all day, thinking about Evan, their wedding plans, the situation with Buddy and the album, the studio, the pharmacy she'd bought just over a year ago and how it now felt like an anchor around her neck.

If only she hadn't invested so much to buy the place, she'd be able to travel with him while he promoted his music. But she was stuck on Gansett for the foreseeable future. It made her sad to feel "stuck" in a place she loved so much, but the idea of being left behind while he went out on tour for months on end made her feel sick. She missed him already, and he hadn't even left yet.

Under the warm spray of the shower, she tried to let go of the anxiety and worries so she could focus on the evening with Evan and their friends. They had today together as well as tomorrow and the next day. There was no point to obsessing about what might happen months down the road. But even as she told herself that, the knot of anxiety in her belly refused to let up.

The shower door opened, and Grace let out a squeak of surprise when Evan stepped in behind her, his arms encircling her waist as he brought her in close to him.

"Where did you come from?" she asked.

His hands and lips were all over her. "Work." Against her back, Grace felt the hard pressure of his erection.

"Evan... I don't have time. I have to get to Jenny's."

"I only need a minute."

"It never takes you only a minute."

"Why, thank you."

Grace laughed at the male satisfaction she heard in his tone. She had absolutely nothing to compare him to, but she knew there was no comparing what she felt for him to anything else she'd ever known.

"I have good news for you."

At that, her heart actually lurched. "What is it?"

"I'll tell you in a minute." He pressed gently on her shoulders, urging her to lean forward. When he had her arranged the way he wanted her, he grasped her hips and surged into her from behind.

Grace remembered the first time they'd done this, and the shock of how incredible it had felt then. It was no less incredible after all the time they'd spent together.

"God, nothing in the whole world feels this good," he said.

She kept her hands flat against the shower wall as the water beat down upon them and he filled her to capacity. In all her wildest dreams, she never could've imagined Evan McCarthy and the joy he brought to her life. The reminder that he'd be leaving her brought tears to her eyes as he kept up the relentless pace.

He reached around her, rolled her clit between his fingers and did the same to her nipple. The combination set her off as it always did. He played her body with the same skill he played the guitar, and she was powerless to resist him.

"*Grace*," he groaned as his hands returned to her hips to hold her still for his fierce thrusts. Still wedged inside her, he helped her to stand up straight and put his arms around her. "I love you so much."

"I love you, too. Now what's the good news?"

Laughing as he withdrew from her and turned her to face him, he kissed her. "I talked to Buddy. I told him the situation, and we agreed to six separate weeks on the road over the next year—none of them in January."

Still a bit sex drunk, it took Grace a second to process what he'd said. "And that's it? Only six weeks?"

"Only six weeks."

When his words finally registered, the flood of relief reduced her to tears.

"Aw, baby, don't cry. You know I hate when you cry."

"Good tears," she said, clinging to him. "I was so afraid of what was going to happen to us if you were gone all the time."

"So was I. That wasn't what I wanted, and I told him so."

"You actually said 'no, thank you' to Buddy Longstreet."

"I did. I want you more than I wanted what he was offering. It's that simple."

Of course that only made her cry harder.

"Gracie… You're killing me here. I thought you'd be happy."

"I'm so happy," she said between sobs.

"You don't look happy."

"I've never been happier in my whole life."

He put his arms around her and held her as tight as he possibly could. "Me neither, baby. Me neither."

JENNY COULDN'T BELIEVE what Maddie, Grace, Stephanie, Abby, Laura and Sydney had accomplished at the lighthouse in only an hour. The lawn was littered with chairs, a fire pit, lanterns and long tables covered with tablecloths that were anchored by white rocks they'd gathered from the beach below. The girls had their guys working just as hard, hauling coolers and ice and taking orders like the well-trained husbands, fiancés and boyfriends that they were.

"You guys are amazing," Jenny said. They'd told her she'd done her part by donating the place, but she'd also made two huge salads and one of her favorite desserts to lend to the cause. It was just as well that she didn't have to do a lot of heavy lifting, because her arms and legs were dead from surfing—if you could call what she'd done "surfing." It was more like falling with style, as Buzz Lightyear would say.

Alex had been a patient teacher, and she'd more or less gotten the hang of it. He told her it would take a lot more practice before she mastered it, and he promised to give her another lesson soon. He'd gone home to check on his mom before the party, and she expected him back any time. She had butterflies in her belly when she thought about taking their relationship fully public with her friends, but she knew they'd be thrilled for her.

She was pretty thrilled for herself, she thought as she cuddled with Thomas, Hailey, Ashleigh and Holden on a blanket spread over the grass. Jenny had volunteered to keep an eye on the kids during the setup. Hailey had crawled into Jenny's lap, and Ashleigh had her head on Jenny's leg as she took a look at Thomas's new board book.

Jenny was so absorbed in the kids and their chatter that she didn't notice Alex approaching her until he was right on top of them. "Oh, hey," she said, her body tingling in delight at the very sight of him. "I didn't see you coming."

He raised a brow in that naughty, sexy way of his and made her laugh.

"Not in front of the children."

"You're a natural," he said, squatting next to the blanket.

"I don't know about that, but I do enjoy them as well as my own nieces and nephews."

"Do you want your own?"

Jenny stared at him, the question arcing between them like a live wire. "I used to. I figured I'd be staring down the teenage years by now." She shrugged off the stab of pain that came with remembering old dreams. "But I'm probably past all that."

"Because you're such an old hag."

"Hey!"

"Come on, Jenny. You're only what? Thirty-six?"

"Seven. And a half."

"Jeez, I had no idea you were so much older than me."

"How much older?" She couldn't believe it hadn't occurred to her to ask him how old he was.

"You've got three and a half years on me."

"Oh my God! I'm a cradle robber."

"What's a cradle robber, Jenny?" Thomas asked.

Jenny bit her lip to keep from laughing. "It's when an old lady like me goes out with a young guy like Alex."

"You're not old, Jenny," Ashleigh said with an annoyed glance at Alex.

"You're my new best friend, Ash," Jenny said.

The dark-haired little girl, who was the spitting image of her gorgeous mother, smiled up at Jenny. "BFFs."

"Forever," Jenny said. "Do you think Mommy will be surprised to find out the party is for her?"

"Yep. Auntie Maddie told her it was a cookout. She lied, but it was a good lie."

"That's right. She lied so she could surprise Mommy, but Auntie Maddie wouldn't lie to your mommy about something important."

"I know. Can we go play with the horseshoes?"

"As long as you stay right there where I can see you, and don't throw the horseshoes at each other."

Holding hands, Thomas and Ashleigh scampered off, leaving Jenny and Alex with Hailey and Holden, who sat in a bouncy chair.

"Don't tell me you've given up on the idea of having kids of your own," Alex said as he took a seat on the blanket.

"Not entirely, but I've tried to be realistic about it. I'm getting older every day, and it's not something I'd do by myself. I'd be a terrible single mom."

"No, you wouldn't." Alex held out a finger to Holden, who curled his pudgy fist around it. "I want kids. I want a family of my own."

As she listened to him and watched his interaction with Holden, Jenny held her breath, waiting to hear what else he would say.

"I bet we'd make really cute babies together."

Okay, that was unexpected. She swallowed hard. "You do?"

Nodding, he reached across the blanket for her hand. "You don't think so?"

"I haven't really thought about it, but now that you mention it, they probably would be pretty cute." Her eyes filled, and she looked away, desperately trying to rein in her emotions.

"What?"

She shook her head.

"Tell me."

"You make me want things I long ago gave up on hoping for."

"You make me want things, too. The same things, I suspect."

"We shouldn't even be talking about this," she said with a nervous laugh. "It's far too soon."

"No, it isn't. We aren't kids. We've both been around long enough to know when something special comes along. Who says we have to spend two years together before it's acceptable to have this conversation?"

"I never said anything about two years, but two months might be practical."

"Screw practical."

"Don't swear in front of the babies."

"Don't dodge the issue."

"Maybe we could continue this conversation later?"

"Yes, I believe we will continue this later."

Trying to hide her trembling hands from him, Jenny snuggled Hailey, her mind racing with the thoughts he'd planted in her brain. The two of them together long-term, having children together and watching them grow up… A powerful sense of yearning filled her, and she had a feeling he knew just how much his words had affected her.

"Hey, you guys," Maddie called. "They're coming."

Alex stood and extended a hand to Jenny. She picked up Hailey, Alex took Holden, and Jenny called for Ashleigh and Thomas to come along with them.

Tiffany and Blaine arrived in his police-issued SUV.

"Are we late or something?" Tiffany asked as she took in the gathering that had grown and multiplied while Alex was rocking her world on the blanket.

"Surprise!" they all said in unison.

"Happy wedding shower," Maddie said to her sister as she hugged her.

Tiffany's mouth fell open. Beside her, Blaine smiled at her reaction.

"We totally got you," Laura said.

"I'm stunned," Tiffany said as she received hugs from her mother and Ned. "You didn't have to do this."

"Oh, we know," Stephanie said with a grin.

Poor Tiffany had no idea what she was in for. It was a good thing they'd set up lots of games and things to keep Thomas and Ashleigh busy during the present stage of the festivities.

After Jenny and Alex returned the babies to their mothers, he stayed close to her, keeping an arm around her shoulders or his hand clasped tightly to hers. He was making a very public statement of their coupledom, which was yet another thrilling moment with him.

Stephanie, Laura and Abby managed to get Jenny away from Alex long enough to pump her for information that she happily gave up.

"I can't believe you kept this from us," Laura said with a teasing smile. "No wonder you didn't click with Mason or Linc."

"I only met Alex the day before I went out with Linc. There was no juggling going on. I swear."

"I'm really happy for you, Jenny," Abby said. "You're positively glowing."

Jenny raised her hands to her face. "Am I?"

"Positively," Stephanie confirmed.

"Are you guys for real?" Tiffany asked loudly as she opened the first of her presents—a skimpy see-through nightgown and an incredibly large dildo. "In front of my *mother?*"

"Relax, dear," Francine said dryly. "Wait till you see what I got you."

"I can't believe you guys did this behind my back in my own store! I wondered why we had such an off-the-charts week. Patty, you're so fired!"

"You can't function without me, boss," Patty retorted.

"That's true, but you're still fired," Tiffany said, adding in a hissing whisper, "*Mr. McCarthy is here.*"

"And he's a big fan of your store," Linda said, making the women laugh and her sons groan in agony.

"I'm going to poke out my mind's eye," Mac said, making a beeline for the beer cooler with Evan, Adam and Grant right behind him.

"Now, boys," Big Mac said with a shit-eating grin. "Don't knock it till you try it."

"Please, shoot me right now," Grant said. "I can't live with that image in my head."

"Take me out while you're at it," Adam said.

"And me," Evan said.

"Stop being a bunch of babies," Abby said to laughter from the others.

"I don't know what I ever did to you to deserve this," Mac said to his wife.

"Um, you only crashed every girls' night we've had for the last two years."

"I'll never do that again. I've learned my lesson."

"I bet you haven't."

The gifts went downhill from there, fueling the guys' mortification. All of them, with the notable exception of Blaine, protested vociferously at being subjected to such shocking gifts.

"No more guys at showers," Adam said. "I'm making it a rule."

"Overruled," all the women said in harmony, laughing and high-fiving each other.

"You girls sure know how to throw a party," Alex whispered in Jenny's ear.

She laughed and leaned her head on his shoulder. "They so deserve it. They're always butting into our business."

"Speaking of butting into your business..." Alex zeroed in on the object Tiffany had pulled from yet another gift bag. "Is that a...um, *plug?*"

"I wouldn't know. I've never seen one. Have you?"

"Um, ah, how to answer that?"

She elbowed his ribs, making him grunt on impact.

"What did you get her?" Alex asked.

Jenny had chosen some relatively tasteful lingerie compared to some of the stuff Tiffany had gotten from the others. "I'll never tell."

"I think we need to make a visit to this store of hers. I had no idea…"

When she thought about Tiffany's store and going there with Alex, Jenny's entire body heated.

Alex spoke directly into her ear. "If that sweet blush is any indication, you seem interested in a field trip to the store."

Jenny was still trying to formulate a reply to him when Ashley and Thomas, apparently bored with their game of Twister, came running over to Tiffany, who sat in a special chair decorated with streamers and balloons.

"Mommy, me and Thomas want to help you open your presents and play with your new toys," Ashleigh said.

"Mac!" Maddie cried as the others lost it laughing. "Do something!"

"Oh, no way, honey," her husband replied. "You made your bed."

"Shall we?" Jenny asked Alex.

"I think we must."

They went over to scoop up the toddlers and took them down to the beach while Tiffany opened the rest of her gifts.

CHAPTER 22

$\mathcal{T}$he party was a smashing success, Jenny decided, as she sat on Alex's lap in a chair at the fire pit while Evan and Owen played for them. Ned and Francine had taken Ashleigh and Thomas home for a sleepover, and Holden and Hailey were sleeping inside in a portable crib with a baby monitor attached to Maddie's hip.

Paul and Jared had come and seemed to be having a great time, which made Jenny happy she'd invited them.

Together, they celebrated Dan and Kara's happy news and enjoyed the retelling of her confrontation with the sister who'd hurt her so badly. Jenny couldn't imagine one of her beloved sisters doing such a thing to her, and it had made her smile to hear that Kara had gotten the chance to tell off her sister.

Jenny's group of friends had reacted with surprise and pleasure to the fact that she and Alex were a couple now. He'd behaved admirably when she talked to Jared. There'd been no comments, scowls or other signs of the green-eyed monster, for which she was grateful. She appreciated that he understood that was something she didn't find attractive and was trying to change.

Paul left at eleven to go home to relieve the friend who'd stayed with his mom so he could go out for a while. Alex had offered to go, but Paul insisted he stay and enjoy the time with Jenny.

"He's being really cool about everything," Alex said after his brother left.

"He told me I'm good for you."

"Did he? Well, you are. I'm glad he sees that, too."

Jenny dropped her head onto his shoulder, loving the feel of his strong arms around her and the clean, sexy scent of him filling her senses. As she sat on his lap in front of the fire with her closest friends surrounding her, the sky above filled with stars and Evan and Owen's music providing a backdrop to endless conversation, Jenny realized she was truly content for the first time since Toby died.

Alex was a big part of the reason for her contentment, but so too were her wonderful friends, her lighthouse and the island where they lived together. As she looked up at the stars, she hoped Toby was looking down at her and was pleased with the life she'd made for herself.

SHE HAD the dream again that night. As always, Toby appeared in living, breathing color, so vital and alive, so handsome in a custommade suit. He got up from breakfast, put his cereal bowl in the dishwasher and poured coffee into a travel mug. Then he went into the bathroom to brush his teeth and returned with the bag he carried to work.

He came over to her and bent to kiss her cheek and then her lips when Jenny turned her face up to him. Looking down at her, his eyes bright with excitement, he said, "I've been thinking."

Jenny held her breath as if she were a third party watching the dream unfold. She'd never gotten this far. She always woke up at the kiss.

"What about?" she asked.

"You should go off the pill now."

Flabbergasted, she stared up at him. "We said we were going to wait a year."

"I don't want to wait. I want everything right now—you, us, our baby. I want it all. Will you think about it?"

Still stunned, she nodded. "Yeah, sure. I'll think about it."

"Good," he said with that irrepressible smile. He knew she was powerless to say no to him when he looked at her that way. "Gotta go. Love you, honey."

"Love you, too."

He came back from the door. "One more kiss."

Amused by him, Jenny hooked her arm around his neck and lost herself in the kiss, opening her mouth to the thrusts of his tongue.

And then he pulled back, looking down at her with eyes gone glassy with desire. "Mmm. I'll need more of that later."

"You got it. Have a good day."

"You, too." After one last short kiss, he was out the door. Gone. Forever.

Jenny woke up sobbing, gasping for breath as the memories flooded her, overwhelming her with the sweetness, the poignancy and the unbearable sadness. And somehow she knew, in her heart of hearts, that she wouldn't have the dream again and felt like she'd lost him all over again.

Her sobs woke Alex. "What, baby? What's wrong?"

She was crying so hard she couldn't speak for a long time.

He held her in his arms, rubbing her back and whispering words of comfort that went straight to her heart.

"I had the dream again," she said as soon as she was able. "I finally remembered what he said that morning."

"Oh God, Jenny. Do you want to tell me? I'd understand if you didn't..."

"I want to tell you." She took several breaths and wiped the tears from her face before she related their last words to him. "All this time... I couldn't remember. I knew it was something big, but I didn't know what. And now..."

"Now you know, and it hurts almost as much as it did the first day."

"Yes." That he understood was an incredible gift at a time when she desperately needed it. Her heartbroken sobs filled the room. He held her until there were no tears left, until her head throbbed and her eyes ached from crying. "Why do you suppose I remembered that the same night you and I talked about children?"

"I don't know. Maybe because you were finally ready to hear what he said?"

"I suppose."

"He was so lucky that you loved him as much as you did. That you continue to love him all these years later. That's an incredible thing."

"I'll always love him."

"I know, baby, and so does he. That's why he decided to finally set you free. He wants you to be happy."

Tears continued to roll slowly down her face. Jenny made no effort to wipe them away. "Do you really believe that?"

"I really do."

"That means a lot to me." She kissed his chest. "And I'm glad you're here. It helps."

"I'm glad, too. I'd never want you to go through anything so painful alone." He continued to caress her back in small, soothing circles. "Do you think you can go back to sleep?"

"I don't know."

"Want to go for a walk or a ride on the bike or something to clear your mind?"

"If it's okay, I think I'd rather just stay here with you."

With his arms tight around her, he kissed her forehead. "It's more than okay."

ON MONDAY EVENING, Jenny met her parents at the ferry and took them for pizza at Mario's before bringing them to see her lighthouse, which they absolutely loved.

"The pictures don't do it justice, honey," her mother said. "It's incredible."

"I love it."

"We can see why," her dad said, taking a close look at her the way he had since her life fell apart. He was always on the lookout for cracks in her veneer. "You look wonderful. I haven't seen you look so good in... It's been a while."

"Yes, it has. Come have a seat. I have stuff to tell you." Over coffee and dessert, she told them about Alex and how excited she was to have found the same sense of connection she'd had once before.

"Oh, Jenny," her mom said with a deep sigh as she dabbed at her eyes. "You have no idea how much we've hoped to hear you say that. It's not that you haven't done fine on your own, but you have so much love to give. And we were hoping... Well, you know."

"Yeah, I know. I think he might be the one." As it had every time since, her belly quivered when she remembered him saying how cute their kids would be.

"Wow," her dad said. "And this happened recently?"

"Yes, and I know what you're going to say—"

"You know what we would've said once upon a time when you were too young to know your own heart. But we'd never say that now."

"Thanks, Mom," Jenny said softly. "I wouldn't have gotten through this without you guys and Emma and Leah. You've kept me going."

"We've taken our cues from you, honey. Your strength has been our strength."

Her father nodded in agreement.

"When do we get to meet your Alex?"

"Tomorrow night at dinner."

"We can't wait."

Jenny drove them to the McCarthy's hotel a short time later and sent a text to Alex before she pulled out of the parking lot.

Coast is clear.

On my way, but I can't stay over. Paul has an early meeting.

I'll take what I can get.

Mmmmmm...

He was there when she got home, and she ran to him, thrilled to see him after the long day without him. She was in so deep and getting deeper all the time. He scooped her up and spun her around, kissing her hard.

"Let's swim."

"I'll go change."

"Let's do it my way." He put her down and turned his back to her, bending at the knees. "Hop on."

Jenny put her hands on his shoulders, and he lifted her onto him piggyback style. As he walked them across the lawn, she kissed and nibbled his neck.

"I'm going to drop you if you keep that up."

"You won't drop me," she said confidently.

"No, I won't."

They reached the beach, and he put her down. Before she knew what hit her, they were on the sand, wrapped up in each other and kissing with heated desperation. The frenzy of their embrace knocked every thought from her mind that didn't involve the sweep of his tongue in her mouth and the press of his rigid cock against her belly.

"I thought I was going nuts waiting for you to text me," he whispered as he kissed his way to the upper slope of her breasts, tugging her tank top down as he went. "All I have to do is think about you, and I'm hard as a fucking rock."

Fueled by the desperation she heard in his voice, she reached down to cup him and discovered he was, in fact, hard as a rock. His groan seemed to come from the deepest part of him, making his chest rumble against hers.

"I thought you wanted to swim," she said.

"I do, but that's not all I want." He started pulling at her clothes, making her laugh at his fumbling attempts to get her naked.

"Quit laughing at me and help."

"Why? It's fun to laugh at you."

Working together, they stripped each other of denim and cotton and lace. When they were naked, he moved fast, hauling her over his shoulder and running for the water as she screamed with laughter.

"This is what you get for laughing at me."

"Alex! Don't!"

But of course he did, and when she came up for air, she blew a mouthful of water in his face.

"A declaration of war." He dunked her again, and she came up sputtering. Then he dove under and grabbed her ankles, pulling her feet out from under her.

Realizing she was outmatched, she called for a time-out and pushed her sopping hair out of her face. "I had no idea you were so mean."

"Don't be a sissy. Fight back."

She saw red at the word "sissy." Eyeing him shrewdly, she plugged her nose daintily and dropped under the water. It was just dark enough that he couldn't gauge her intent until she took his hard cock and a gallon of water into her mouth. Since she hadn't touched him anywhere else, she could tell she'd completely shocked him, because he went rigid. She dragged her teeth gently along his length until he popped free of her mouth, and she floated to the surface, looking up at him triumphantly. "Sissy?"

He shook his head, his eyes wide with pleasure and shock. "That was crazy hot. Do it again."

She did it again and again and again, until he released into her mouth under the water. Jenny came up for air and a sanity check. Who had she become since she met him? Someone who ran around naked outside, gave underwater blowjobs and was happier than she'd been in years. That's who.

He dropped down into the water and gathered her into his tight embrace. "If I wasn't already flat on my fucking face in love with you, I would be after that."

"You called me a sissy."

"I'll never make that mistake again—or maybe I will. The punishment was well worth the crime."

"You're flat on your fucking face in love with me?"

"You have to ask?"

"I do like the way you say things, but if you could leave the F bombs at home when you're with my parents tomorrow night, I'd appreciate that."

"I'll try my best," he said, sounding like a chastised little boy.

"Try very hard."

"I am very hard."

"Again?"

"Always, when you're around."

"I thought you had to go home."

"I do," he said as he lifted her and brought her down on his cock.

Jenny gasped and shuddered as she stretched to accommodate him.

"But not until I take care of you—a couple of times."

SHE HAD no reason to be nervous about her parents meeting Alex. They would love him because she did. But the nerves had been with her all day as she showed her parents around the island, introduced them to several of her friends and took them to lunch at the Oar Bar, which they loved.

By the time they walked into the Lobster House to meet Alex at seven, Jenny was a hot mess. In her twisted mind, this evening had been blown up into something much bigger than it should've been.

He stood and took her breath away with the way he looked at her with relief and pleasure and appreciation for the dress she'd chosen. He looked handsome in khaki pants and a light-colored dress shirt that highlighted his deep tan.

She'd been so caught up in him that she failed to immediately notice that Marion was with him.

"Paul and I got our wires crossed," he said quietly. "I was hoping you wouldn't mind."

"Of course I don't. Hi, Marion. It's so nice to see you again."

"Who are you?"

"I'm Jenny, Alex's friend. We've met several times recently."

"Jenny."

"Yes, and these are my parents, Hugh and Karen Wilks. Mom, Dad, this is Alex Martinez and his mother, Marion." Jenny hadn't mentioned Marion's dementia to her parents, but they had experience with the ailment and would recognize it for what it was.

"I don't know these people," Marion said stiffly.

"They're new friends, Mom," Alex said with endless patience, even though Jenny could see the tension in the set of his jaw and shoulders. "Jenny is my girlfriend, and these are her parents." He shook hands with her parents. "So nice to meet you. Jenny talks about you all the time."

"Good stuff, I hope," her dad said, making Alex laugh and breaking the ice.

"All good."

They were shown to their table, which Alex had upgraded from a four-top to a five before she arrived. He sat between her and his mother, but as soon as they were seated, he reached for Jenny's hand under the table, which calmed and settled her. It would be okay. He loved her, and her parents were thrilled to know that, so Jenny had no need to worry.

"I don't know these people, Alexander," Marion said after they'd ordered drinks and dinner. "Where's Daddy?"

"He couldn't come, Mom."

"Why not? I never go out to eat without him."

Jenny's heart broke for Alex and the pain it caused him whenever he had to remind his mother that his father had died.

"He's working late tonight, Marion," Jenny said. "He'll see you at home."

Alex sent her a grateful smile.

"Who are you?"

"I'm Jenny, and these are my parents, Hugh and Karen."

Marion seemed appeased for the moment with the introductions and took a bite of the roll that Alex had buttered for her.

"What do you think of our island so far?" Alex asked her parents.

"It's breathtaking," Karen said. "I can see why Jenny loves it so much." As her mother said the words, she looked directly at Alex, and the double meaning wasn't lost on Jenny. Her mother liked him, and Jenny had no doubt her parents respected the gentle way he handled his mother and her condition.

The dinner was a trial for Marion. Her confusion was worse than Jenny had ever seen it before. Under his breath, Alex told her it was a difficult time of day. "Maybe we should go home and catch up with you guys tomorrow."

"Where's George?" Marion said. "He should be here. I don't go out to eat without George. Who are these people? Why are we here?"

Since Alex seemed on the verge of breaking, Jenny leaned across him. "Marion, would you like to go for a walk to the ladies' room with me?"

"Who are you?"

"I'm Jenny, Alex's girlfriend."

"Alexander doesn't have a girlfriend. He's too young for such things." Her gaze narrowed as she studied Jenny. "Are you sleeping with him? I'll have you arrested! You're taking advantage of a boy!"

Alex's audible gasp caught the attention of diners all around them. "I'm so sorry. We're going to call it a night. It was great to meet you. I hope to see you again while you're here."

"It was great to meet you, too, Alex, and Marion," Karen said. "I'm sure we'll see you again before we leave."

Jenny got up to walk them out, but he stopped her with the gentle press of his hand on her arm. "It's okay. Stay with your folks. I'm really sorry about this."

"There's nothing to be sorry about. I'll call you later?"

"Yeah, I guess." Without looking back, he escorted his mother from the restaurant.

As Jenny returned to her seat, she told herself it didn't matter that he'd gone out of his way not to look at her as he said good-bye. The belly that had once fluttered with nerves now sank with dread. His good-bye had felt awfully final.

"Well," she said to her parents, "that's Alex. And his mom."

"She's so young," Karen said, her eyes soft with compassion.

"I know."

"Does he have siblings?"

"He has a brother. They've been managing her situation on their own while trying to run their landscaping business. It's been a struggle."

"He's very good with her."

"Yes, they both are. It's impressive, but it's a lot on them, especially living here where there're no facilities or anything like that. They're in the process of hiring a nurse to come here to help them."

"They say the measure of a man is in the way he cares for his mother," Hugh said. "If that's the case, then it seems like you've found a man truly worthy of your affection."

Jenny couldn't agree more, but she also couldn't shake the feeling of impending doom that had come over her as he'd walked away from her.

CHAPTER 23

*T*he discomfort grew with every minute Jenny spent away from Alex. At nine-thirty, she sent him a text.

Just dropped my parents at the hotel. Are you around?

She waited several minutes, and when he didn't reply, she headed home. Halfway there, she executed a U-turn and went to his house instead. Her heart pounded so hard she wondered why she didn't pass out. He was upset about what'd happened at dinner, and understandably so, but she couldn't stop thinking about the future they'd dreamed of together. Those dreams had her turning into the driveway that led to Martinez Lawn & Garden, even if she wasn't entirely sure she'd be welcome.

The house was dark except for a single light glowing in the living room. Jenny parked her car and got out, heading for the porch on trembling legs.

"What're you doing here?"

His voice in the dark startled her. "I came to see you."

"Why?"

Jenny followed his voice to the rockers on the porch. "Because I wanted to see if you're okay."

"I'm great, so you don't need to stay. You should go spend time with your folks while they're here." His voice was so cold, so devoid of the emotion she'd come to expect from him that it made her shiver despite the warm summer night. In the silence that stretched between them, the only sound she could hear was that of crickets chirping. "Go, Jenny. There's nothing for you here."

His words sliced through her recently healed heart with the precision of a surgeon's scalpel. She bit back a gasp from the pain that gathered in her chest and radiated through her entire body. If she walked away from him now, she sensed she'd never see him again.

Because never seeing him again simply wasn't an option, she moved toward him rather than away. Her eyes had adjusted to the dark, so she was able to see the white shirt and khakis. Moving quickly, before she could change her mind, she slid onto his lap.

He stiffened in resistance. "What're you doing?"

She put her arms around him and laid her lips on his. "This." Turning her head, she kissed him again. "And this." With her hand cupping his cheek, she ran her tongue over his bottom lip and felt his resistance begin to give way.

He turned his face. "Don't."

"Why not? I love you. Why wouldn't I kiss you and touch you and be with you when you're upset?"

"Because!" The single word burst free with the power of a gunshot blast. "This is my life. Right here. I was fooling myself to think I could have you, too. It's not fair. You've been through so much. You don't need this."

"Is that what you think? That your mother's illness is too much for me?"

"Hell, it's too much for *me*, and she's *my* mother! What she fucking said to you, in front of your parents…" His voice broke on the last word, breaking her heart right along with it.

"Alex, we've been there, remember? My grandmother had it, too. Nothing your mother said or did tonight bothered us."

"It bothered me. It fucking infuriated me. That she'd say that to you. And don't tell me it's the disease. I know that. But she's my mother, and she basically called the woman I love a whore in front of her parents. Is that the life you want?"

"If it includes you, then yes, it is."

He shook his head. "I care about you too much to do that to you."

"So you're doing this instead? You get me to fall in love with you and then you walk away the first time it gets hard?"

"That's not what I'm doing."

"Isn't it? When I lost Toby, that was the worst thing I've ever been through, but at least I know he didn't leave me because he wanted to."

"And you think I do? You're the only thing keeping me sane. But I have to be fair to you, and this…" He gestured toward the house, where his mother presumably slept. "This isn't fair."

Jenny's composure began to waver at the finality she heard in his voice. "Please don't decide that for me," she said softly, leaning her forehead against his. "Please."

"I need some time to think. What happened tonight… It was like a slap in the face and a wake-up call all at once, a reminder of where my obligations are and where they'll be for the foreseeable future."

"Have I ever given you any indication that I don't understand where your obligations are?"

"No, you've been awesome and amazing and incredible about it."

"I guess I fail to see the issue, but I'm not going to force myself on you." She stood and immediately mourned the loss of his heat and his touch. "You know where I am if you figure out that it doesn't have to be one or the other. It can be both, and we can make it work, but only if it's what you want, too. I won't bother you again."

"Jenny."

If only she couldn't hear his anguish in the way he said her name.

"I'm sorry," Alex said. "I hate myself for doing this to you, but it's for the best. You'll see that."

Because there was simply no way to convey to him that she'd never see how this was for the best, she left him on the porch and went to her car, feeling like a robot.

Jenny drove home on autopilot and, except for the time she spent with her parents before they left, when she faked a cheerful veneer so they wouldn't worry about her, she stayed there for the next week. Unfortunately, she was very well trained in hiding heartbreak from the people closest to her.

She refused to allow in the pain that hovered on the edge of her consciousness as she forced herself through a daily routine that consisted of sleep, enough food to stay alive and more sleep.

She dodged her friends, didn't go to work at the store and didn't take the calls from Paul that stopped after the third day. The only Martinez brother she wanted to hear from didn't call.

Sydney came on the fifth day, marching in the mudroom door and up the stairs, calling out for Jenny on the way up. "Where are you?"

Jenny was on the sofa in the sitting room, still wearing the pajamas she'd changed into after her last shower two days ago. "Here."

"What the hell is going on?" Syd asked, zeroing in on her on the sofa. "You're not taking our calls. No one has seen you. What gives?"

"He broke up with me."

"No... *Why?*"

Jenny moved her feet so Syd could sit on the other end of the sofa. "Because of his mother and his guilt and his sense of obligation that apparently doesn't extend to me."

"I don't get it. He's crazy about you. We all saw that. It's all we've talked about since Saturday. Grace is trying to take credit for it. She thinks she introduced you to him at the Tiki. I didn't tell her otherwise, but you'd be doing us all a favor if you could set her straight at some point."

Jenny knew her friend was trying to cheer her up with the silly story. However, nothing could cheer her up except an indication from Alex that he'd changed his mind, but she'd given up on that happening a couple of days ago. Her eyes welled with tears, which was funny because she would've thought her tear ducts had run dry by now.

"God, I'm so sorry, Jenny. This totally blows."

"It reminds me far too much of another time in my life. I never thought I'd feel that bad again, but this is..." There were no words for what this was. "I love him so much. I love everything about him. I even love his brother and his mother. I don't care that she's sick or that she might need me or he might need me. I don't care about any of that."

"And you told him so?"

Jenny nodded. "It didn't matter."

Sydney blew out a deep breath. "Well, if that's the way he wants to be, you'll have to show him it doesn't matter."

"And how do you propose I do that?"

"You need to get right back on the horse and start going out again. There's no way we're going to let you hole up here by yourself."

"I don't know, Syd. I'm not really in the mood to be out and about."

"I know, honey, but I won't let you go backward. Not after all the progress you've made. Why don't you pack a bag and come spend a couple of days with us? We'll keep you company and get you through this."

"That's very kind of you, but you and Luke have baby-making to do, and you don't need me underfoot for that."

"Oh, please," Syd said with an inelegant snort. "He can wait a few more days."

"The poor guy has waited long enough, and besides, I'm comfortable here. I promise I'll call you every day, though, and I'll be back out to play before too long."

"All right, but I'm holding you to that."

"I wouldn't expect anything less."

Jenny got up to walk her friend to the stairs and gave her a hug. "Thanks for coming to check on me."

"It's his loss. You know that, right?"

"Of course I do. I'm awesome."

"Yes, you are, and you're going to find an awesome guy who deserves you."

Jenny didn't tell her that she'd already found that guy. Too bad he didn't think he deserved to be happy.

JENNY DISCOVERED sleep was hard to come by when your heart is broken. She found herself sleeping for hours at a time in the middle of the day and lying awake in the middle of the night. Ten days had passed since she'd last seen Alex, and she was beginning to tire of her own company.

She'd kept her word to Sydney and called every day and was considering Syd's invitation to a cookout the next night, which Jenny suspected had been thrown together as an excuse to lure her out of hiding. She'd probably go. She couldn't hide out forever, and she wasn't about to let a man ruin a life that had been more than satisfying before she met him.

The sun was beginning to rise in the east when she finally dozed into restless sleep that was ended a short time later by a roar outside her window. Jenny's eyes flew open as she tried to figure out where the hell she was and what the hell was making so much noise.

And then she knew. The *beast*. She bolted from her bed and ran to the window like she had weeks earlier, and there he was, riding on the back of the beast as if he hadn't a care in the world, like he hadn't shattered her. As usual, he was shirtless and too hot for his own good.

How dare he show up here at… 5:45 a.m. like he has a right to be here! He had no right after what he'd done to her! Enraged, she charged down two flights of stairs and out into the same pearly dawn light as the last time. Like before, she wore only a thin tank and skimpy underwear. And just like before, she went straight for the ripening tomatoes and started hurling them at him, one after the other. Three in a row hit him—one on his back, another on the side of the head and the third, square in the ass.

Her heart might be broken, but there was nothing wrong with her aim.

He killed the engine and slowly turned to her, grinning like a loon.

She threw another tomato that splatted against his chest.

He began walking toward her with the kind of determination that had her taking a step backward because she was out of ammo. "Still not a morning person, huh?"

"You've got some nerve showing up here."

"Why? It's my job to cut your grass, so I'm cutting your grass."

"You could've sent someone else. You should've done that."

"Maybe so." His gaze took a slow perusing journey from the top of her head to her chest, where he lingered for a moment before he continued on down.

He may as well have touched her, because he set her on fire with those dark-chocolate eyes that seemed to see right through her.

"Don't come any closer." Jenny wasn't sure if she was happy or sad when he did as he was told and stopped with six feet between them. "Why are you here?"

"I told you. I came to cut the grass."

"Why you and not someone else?"

"Because I couldn't take the chance that one of the other guys might see you in that getup. You know how jealous I am."

"You have no right to say that to me. Not anymore."

"Yes, I do," he said coming toward her again. Even with tomato remnants in his hair and stuck to his chest, he'd never looked better to her.

Self-preservation had her backing up until her back was against the mudroom door and he was standing a foot from her. Looking up at him, trying to gauge his mood and intentions, she licked her lips and ignited a flashpoint of desire in his eyes.

His mouth was on hers before she had a chance to react. Unlike last time, he didn't give her the chance to say no. He simply took what he seemed to want urgently, if his ravenous kiss was any indication.

Jenny flattened her hands against his chest and pushed him back. "No," she said, sputtering with outrage and despair. "You can't do this to me. I won't allow it. You sent me away like I meant nothing to you."

"You never meant nothing to me. You meant too much. That was the problem."

"Well, great. That makes me feel so much better."

"I love you desperately. I've missed you more than I've ever missed anyone in my entire life. Every day I had to force myself to stay away from you when everything in me yearned for you."

Okay, she had to admit that was some pretty good groveling. And it was a tremendous comfort to know he'd been every bit as miserable.

He focused on something over her shoulder. "I was embarrassed. For the first time since my mother got sick, what she did… I was embarrassed by her." He released a deep sigh. "And I was furious with her. I'd never felt either of those things in all the time we've been dealing with her illness, but it wasn't about me anymore. It was about you and how it affected you. So I figured if I pushed you away, I could protect you from getting hurt."

"Just FYI, that strategy totally backfired."

"I know that now."

"So what changed?"

"Nothing other than I've run out of willpower. I guess I'm a selfish bastard after all, because I don't care anymore if I'm being fair to you by bringing you into my chaotic life. I don't care if it's fair that my mother basically called you a whore in front of your parents. I don't care about anything other than finding a way to spend as much of every day with you as I possibly can."

Jenny stared up at him, trying to decide if this was really happening or if she was having one of her vivid dreams.

And then he smiled, and she melted. "I'm just a guy, standing before a girl, asking her to love him."

Jenny's composure broke, and she stepped into his embrace. "She does love him every bit as desperately as he loves her."

He hugged her so tightly she could barely breathe. "I'm so sorry I freaked out. Once the dust settled and I realized how stupid I'd been, I drove everyone crazy until Paul begged me to come cut the grass and fix this with you, if I still could. And he said to tell you he needs you at the store as badly as I need you in my bed."

Jenny raised a brow. "Was that a direct quote?"

"I paraphrased just a tiny bit."

"I had a feeling," she said, laughing. "Are you going to freak out again the next time your mom says something to me that she shouldn't?"

"I'll try not to, but even if I do freak out, I won't push you away again. I promise you that."

"You broke my heart."

Wincing, he said, "I know. I hate myself for that. It was the last thing you deserved after you took such a big chance on me. I never want to cause you another second of pain."

"Then don't. Let me take this walk with you and hold your hand along the way and help you deal with whatever comes up the same way you will for me."

"You make it sound so simple."

"It is simple. I love you. You love me. What else matters?"

"Nothing, I suppose. There's apt to be more hand-holding on your part than there will be on mine."

"We have no way to know that, do we?"

"All I know is I'll do whatever it takes to get you to forgive me."

"I forgave you a while ago, actually. What's not to love about a man who puts his ailing mother ahead of everything else in his life?"

"What's not to love about a woman who puts up with a man who thinks he can survive without her when he should've known better?"

"She does sound pretty awesome. You should come inside and make love with her so she'll believe you mean all these pretty words you're throwing at her."

"Oh, I mean them, and I'd like nothing more, but can I borrow her shower first? I had a little trouble with some tomatoes."

Jenny laughed and then squealed when he picked her up and swung her around. She held on tight to him until he put her down, took her hand and led her inside to begin the rest of their lives together.

EPILOGUE

"*S*o I have this big idea," Alex said, much later that night. They'd spent the entire day in her bed making up for the time they'd lost when they were apart. Alex said he figured they'd be caught up in another couple of days. Then they could start over again.

Facedown on the bed, Jenny hugged a pillow and looked over at him. "What's your big idea?"

"We own quite a bit of property behind the greenhouses. It occurred to me that we could build a place of our own back there so we'd be close to my mom but still have our own space."

She couldn't believe what he was saying. "You want to build a house."

"For us. Yes. What do you think?"

"It's a wonderful thought, and maybe by the time it's built, I'll be ready to move in with you."

"Oh, well, um, see the rest of my plan would involve you moving in with me now so we can get busy making those babies you want so desperately. The babies you thought you'd never have." With a teasing grin, he added, "You're getting, you know…"

Her scowl discouraged him from finishing that thought. "Since I've only recently forgiven you for breaking my heart, I'm going to pretend I didn't hear you infer that I'm old."

"All kidding aside, do you want to wait another year to get started on what we both want?"

Jenny didn't need long to consider her answer. "No, I guess I don't."

"Then it's settled. You'll move in with us, we'll make babies and build a house."

"I don't want you to think I'm old-fashioned or anything, but if we're going to actively try to make babies—"

"We're going to *very* actively try," he said, earning a pillow to the face.

"If we're going to do that, shouldn't we, you know, at least talk about..." The stinker watched her, enjoying her discomfort when he knew damned well what she was getting at. "Are you going to make me say it?"

"I think maybe I am," he said with a smug grin.

"I'd want to be married if I'm going to have a baby."

"Married to me, or will anyone do?"

"I'm beginning to think anyone will do."

He pounced on her and rolled her so quickly she had no idea how he managed to end up on top of her, their bodies aligned. "*I'm* going to forget that *you* said *that*."

Jenny reached up to place her hands on his face, drawing him into her kiss. "No one else will do."

"Then I guess you have no choice but to marry me."

"And won't that go down as the most romantic proposal in history?"

"No, but I hope this one will." He slid off the bed, dropping to his knees before her. Taking her hand, he brought it to his lips and bent his head over their joined hands for a second, seeming to gather his composure.

Jenny had to remind herself to breathe while she waited to hear what he would say.

"I want you to know I think you're probably the best person I've ever known. You have the face of an angel, the heart of a warrior and the backbone needed to put up with me. I would like for you, Jenny Wilks, to come along with me the rest of the way, to build an amazing future together that also pays homage to the past you shared with Toby. I want to bring him with us, too, because he's part of you and thus part of who we are together. I love you, I need you, I believe I've proven I want you, but I'm available to provide additional evidence upon request."

Jenny laughed as she wiped away tears.

"I know I'm asking a lot of you by bringing you into my family at this particular juncture, but I'm hoping you'll be by my side wherever this journey we're on with my mom takes us."

"Alex…"

"Wait, I'm not finished. This is the important part. I want us to have a family together and watch them grow up and then get really, really old together, but still have a lot of sex. I'll take the little blue pills if necessary, but let's hope to God it doesn't come to that."

She laughed even harder. "You've landed your spot in the history books as the first guy to bring erectile dysfunction into a marriage proposal."

"I believe these things should never be left to chance," he said gravely.

"Are you done now?"

"I think I might be."

She leaned forward to give him a lingering kiss. "You had me at the best person you know, and you sealed the deal with Toby."

"So, wait… I could've skipped the rest of it?"

"Not on your life, buster. That would've been the most romanti-cally hilarious proposal in recorded history, except for *one* small detail."

"What small detail?"

She rolled her eyes. "I can tell you've never done this before."

"You're damned right I've never done this before, and I can't believe you're actually critiquing me."

His righteous indignation sent her into hysterical laughter. "You never asked the question, dummy!"

"Yes, I did."

"No, you didn't. I would've remembered that."

"Fine," he said with a scowl. "Are you going to marry me or not?"

Jenny raised a brow, letting him know he'd have to do better than that.

"Will you officially be my ball and chain so all the pain you inflict upon me will come with legally required sex?"

She shook her head, shaking with silent laughter.

And then he brought her hand to his lips, his face serious and earnest and as handsome as she'd ever seen it. "Jenny Wilks, best person I've ever known, masterful chucker of tomatoes and the only woman I've ever truly loved, will you put me out of my self-inflicted misery and do me the tremendous honor of being my wife?"

"Yes," she said softly. "Now, was that so hard?"

"I'll tell you what's hard," he muttered, making her laugh again as he got back in bed with her.

"You're nothing if not predictable, Martinez."

"And you love my endless desire for you."

"Yes, I do."

"I'll get you a ring. As soon as I can."

"You don't have to do that."

"Since I only plan to endure this torture once, I'm doing it right."

Jenny batted her lashes at him. "When you put it so sweetly, how could a girl say no?"

He looked over at her, his heart in his eyes. "I'm sorry I hurt you. I'll never do it again."

"Yes, you probably will, but I'll always forgive you as long as you grovel so beautifully."

"I'm getting pretty good at that since I met you."

She wrapped her arms around him, cradling his head to her chest. "Then we ought to do just fine."

Thanks so much for reading *Meant for Love*! I hope you enjoyed it.

Check out *Chance for Love*, Jared and Lizzie's story, available now. Turn the page to read Chapter 1!

CHANCE FOR LOVE

Chapter 1

It's high time to end the pity party. That was the thought Jared James woke up with on the fortieth day after the love of his life turned down his marriage proposal.

On that Friday morning in late July, Jared woke to the sound of seagulls and surf pounding against the rocks that abutted his property on Gansett Island—and to this somewhat major development in the midst of his retreat from real life. As he did every morning, he thought of his girlfriend, Elisabeth—"with an S," she always said. His ex-girlfriend now…

He'd called her Lizzie, a nickname she'd always hated until he decided she was *his* Lizzie. Over time, he'd convinced her she loved the nickname as much as she loved him. As he had every day since it all went so bad, he thought of the night he'd taken her to a rooftop restaurant in Manhattan, which had been reserved just for them. He recalled his carefully planned proposal and the look of utter shock and dismay on her face when she realized what he was asking.

She'd shaken her head, which meant *no* in every language he spoke. *She actually said no.* That was the part he still couldn't believe more than a month later. He hadn't seen that coming. It hadn't occurred to him for a second that she'd say no. When he'd gotten down on one knee, he'd pictured an entirely different outcome. He'd imagined a tearful acceptance, kissing and hugging and dancing.

There'd been champagne chilling for the celebration that hadn't happened. He'd had the company Learjet waiting at Teterboro to whisk her off to Paris for a romantic long weekend. She'd always wanted to go there, and he was set to make all her dreams come true, starting with that one.

She'd said *no*.

He hadn't heard much of what she said after she shook her head in reply to his heartfelt question. The movement of her head in a negative direction had hit him like a fist to the gut. There'd been tears, not the happy kind he'd hoped for, but rather the grief-stricken sort, the kind that come when everything that could go wrong did. He knew about those tears. He'd shed a lot of them over the last five weeks.

In all his thirty-eight years, he'd never shed a tear over a woman until he'd finally given his heart to one, only to see it crushed to smithereens after the best year of his life. He had vague memories of standing up, of staring at her tearstained face as she continued to shake her head and tried to make him understand.

But he hadn't heard a word she said. It was all noise that refused to permeate the fog that had infiltrated his brain. He'd walked away and taken a cab to the garage where he kept his car. He'd driven for hours to get the first ferry of the morning to the home he'd bought on Gansett Island a couple of years ago and had barely seen since. He'd been too busy to spend time on the island.

Now he had nothing but time after taking an indefinite leave of absence from work.

Lizzie had called him a couple of times since that night, but he hadn't taken her calls. What did it matter now? What could she possibly say that would make a difference? He'd erased her voice-mail messages without listening to them. The last thing he needed was to hear her voice and be set back to day one, when he'd honestly wondered if he was going to be able to continue breathing without her.

Yeah, he was a mess, and he was sick to death of being a mess. He was sick to death of himself. He got up and pulled on shorts and a tank, shoved his feet into an old pair of Nikes and headed out to run on the beach, something he'd done nearly every day he'd been here. What the hell good was owning waterfront property if you didn't take advantage of the chance to run on the beach?

He hadn't taken the time to appreciate most of the perks of making a billion dollars before his thirty-fifth birthday. He'd been too busy making more money to enjoy what he'd already accomplished. Those days were over, too. In the weeks he'd spent on Gansett, he'd been able to *breathe* for the first time in longer than he could remember. Without the constant pressure of work, work and more work, he'd discovered he had absolutely no life away from work.

He didn't have a single hobby, and he didn't have many friends who weren't affiliated in some way with his job. His clients were among his closest friends. How screwed up was that? Lizzie had been the exception. He'd met her at a benefit for the homeless shelter she ran for women and children in crisis. One of the guys from work had talked him into sponsoring the event, which was how he'd ended up in a monkey suit on a Wednesday evening, working the ballroom in the Ritz-Carlton at Central Park.

If he lived forever, Jared would never forget the first time he saw her. He'd been talking with some friends, guys he knew from the financial rat race, while his gaze swept the room and landed on her. She'd worn black—slinky, sexy black—that showed off her subtle curves.

However, her curves, as captivating as they'd been, hadn't been the thing that made him walk away from a conversation mid-sentence. No, it had been her smile and the way it lit up her entire face that had him making his way across the crowded room, like a magnet drawn to the most precious of metals.

"Why am I thinking about that?" he asked himself as he pounded his footprints into the sand. "I'm done thinking about her, reliving every minute I spent with her. It's over, and it's time to accept that and stop acting like a pussy-whipped, pathetic, ridiculous fool. She doesn't want you. Plenty of others do."

Except… He didn't want anyone else. He'd never wanted anyone the way he wanted her, and it was going to take a lot more than forty days for the yearning to subside. Still, that didn't mean he had to walk around like a lovesick dickwad in the meantime.

He barely noticed the gorgeous scenery that unfolded before him as he hit the mile mark and turned back, a plan forming as he went. He'd invite some people over for dinner. They'd have a cookout like normal people did this time of year. David and Daisy would come, and he'd ask Jenny Wilks and her fiancé, Alex Martinez. He'd tell them to bring others who'd like a free steak and a couple of beers.

People, he thought. That's what he needed. David and Daisy had been exceptionally good friends to him, dragging him along on many a date night and letting him be their official third wheel. The least he could do was make them dinner to thank them for their extraordinary compassion as he nursed his broken heart.

He came to a halt at the stairs that led to his house, bent at the waist to catch his breath and then walked slowly up the stairs and across the lawn, past the inground pool he'd never used. A guy came out from the mainland every week to tend to it. Perhaps it was time someone actually swam in the crystal-clear water he paid a small fortune to maintain.

Grasping the hem of his tank, he brought it up to wipe the sweat off his face. When he let the shirt drop, he noticed David coming down the stairs from the garage apartment.

"Off to save some lives, Doc?" Jared asked his friend, who was dressed in khakis and a blue dress shirt—or what Daisy called his doctor uniform.

"You know it," David said, his face lifting into the engaging grin that had become familiar to Jared in the last few weeks.

"Hey, so why don't you and Daisy come for a cookout tonight? You can take a swim and have a steak. If you want to."

David eyed him skeptically. "Who's cooking?"

"I am," Jared said indignantly. "I'm not totally useless."

Laughing, David said, "No comment. Daisy will want to know what we can bring."

"You don't have to bring anything."

"That won't fly with her. How about a salad?"

"Sure." Jared had come to know Daisy well in the last few weeks and recognized defeat when he saw it. "Sounds good."

"Great. What time?"

"Six thirty?" That sounded like a good time for a cookout, didn't it?

"We'll be here."

"If there's anyone else you want to bring, feel free."

"Maybe I'll ask Victoria at the clinic. She's fun."

"Not a fix-up, right?"

David tossed his head back and laughed. "Hardly. She's hot and heavy with an Irishman."

"Tell her to bring him."

"I'll do that." David gave him a perusing look. "You seem better."

"I think it's more that I'm sick of feeling like shit. That gets old after a while."

"Yes, it does."

David had shared what he'd gone through after he'd screwed up his relationship with his fiancée and then had to sit on the sidelines and watch while she married someone else.

"Does it ever stop hurting like hell?" Jared asked.

"Eventually."

Hands on his hips, Jared nodded. "Good to know. See you tonight?"

"We'll be there. Thanks for the invite."

"Thanks for everything. You and Daisy have been… You've been great. Really great."

"I'm glad to finally get to know the guy I've been sending my rent checks to all this time," David said with a smile as he headed for his car with a wave from Jared.

Clinging to the upbeat attitude he'd woken with, Jared went to the outdoor shower to rinse off the sweat and sand. He'd owned the house for three years but hadn't discovered the outdoor shower until he'd arrived earlier in the summer.

"I need to remember how to enjoy life," he muttered as he stood under the cool water and looked up at the bright sunshine. Other than the incredible time he'd spent with Lizzie, he'd given everything he had to his work for so long he'd forgotten the simple pleasure of an early morning run on the beach. It was quite possible that he'd never get over losing Lizzie, but there was no sense in letting what remained of his life be ruined by her rejection.

He'd recently reconnected with Jenny Wilks, a woman he'd known at UPenn's Wharton School where he'd studied for his MBA. Jenny had lost her fiancé, Toby, who Jared had also known at Penn, in the 9/11 attacks on New York City. The reminder of Toby's untimely death made Jared feel guilty for spending glorious summer days grieving for a woman who clearly didn't love him as much as he'd loved her.

Jared sat on a lounge chair by the pool and let the warm sun dry him as he plotted his day. First stop, grocery store. Second stop, liquor store. When was the last time he'd been anywhere near a grocery or liquor store? He couldn't recall. In the city, he had a household staff who took care of such things for him. Here on the island, his cleaning lady started bringing groceries with her when she realized he wasn't eating much of anything as he nursed his broken heart.

"Enough with being a pathetic loser." He got up to go get dressed and head out on his errands. He had a party to get ready for.

On the way into town, Jared's attention was drawn to an Open House sign outside the Chesterfield Estate, which he'd read about in the *Gansett Gazette*. The twenty-acre parcel had been for sale for quite some time, and he had to admit he was curious, especially after hearing Alex and Jenny talk about it.

Since he had all day before his guests were due to arrive, he decided to indulge the curiosity and pulled down the long driveway that led to the enormous stone house on the Atlantic coast.

Jared had seen some incredible houses in his time, had been a guest at some of the most exceptional seaside homes in the Hamptons, but he'd never seen anything quite like this one. A blonde woman dressed in a sharp black suit worked the door. Jared noticed she took a quick look at him, dressed in faded cargo shorts and an old polo shirt, and dismissed him on first glance.

Part of him wanted to tell her he could buy the estate a thousand times over if he so desired, but he resisted the urge to brag and took the brochure that she handed to him.

"Make yourself at home," she said with a tight, disinterested smile.

"Thank you." Jared had the house to himself as he wandered through spacious, airy rooms. In the brochure, he noted that Harold Chesterfield, an oilman, had built the summer house in 1932 as a surprise for his bride, Esther, who had died a couple of years ago. A black-and-white photo of the happy couple tugged at Jared's broken heart.

When he thought about all the things he could've given his beloved Lizzie… Except she'd never wanted such things from him. Her discomfort with his affluence and fondness for the finer things in life had been the only source of discontent in what had been an otherwise blissful relationship. He'd wanted to give her everything, to shower her in diamonds and whisk her away to places she'd only dreamed of visiting.

Over and over again, however, she'd told him she didn't want those things. She wanted him but had no interest in his extravagant lifestyle. The one comment that had permeated the fog after the proposal-gone-wrong had haunted him ever since: *"I can't live like you do. I just can't."*

"Why are you thinking about her again?" Jared muttered to himself. He'd be a raving lunatic by the time he finally emerged from his self-imposed exile. That was what she'd reduced him to.

As he walked through one incredible room after another, an idea occurred to him and solidified when he reached the grand staircase in the center of the magnificent house.

"Are you finding everything all right?" the frosty blonde asked when she found him in the drawing room, staring at the brochure like he gave a damn about the Chesterfields and their "storybook" romance.

"What's the asking price?" It was the one thing he couldn't find anywhere in the literature.

"It's listed at fifteen nine."

Jared wondered how Jenny and Alex would feel about getting married here. They'd lamented that nothing was available on short notice for a wedding this summer. Ironic, right, to be thinking about another couple's wedding when he'd expected to be planning his own. *You're not thinking about that...*

"Would they take fourteen five?"

The blonde's mouth fell open in shock and then closed just as quickly when she recovered her composure. "And you are?"

"Jared James."

"Oh! Mr. James! I didn't recognize you! I'm so sorry. I'm Doro Chase, representing the Chesterfields' heirs."

Jared shook her hand but only because she'd thrust it practically into his chest in her excitement.

"I can't believe I didn't recognize you!"

"Anyway, about the offer... Are your clients willing to negotiate?"

"I'm sure they'd be willing to entertain your offer. I'd be happy to discuss it with them if you're serious."

Jared took in the view of the ocean, the sweeping stairway, the incredible woodwork, the huge rooms, the hardwood floors. The place called to the businessman in him and filled him with the kind of enthusiasm he hadn't felt in weeks. "I'm serious."

Chance for Love is available in print from *Amazon.com* and other online retailers, or you can purchase a signed copy from Marie's store at *shop.marieforce.com*.

OTHER BOOKS BY MARIE FORCE

Contemporary Romances

The Gansett Island Series

Book 1: Maid for Love (*Mac & Maddie*)

Book 2: Fool for Love (*Joe & Janey*)

Book 3: Ready for Love (*Luke & Sydney*)

Book 4: Falling for Love (*Grant & Stephanie*)

Book 5: Hoping for Love (*Evan & Grace*)

Book 6: Season for Love (*Owen & Laura*)

Book 7: Longing for Love (*Blaine & Tiffany*)

Book 8: Waiting for Love (*Adam & Abby*)

Book 9: Time for Love (*David & Daisy*)

Book 10: Meant for Love (*Jenny & Alex*)

Book 10.5: Chance for Love, *A Gansett Island Novella* (*Jared & Lizzie*)

Book 11: Gansett After Dark (*Owen & Laura*)

Book 12: Kisses After Dark (*Shane & Katie*)

Book 13: Love After Dark (*Paul & Hope*)

Book 14: Celebration After Dark (*Big Mac & Linda*)

Book 15: Desire After Dark (*Slim & Erin*)

Book 16: Light After Dark (*Mallory & Quinn*)

Book 17: Victoria & Shannon (Episode 1)

Book 18: Kevin & Chelsea (Episode 2)

A Gansett Island Christmas Novella

Book 19: Mine After Dark (*Riley & Nikki*)

Book 20: Yours After Dark (*Finn & Chloe*)

Book 21: Trouble After Dark (*Deacon & Julia*)

Book 22: Rescue After Dark (*Mason & Jordan*)

The Green Mountain Series

Book 1: All You Need Is Love (*Will & Cameron*)

Book 2: I Want to Hold Your Hand (*Nolan & Hannah*)

Book 3: I Saw Her Standing There (*Colton & Lucy*)

Book 4: And I Love Her (*Hunter & Megan*)

Novella: You'll Be Mine (*Will & Cam's Wedding*)

Book 5: It's Only Love (*Gavin & Ella*)

Book 6: Ain't She Sweet (*Tyler & Charlotte*)

The Butler Vermont Series
(Continuation of the Green Mountain Series)

Book 1: Every Little Thing (*Grayson & Emma*)

Book 2: Can't Buy Me Love (*Mary & Patrick*)

Book 3: Here Comes the Sun (*Wade & Mia*)

Book 4: Till There Was You (*Lucas & Dani*)

The Treading Water Series

Book 1: Treading Water

Book 2: Marking Time

Book 3: Starting Over

Book 4: Coming Home

Book 5: Finding Forever

Historical Romances
The Gilded Series

Book 1: Duchess by Deception

Book 2: Deceived by Desire

Single Titles

How Much I Feel

Five Years Gone

One Year Home

Sex Machine

Sex God

Georgia on My Mind

True North

The Fall

The Wreck

Love at First Flight

Everyone Loves a Hero

Line of Scrimmage

Erotic Romance

The Erotic Quantum Series

Book 1: Virtuous (*Flynn & Natalie*)

Book 2: Valorous (*Flynn & Natalie*)

Book 3: Victorious (*Flynn & Natalie*)

Book 4: Rapturous (*Addie & Hayden*)

Book 5: Ravenous (*Jasper & Ellie*)

Book 6: Delirious (*Kristian & Aileen*)

Book 7: Outrageous (*Emmett & Leah*)

Book 8: Famous (*Marlowe*)

Romantic Suspense

The Fatal Series

One Night With You, *A Fatal Series Prequel Novella*

Book 1: Fatal Affair

Book 2: Fatal Justice

Book 3: Fatal Consequences

Book 3.5: Fatal Destiny, *the Wedding Novella*

Book 4: Fatal Flaw

Book 5: Fatal Deception

Book 6: Fatal Mistake

Book 7: Fatal Jeopardy

Book 8: Fatal Scandal

Book 9: Fatal Frenzy

Book 10: Fatal Identity

Book 11: Fatal Threat

Book 12: Fatal Chaos

Book 13: Fatal Invasion

Book 14: Fatal Reckoning

Book 15: Fatal Accusation

Book 16: Fatal Fraud

ABOUT THE AUTHOR

Marie Force is the *New York Times* bestselling author of contemporary romance, romantic suspense and erotic romance. Her series include Gansett Island, Fatal, Treading Water, Butler Vermont and Quantum.

Her books have sold nearly 10 million copies worldwide, have been translated into more than a dozen languages and have appeared on the *New York Times* bestseller more than 30 times. She is also a *USA Today* and *Wall Street Journal* bestseller, as well as a Speigel bestseller in Germany.

Her goals in life are simple—to finish raising two happy, healthy, productive young adults, to keep writing books for as long as she possibly can and to never be on a flight that makes the news.

Join Marie's mailing list on her website at marieforce.com for news about new books and upcoming appearances in your area. Follow her on Facebook at www.Facebook.com/MarieForceAuthor and on Instagram at www.instagram.com/marieforceauthor/. Contact Marie at marie@marieforce.com.

Made in the USA
Middletown, DE
07 July 2020

12187692R00188